So Wild a Heart

CANDACE CAMP

So Wild a Heart

MIRA®

MIRA®

ISBN 0-7394-2320-7

SO WILD A HEART

Copyright © 2002 by Candace Camp.

Printed in U.S.A.

1

She reached up toward him, arms outstretched, eyes wide and pleading, mouth contorted in a death grimace. She was pale, her skin white with an undertone of gray, and water coated her skin and clothes. Dark seaweed wrapped around her chest, seemingly pulling her down into the roiling water.

"Dev! Help me! Save me!" Her shrill words echoed through the darkness.

He reached out for her, but her hand was inches from his, and he could not move forward. He stretched, straining every fiber of his being but she remained frustratingly beyond his reach.

She was sinking into the black water, her eyes closing.

"Don't!" he yelled, grabbing futilely for her. "Don't! Let me help you!"

Devin's eyes flew open, blank at first, then slowly gaining understanding. *He had dreamed about her again.*

"Christ!" He shivered, feeling cold to the bone, and

glanced around. It took a moment for him to realize where he was. He had fallen asleep sitting up in his bedroom, dressing gown wrapped around him. A bottle of brandy and a gracefully curved snifter sat on the small table beside his chair. He picked up the bottle and poured some into the glass, his hand trembling so hard that the bottle clinked against the rim.

He took a quick gulp of the drink, warming as the fiery liquid rushed down his throat and exploded in his stomach. He ran his hand back through his thick black hair and took another drink. "Why didn't you tell me?" he murmured. "I would have helped."

He was still cold, despite the aid of the brandy, and he stood up and walked over to the bed, his gait a trifle unsteady. *How much had he had to drink last night?* He couldn't remember. Clearly it had been enough that he had fallen asleep sitting up instead of crossing the few feet to his bed. It was no wonder, he told himself, that he had had bad dreams.

He crawled into bed, the covers having been neatly turned back by his valet before he left last night, and wrapped the blankets around him. Slowly, between the brandy and the warmth of the bedspread, his shivers slowed down, then stopped. It was June, not really that cold, even for sleeping in only one's dressing gown, but Devin knew that his bone-chilling coldness had less to do with the temperature than with his most persistent and discomfiting nightmare.

It had been years. He had thought the dream would have stopped recurring by now. But he could depend on it popping up here and there throughout the months, at least two or three times a year. Devin grimaced. *He could not seem to keep a farthing in his pocket, but a bad dream he could hold on to for years.*

The shivering ceased, and his eyes drifted closed. At least, after all these years, he could sleep after the dream. When he'd first had it, he had stayed awake all night. *Time might not heal all wounds, but apparently, with a little help from brandy, it could make them more easily forgotten.* With a faint sigh, he slid into sleep.

It was several hours later and the sun was well up when his valet shook his arm gently and whispered, "My lord. My lord. I am sorry to awaken you, sir, but Lady Ravenscar and Lady Westhampton are below, asking for you."

Devin opened one eye and rolled it up to focus with bloodshot malevolence on his servant, hovering at the side of his bed. "Go away," he muttered succinctly.

"Yes, my lord, I quite understand. 'Tis a dreadfully early hour. The thing is, her ladyship is threatening to come up here and wake you herself. And one feels it beyond one's duties to physically restrain your lordship's mother."

Devin sighed, closing his eye, and rolled onto his back. "Is she weeping or warlike?"

"No sign of tears, my lord," his valet responded, furrowing his brow in thought. "I would say more... determined. And she brought Lady Westhampton with her."

"Mmm. Makes it harder when my sister joins forces with her."

"Just so, my lord. Shall I lay out your clothes?"

Devin groaned. He felt like hell. His head was pounding, his body ached, and the inside of his mouth tasted as foul as a trash bin. "Where was I last night, Carson?"

"I'm sure I couldn't say, sir," his valet replied blandly. "I believe that Mr. Mickleston was with you."

"Stuart?" Devin summoned up a faint memory of a visit from his longtime friend. It seemed that Stuart had been uncharacteristically flush in the pocket. That explained the hangover. They had probably visited half the hellholes in London last night, celebrating his good fortune—and no doubt disposing of at least half of it.

He sat up gingerly, swinging his legs out of the bed, and waited for the rush of nausea to subside. "All right, Carson. Lay out my clothes and ring for shaving water. Did my mother indicate what she wanted?"

"No, sir. I spoke to her myself, but she was quite reticent as to the object of her visit. She would say only that it was imperative that she see you."

"No doubt." He looked at his valet. "I think a cup of strong tea would be in order."

"Indeed, sir. I will fetch it myself."

Thirty minutes later, shaved, impeccably dressed in the plain black suit and crisp white shirt that he favored, cravat knotted fashionably under his chin, Devin Aincourt made his way downstairs, looking every inch the sixth Earl of Ravenscar.

He walked into the drawing room, decorated tastefully in masculine tones of beige and brown by the selfsame sister who sat there now. An attractive woman in her late twenties, she had the black hair, green eyes and well-modeled features that were characteristic of the Aincourt family's handsomeness, and was possessed of a charming dimple in her cheek. She looked up at his entrance and smiled. "Dev!"

"Rachel." He smiled back at her despite the low-grade pounding in his head. She was one of the few people who was dear to him. The smile faded as he turned toward his mother, a slender blond woman whose exquisite taste in clothes and regal carriage elevated her looks above an ordinary prettiness. He bowed formally toward her. "Mother. An unexpected pleasure."

"Ravenscar." His mother nodded to him. She had always preferred formality even in dealings with her own family, believing that to behave otherwise would undermine one's importance—and whatever had befallen the Aincourt family over the years, they *were* important.

"I am relieved to see you alive," Lady Ravenscar went on dryly. "Given the reaction of your servants to the thought of your receiving us, I was beginning to wonder whether you were."

"I was still asleep. My servants are understandably reluctant to pull me out of bed."

His mother raised her eyebrows. "It is almost one o'clock in the afternoon."

"Exactly."

The older lady sighed resignedly. "You are a heathen. But that is not the issue at hand." She waved the matter away.

"I presumed not. Precisely what matter has brought you into this den of iniquity? It must be of great urgency."

Lady Ravenscar made a little moue of distaste. "I suppose that is your idea of a jest."

"Very faint, I will admit," Ravenscar said in a bored tone.

"What brings me here is your marriage."

His eyebrows rose. "My marriage? I am afraid that I have no knowledge of any marriage."

"You should," his mother retorted bluntly. "You are desperately in need of one. You should have been casting about for a suitable girl these ages past. But since you have not made the slightest push in that regard, I have found one for you."

Devin cast a look at his sister and murmured, "*Et tu,* Rachel?"

"Dev..." Rachel began in an unhappy voice, looking abashed.

"Don't be nonsensical," Lady Ravenscar interrupted crisply. "I am serious, Devin. You must marry—and soon—or you shall find yourself in debtors' prison."

"I am not run off my legs yet," he said mildly.

"You are not far from it, if I understand your vulgar expression correctly. Your estate is in dreadful shape, and Darkwater is literally falling down about our heads. As you would know if you ever made the least effort to visit your lands."

"It is very far away, and I am not fond of visiting places that are about to come down around my head."

"Oh, yes, it is easy for you to jest about it," Lady

Ravenscar returned feelingly. "*You* are not the one who has to live there."

"You do not have to live there," he pointed out. "Indeed, I believe you are residing in London right now, are you not?"

"Renting a house for the Season," his mother said in the tone of one suffering the utmost humiliation. "We once had a house in Town, a lovely place where we could hold the most elegant parties. Now I can rent a house for only two months, and it's of such a size that I can barely have a dinner for over eight people. I haven't thrown a decent rout in years."

"You could live with me," Rachel told her.

"I already live on your husband's charity enough. I have him and Richard to thank for the clothes on my back. That is enough without making Westhampton put me up, as well. It is Devin's responsibility. He is the Earl of Ravenscar."

"So I must marry to give you a house in Town?"

"Don't be obtuse, Devin. It doesn't become you. You have a duty—to me, to your name—to yourself, for that matter. What is to happen to Darkwater? To the Aincourt name? It is your duty to marry and produce heirs—how else are the name and title to continue? And what about the house? It's been standing since Queen Elizabeth was a child. Are you going to let it fall into complete ruin?"

"I am sure the title will go on."

"Oh, yes, if you don't mind that rat-faced little Edward March succeeding to *your* title. A third cousin, I ask you—and he hasn't the least idea how to conduct himself, I assure you."

"I would have said that you thought *I* hadn't the least idea how to conduct myself, either."

His mother cast him a long, pointed look. "You haven't. But at least you are direct in line. And you don't resemble a weasel." She sighed. "It pains me to think of a rodenty Ravenscar. Whatever else one might say about them, at least the Earls of Ravenscar were always handsome creatures."

"So I am to be the sacrificial lamb on the altar of family, is that it?"

"There is no need to be dramatic. It isn't as if it isn't done every day. Love matches are for the lower classes. People like us make alliances. It is what your father and I did. And look at your sisters. They married as they should. They didn't whine, they just did what the family needed. As head of the family, I can scarcely see how you can do any less."

"Ah, but doing less is something I am remarkably good at."

"You are not going to divert me with your jests." His mother pointed her index finger at him.

"I can see that," Devin replied wearily.

"You have wasted your entire inheritance since you came into it," Lady Ravenscar went on relentlessly. "How can you think that you should not be the one to recover it?"

"Mother, that's not fair!" his sister cried. "You know that every Earl in memory has squandered his money. The blame isn't all to lay at Dev's door. If you will remember, it was actually Papa who sold the house in town."

"I remember it quite well, thank you, Rachel. You

are right. The Aincourts have never been good with money. That is why they always married well." Having made her point, she folded her hands in her lap and waited, watching Devin.

He rubbed his temple, where the throbbing had picked up in both speed and intensity. "And who is it you wish me to shackle myself to? Not that gap-toothed Winthorpe girl, I hope."

"Vivian Winthorpe! I should say not. Why, the settlement her father will lay on her would do little more than pay off your debts. Besides, the Winthorpes would never agree to tying their name to yours—they cannot abide scandal. You can scarcely expect a father to agree to give his daughter to a man who...well, who has had the sort of liaison you have had for years." Lady Ravenscar's lip curled expressively.

"Who, then? A widow, I suppose."

"I am sure that you could win one of them over if you put your mind to it," the older woman agreed dispassionately. "But it would require dancing attendance on her, and frankly, I doubt you would carry through on it."

"Your faith in me is astounding."

His mother went on, ignoring his sarcasm. "The girl I am thinking of is perfect. Her fortune is huge, and her father is hot for the match. He fancies his daughter being a countess. You should have seen the way his eyes lit up when I started talking about Darkwater. It seems there's nothing he wants more than the chance to restore an old mansion."

"You're talking about a Cit?" he asked, surprised.

"No. An American."

"What?" He stared at her blankly. "You want me to marry an American heiress?"

"It is a perfect situation. The fellow made a ludicrous amount of money in furs or some such thing, and he is willing to spend it on the estate. The man is enamored of a title. And because they don't live here, they don't know a thing about your reputation."

"You astound me. You want me to tie myself to some fur trapper's daughter—someone who cannot speak proper English and probably doesn't even have any idea which fork to use, and who no doubt looks as if she just stepped out of the backwoods."

"I have no idea how she looks or acts," Lady Ravenscar replied, "but I am sure that Rachel and I can clean her up. If she's a complete embarrassment... well, I am sure she will be happy living in Derbyshire with her father putting Darkwater in order. Honestly, Devin, don't you realize that everyone who is anyone in this country knows that you are steeped in sin? It pains me as a mother to have to say this, but no self-respecting Englishwoman would be willing to marry you."

Devin made no reply. He knew as well as his mother that her words were true. Since adulthood, he had a led a life that had scandalized most of the people of his social class. There were several hostesses who would not receive him, and the majority of the others did so only because he was, after all, an earl. Fortunately, he had no desire to mingle with most of the peerage and their disapproval left him unmoved. He had also years ago accepted the fact that his mother shared Society's opinion of him—and his father had considered him blacker of soul than everyone else did.

"I don't know why you should worry about the American's social blunders, anyway," his mother plowed on. "I am the one whose standing could be ruined by a rustic daughter-in-law."

"Let me remind you that I am the one who would be legally bound to her. I can see her now—too homely to catch a husband back home, even with all her money, wearing clothes ten years out of date, and not an interesting bit of conversation in her head."

"Really, Devin, I am sure you are exaggerating."

"Am I? Why, then, did they come to England for a husband? To find someone with a crumbling estate and a vanished fortune, desperate enough to marry anyone with money! Really, Mother, that is the outside of enough. I won't do it. I'll find some way to get along. I always have."

"Gambling?" his mother retorted. "Pawning your watch and your grandfather's diamond studs? Oh, yes, I know how you've scraped by the last few months. You have sold everything that isn't encumbered and has any value. We've laid off half the staff at Darkwater. You have lived a ruinous, licentious, extravagant lifestyle, Devin, and this is the consequence."

Devin turned toward his sister, who had held her silence through most of the conversation. "Is this what you want for me, Rachel? To marry some chit I've never laid eyes on? To have the same sort of happy marriage you do?"

His sister stiffened, tears springing into her eyes. "That is cruel and unfair! All I want is your happiness.

But how happy are you going to be when you have to give up this house and live in some one-room flat? You know how much money you spend, Devin. I dare swear it's far more than what Strong sends you from the estate, and that is only going to get smaller and smaller. You have to put some of that money back in to your lands if you want to keep them profitable, and neither you nor Father ever did that. I know that when Papa cut you off you scraped by on your card-playing skills and the money Michael and Richard gave you. But you won't want to do that the rest of your life.''

He looked away from her, his silence an assent. Finally he said, ''I am sorry, Rachel. I shouldn't have said that.'' He glanced at her, and a faint smile warmed his face. ''I have a damnable headache, and it goads me into sarcasm. I know you sacrificed your happiness for the sake of the family.''

''What nonsense,'' Lady Ravenscar put in exasperatedly. ''Rachel is one of the most envied women in London. She has an exquisite house, a lovely wardrobe and a most generous allowance. A large number of woman would be quite happy to have made that sort of 'sacrifice.' ''

Devin and Rachel glanced at each other, and amusement glinted in their eyes. Happiness for Lady Ravenscar would indeed consist of just such things.

''As for you, Devin, I am not asking you to offer for the girl. I merely ask that you consider the proposition. I am having a dinner tonight at my home, and I have invited her to come. The least you can do is come to dinner and meet her.''

Devin let out a low groan. A dinner at his mother's

house ranked almost as low on his list of preferred things as meeting an American heiress.

"I will be there, too," Rachel put in encouragingly. "Do say you'll come, Dev."

"Oh, all right," he said grudgingly. "I will come tonight and meet the girl."

The "girl"—much to Lord Ravenscar's astonishment, if he had known it—was at that very moment engaged in a war of words with her family along the same lines.

"Papa," Miranda Upshaw said firmly, "I am not marrying a man I've never even seen, no matter how eager you are to get your hands on a British estate. It's positively medieval."

She crossed her arms over her chest and looked at her father implacably. Miranda was a pretty woman, with large, expressive gray eyes and a thick mane of chestnut hair. Her figure was small and compact, nicely curved beneath the high-waisted blue cambric gown she wore, but her force of personality was such that people often came away with the impression that Miranda was a tall woman.

Joseph Upshaw gazed back at his daughter, his arms and face set in a mirror image of hers. He was a barrel-chested man not much taller than his daughter, whose lithe build had obviously come to her from her mother. He was as used to having his way as his daughter was, and they had gone head-to-head with each other on more than one occasion.

"I'm not asking you to marry him tomorrow," he said now in a reasonable tone. "All you have to do is go to his mother's house tonight and meet the man. After that, you can take all the time you want getting to know him.''

''I doubt I shall want to get to know him. He probably has spindly calves and squinty eyes and...and thinning hair. Why else is his family so eager to marry him off? Even without money, an earl should be a good catch. Surely there are wealthy Englishmen who would be willing to sell their daughters for a title.''

''Are you saying I'm selling you?'' her father retorted indignantly. ''That's a fine thing to say about a man who's trying to give you one of the oldest and best names in this country. If there's any selling going on, I'm the one buying him for you.''

''But I don't want him.'' Miranda knew as well as her father did that in reality he was wanting to buy a son-in-law for himself more than a husband for Miranda. Ever since Miranda could remember, Joseph had been an Anglophile, reading everything he could get his hands on about the English aristocracy—their rankings, their histories, their estates. He was fascinated with English castles and mansions, and wanted desperately to get his hands on one.

''How can you turn him down when you haven't even seen the man?'' he asked her now. ''He's an earl. You would be a countess! Just think how pleased Elizabeth would be. As soon as she's feeling not so under the weather, I'm going to tell her all about it. She will be thrilled.''

''I am sure she will,'' Miranda replied dryly. Her stepmother, Elizabeth, herself English, was even more enamored of the idea of Miranda marrying British nobility than Joseph was. She had come from a 'good family' herself, she was fond of telling whoever would listen; and the improvident, impetuous husband who had brought her to New York, then committed the final folly of catching a chill and dying, leaving her stranded in the New World with a baby daughter, had come from a family even higher up the social scale. Her dream was for her daughter Veronica, now fourteen, to live in the world of British aristocracy—to have her coming out, to hobnob with the members of the *Ton*, to marry a suitably noble husband. The easiest method of accomplishing this dream, she had decided, was for Miranda to marry into the aforesaid aristocracy and then bring Veronica out in a few years.

"You know how fond I am of Elizabeth," Miranda went on. "She is the only mother I've ever known, and she has always been quite kind to me." Possessed of a kind, easygoing, and rather lazy nature, Elizabeth had never mistreated her stepdaughter or tried to take away control of the household from her. Indeed, Elizabeth much preferred letting someone else handle all the troublesome details of keeping a large house with numerous servants running, for it allowed her to concentrate on her various "illnesses." "And I love Veronica, too."

"I know you do." Her father beamed at her. "You've always been like a little mother to that child."

"But that doesn't mean," Miranda went on firmly, "that I am going to marry someone just because Elizabeth wants Veronica to make her debut in London society."

"That's not the only reason," Joseph protested. "There's a grand estate in Derbyshire. And a house—not a castle, grant you, but almost big enough to be one. *Darkwater*. Now there's a name for you. Doesn't it conjure up history? Romance? The Earl of Ravenscar. My God, girl, is your heart dead?"

"No, Papa, it is not. And I will be the first to admit that it's a very romantic name—although, I might point out, a wee bit spooky."

"All the better. There are probably ghosts." Her father looked delighted at the thought.

"Happy thought."

"Yes, isn't it?" Joseph Upshaw was immune to irony at the moment. His eyes sparkled and his face positively glowed as he began to talk about the house he had spent the evening before discussing with Lady Ravenscar. "The house was built by one of Henry VIII's closest friends and supporters. He built the main hall during Henry's reign. Then, when his son inherited and grew even more prosperous during Elizabeth's rule, he added two wings onto it to form the classic E-shaped Elizabethan mansion. It's grand, but it's falling into complete ruin. Rot in the wood... tapestries in shreds...stone crumbling." He related the problems of the house with zest, ending, "And we can restore it! Can you imagine the opportunity? The house, the grounds, the estate. We could rebuild it all."

"It does sound delightful," Miranda agreed truthfully.

Real estate was one of her primary interests. During her father's years of dealing with John Jacob Astor, she had had many conversations with that shrewd gentleman, and she had wisely followed his advice and had invested much of her father's profits in real estate in Manhattan. The risks had already paid off handsomely, and Miranda was sure they would provide even more income in the future. The speculation of buying land to sell at a future date for high profits was fun, but what she truly enjoyed was developing projects—buying land and building something on it that she could then rent to someone, or investing in another's plan to build or expand or create.

So the thought of restoring a grand old house to its former glory did appeal to her, and she had lived with her father for too long not to have absorbed a great deal of interest in British history and architecture. But she did not want to renovate an estate so much that she was willing to marry to acquire it.

With the look of one delivering the coup de grace, her father went on proudly, "It even has a curse."

Miranda raised her eyebrows. "A curse? That would be splendid, I'm sure."

"Oh, it is indeed. 'Tis a wonderful curse. There was a powerful abbey in Derbyshire, you see—Branton Abbey—and during the Dissolution, when Henry VIII seized all the monastic lands and goods, he took this abbey and gave it to his good friend Edward Aincourt. Well, the abbot at Branton was a tough old coot, and he didn't go easily. As they dragged him out of the church, he cursed the king and he cursed Aincourt. He cursed the very stones of the abbey, saying that nothing would ever prosper there and 'no one who lives within these stones shall ever know happiness.'"

He looked at her triumphantly.

"Well. That *is* an impressive curse," Miranda admitted. She knew her father's love of drama and romance too well to be surprised to think that he would find a ruined, cursed house the perfect spot for his beloved daughter to live. To Joseph Upshaw, such a place would be a treasure.

"Isn't it? They say that Capability Brown did the original gardens. Miranda...how can you pass up an opportunity like this? It isn't only the house and grounds that need restoring, you know. Apparently the whole estate is also a financial wreck. You could rebuild that, as well. It could be one of your projects."

Miranda chuckled. "That all sounds very delightful, I'm sure, but there is still the fact that in order to get my hands on the house and the estate and all that, I would have to marry a complete stranger."

"He wouldn't have to be a stranger by the time you married him," Joseph pointed out. "You could have a long engagement, if you wish. We could start to work on the house in the meantime."

Miranda smiled at her father and shook her head. "I am not marrying, Papa, just because you are bored. Talk about wanting a project..."

"But this would be the project of a lifetime! And it's not just because I'm bored since I sold out to Mr. Astor. You know I've wanted to get my hands on a grand old house like that for years." He paused, considering her, then went on in a wheedling tone. "Anyway, Miranda, my love, I'm not asking that you marry the fellow tonight. All I want is for you to meet him. See what he's like. Consider the possibilities."

"Yes, but then you'll be asking me about how I feel and 'couldn't you just give the man another chance' and wanting me to go to this Darkwater place to see it, and..."

Her father put on a shocked face. "Miranda! You do say the most terrible things about me. As if I would badger you..."

Miranda quirked an eyebrow at him, and Joseph had the grace to smile. "Well, all right, I do badger you sometimes. I admit it. But not this time—I promise. Just meet the man. It will be nothing but going to an elegant dinner party and making polite conversation and taking a little look-see at him. Couldn't you do that much for Elizabeth and me?"

Miranda sighed. "Oh, all right. I guess I can meet the man. But I'm not promising anything. You understand?"

"Of course, of course!" Joseph agreed happily, coming over to his daughter and enveloping her in a bear hug.

"Oh, my," said a soft voice from the doorway. "What joyous thing has occurred?"

The two of them turned at the sound of Mrs. Upshaw's voice. Miranda smiled at her stepmother, and Joseph beamed. Elizabeth Upshaw was a short blond woman who fluttered whenever she walked—hands, hair, ribbons, laces, the ends of her shawl. When Joseph had met her, she had been a pretty young woman, but over the years, time and inactivity had taken their toll on her, blurring the lines of her face and figure with fat. With a matronly cap on her head and wrapped in shawls as she always was, she looked several years older than her actual age. Though only ten years separated them, there were many who assumed upon meeting them that Elizabeth was Miranda's mother.

"Elizabeth!" Joseph exclaimed, going to take his wife's elbow and escort her to the sofa as if she were too weak to walk. Elizabeth had long suffered from a variety of real and imaginary illnesses, and her husband entered happily into her presentation of herself as a fragile woman. Miranda could not quite understand why Elizabeth enjoyed spending her life reclining on couches and beds, bearing her ills with a gentle smile, but if that was the way Elizabeth chose to live, it didn't bother her. She was quite fond of her stepmother, whose kind heart more than made up for her litany of gentle complaints.

"The grandest thing has happened," Joseph went on, settling his wife on the couch and making sure her shawl, an afghan and several pillows were settled around her. "I didn't want to wake you this morning to tell you, not as poorly as you've been feeling from crossing the Channel."

"I know. I've always been sadly affected by *mal de mer,*" Elizabeth Upshaw agreed in a die-away voice. "I dread returning to New York because of it."

"Perhaps you won't have to," Joseph said happily. "Or at least, not for some time."

"Why? Whatever do you mean?"

"Miranda just may marry an earl."

"An earl!" Elizabeth exclaimed, sitting up so straight in her interest that her shawl slid down from her shoulders unnoticed.

"Papa!" Miranda said in exasperation, putting her

hands on her hips. "There you go. I told you I would meet the man. I have no intention of marrying him."

"But an earl!" her stepmother breathed, one hand going to her chest as though the news were too much for her heart. She looked wide-eyed at Miranda. "You would be a Countess. Oh, Miranda, that is more than I ever hoped for."

Miranda sighed inwardly, wishing that she had not let her father wheedle her into agreeing to meet this nobleman. Joseph would not have to badger her; after this news, her stepmother would take care of that for him.

Elizabeth's eyes sparkled, and her face was lit with an animation unusual for her. "Just think—the parties, the wedding—" A thought struck her, and she turned toward her husband. "Do they have a house in Town?"

"No, the Countess told me last night that her husband had to sell it. I believe her son, the Earl, keeps a small bachelor house, but she has to lease a home during the Season. It sounded to be a sore trial to her."

Elizabeth nodded sagely. "It would be. Having to give up one's no doubt magnificent home and make do with a rented house every summer. Knowing that everyone knows it... It's too bad not to be able to have the wedding party in a grand house." She brightened. "But you can buy one, dear. I mean, we will have to have a house in London if we are to stay here any length of time, and—"

"Elizabeth, please," Miranda put in gently. "I'm not planning to marry the Earl of Ravenscar. I just said—"

"What?" Her stepmother stared at Miranda, her face suddenly pale and her eyes wide. "What did you say? Who?"

"The Earl of Ravenscar," Joseph put in. "That's the fellow we're talking about Miranda's marrying— er, that is, meeting. Devin Aincourt's his name."

"Oh, my God." Elizabeth rose to her feet, her hands clenching together. "You cannot marry him. The man is a devil!"

2

This pronouncement had the effect of rendering her audience speechless, as Miranda and her father stared at Elizabeth. Under their gaze, Elizabeth colored a little self-consciously and sat back down.

"That is, well, I mean, I don't think that it would be a good idea for Miranda to marry him. He is, well, he has a...an unsavory reputation."

"Do you know him, dear?" her husband asked.

"Oh, no. He was far above my touch, of course. But...I had heard of him. Everyone had heard of him. He had a scandalous reputation. That was before he was the earl, of course. His father was Ravenscar then."

"What was wrong with him?" Miranda asked curiously. "What did he do?"

"Oh, the usual things that young noblemen do, I imagine," Elizabeth replied vaguely. "Not the sort of thing suitable for your ears."

Miranda grimaced. "Oh, Elizabeth, don't be stuffy. I am twenty-five years old and not a bit fainthearted. I am not going to collapse in shock."

"Yes, what did he do, Elizabeth?" Joseph prodded.

"Well, he gambled and...consorted with unsuitable types."

The other two waited expectantly, and when she said nothing more, Miranda asked disappointedly, "Is that all?"

Elizabeth shifted uncomfortably. "He was, they say—" her voice dropped "—a womanizer. He seduced young women, led them astray."

She colored at speaking so plainly and began to ply her fan.

"Ha!" Joseph let out a short bark of laughter. "I'd like to see him try anything with my Miranda. Besides, if he's marrying her, you can scarcely worry about him ruining her reputation."

"I suspect she is worried more about his *faithlessness,* Papa," Miranda pointed out wryly.

"Faithless? To you?" Joseph's brows rushed together, and he said again, "I'd like to see him try! Trust me, my dear, I'll make sure he knows what's expected of him."

"Nothing is expected of him," Miranda stuck in pointedly. "I'm not marrying him."

"Of course, dear, not unless you want to," Joseph replied easily. He turned to Elizabeth. "Besides, Lizzie, that was years ago. He was just a boy then. Lots of men are wild in their salad years, but they straighten out as they get older."

"Yes, I know." Elizabeth agreed, but her forehead remained creased with worry.

"Besides, we would make sure it was all wrapped up right and tight before she married him. You know we would not allow a wastrel to endanger Miranda's fortune.''

"It wasn't her fortune I was thinking of," Elizabeth retorted with an unusual touch of asperity. "It was her happiness."

"I know." Touched by her stepmother's putting Miranda's happiness over her own desire for her to marry a peer of the realm, Miranda went to Elizabeth and sat down beside her, taking her hand. "And I appreciate that. Truly."

"Miranda can hold her own with any man," Joseph said confidently.

"Yes, I can," Miranda replied with a grin. "And that includes you...so don't go thinking that you've won me over." She squeezed Elizabeth's hand. "I only agreed to meet this earl, and I have no intention of marrying him, I assure you."

Her stepmother retained her worried expression. "But you haven't seen him yet. He's, well, the sort who can change anyone's mind."

"Handsome, is he?" Joseph asked. "Well, that's good, isn't it, Miranda?"

"And charming—or so I understand," Elizabeth added.

"That was fourteen years ago," Miranda pointed out. "Fourteen years of dissipated living can do a lot to change one's looks."

"That's true." Elizabeth brightened a little.

"Anyway, I am not about to be swayed by a pretty face. You must realize that. Remember how angelic looking that Italian count was? And I wasn't the least tempted to accept his offer."

Elizabeth did not look entirely reassured, but she smiled faintly at Miranda. "I know. I can still see the shock on his face when you turned him down."

"And this one will look the same," Miranda told her confidently. "You'll see."

Devin could not get the idea of the American heiress out of his mind after his relatives left. Finally he picked up his hat and left the house. He walked, hoping that the air would clear his still-aching and foggy head, but when he arrived a few minutes later at Stuart's apartment, he felt little better. Stuart's valet answered the door and looked a trifle shocked when Devin suggested he awaken his master.

With an impatient noise, Devin pushed past him and took the stairs two at a time up to Stuart's room, the valet running at his heels, squawking anxiously. The noise awakened Stuart, and he was sitting up in his bed, sleeping cap slipping to the side, looking both annoyed and befuddled, when Devin opened the door and stepped into the room.

"Hallo, Stuart."

"Good Gawd, Ravenscar," his friend replied without any noticeable appreciation of his visit. "What the devil are you doing here? What time is it?"

"It's two o'clock in the afternoon, sir," the valet put in, wringing his hands. "I beg your pardon, sir, I could not keep him out."

"Oh, give over." Stuart waved the nervous man out of the room. "I'm not blaming you. No one can keep Ravenscar out if he decides to come in. Just go fetch me some tea. No, make that coffee. Very strong."

"Very good, sir." The man backed subserviently out of the room.

"When did you get him?" Devin asked, strolling over to a chair and flopping down in it. "Nervous sort."

"Yes. I know. Afraid I'll let him go. I will, too," Stuart went on meditatively, "if he don't stop messing up my ascots. I miss Rickman. Damn that Holingbroke for stealing him away from me."

"Hardly stealing," Devin pointed out mildly. "I believe he offered to actually pay the man."

Stuart grimaced, muttering, "No loyalty." He rubbed his hands over his face and sighed. "Damn, Dev, what are you doing here? I have the most ferocious headache."

"Mmm. Not feeling too well myself. But my mother and sister visited me an hour ago."

"No excuse to inflict yourself on me," his friend pointed out reasonably.

"Lady Ravenscar wants me to marry."

Stuart's eyebrows rose. "Anyone in particular?"

"An American heiress. Fur trader's daughter or some such thing."

"An heiress, eh? Some people have all the luck. What's her name?"

"I have no idea. I have no intention of marrying her."

"Good Gawd, why not? You're on your last legs. All of London knows it."

"I'm not done in yet," Devin protested.

Stuart snorted. "You owe at least three gentlemen of our acquaintance gambling debts, and you know your name will be blackened if you don't pay them soon. Last night we had to leave by your back door, if you'll remember, because that damned bill collector was hanging about out front. No need to pay a trades-man, of course—won't ruin your name. But it's a damned nuisance, tripping over those fellows all the time."

Devin sighed. "I know. It's worse than it was that time Father cut me off. At least then everyone knew I had an inheritance coming when he died. Between gambling and putting people off, I did all right."

"Not the same now, though. There's no blunt lying in your future. I've experienced it for years—younger son, they know I won't inherit, never give me an inch. It's bloody unfair, but there you have it. Tailors are the worst. As if it don't bring them plenty of other business, my wearing their suits."

Devin smiled faintly at his friend's logic. "That's true. It's terribly selfish of them to want to get paid."

"That's what I told that Goldman chap, but he just kept chattering about payment. Finally had to give him a few guineas to shut him up." He brightened a little. "Mayhap I'll pay him off, now that I won that pot." He stopped, frowning. "But no, there's that gold-handled cane I saw yesterday—rather spend it on that. What's the use of paying for something you already have?"

"Good point. I am sure Goldman will understand."

"Oh, no." Stuart, not given to sarcasm, especially upon waking, shook his head. "He'll squawk. I may have to start going to another chap. Pity. Fellow knows how to make the shoulders of my coats exactly as I like them.''

''Padded?''

Stuart rolled his eyes. ''Why did you say you came here?''

''The American heiress.''

''Oh, yes. Are you saying you're thinking of not jumping on the offer?''

''The last thing I want is a wife.''

''Yes. Damned nuisances, usually. Still…hard to argue with having coins in your pocket. What else are you going to do, anyway? You've run through your entire fortune. Told me so yourself.''

''Such as it was. The earls of Ravenscar have been improvident for years. Even my father, holy soldier that he was, spent money like water.''

''There you have it. Have to do something to recoup the family fortunes. It's your duty as an Aincourt and all that. That's the good thing about being a younger son. Don't have to worry about family duty much. Usually involves doing something boring, duty does.''

''Yes.'' Dev was silent for a moment, then said quietly, ''What about your sister?''

''Leona?'' Stuart looked at him uncomprehendingly. ''What does it have to do with her?''

Dev raised an eyebrow and looked at him pointedly.

''Oh, that. Well, it makes no difference if you're married, does it? Leona's shackled to Vesey. Been that way this whole time, hasn't she? Why shouldn't you be married, too? This fur trapper's daughter won't change anything. Get an heir on her and pack her off to Darkwater and enjoy her money.'' He looked up as the door opened and his valet entered with a tray. "Ah, there you are. Set it on the table and fetch my dressing gown. Dev, be a good chap and look in that cabinet. There should be some Irish whiskey in it. Make the coffee palatable."

"Of course." Devin went over to the small Oriental cabinet and rummaged about in it until he found a small bottle of whiskey. He didn't know why he worried about such things, he thought as he pulled out the bottle and added liberal splashes of alcohol to the cups of coffee the valet had poured for them. Stuart, and nearly everyone else he knew, would not give a moment's thought to marrying this woman. And if they did hesitate, it would be only at the thought of mingling their blue blood with her common sort. Once they were married, he would, of course, have control of her money, and there would be nothing to stop him from leaving her at Darkwater as Stuart suggested, while he went back to his life in London—with Leona. Nor would he be technically disloyal to Leona. She *was* married, after all. And one could hardly expect him to let the line of Aincourts fail just because he loved a married woman.

It was foolish of him to balk, he told himself. It was scarcely as if he lived the life of an honorable man. He lived, as his father had pointed out many times, among the dregs of polite society, consorting with cardsharps, drunkards and bawdy women. It seemed absurd to hesitate about taking a wife because of his mistress—or because he would undoubtedly make this rustic heiress miserable.

"You're right, no doubt," he told Stuart, taking a

sip of the liberally laced coffee. His stomach shuddered a little when the strong mixture hit it, but then it calmed, and the rest went down smoothly.

"'Course I am. You going to offer for her?"

"I'm not sure. I told Mother I would meet her. Dinner at Lady Ravenscar's tonight."

"Grim." Stuart made a face at the thought. "Much better go with us. Boly and I are visiting Madame Valencia's."

"I am sure a brothel *would* be more entertaining," Devin agreed. "But I ought to meet this chit, I suppose."

"Well, if you don't offer for her, give me her name," Stuart told him, grinning. "I'll take her—squint, bow legs, spotty skin and all. I'm always short of the ready."

"I shall keep you in mind," Devin told him gravely, and they settled down to the far more enjoyable business of drinking and discussing a curricle race they had attended the week before.

Miranda leaned closer to her father and whispered in his ear, "I believe this little dinner to meet Lord Ravenscar might have been more of a success if Lord Ravenscar had actually attended it."

"Now, Miranda, my love," Joseph said ingratiatingly, "he might still come. It's only—" he sneaked a glance at his pocket watch "—ten-thirty."

"The invitation was for nine," Miranda reminded him. The party had waited for Lord Ravenscar for almost thirty minutes before they went in to eat. But the elaborate, multicourse dinner had now drawn to a close, and the company had retired to the music room, where one of the guests, a blond, rather toothy woman, was butchering Mozart.

"Unless the man was run over by a wagon or something of equal severity," Miranda went on in a whisper, "he is at the very least excessively rude. Personally, I am putting my money on his not showing at all."

The female pianist stopped, and everyone applauded graciously. Fortunately, she did not offer to play another piece. Lady Westhampton turned in her seat so that she was facing Miranda and smiled. "Miss Upshaw, I am so sorry," she said sweetly. "I must apologize for my brother. I cannot imagine what has detained him."

"From what I have heard about him, I imagine it was a game of cards," Miranda replied crisply.

"Miranda!" Joseph turned to Rachel. "I beg your pardon, Lady Westhampton. My daughter is not usually so...so..."

"Truthful?" Miranda put in helpfully. "No, I'm afraid that I am, Papa. But I am sorry, Lady Westhampton, if I offended you. I like *you* a great deal. You are by far the nicest member of the *Ton* that I have met."

Rachel smiled. "Thank you, Miss Upshaw. And I have to admit that I understand perfectly your feelings at the moment toward my brother. It is terribly impolite of Devin to be this late." She looked pained. "You are probably thinking that he will not make an appearance at all, and you may be right. You can see that he needs someone to take him in hand."

"No doubt he does. However, I am not looking for a husband, let alone one who must be schooled like a child. I came here only because my father was eager for me to meet Lord Ravenscar, and I feel that I have done enough to satisfy my obligation to him. Papa?" She turned to Joseph. "I am ready to take our leave now."

"Oh, surely, not," Joseph protested immediately. "Why, there's, uh..."

"Cards, later, in the drawing room," Rachel supplied. "I believe Lady Ravenscar promised your father a game of whist."

"Yes, that's it. Whist. Quite looking forward to it."

"Very well, then," Miranda said reasonably. "I shall take the carriage home and send it back for you later."

"Please." Rachel reached out impulsively and took Miranda's hand. "Can I not persuade you to remain a few minutes longer? My brother is rude, I agree, but he is a good man at heart, I promise you. He is, as you doubtless are, reluctant to enter into this sort of relationship."

"I must think the more highly of him for that," Miranda agreed. "However, if *he* is reluctant and *I* am reluctant, there seems little purpose in our meeting. No doubt he realized it, and that is why he did not come tonight. But it would be foolish of me indeed to linger here in that case."

Rachel sighed. Miranda squeezed her hand and smiled. She had liked Lord Ravenscar's sister from the moment she met her. The young woman had a pensive, lovely face, her big green eyes touched by a hint of sadness, and there was a quiet warmth in her manner that made her seem approachable despite her beauty, and her fashionable hair and attire.

"Lady Westhampton, I truly do like you," Miranda went on. "And I think more of your brother that he is reluctant to attach himself to any rich woman who comes along. However, like him, I have no desire for this marriage, and it seems quite useless for me to remain."

"I would so like for him to meet you. Now that I have met you myself, I—I am even more in favor of his marrying you. He is a very charming man, really. You would be bound to like him. And he would be so sur—well, pleased to meet you."

"Surprised, you started to say?" Miranda asked, a smile curving her mouth. "Why? Did he think I was an untutored rustic?"

Color rose in the other woman's cheeks. It's… well…possible. You see, we didn't know." She sighed and raised her hands in a gesture of surrender. "I am sorry. I am making even more of a hash of it. But I admit, I had not expected you to be…so fashionably dressed or to speak so, well, almost like an Englishwoman."

"My stepmother is English," Miranda replied. "She always made certain we spoke correctly and behaved politely."

"Oh, I see." Rachel colored even more. "Now I feel even more the fool. I—is your stepmother here? I don't remember meeting her." Rachel glanced around the room.

"No. She wasn't feeling quite the thing this evening. She is often a trifle ill, I'm afraid."

"I'm sorry." Rachel looked at her for a moment, then said, "Miss Upshaw, may I be quite frank with you, as you were with me a while ago?"

"I prefer it."

"I am afraid that we seem very different to you, this way we marry for alliances rather than for love. It is somewhat cold, I admit. But that is the way it has long been among us—the aristocracy, I mean. We have a duty to our family, our name, the very house where we were born and all the people who work there, who live there. We are not always able to do as we choose. I, too, married as my parents wished."

Miranda wondered curiously how that marriage had worked out. She had not met a Lord Westhampton here tonight.

As if seeing Miranda's thoughts on her face, Rachel added, "You have not met my husband. Lord Westhampton resides at our country estate most of the year." She hesitated, then went on, "Surely you can see that sometimes it is a necessity to marry well, not to marry as one desires. It seems that you would encounter the same sort of thing in the United States. Your father's business will need someone to take his place when he dies, will it not? If you did not have a brother or uncle or whoever to run the business, then wouldn't you feel the obligation to marry someone who could take it over?"

"I have no brother or uncle. But when my father dies, *I* will take over his business. I will not need a husband to do so."

Rachel stared at her for a long moment. "You will run it?"

"Yes, of course. There is no one who knows more about it than I. I have been helping my father with his work since I was seven years old and totted down the numbers and prices for furs when he was trading with the trappers. I know the fur business from the ground up, and now that he has sold it to Mr. Astor, frankly, the business that he has now is more my doing than his. I invest the majority of his money for him in real estate and businesses and such."

"But I— You deprive me of speech, Miss Upshaw. I am amazed."

"It will be mine one day, mine and Veronica's. It would seem very foolish not to know all I can about it. Besides, it's quite a bit more interesting than paying calls all day. Oh! I'm sorry. I didn't mean to imply..."

"That what I do is useless and boring?" Rachel finished her sentence for her. "Don't worry. I'm not angry. It's the simple truth. What I do *is* rather useless and often boring." She smiled, a dimple popping into her smooth cheek. "But I am afraid I would not have the slightest idea how to run the estate or how to make money to repair it. And, besides, here it would not be considered proper."

"Oh, I doubt it is considered proper where I live," Miranda replied cheerfully. "But if I lived my life by what society matrons considered proper, I would scarcely ever get to do anything I enjoyed. I am not a very proper person, I'm afraid, so you can see that it is just as well that your brother does not marry me, for I would doubtless be forever doing things that would shock everyone.''

Rachel smiled. ''But life would be much more entertaining for us.''

''Perhaps.'' Miranda smiled back and rose to take her leave.

Lady Ravenscar came over at her daughter's signal, smiling in her rather stiff way and saying, ''Oh, no, you must not leave us so soon, Miss Upshaw. Why, you have not yet met my brother. Rupert...'' She turned and gestured toward an older gentleman standing a few feet away. ''Do come here and meet Miss Upshaw. This is my brother, Rupert Dalrymple, Miss Upshaw.''

Rupert Dalrymple was an affable gentleman, far more genial than his sister, a trifle portly, with an almost completely bald pate, which he strove to make up for by cultivating a luxuriant white mustache that curved down far past his upper lip. He, too, strove valiantly to convince Miranda to stay, offering card games and more music as amusements and assuring her that his nephew Dev was one who tended to lose track of time— ''no insult intended to you, I can assure you'' —and would soon appear.

Miranda smiled but stood her ground, and a few minutes later she was outside Lady Ravenscar's door, waiting for her carriage to pull up in front.

Lady Ravenscar's house, for all her complaining about its inadequacies, was a pleasant white house of the Queen Anne style, and, while not large, it sat on a crescent-shaped street, the other side of which held a small park, protecting the little street from a larger thoroughfare. After the carriage pulled up and Miranda climbed into it, they drove forward, curving around the crescent and joining the large thoroughfare, empty of traffic at this time of night.

Miranda pulled back the curtain to look out into the night. Most people, she knew, preferred the privacy of the curtains, but on such a pleasant night as this, warm and not rainy, it seemed a shame to sit in a stuffy, enclosed carriage. She would frankly have preferred to walk the few blocks home and enjoy the balmy evening up close, but the sort of soft evening slippers she wore were not made for walking, and, besides, she knew that her stepmother would suffer a collapse at the thought of Miranda walking alone at night amid the dangers of London.

As her driver turned right at the next street and started up the block, Miranda saw a man strolling down the street toward them. He was dressed in elegant evening attire, his hat set at a rakish angle on his head. Miranda noticed that as he walked along, his steps were less than straight. Though he did not stagger or lurch, he was, Miranda decided, definitely "bosky." There was something about the overly careful way he strode along, his steps meandering first one way and then the other.

A gentleman coming home from his club, she thought, and wondered if he was walking in the hopes that the evening air would sober him up a bit before he had to face his wife. She had noticed the propensity of the aristocracy to drink, but it was a trifle early for a gentleman to be quite this far in his cups. He must have started rather early.

He passed a narrow strip of black that indicated a passageway between two of the houses, and as he did so, three men erupted from the little alley and launched themselves at him. He fell to the ground under their attack, the others on top of him. It was scarcely a fair fight, even if the man under attack had been sober, and Miranda's innate fairness was aroused. Sticking her head out the window, she shouted at her driver to hurry toward the knot of men.

"But, miss!" the driver exclaimed, shocked. "They're fighting. You don't want to—"

"Do as I say," Miranda replied crisply. "If you favor keeping your job."

Having driven the Upshaw family for a week now and having a fair idea how things stood with them, the driver did not hesitate to obey Miranda. He shouted to his horse, slapping the reins, and they clattered forward. Miranda glanced around the inside of the carriage for a weapon, and her eye fell upon an umbrella in the corner, kept handy for the inevitable rain. She grabbed it, threw off her light shawl, and, when the carriage pulled to a halt, she opened the carriage door and leapt down, shouting to the driver to follow.

She ran to the knot of men, who were rolling across the sidewalk, punching and kicking. Without hesitation, she raised her umbrella, grasping the shaft with both hands, and brought it down hard, handle side down, onto the back of the nearest assailant. He let out a cry of surprise and pain and whirled around, rising to his knees as he did so. It was a foolish move, for it exposed his front without giving him the leverage of height, and Miranda quickly took advantage of his move. She whipped the umbrella around so that she held the heavy curved handle and thrust it hard into the attacker's midsection. His initial expression of outrage was quickly followed by one of astonishment upon seeing that it was a well-dressed woman who had hit him and then by one of intense pain as the pointed end of the umbrella poked into his belly.

He rose with a howl of pain and grabbed for the umbrella, but Miranda stepped neatly backward and whacked the umbrella shaft across his outstretched arm. At that moment the carriage driver, having paused to secure his horses, arrived at the fight, carrying the short, thick club that he always kept tucked beneath his seat. He used it now to good effect, bringing it down on the back of Miranda's opponent's head just as he managed to grab the other end of Miranda's umbrella. The ruffian's eyes rolled up, and he slumped to the ground without a sound.

Meanwhile, the drunken gentleman landed a fist in the gut of the third man, who rolled away, gasping for breath and holding his stomach, while the gentleman was able to pull away and stagger to his feet. He reached down and jerked the man up by the front of his shirt, punching him in the stomach and finishing it with a quick right to the jaw. The man crumpled and went down. The gentleman turned toward the first assailant, as did the coachman. The ruffian, seeing the two of them coming toward him, quickly jumped up and ran off.

The gentleman grinned at the other man's flight. He dusted off his clothes as he turned to the carriage driver. "My thanks, sir." His voice was deep and well-modulated, only a slight slurring indicating his inebriation.

He turned past the coachman to face Miranda and stopped, his expression one of comical surprise. "A lady!"

Quickly recovering, he swept her an elegant bow. "My deepest gratitude, madam, for coming to my rescue. You saved my life."

She had not seen his face clearly before, and now Miranda stared at him, stunned by the jolt of feeling that ran all through her. She was at once breathless, tingling all over, and so giddy she wanted to giggle. The man was undeniably handsome. His thick black hair, tousled from the fight, dangled down over his forehead; that, coupled with the twinkle in his eyes, gave him an undeniably rakish look. His face was strong, with a firm chin and square jaw, and cheekbones that looked sharp enough to cut paper. The almost fierce lines of his face were softened, however, by a full, sensual mouth, curved now into a grin, and by the thick black lashes that framed his eyes. He was tall and leanly muscled, his shoulders inside the black evening suit impressively wide. A red mark blazed on his cheek where one of the men had hit him, and blood trickled down from a split lip, but even those marks could not detract from his appeal.

However, it was not just the fact that he was handsome that made her feel as if she had been hit by a bolt of lightning. She had seen good-looking men before. But never before had she felt that sizzle of excitement, that elemental pull of lust—or the strange, deep connection, as if somehow she knew him. Crazily, the thought that had come into her mind was that this was the man she wanted to marry.

That, of course, was absurd, she knew. It was just a strange quirk of thought. However, he was certainly intriguing. He was unlike any aristocrat she had met so far in Europe or England. He was as handy with his fists as any man she had met among the trappers in the backwoods, and there was an impish humor that gleamed in his eyes. He was dressed fashionably but with none of the extremes of a dandy, and the admirable set of his clothes on his body owed more to the firmness of his muscles than to the padding of shoulders and legs that she had seen on other gentlemen. Obviously surprised to find that he had been rescued by a woman, he had managed not to spoil his thanks with any remark about the impropriety of her doing so.

"You seemed handy enough with your fists," she replied, glad to find that her voice came out more casually than she felt.

"They caught me unaware, however, and, I confess, not at my best." Again the charming smile lit his face, encouraging her to smile back. "I am fortunate that you were gallant enough to stop."

"I could scarcely drive by when there were three of them to your one," Miranda pointed out. "Hardly fair."

"Indeed. I think that was the idea."

"Did you know them, sir?" the coachman asked, going over to one of the unconscious men and peering down into his face. "A right vicious-lookin' one, this 'un."

"No, I've never seen them before." The man shrugged. "No doubt they were simply thieves hiding in wait for the first person to happen by."

"Not usually an area for thieves," the coachman remarked, glancing around at the expensive houses on both sides of the street.

"No," the man agreed without much interest. "They must be growing bolder."

He dusted off his coat again, without much success. "I am afraid my valet will be quite perturbed to see what I have done to his careful work."

"You are bleeding," Miranda observed, fishing her lace-trimmed handkerchief out of her pocket and stepping forward to wipe away the blood that trickled down from his mouth.

It was unnerving to stand this close to him. She could feel the heat of his body, smell the liquor on his breath. Miranda looked up into his face. She could not see the color of his eyes in this dim light, but they were warm and compelling...and, at the moment, somewhat unfocused. He swayed a little, and Miranda grabbed his arm to steady him.

"Sir? Are you all right? Beldon..." she called to the coachman, and he came up to close his large hand around the man's other arm.

"Yes. Yes, I'm fine. Just a moment's dizziness, that's all."

"Perhaps you ought to let us take you home," Miranda suggested. "My carriage is right there."

"Miss..." the driver said warningly.

"Yes, yes, I know," Miranda said impatiently. "It wouldn't be the thing for me to give a stranger a ride. But I don't think he is going to harm me. I mean, really..."

"You are a woman of warmth and courage," the gentleman said, "but you need not worry. I can make it without help. I am only going another block or so, to my mother's." He looked in the direction from which Miranda had come, then frowned and said, "Well, perhaps not. I am a trifle late. I fear I stayed too long with my friends. And in this condition... But it isn't far back to my house, either. I shall be fine."

"I insist on driving you. You have received some blows to the head, I warrant, and even with a hard head, that is bound to affect you."

He smiled faintly at her jest. "Perhaps you are right. I must admit, it is beginning to pound—though I'm not entirely sure if that is due to fists or to too much brandy."

He went with them to the carriage, but, agreeing with the driver that it would not be seemly for the lady to ride with a stranger, he opted to climb up beside the coachman. They drove the few blocks to the address he gave them, and as she rode in the carriage, Miranda considered the situation. He had said he was going to his mother's and had pointed in the direction of Lady Ravenscar's house. Could the man she had rescued be the man she had been supposed to meet tonight? Was it possible that this handsome, rather charming man who was good with his fists was the Earl of Ravenscar? It made sense. And his state of inebriation would certainly explain his tardiness, as well as match what she had heard of him. *And Elizabeth had said he was charming and handsome— though mere words could not convey the intensity of his roguish appeal.* There had been a strange moment when her entire being had thrilled to him, when she had thought that she belonged with him... This was the sort of man who could make a woman forget all else.

They came to a stop in front of his house: a small, graceful abode in the fashionable district, just the sort of house a bachelor of means and name might live in. The gentleman climbed down with the coachman's help, and Miranda opened the door of the carriage and leaned out.

"Good night, sir." She was reluctant to let him go, she found, another odd sensation for her. *If only she knew if he was the Earl of Ravenscar...* But she did not want to introduce herself to him. If he was Ravenscar, she did not want him to know that she was the heiress he had spent the evening drinking to avoid.

"Madam." He bowed again, but she noticed that he was rather more unsteady now. "You are an angel from heaven."

"That is a rather large exaggeration, but I thank you," Miranda replied wryly.

He turned and made his weaving way up the steps of the house. A moment later, the door opened, and he went inside.

"Let's go home, Beldon," Miranda said, and the carriage rolled forward.

As she drove home, her thoughts circled around the

man she had just rescued. *Was he Ravenscar? And what would have happened if he had not been late to the party tonight?* One thing she was certain of: if this man had been there, she would not have left early.

3

"Good evening, sir." Carson, Devin's valet, opened the door. He took in his employer's disarray, more alarmed by the rumpled cravat and the rent in his coat than by the marks of fighting on Ravenscar's face. "I say, my lord, are you all right? Did something happen?"

"Bit of a dustup," Devin admitted. "A cold cloth for my face would be nice."

"Of course, sir." The servant hurried off to do his bidding.

Devin sighed and ran his hand back through his hair. He wondered if it had been simple thieves, as he had assured his fair rescuer. The coachman was right in saying that it wasn't an area where thieves and ruffians were wont to linger. There were one or two of his creditors whom he would not be surprised to find were behind the attack. He suspected that if his rescuers had not routed the fellows, they might have told him to pay up if he didn't want more of the same.

He would have to be more careful now...perhaps

carry his little pistol, though that would mar the line of his coat. Carson would protest.

His thoughts wandered to his rescuers, and he smiled to himself. *What an odd sort of woman!* He had been somewhat distracted by his own fight, but he was almost sure that she had waded right into the melee and whacked one of the miscreants with her umbrella. *A pretty thing, too.* He wished the light had been better—and his vision not so impaired by alcohol. Her hair had been brown, and he had been unable to determine the color of her eyes, but they had been large and bright, and she had had a merry, laughing mouth. He remembered more distinctly the generous curve of her breasts above the neckline of her evening gown. He remembered, too, the unmistakable response of his body when he looked at her.

He wondered if she was a member of the demimonde. She had spoken and dressed like a lady, but he could not imagine any lady of his acquaintance wading into a fight like that. And there had been something odd about her speech. He could not quite put his finger on it, but there had been a certain inflection that was not quite right. Perhaps she had taught herself to speak like a lady, and an attractive bird of paradise could easily have a carriage and dress well. It would explain the actions, so unlike a woman of aristocratic breeding.

He toyed with the idea of trying to find out the woman's name. She intrigued him. In general, Leona didn't squawk about his brief dalliances with other women. She knew that he would never stray far. But, he remembered with a sigh, there was the lowering thought of the state of his finances. He could never hope to lure some ladybird from her obviously generous patron when his own pockets were to let. And the way to remedy that lay back at his mother's house where, he suspected, he was something of a *persona non grata* at the moment.

His failure to appear tonight was something that could be remedied, he supposed, with some effort on his part, but, as always, he rebelled at the thought. Something inside him quailed at the idea of spending the rest of his life shackled to a woman for whom he felt at best indifference...and, at worst, active dislike. He had seen enough loveless marriages made for the sake of name and family—including that of his own parents, not to mention Rachel's and Leona's—to know that he did not want that state for himself. He was not, he hoped, such a romantic fool as to wish for love in a marriage—or, at least, he had not been for many years. However, he was fairly sure that it was better not to marry at all than to live in the sort of quiet loneliness that was Rachel's and Westhampton's lot.

Carson returned, carrying a cool, damp cloth on a small silver tray. Devin took the cloth and held it against the cut on his lip, remembering as he did so the way the woman tonight had wiped away his blood with her handkerchief. He could smell again the faint scent of roses that had clung to the lace-trimmed cotton. He wondered if she, too, smelled of roses.

''A note arrived for you tonight, sir,'' Carson said and went over to the small table in the foyer, where another small salver held a square white piece of paper, folded over and sealed. ''Ravenscar'' was all that was written on the front, in the bold, loopy handwriting that he recognized instantly as Leona's.

A familiar sense of anticipation snaked through him as he took the note from the tray Carson offered him. He split the seal and unfolded the note.

Darling,
    Tonight after midnight. I have a surprise for you.

It was a message typical of Leona—brief, unsigned and faintly mysterious—and it immediately wiped out all thoughts of the woman he had met earlier this evening.

''What time is it, Carson?''

''Why, a bit after eleven, I believe.''

''Good. We have enough time. I need to clean up before my visitor arrives.''

Both of them knew who that visitor was, but neither would, of course, say it aloud. His relationship with Leona existed behind a veil of secrecy, however flimsy that veil might be. Though every gossip in London society knew about them and whispered about their long-standing affair behind their backs, it was still only gossip and not proven fact as long as they maintained their secrecy. Lord Vesey did not care what his wife did—they went their own ways quite happily—as long as he was not subjected to public ridicule.

So, as it had been for many years, Devin saw Leona only now and then in public—perhaps making one of her party at the theater or opera, or attending a ball to which she was also invited—never by a word or gesture indicating that she was anything other than a friend. He did not go to her house except when he went with her brother Stuart. They met late at night when she left her house or whatever party she was attending and, thoroughly hidden in a hooded cloak, took a hack to his house, slipping around the side and entering through the garden door. At those times, he waited for her by the fire in his bedroom as he would tonight, a glass of brandy on the small table before him, his pulse thrumming with expectation.

There were evenings when she did not come. One never knew with Leona—it was one of the things that kept any relationship with her from becoming mundane. Sometimes she could not get away. And sometimes she simply liked to keep matters unsettled. Over the years, Devin had reached the point where her absences no longer drove him nearly mad, but he had never been able to quite get rid of the prickle of jealousy, the thought that she had not come because of some other man—her husband, who, despite their avowed disinterest in each other, still had first call on her, or perhaps a new swain, some fresh-faced lad who hoped to attract the attention of the most desirable lady in London. Earlier in his career, Devin had settled matters with one or two of them. His blood no longer ran so hot or so fast, but still, the thought of her being with another man, even just to talk, carried a sting.

The secrecy and mystery, that sting of jealousy, the uncertainty of their rendezvous, all had served to keep alive the excitement of their affair through the years that they had known each other.

He took the stairs two at a time, his valet trailing after him, and went to his room. It did not take him long to clean up, and even though Carson was meticulous to the point of irritation about his ascot being tied just so, he was also nimble-fingered about it, and so, several minutes before midnight, he was once again impeccably dressed and groomed. He sent Carson off to bed and settled down before his fire to wait, pouring himself a small snifter of brandy.

He had a good deal of time to wait. It was almost one o'clock before there was the soft scrape of a shoe outside in the hall and the door to his room opened. Devin rose to his feet as a woman slipped inside. She closed the door behind her and turned to him, reaching up slowly to push the hood back from her face. As many times as it had happened this way, his pulse still beat a little faster. Leona looked at him, a faint smile hovering about her lips.

She was aptly named, Devin had always thought, with her tawny golden hair, rounded, sherry-gold eyes, and lioness spirit. Leona was a wild creature, barely tamed by the rules and strictures of English society. She paid them lip service and nothing more, in private going her own way.

Devin had met her when he was eighteen and first came to London from his father's estate. The world had opened up to him then, the sophistication of the city replacing the stultifying life he had known at Darkwater. Instead of his father's prayers and moralizing, there had been gambling and boon companions and late nights spent in clubs and taverns. Instead of daily lessons, there had been hours of time to do with as he wanted. And instead of boring country misses, there had been...Leona.

He first saw her at a ball at Lady Atwater's. She had been wearing a dress made of gold tissue that clung to her every curve, and her skin had gleamed in the candlelight, her eyes reflecting the glitter of her dress. He had wanted her with a rush of lust he had never before experienced. She had played him like the green lad that he was. Looking back on it, Devin could see that, but, these years removed, the fact that she had done so only amused him. He had stumbled all over himself, trying to get her into his bed, but she had teased and eluded him for over a year, rejecting him until he was on the verge of giving up, then subtly sparking his desire into flame again with a look, an accidental brush of her bosom against his arm, a quick kiss in the garden.

His pursuit of the married Lady Vesey had been a scandal, of course—one of the many scandalous things he had done in Town that brought down his disapproving father's wrath, driving an ever-widening wedge between the two of them. But he had not cared for scandal. Most of the things he enjoyed in life, he found, were a scandal. As Leona had pointed out to him, he and she were not like other people.

"Hello, Dev," Leona said in her distinctive, throaty voice.

"Leona." Devin strolled over to her, his eyes roaming over her face and down her throat to her chest, where the full globes of her breasts swelled up over the neckline of her dress. Leona, like some of the other "wild" set of ladies, often dampened her thin dresses, so that they clung to her voluptuous body more tightly. Tonight he could see the dark circles of her nipples through the thin material of her virginally white muslin dress, and his loins tightened in response. Trust Leona to dress like a maiden making her debut, yet somehow manage to look like a wanton.

He bent and brushed his lips against hers. "You are looking lovely tonight."

It amazed him sometimes how well she had kept her looks. He did not know the hours and expense that were put into creams and cosmetics and hennas. Nor had he realized that in the past two or three years, he had almost never seen Leona in full daylight, their times together kept to evenings lit by softening candlelight.

He cupped his hand beneath her breast and trailed his thumb across her nipple, so that it hardened and pointed. "Did you wear this to a party?"

"Yes. Nearly caused a riot at Lady Blanchette's soiree—or at least one would think so, from the freezing way she talked to me. But the men all seemed to enjoy it."

"I am sure they did." He chuckled, and his hands dropped to her waist, pulling her to him for a kiss. He winced slightly as their lips touched, and Leona drew back.

She looked up into his face, her eyes going to his lip. "What happened? Does it hurt?"

He shrugged. "Some men jumped me, but I got away. It bled a little, but it's all right."

Leona's eyes darkened seductively, and she went up on tiptoe until her lips were only a breath away from his. "I never minded a little taste of blood," she murmured, and her tongue flicked out to run across his lips.

He pulled her hard against him and buried his mouth in hers. After a long, thorough kiss, he released her. Leona leaned back, looking seductively up into his face. "Mmm. I have a surprise for you tonight," she purred.

His loins tightened. "Do you?" Leona's surprises were always sensual delights, worth the teasing she usually insisted upon before revealing them. "A pleasant one, I hope."

"Most pleasant." She smiled, walking her fingers down his chest. She hooked her hand in the waistband of his trousers, then pushed him away from her. "But first, I think, a bit of brandy would be in order."

"Of course." He had learned to enjoy Leona's cat-and-mouse games, enjoying the mounting pleasure and anticipation, even the frustration, knowing that it would lead to intense pleasure. He turned away easily and poured her a glass of brandy.

She took the snifter from him and gestured to him to sit down in the chair. He did so, and she took a seat on his lap, turning sideways. She sipped at her drink, then set it aside. She began to play idly with the buttons of his shirt, undoing them slowly one by one and slipping her hands in between the edges of his shirt.

"I heard about your American heiress," she said after a moment, tweaking one of his nipples.

"What? I don't have an heiress, American or otherwise."

"I heard differently. It was all the talk at Lady Blanchette's. The daughter of a clothier, I believe."

"He deals in furs." Devin smiled. "Jealous, my love?"

"Me? Jealous of a fur trader's daughter?" Leona asked scornfully. "Hardly. Interested, more like. Does she really want to marry you?"

"According to my mother, the father is panting for it. Wants to get his hands on an earl's estate." Devin picked up Leona's discarded drink from the small table beside the chair and drank from it. "They are, apparently, swimming in money. They could save Darkwater."

"Oh, Darkwater." Leona dismissed the estate with a wave of her hand. "They could save *us.*"

"Save *us?*" Devin looked at her, a trifle taken aback by her words.

"Yes. From financial ruin." Leona stretched, arching her back so that her breasts thrust even more boldly against the sheer material of her dress. Then she slipped her hand inside Devin's shirt and let her hand roam freely over his chest as she talked. "Vesey says he refuses to pay any more of my gambling debts. He says Croesus himself could not keep up with my spending habits." Her fingers settled on his nipple, caressing and squeezing it, circling it teasingly. "I reminded him that I scarcely married him for his charming manner. He was to supply the funds, and I would provide the veil for his, uh, true sexual proclivities. But he said that no amount of behavior on his part could possibly be worth the amount of money I waste.''

Leona's full mouth settled into a luscious pout. ''Do you think this dress is a waste?'' She stroked her fingertips across the neckline of her dress.

''Not on you,'' he replied, his eyes following the movement of her fingers. His hand slid up her body to cup her breast and caress it, his eyes glittering with desire as he watched her nipple tighten in response to his touch.

''But, then, nothing over fourteen attracts Vesey's notice,'' Leona added with a shrug. ''I mean, really...I find a schoolboy exciting now and then—there is something quite stimulating about that wide-eyed eagerness. But as a steady diet?'' She shook her head. ''But I am straying from the subject.'' She stretched up to brush her lips against his. ''We were talking about your American heiress.''

''I told you, she's not my American heiress,'' Devin responded. ''I have no desire to marry her.''

''Of course you don't. Don't be silly. Who would want to marry some boring little chit from the back of beyond? But...needs must.''

'''Needs must?' '' Devin repeated in some astonishment. His hand went up to cup her chin, tilting her face so that she had to look into his eyes. ''Are you saying *you* think I should marry this girl?''

''Of course,'' Leona replied reasonably. ''What else are you going to do? What else are *we* going to do? Much as I love the taste of you, my pet, we cannot live on it. We need money to survive. You haven't a cent. You told me what your uncle said the last time you asked about the estate. It *loses* money and has for years. Your funds have long since been depleted. What are you going to do—take up clerking?''

''I know how little money I have,'' Devin growled. ''Everyone has been kind enough to remind me of it. Certainly marriage would solve that problem. But then I would have a *wife*.''

''A minor inconvenience, surely.'' Leona waved her hand airily, dismissing the problem. ''Many men have wives, and one would scarcely know it. Send the boring little colonial off to Darkwater and let her live there. No doubt she will be quite happy living there— she's spent her whole life in a backwater, after all. She wants to be *Lady* Ravenscar, and she will have that. She will have her little 'domain,' and the poor naive creature will probably think she is living the life of the *Ton*. Heavens, Dev, I doubt she would be able to live anywhere except immured at Darkwater. She probably can't keep up a minute's conversation on any topic but housekeeping or some such thing, and she would be lost trying to determine what to do with an oyster fork. Can you imagine taking the chit out into Society? Let your mother take her to Darkwater and oversee her education.''

''Perhaps that is not the life she imagines,'' Devin pointed out. He stood up abruptly, setting Leona aside. ''What if she wants to live in London and foist herself on Society in all her rustic glory?'' Devin asked. ''Am I to endure my wife making a laughingstock of the Aincourt name?''

''Don't be absurd. What will it matter what she wants? Once you are married to her, her money is yours. You are her husband, her lord and master. She will do as you say.''

''Mmm. No doubt just as you do what your lord and master says.''

''How absurd—to compare me with a fur trapper's daughter.'' Leona laughed, her rather short upper lip pulling back charmingly over white, even teeth. ''Really, Dev, you make me laugh.''

''I am glad you find it so amusing,'' Devin replied sourly. ''I thought you, of all people, would not urge me to marry this chit. Does it bother you not at all to think of my having a wife? Of my bedding her and producing heirs?''

''Really, Dev, don't be so plebian. Your getting a few puling brats on some insipid cow has nothing to do with us. What could it possibly matter?'' She went to him, sliding her arms about his waist and leaning her head upon his chest. ''I can remember more than once when you have had another woman...even at the same time. As I remember, we both found that rather stimulating.''

''It was a different matter altogether,'' he said gruffly, his mind involuntarily going back to the debauched evening she had mentioned. His loins stirred at the memory. ''I did not marry the other woman. I had no obligation to her, no ties beyond money.''

''And what binds you to this one besides money?'' Leona returned. She slid her hands down the small of his back and onto his buttocks, digging in with her fingertips. ''Come, enough talk. I think it is time for my surprise, don't you?''

He bent and kissed her in agreement. Leona slipped

out of his arms and went to the door. She opened it and stuck her head out, then came back in. A moment later, a figure wrapped in a hooded cloak entered the room. The person was small; he assumed from the stature that it was a woman. The only other noticeable thing about her was that her dainty feet were small, tanned and bare.

As he was taking in this unusual fact, Leona closed and locked the door into the hall and came back to Devin. She took his hand and led him to the bed. Taking off their shoes, they climbed onto the high bed, where Leona directed him to lie on his side. She snuggled up behind him, propping herself up on her elbow so that she could see.

The cloaked woman padded over to the side of the bed, taking up a place a few feet away from them. She untied the cloak and pulled it off, revealing herself as a small dark woman dressed in a brief top that covered only her breasts and loose trousers made of gauzy material that gathered at her ankles. Slender gold chains hung at her bare waist and around her neck, and looped across the narrow top. Tiny bells hung in a row around the hem of the top and across the waistband of her trousers. They dangled from a ribbon braided into her thick black hair, and on bracelets and anklets. With every movement they tinkled musically. Over her flimsy garments were wrapped a multitude of colorful scarves, all of the same flimsy material. Just looking at her sent a jolt of desire through Devin's loins.

She looked downward almost shyly as she raised her arms above her head and began to click her fingers together, making a rhythmic metallic sound with tiny cymbals. Then her hips began to move in an undulating motion, setting up the jangle of the bells. She began to dance, her feet and hips moving rhythmically. She moved in a small space, swaying and writhing and twisting.

"Stirring, isn't she?" Leona whispered into his ear, her breath sending shivers through him. She took the edge of his ear between her teeth and worried at it gently. While the girl danced, Leona's hand slipped beneath the open sides of his shirt and began to roam his chest, and the combination of the erotic sight and Leona's touch made the pulse begin to roar in his head.

The girl danced on, her hips pumping, breasts jiggling, setting all the tinny bells dancing, punctuated by the rhythmic clicking of the cymbals on her fingers. And Leona stroked him, her fingers teasing over his chest and stomach, then down over the cloth of his trousers. She let out a low, throaty laugh at the tumescence pressing against the fabric.

"Would you like more?" Leona breathed against his ear. "Perhaps you want to see her more clearly?" Raising up a little, she clapped once sharply.

The dark-haired dancer reached up, never stopping the movement of her hips, and detached one scarf. She let it fall, drifting slowly down over her legs to puddle at her feet. Slowly, as she twisted and turned, undulating to the rhythm of her cymbals, she undid the scarves one by one.

Devin watched her undress, his breath rasping in his throat, the heat rising in him, as Leona caressed him, her hand slipping beneath his trousers to wrap around him.

"Mmm," she murmured. "Still hard as you were as a lad. I like that." Her tongue flicked out and traced the whorls of his ear, sending a long shudder through him. "What does it matter if you take a wife when we will still have this? Who cares if some peasant from the colonies can claim to be your wife? Go to Darkwater once a year and bed her for an heir, then return to me...and all the pleasures you are used to."

"Leona..." Devin let out a laugh of disbelief and turned to look her in the face. "I cannot believe that even you—you are seducing me into asking another woman to marry me."

"I am asking you to make it possible for us to continue as we always have," Leona snapped back, her eyes flashing. "I told you Vesey is limiting me to a paltry allowance. If my lover, too, is without funds..."

His eyes narrowed. "Are you threatening to take another lover? He won't last long if I call him out."

"Don't be absurd. I would do what I had to. Because you refuse to do what *you* should."

"Dammit, Leona, if you dare..."

"I wouldn't replace you, darling. You would always have a place in my bed. I would simply have to give you less time."

"Christ! You talk like a whore." He pulled away from her, rising to his feet.

The dancing girl stopped and stepped back uncertainly, her eyes going up to Devin's suddenly stony face.

"Oh, Dev, stop acting like a spoiled child." Leona

slipped off the bed, too, making a quick motion with her hand to the dancer to continue.

The woman began to dance again. Leona walked over to her and, as the girl slowly undulated, she slid her hand over the other girl's chest, now slick with perspiration, and unfastened another of the scarves. Leona looked up at Devin, her face challenging, her eyes lit sensually. "Come, Dev, my love, you know what I am. I have never pretended to be anything else."

As she talked, she caressed the other woman's body, setting scarf after scarf adrift, until the woman was clothed only in the sheer pants, brief top and delicate gold chains. "I am wicked," Leona went on. "And so are you. You enjoy this, just as I do. Just as you enjoy all the things we do—things no decent person enjoys."

He watched her, no more able to look away from the erotic scene than he was to suppress the hot pulsation in his manhood. His eyes were glued to Leona's nimble fingers as they unfastened the top and pulled it away, leaving only the gold chains draped over the woman's small tanned breasts. She caressed the woman's breasts delicately, circling each nipple with her forefinger.

"Don't you want to take her now, Dev?" Leona purred. "Don't you want to drive yourself into her? I'd like to see it. You'd like me to watch, wouldn't you? Do you think that's normal? It's wicked. Wicked, the way you and I are."

With an abrupt, fierce movement, she jerked at the waistband of the sheer harem trousers, opening them, and let them fall down to the dancer's feet. "What do you think, Dev? Will you take her?" She stepped away from the woman. "Or would you rather take me?"

She unbuttoned the front of her dress and peeled it back, revealing her breasts, firm and full, centered by large dark nipples, pointed with desire. She pushed the dress back off her shoulders and let it fall to the floor, revealing her naked body beneath. Running her hands provocatively down her body, she looked at him, arching one brow.

"Well, Dev, do you want me? Or maybe you want both of us. Or are you too pious, like your father?"

"Damn you," he growled, reaching out and pulling her to him. "You know I want you."

Leona smiled and rubbed her body against his. "Then admit it. Admit that you are wicked. You don't give a damn about that silly American chit or whether she enjoys living at Darkwater. You don't give a damn about the Aincourt name. Not as long as you can have plenty of money. And this." She looped one leg around his, rubbing herself suggestively against him. "Well, Dev, do you?"

"You know I don't," he replied thickly, swinging her up into his arms and dropping her none too gently on the bed. "You're right. We're steeped in sin," he said as he unbuttoned his trousers and peeled them off. "And I will marry the damned heiress, if that is what you want."

4

Miranda settled her spectacles on her nose and suppressed her sigh. For once, the accounts in front of her bored her past speaking. She had been feeling faintly blue all day. She knew that the feeling had to do with the stranger she had met last night. The more she thought about it, the more she was convinced that the man who had been attacked was the very man whom her father had wanted her to meet. It should have been a fortuitous thing that that man had turned out to be the first man who had sparked her interest since she had been in England. Instead, it was rather depressing, since it was clear that he obviously was so set against her that he had not even been willing to attend his mother's party to meet her. Of course, she had felt pretty much the same, so she could hardly hold it against the man. In fact, it showed that he was not the weak, shallow sort that she had assumed him to be. However, she could not help but feel a trifle miffed, no matter how silly she told herself that was.

She would never admit such a thing to anyone, of course. Indeed, she had not even told her father that she thought she had actually met the elusive Earl of Ravenscar the night before. If he knew that she had found his candidate for a husband in any way intriguing, he would never let up his campaign to get her to marry the man. And, of course, she had no intention of doing anything like that, no matter how attractive she had found the earl. She still felt the same way. She could never marry a man whom she did not love. She wanted the kind of marriage her father and Elizabeth had—they had been devoted to one another from the day they met. And while she certainly was not the sort of dependent, clinging female that her stepmother was, she wanted to experience that same sort of firm, long-standing feeling.

She wanted her eyes to shine every time she saw her husband the way that her father's did whenever Elizabeth came into the room. She wanted to miss him when he was away and greet him with unfeigned delight when he returned, the way she had seen Elizabeth do with her father. Otherwise, what use was marriage? She could do very well on her own without a husband. She was used to taking care of things herself, and she had an ample fortune. She did not need to marry the way most women did, and she certainly did not feel, as Lady Westhampton had said about herself, that she must marry out of duty to her family. She might want to please her father, but it would not harm him or the Upshaw name if she did not.

She had told herself that she was being uncharacteristically foolish about the matter of the man she had rescued last night, and so, after picking her way through her breakfast, she had decided to spend the remainder of the day doing something useful—as well as something that usually kept her thoroughly engrossed. So she had pulled her hair back into a plain, no-nonsense bun and slipped into one of the older, much washed sacque dresses that she was accustomed to wearing when she did the accounts or wrote business letters. She was far too likely to get splotches and smudges of ink on her clothes when she worked to wear one of her nicer dresses. Then she had gone downstairs to the study, put on the small round spectacles that she wore when she did close work, and settled down to work with her father's assistant, Hiram Baldwin.

Much to her dismay, she had found that she could not seem to shake her mood. Worse, she could not get interested in the sheets of numbers that Hiram had laid out before her. Usually she and Hiram shared an abiding interest in financial dealings, but today his voice droned on unmercifully, and she found her attention wandering back to the events of the evening before. Time and again she had to pull her mind back and apply it to the business at hand.

It was something of a relief when the door opened early in the afternoon and her father bustled in, grinning from ear to ear. Miranda smiled back at him; it was difficult not to, when her father smiled like that. Besides, she was more than ready to have a legitimate reason to be distracted from her work.

"Hello, Papa," she greeted him. "You certainly look like the cat that ate the canary."

"Indeed?" Her father's grin grew even broader. "Well, I have every reason to be, my girl. I've been talking with a gentleman, and it seems he would like to pay his addresses to you. I told him I was amenable to it, of course.''

''What?'' Miranda jumped to her feet. ''What are you talking about? What gentleman? Papa, what have you done? If you have found some other puffed-up nobleman to try to shackle me to, I swear I'll—''

''No, no,'' Joseph hastened to assure her. ''It's no new gentleman. It's the same gentleman. Lord Ravenscar.''

Miranda stared. ''What? Here?'' Her hand flew to her hair. *She must look like a fright!* Her hair was not arranged becomingly at all, and the dress she wore was so old and outmoded that she was embarrassed to be seen in it. ''Papa! No! I can't—he mustn't.''

''Pish-posh, girl,'' Joseph replied cheerfully. ''I've already told him he could speak to you. Wouldn't be polite to send him packing now. Won't take but a minute.'' He turned and walked toward the door. ''Come, Hiram, you and I had better leave the girl alone.''

Hiram, with a single puzzled glance at Miranda, who was standing as if turned to stone, stuck his pen back into the inkwell and followed his employer out the door.

''No, wait!'' Miranda hurried toward the door. *She couldn't let Ravenscar see her like this!* But she had not even reached the doorway when it was filled by a large, well-dressed gentleman.

Miranda's first thought was that she had been right. The man standing before her, handsome and tall, was the same man whom she had helped to escape his attackers last night. Her second thought was to wonder what had happened to all that man's charm.

This man's face was faintly bored and settled into lines of aristocratic hauteur. He was handsome, certainly, and his figure was slim and well-muscled in his perfectly tailored clothes, but the green eyes held no laughter or excitement now as they flickered coldly around the room and settled on her briefly.

"Miss Upshaw," he drawled as he made an elegant bow in her direction.

"Lord Ravenscar," Miranda replied in a tone as cool and distant as his face. She wondered if the excitement of the evening before had addled her brain that she had been drawn to this man. The Earl of Ravenscar seemed to be like every other arrogant nobleman she had met—if not worse.

Devin glanced at Miranda again. He hated being here. It was humiliating, degrading. It grated at his soul to be reduced to this—for however Leona or his mother or Rachel might phrase it, it still boiled down to his selling himself for this woman's money. It was proof, he knew, of just how low he had sunk. *Well, as Leona had pointed out, he was in the mire now, had been for years; he might as well wallow in it.*

Still, it was hard for him to do. He had felt shamed as he had spoken to the girl's father; he felt even more so now, facing the girl herself. But he had enough pride left that he would not allow them to see the way the humiliation scored his soul. His family, he reminded himself, had walked and talked with kings; he was not about to let some fur trapper or his daughter see him humbled. He lifted his chin and cast another look at the homely creature before him.

She was much as he had imagined her: dowdy in an old-fashioned, rather shapeless dress, her hair skinned back into an unfashionable bun, a pair of spectacles perched on her nose. She was without mistake a spinster, a plain woman who would be married only for her money. No doubt her speech and manners would be just as bad as her looks—a grating American accent and no idea what to do or say in polite company.

His eyes skimmed away again as fast as they had settled on her. He could not bear to look at her as he did this, so he fixed his gaze on a point just over her left shoulder and began his speech. "Miss Upshaw, I have asked your father's permission to pay my addresses to you, and he graciously gave it to me." He drew a breath and plunged on. "It would give me great pleasure if you would do me the honor of consenting to be my wife."

He paused, waiting. Miranda stared at him for a long moment, scarcely able to believe what she had heard. She was so furious, she could hardly make a coherent sentence.

Finally, flatly, she said, "No."

His mouth dropped open comically, and for the first time he stared straight at her. "What?"

His look of astonishment was so great that Miranda let out a giggle. "I said, 'No,' Lord Ravenscar," she repeated.

"*You* are refusing me?" *Not only that, the silly cow had the nerve to laugh at him!*

"Yes, I am."

"Good God, woman!" he burst out. "I hope you don't think that you are going to receive a better offer!"

"My dear sir," Miranda said crisply, "*any* offer would be better than the one you just made me."

She whipped off her spectacles and strode forward until she was standing only a foot away from him. She looked pugnaciously up into his face. "I have never heard a more graceless speech in my entire life. I can assure you that there is not a woman on earth who would marry you if you approached her like that. Who do you think you are? Do you think that any woman would just fall down in gratitude before you because you had decided to let her be your wife? You are the rudest, most arrogant man I have ever had the misfortune to meet, and I would rather live and die alone than to tie myself to the likes of you!"

Dev looked down into the wide gray eyes, snapping with fury, and he had the second great surprise of the afternoon. "You! Why, you are the woman who—"

"Yes," Miranda replied crisply. "I am the woman who saved your unworthy hide last night. If you were not so thoroughly arrogant and conceited, no doubt you would have realized it sooner. And I can tell you that I am rapidly regretting that I made the effort. A drubbing at the hands of those ruffians would probably have done you a world of good. Indeed, I am inclined to think that perhaps they were hired by some other woman who you insulted with a marriage proposal."

"Insulted!" Devin exclaimed, fury surging up in him. He wasn't sure what annoyed him more—this woman's disdain, or the fact that his body remembered quite suddenly and vividly the desire that had stirred in his loins last night when he had looked at her. "You dare to say that I insulted you by asking you to marry me? I am the sixth Earl of Ravenscar. I can trace my bloodlines back to the twelfth century. I dare swear *you* would be hard put to know who your grandfather was."

"That is a colossally foolish argument," Miranda said dispassionately. "Everyone's ancestors go back that far. The fact that you know the names of yours means nothing except that your family kept good records. The Lord only knows what sort of man your ancestor was—he may very well have been the most evil fellow around. And it certainly doesn't mean anything about *your* character. That is something that you make yourself, and from the things I have heard, you have not done a very good job of it."

"You dare—" Ravenscar looked at her through narrowed eyes. "Good God, if you were a man, I'd call you out for that." He moved even closer, glaring down into her face.

"Another supremely silly thing to bring up, since I obviously am not," Miranda pointed out, standing her ground. She was not about to let him intimidate her by looming over her this way. Her temper was up, and she was enjoying herself. This man deserved to be taken down a peg or two, and she was quite happy to be the one to do so. Lifting her chin defiantly, she glared back at him, only inches away from his face.

"You impudent little—" Ravenscar broke off his words, and suddenly his hands went around her arms like steel. He jerked her up and into him, and his mouth came down on hers.

Miranda stood stock-still for a moment, unable to move. She had never been treated like this before in her life, handled so roughly or kissed so thoroughly. No other man would have had the arrogance—or the courage. Indignation shot through her. But at the same time, every fiber in her being thrilled to the sensations that coursed through her. His mouth was hot and demanding, and the taste of it intoxicated her. His lips pressed into hers, fervent, velvety, searing. Then his tongue was in her mouth, invading her. A tremor of excitement shot through her, a vibration that sizzled down every nerve ending in her body in a way that she had never experienced—indeed, had never even imagined existed.

An ache started low in her abdomen, warm and pulsing, insistent. She sagged against him, lost in the heat and pleasure, her anger and indignation burned away by the desire that swept through her. Her breasts felt full and soft, the nipples prickling with longing, and she was aware that she wanted to feel his hands on them, to have him touch her everywhere. She shuddered, her moan swallowed by his voracious mouth.

Then, suddenly, shockingly, his mouth was gone from hers. He pulled back and looked down into her passion-softened face. His eyes glittered, green as glass.

"There," he muttered huskily, his hands falling away from her arms. "Now you know what you could have had but were too much a fool to take."

His caustic words cut through the haze of pleasure,

and Miranda's spine stiffened. Anger and a fierce self-dislike seized her. She lifted her hand and slapped him hard.

"Get out," she snapped. "Get out of this house, and never show your face here again."

"With great pleasure," he responded sardonically and turned on his heel to stride out of the room.

Miranda's knees were suddenly too weak to stand, and she sank down in the nearest chair. *Dear God, what had just happened?*

In an instant her whole life had been turned upside down. She coursed with fury and indignation and a fire that was completely new to her. Her hand stung from slapping him. She was glad she had; she wished he were back here so she could slap him again. At the same time, her insides felt jumbled and hot and hungry, and she wanted to feel again the pleasure that had surged in her when he kissed her.

The man was arrogant and rude—no, he was beyond arrogant and rude; he was something so irritating and provoking that she could not think of a name for it. She hated him, and she hated him all the more because she had thrilled so to his kiss. She had weakly wanted to lean against him, had wantonly wished that the kiss would go on and on forever. She had enjoyed it, even though everything in her screamed not to. She had wanted him with a fierce and urgent ache that she had never felt for any other man. And it was infuriating that he had made her feel that way quite against her will.

The man was the very devil, she thought, and she hoped that she would never have to see him again.

But, no, she realized immediately, that was not true. She hoped she would see him again—and soon—so that she could tell him exactly how much she despised him!

Devin strode down the street, his feet keeping pace with the rapid tumbling of his brain. *The nerve of the wench! To slap him, to tell him he was not good enough to be her husband! Who did she think she was? He was an Aincourt of Darkwater, and she was a nobody, puffed up in importance just because her father had made a pile of gold selling animal skins—as if that made her anyone of consequence!*

He thought of a dozen scathing things he should have said to her. He should have told her how little her refusal of his proposal had meant to him. *He had not wanted to ask her to marry him in the first place— he had only done it because everyone kept hounding him to.* He should have pointed out to her that she was no prize for any man, least of all an earl. *But, damnation, she had felt so soft and yielding against him. And her lips had tasted of honey, and the scent of roses that clung to her had filled his nostrils in the most delightful, heady way.*

He let out a growl of frustration, startling a passerby and making the man move quickly to the opposite side of the street. It seemed too bizarre, too absurd, that she could possibly be the fetching woman who had rescued him last night. He had been in his cups, of course, and he'd had only a hazy memory of the woman's face, but he'd remembered those wide, expressive gray eyes and the way they had lit with laughter and excitement. *How could she have been the same person as that drab, infuriating creature he had forced himself to propose to this afternoon?*

It had been the woman from last night who had responded to his kiss. He had felt the warmth and excitement in her, the same passion that yesterday had sent her flying into the midst of a fray. He smiled a little as he thought about the kiss, remembering the warmth of her lips, the sweet eagerness. He wasn't sure why he had done it—he had wanted to get back at her in some way. She had been so infuriating, so cold and controlled, so contemptuous of him, that he had wanted to show her that he had the upper hand. And he had done so, despite the slap. The slap only showed how much he had struck a nerve with her; he suspected that she was more furious at herself for responding than anything else.

He knew, too, that he could make her respond again. *Hell, if he put an effort into it, he could make her fall in love with him.* Devin knew that he could be charming. There had been many women over the years who had succumbed to that charm—even some who most people would have said were far too circumspect to have anything to do with a rake such as Devin Aincourt. Generally, he simply did not make the effort to woo a woman who resisted him; there were too many others who were quite happy to climb into his bed…and there was, of course, Leona, who always retained first hold on his affections.

But this time, he thought, this time it just might be worth the trouble. *So the American wench thought that he was poor husband material…. Any other proposal would be better than his.* He wondered how she would feel about that after a few days of determined wooing. The smile that touched his lips at that thought was not pleasant. He would be charming and attentive; he would seduce her with great care and tenderness. It wouldn't be difficult, not with the kind of passion that he had felt in her this afternoon. And when he had her deeply in love with him, telling him that she wanted more than anything to marry him...well, then he would smile and say that he was sorry, he never offered more than once.

Just the thought of the scene brought him a great feeling of satisfaction. He was, he thought, a wicked man at heart, just as Leona had said last night. Breaking the American chit's heart had a great deal more appeal for him than marrying her.

He changed the direction of his path, heading now for his sister's town house, a stately white affair that took up most of a block in Mayfair. The footman knew him and merely bowed as Devin walked past him and took the stairs to his sister's sitting room upstairs. He was relieved to find her alone rather than receiving callers, frowning over a framed circle of needlework.

She looked up at the sound of his footsteps, and a smile broke across her face. ''Dev!'' She rose quickly to her feet and started toward him, holding out both her hands. ''I am so happy to see you—although I should scold you for the what you did last night, or, I should say, didn't do. It was terribly embarrassing. I felt a fool trying to tell Miss Upshaw that you were really a very nice man.''

''No need to lie about me, Rachel,'' Devin said with

a smile, greeting his sister with a kiss on the cheek. "You know I am anything but a nice man."

"Well, everyone else in Town will tell her *that*. I was hoping to present a counterargument. But it was a little difficult when you did not even have the courtesy to show up."

"Well, I made up for it today. I went to her house and asked her father for her hand."

"Dev!" Rachel's green eyes, a warmer, feminine version of her brother's, lit with delight. "You never did! Really? Oh, I am so happy. I liked Miss Upshaw on sight. I think she will make you a wonderful wife. I know this is the right thing—you will be so happy."

"Not if my happiness depends on marrying her. She turned me down."

"Turned you down?"

Devin chuckled. "Well, it soothes my wounded feelings somewhat to see you look so shocked at the notion. I am sure our esteemed mother will tell me that it serves me right."

"Well, it probably does," Rachel admitted. "But, oh, this is so disappointing. I had really hoped..."

"Don't give up hope, my love. I have a plan."

"A plan?" The look Rachel turned on him was tinged with suspicion. "What do you mean? A plan for what?"

"For turning the tables on our Miss Moneybags," Devin replied lightly. "I intend to woo the chit. Get her to take back her refusal."

Rachel frowned. "But why? I thought you didn't want to marry her anyway? I would have thought you would be glad she turned you down."

"Glad to have an American nobody tell me I was not good enough for her?" Devin asked coolly. "I think not, dear sister. I am happy not to shackle myself to her, but that doesn't mean I was pleased to be rejected."

Rachel's frown deepened. "Devin..."

"What?" He looked at her with great innocence. "I thought you would be happy for me to make a push to fix her interest."

"I would be if I thought you were serious. But it sounds as if it is a game for you, and it seems a cruel game."

"Don't worry about the American. Just think of all that lovely money waiting for us to snatch it up."

"Devin! You make us sound so..."

"So what? Mercenary? Well, aren't we? Haven't we always been aimed in the direction of money? Was it not the prime objective of your marriage? And Caroline's? Haven't I always been the slackard who would not do his family duty of wedding an heiress? The Aincourt coffers, after all, are a bottomless pit."

"I hate it when you talk that way," Rachel said, her face saddening. "Caroline and Richard loved each other. He has been heartbroken ever since her death, and you know it."

"I know." His face softened a trifle. "And I am a wretch to remind you of your own sacrifice. Especially when I have always been too selfish to match it."

"I don't want you to sacrifice your life, Dev. I want your happiness. That is all that I care about."

"Well, it will make me happy to win over your

Miss Upshaw. And that is why I want you to have a party and invite her to it.''

''Have a party?''

''Yes. A party which I shall attend—and where I will endeavor to repair the damage I have done to Miss Upshaw's opinion of me.''

Rachel gave her brother a long, considering look. The hard light in his eyes frightened her a little, and she wondered if she would be doing the American girl a serious disservice by helping Devin try to charm her into accepting him. But then she thought about Miss Upshaw and their conversation of the night before, and it occurred to her that Miranda Upshaw was capable of holding her own with anyone, including Devin.

''All right,'' she said finally. ''I shall throw a ball for Miss Upshaw. She can scarcely refuse to attend a party designed to introduce her to the *Ton*.''

''Thank you, dear sister.'' Devin threw her a playful bow. ''I am eternally in your debt.''

''I shall hold you to that promise,'' Rachel retorted in the same vein, then added, more thoughtfully, ''It will be interesting to see which one of you wins out.''

Perhaps, with any luck, they both would.

5

Miranda turned first this way, then that, looking at her reflection in the mirror. Behind her sat her stepsister and stepmother, observing her. Her father paced impatiently up and down the hallway, sticking his head in from time to time to see how things were progressing.

"You're beautiful," Veronica said, gazing up at her with stars in her eyes.

"She's right," Elizabeth agreed. "That seafoam green sets off your hair perfectly. I am so glad we decided to get it."

"I am, too," Miranda admitted. The dress was lovely. Made of layer upon layer of the palest green gauze, scalloped around the hem, it did indeed look as if she were rising from a layer of sea-foam. Tied by a wide silver ribbon beneath the bust, it accentuated the firm thrust of her breasts, and the low, round neckline showed off their creamy tops to advantage. Around her shoulders she wore a wrap of silver, so thin as to be almost nonexistent. Her chestnut hair was swept up and artfully arranged in a cascade of falling curls, through which a matching silver ribbon was twined. She did, she thought with a satisfied smile, look her best. Lord Ravenscar would not find her plain or dowdy tonight.

That, she knew, was the main reason why she had decided to attend Lady Westhampton's ball tonight. When she had first received the invitation, she had told her father flatly that she would not go.

"It is only a ploy to force me to meet Lord Ravenscar again, and nothing could impel me to do that," she had said, ignoring Joseph's pleading expression.

"Now, we don't know that."

"Why else would Lady Westhampton have invited us? Obviously she loves her brother dearly, despite the fact that the man is a pig. She must hope that he will be able to persuade me the second time around. Or perhaps she thinks that she can dazzle me with a taste of the glittering life of London society, hoping I will marry him just to be able to attend such parties."

"I am sure that wasn't the reason. She likes you. Didn't you tell me that you liked her?"

"Yes. But not enough to marry her odious brother."

"Now, Miranda, my love, was he really that bad?" Joseph had asked in a wheedling tone.

"He was the rudest, most arrogant man I have ever had the misfortune to talk to. Why, he barely even glanced at me the whole time he was talking. It was quite clear that he considered me far beneath him and was offering only because he was desperate. If I had to live with a man like that, one or the other of us would be dead within a month, I am sure."

"Perhaps he was nervous," Joseph suggested. "Asking for a woman's hand will do that to a man."

"I have never met a man less nervous."

Miranda had not told her father about the way Lord Ravenscar had jerked her to him and kissed her forcefully. She was not exactly sure why. She knew that such a revelation would end her father's questions and pleadings immediately. However, she had found herself reluctant to tell him about it. It was embarrassing; she could scarcely even think about the incident without blushing. Also, she was not sure exactly how her father would react. He was not a man with an excessive temper, but an insult like that to his daughter was something that could make him fly into a rage, and if he did, she was fairly sure he might do something rash like march over to the Earl's house and lay into him with his fists. While that was something that the man richly deserved, she suspected, having seen the Earl in action the other night, that her father would be the one who came out the worse for the fisticuffs, and she certainly did not want him to get hurt.

But Miranda knew that there was something more than these things that had kept her from revealing Ravenscar's scandalous behavior. She was not sure of the reason; she knew only that she wanted to keep the information to herself. His kiss had left her confused and uncertain, a condition to which she was not accustomed, and she was reluctant to let anyone see that.

She thoroughly disliked the man, just as she had told her father, and she felt certain that even a few minutes in his company would make her furious again. What did she not reveal, however, was that she could not stop thinking about his kiss, and there was something inside her that wanted with equal intensity to experience it again. She did not want to tell Joseph, of course, but she knew that deep down she was intrigued by the thought of meeting Ravenscar once more.

Lord Ravenscar would find no dowdy girl with spectacles tonight, she thought, and smiled to herself, taking a last look in the mirror before turning away to pull on her long evening gloves. The whole evening would be worth it just to see his expression.

Joseph popped into the room again, evening gloves in one hand and his gold watch in the other. "Time to go," he said, then stopped, looking at his daughter. "Well! I'll be having to fight them off tonight, I can see that."

Miranda chuckled. "Thank you, Papa."

"Don't you have anything you can put in that neckline to cover you up some?" he went on, frowning. "Ruffles or lace or some such?"

"It is an evening gown, Papa. That's the way it's supposed to look."

"Yes, dear," Elizabeth agreed placidly from her position on the couch. "It is the very height of fashion."

"I think it's perfectly grand," Veronica stuck in, sighing. "I wish I could go with you. To think of meeting all those people—the wealthiest and toniest of English society."

"The phoniest and silliest is more like it," Miranda replied and ran a loving hand down the girl's brown hair. "Just wait, you shall get your chance."

"Yes, your sister will see to your coming out," Joseph promised. "Once we've got her all settled."

"Papa..."

"You know, Joseph, you should not push her," Elizabeth put in softly. "She does not need to marry Lord Ravenscar. Indeed, you know that I think she should not."

"I know, Elizabeth," Miranda told her stepmother with a smile. "Believe me, I have no intention of agreeing to become Lady Ravenscar."

"I think that is a wonderfully romantic name," Veronica said, heaving another sigh of admiration. "Ravenscar. It sounds so—so wild and exotic.

"Mmm." Miranda picked up her fan from the table nearby. "Far too wild and exotic for a plain thing like me, I'm sure. All right, Papa, I'm ready."

"Finally." He went to his wife and bent to kiss her cheek. "I wish you would go with us, Elizabeth. It seems a shame that you're missing all these parties."

"It doesn't matter. I'm really not feeling up to it tonight. I want to go to the opera in a few days more."

"I am sure it will be much more enjoyable—and far less tiring," Miranda agreed, also going to her stepmother and kissing her on the cheek.

Her father offered her his arm, she took it, and they proceeded out the door and down the stairs to where the carriage awaited them outside. Her father was uncharacteristically silent on the drive over to Westhampton House, staring thoughtfully out the window.

Finally he said, "You know, I would not want you to do anything that would make you unhappy."

"I know that, Papa." Miranda reached over and patted his knee.

"Perhaps Elizabeth is right—I am just thinking of myself and not you."

"Well, I am quite capable of thinking of *my*self, and, believe me, you will not be able to bully me into doing something I don't want to." She smiled. "Surely you don't think that I have turned weak and biddable the last few days?"

A grin flashed across his face as he swiveled his head to look at her. "No, that I don't."

"Then there's nothing to worry about. I am just as bullheaded as you, so you may argue with me to your heart's content and you won't budge me past what I wish to do. Now, Veronica is a different matter."

"Veronica!" Her father looked shocked. "Why, I would never try to bully Veronica into anything. She's, well, she might do it just to please me and then be miserably unhappy."

"You see? You know with me you don't have that worry."

"You're right." He took her hand with a smile. "It is a comfort to me to know that you never pay the least heed to me."

Miranda chuckled and gave his hand a squeeze.

Westhampton House, when they reached it, was packed with people. Miranda had hung back on purpose, dithering over her clothing as she never did, because she wanted to make a grand entrance. It was disappointing, therefore, when she swept down the grand staircase on her father's arm and realized that Ravenscar was not standing at the bottom of it to watch her descent. The man had gotten the better of her, she thought disgustedly, as her eyes roamed quickly and discreetly around the great ballroom. She did not see him anywhere. *Could it be that this party was all just a result of his sister's wishful thinking and he did not plan to try to press his suit with her at all?*

It was a lowering thought. She had been counting all week on another opportunity to give the arrogant man a set-down. However, she put the best face on it that she could, greeting Rachel, who stood receiving at the foot of the stairs, with a smile.

"Miss Upshaw!" Rachel's green eyes lit up, and she took both Miranda's hands in hers in a friendly grasp.

Now that she had met her brother, Miranda could see the resemblance between the two of them. Like her brother, Rachel was tall, with a femininely broad-shouldered figure that made clothes hang beautifully on her. Her thick, lustrous hair was black, like his, and her eyes the same leaf green. But warmth made her eyes soft and inviting and touched her features with a friendliness that was completely missing from Lord Ravenscar's face.

"I am so glad you came this evening. I was afraid my brother's intolerable behavior would keep you away. I can assure you that he regrets it deeply."

Miranda held her own counsel about that. She had her doubts about the Earl of Ravenscar ever regretting anything, but one could scarcely blame his sister for not seeing his true character.

Rachel greeted Miranda's father warmly, too. Beyond her stood her mother, Lady Ravenscar, who unbent enough to smile at them, although the gesture did not reach her eyes. She, Miranda thought, was more like the Earl—hating the notion that she had to stoop to allow mere peasants into her family. Miranda replied to Lady Ravenscar with as much warmth and enthusiasm as her ladyship exhibited. Then she started to move on with her father into the crowd.

But Rachel was not about to let her get away so easily. She moved up beside them and linked her arm through one of Miranda's. "Let me introduce you to some of my friends," she told her, guiding Miranda in the direction of a knot of young matrons.

Rachel introduced her to all the women. Some were as warm as Rachel in their greetings, others almost frosty. Miranda could feel their eyes running over her gown, assessing style and cost. She knew that it had been made by one of the premiere modistes in London, so she had no fears on that score. No doubt the ones who wanted to would find something to criticize about her manner or speech, but Miranda did not care. She knew that she had dressed for only one person here tonight—and it seemed as if it might all be a waste. There was no sign of the Earl of Ravenscar anywhere.

She knew that people were talking about her. She saw the sidelong glances and heard the whispers behind hands and fans as Rachel led her along, introducing her to a dizzying array of girls dressed all in white, matrons in magnificent dresses and black-clad dowagers lined up in chairs against the wall. Every now and again, when Rachel turned away to speak to someone else, she could hear snippets of conversation:

"...so wild only an American would marry him..."

"…nothing but gambling dens and houses of ill repute…"

"Well, what can you expect? He's run through all his fortune—cards, liquor and women."

"…handsome as Lucifer himself, of course."

"Thank heaven he never cast his lures to my Marie."

"Well, she'll be sorry."

It was almost enough to make one feel a trifle sorry for the man, Miranda thought—if one were not already completely set against him. She also found it a bit irritating that everyone seemed to assume that if he offered, she would accept, as if an American would be happy to get a British aristocrat, no matter how low and vile he was. It was an attitude that she had encountered several times during their stay here. Back home, she and her family were counted among the highest of society; here, they seemed to be merely tolerated as something of an oddity. She found it distinctly peculiar that success in life counted for little compared to the name one carried. It was the same attitude that Ravenscar had held; the distaste and contempt at having to offer for a nobody from the former colonies had been apparent in his speech and manner. She supposed it was inevitable, having grown up among these people, that he should have turned out to be so arrogant.

She had been here almost an hour by now, and it seemed even longer, given the stultifying conversations that she had had the misfortune to be a part of. If the man did not show up soon, she thought, she was going to go home early and settle down with a nice book. It would be bound to be more entertaining than this.

At that moment, a deep voice spoke behind her and Rachel.

"My dear sister," Ravenscar began. "A successful crush, as always."

"Hello, Dev." Miranda felt Rachel's arm tense against hers, but she knew already who it was by the voice. It was the deep, wry tone of the man she had rescued, the faintest hint of amusement tingeing his voice, not the haughty drawl of the Ravenscar who had asked her to marry him.

She turned as Rachel did to face him. "And who is thi—" He stumbled gratifyingly over his words as he took his first look at Miranda. She saw the widening of his eyes and the quick way they swept down her body and back up, and she knew that her dress and hair had had exactly the effect she had hoped for. "—this lovely lady," he went on, smoothly covering the brief hitch in his words. "Ah, but I recognize you now, Miss Upshaw. It is a pleasure to see you again."

"It could scarcely be less of a pleasure than it was the last time we met," Miranda replied in a voice equally smooth. "How do you do, Lord Ravenscar?"

"Better now that I have seen you." He turned slightly toward his sister. "Rachel, I must take your guest from you. You have been monopolizing her time far too long. There is a waltz about to start, Miss Upshaw. If you would do me the honor...?"

He held out his hand, his eyes challenging in his handsome face. He knew that she would have liked to refuse him, but it would have been excessively rude, with his sister, the hostess of the party, standing right there beside them.

"I have scarcely had a chance to chat with Lady Westhampton," Miranda lied, making an attempt to get out of the invitation.

But Rachel was too quick for her. "Oh, heavens, don't consider me, Miss Upshaw. I have been neglecting my guests, I have so enjoyed speaking with you. Go ahead and dance with Dev. I can assure you, whatever his other faults, he is a divine dancer. You and I will have a chance to talk again later."

"Of course." Miranda could do nothing now, with everyone watching them, except to give in gracefully.

She took the arm he proffered and walked with him out onto the dance floor. They turned to face each other, and he took her hand in his, slipping the other lightly around her waist. She looked up at him, her heart beating faster than she would have liked. *The man was undeniably handsome.*

He swung her onto the floor as the first notes of the waltz began, and for the next few moments they did not speak, only moved with the music, concentrating on adjusting their steps to each other. It was easy to dance with him, Miranda found. He was, as his sister had said, an excellent dancer—moving gracefully and leading her with the slightest of guidance, not shoving and jerking one about as some men were prone to do. After they had settled into the rhythm of the dance, Devin smiled down at her a trifle ironically.

"Well, quite a transformation, I must say."

"Not so much so—if one bothers to look beneath the surface of things."

"Ah, a direct hit, Miss Upshaw. You have me there. I was careless the other day."

"You were rude," Miranda corrected him crisply. "Arrogant and rude and thoroughly dislikable."

"Yes. I confess I was all that. And after you had come to my rescue the night before. It was very boorish of me."

His ready admission of his lack of manners took Miranda by surprise. She had expected him to argue, or deny her statement—or perhaps simply ignore it. She was unprepared for him to agree with her. It left her, she found, with little to say.

He smiled at her expression. "You see, at least I am honest. You can give me credit for that."

"That counts for something, I suppose.... A very small something."

"At least I have something to build on, then. Perhaps I can make up for my lack of manners the other day."

"I am not sure if that is possible. One would always know, you see, that your polished manners were merely a facade, and behind them lay the same fellow who behaved so badly."

"No excuse will do, then? No apology suffice? Is there to be no allowance for improving oneself?"

"Improving oneself is a good thing, as long as it is real."

"You obviously doubt my ability to do so...or my veracity."

"I do not really know you well enough to say, Lord Ravenscar. The situations in which I have seen you..."

"I know. I have not appeared at my best." A grin quirked one corner of his mouth. "Although there are many who would say that I have no best."

"Indeed? So far you are not making a very good case for yourself."

"No, I am not, am I? I think that it must be you, Miss Upshaw. I am usually much more glib. You leave me tongue-tied."

"Indeed? I am amazed that I have such power over you. Especially given that you are the sixth Earl of Ravenscar, and I am just a provincial nobody who scarcely knows who her grandfather was." She smiled up sweetly at him.

Ravenscar let out a groan. "You aren't going to let me forget that, are you?"

"No, I don't think so."

"Let me make my apologies, Miss Upshaw."

"All right." She looked up at him expectantly. "Go ahead. Make them."

Her words seemed to fluster him. He glanced away, saying, "Well, ah..."

Miranda suspected that apologizing was something the man rarely did. "Yes?"

"I apologize," he said finally, and looked back down at her. "I should not have acted the way I did or said the things I did. I have no excuse, except...frankly, I was angry, and I am afraid that I took it out on you."

Ravenscar looked faintly surprised, as if he had not expected to say what he had—or perhaps had not realized the truth of it until this moment. He hesitated, then said, "May we talk?"

"I thought that is what we were doing."

"No, I mean—" he guided them to the edge of the dance floor and stopped "—let's take a stroll, get a breath of fresh air. And talk."

"All right," Miranda agreed. She wasn't sure what Ravenscar was up to, or exactly why he had this sudden urge to talk. She supposed that he was working on some way to get her to accept his proposal. She would not put it past him to try some nefarious scheme to get her to marry him—such as ruining her reputation—but she was confident that she could outwit him. And she was interested in finding out what he had devised to convince—or force—her to accept his proposal.

She put her hand on his arm and walked with him around the perimeter of the room until they reached the wide double doors open onto the terrace of the spacious house. There were other people on the terrace, escaping the hot, confining air of the ballroom. Some strolled along as they did, and some stood in knots of conversation. Miranda saw more than one pair of eyes slide in their direction and away, and she glimpsed just as many hands raised to cover whispers. She felt sure that everyone was talking about them. She did not know exactly what the gossip was or how much everyone in Ravenscar's set knew about his proposal, but it was obvious that there had been rumors flying.

Ravenscar smoothly guided Miranda away from the other occupants of the terrace and down the shallow steps onto one of the garden paths, lit by lanterns placed here and there among the trees.

"I did not want to have to marry," he said to her. "That was why I was angry—and embarrassed. So I acted the fool." He cast a sideways glance at her. "If I had known who you were, it would have been entirely different."

"Indeed?" Miranda responded coolly. If the man thought that this was an adequate apology, then he had a great deal to learn.

He came to a stop, so that she had to stop, too, and turned her to him. Miranda looked up into his eyes, dark in the dim light of the garden, and suddenly her knees felt a trifle weak. *Perhaps this apology was quite enough, after all.* She felt a rush of sensations that had nothing to do with holding a grudge against the man.

"Why, yes. The mystery woman who came so boldly to my aid...the beautiful woman I see before me...how could I be anything but intrigued?"

"Despite being those things," Miranda replied, "I am also still the American nobody whom your mother is forcing you to marry."

His eyes flashed. "I am not forced by my mother to marry you. She hasn't the power."

Miranda turned away, hiding a smile. *It was almost too easy to goad him.* She had found that when others underestimated her, it was much simpler to manipulate them. It had often worked to her advantage when dealing with men who thought her incompetent simply because she was a woman. It was just as easy with these British aristocrats, who thought her unsophisticated and even dull-witted simply because she was an American.

"I am sorry. I should have said, whom you were forced to marry to keep out of—how is it you say it here?—*dun territory?*"

"If you wish to put it that way," he said, irritation grating his voice. "Miss Upshaw, I am my own man. I shall marry as I choose."

He came closer, moving around her so that he faced her again. Miranda kept her face downcast, more to hide the dance of humor in her eyes than out of any shyness. Ravenscar put his hand beneath her chin and tilted it up so that she looked up into his face.

"I rushed my fences with you," he said, smiling faintly. "I apologize. I am not usually so cow-handed. Please accept my apologies and allow me to pay court to you."

He reached down and took her arm in his hand, lifting it and bending to plant a gentle kiss on the inside of her wrist. "Let me show you the man I can be. Give me a chance. Give *us* a chance."

As he spoke, his lips moved in soft kisses up her arm to her elbow. The cultivated charm of his words irritated Miranda, but she could not hold back the deep rush of pleasure at the touch of his lips on her flesh. She did not know how the merest feather of a kiss on the sensitive skin of her inner arm could make her abdomen flood with heat and her skin tingle.

"My lord," she said, embarrassed to find that her voice trembled, "this is scarcely proper. We are in the garden alone."

"Yes, we are." His voice was husky. His hands slid around her waist and gently pulled her closer.

"People will—"

"Damn people." He lowered his head and kissed her.

Desire thrilled through her as it had the first time he kissed her, startling and alarming her even as she melted against him. He wrapped his arms around her, pressing her body into his. His body was hard and masculine, delightfully different from her own. Miranda had never felt the strength and power of a man's body pressing into her this way; no man she knew would ever have dared to be so presumptuous. The fact that this man had no fear of her added somehow to the quiver of pure lust that darted through her. She tasted his mouth, hot and hungry, felt his heat as it rushed through his body. She trembled, her fingers curling into the lapels of his jacket, holding on to him in a suddenly unstable world.

Devin made a noise low in his throat and gathered her to him even more closely, the carefully calculated kiss turning unexpectedly into one of passion. His lips dug into hers, and she answered him with an equal enthusiasm, surprising him into an explosion of desire deep within. He had wanted to seduce her, to manipulate her into wanting him. Suddenly all he wanted was to feel her naked beneath him.

He slid his hands down her back and over her rounded buttocks, squeezing and lifting her up into him. Miranda could feel the hard length of him against her, and though she had had no experience in such things, she knew instinctively what it was, and the thought made her loins ache. Her arms went up and around his neck, and she strained against him. He groaned, his hands running wild over her back and hips.

Miranda clung to him, aware of little else except the intense pleasure coursing through her. Her breasts ached and tingled in a way she had never imagined, and her loins throbbed heavily. She wanted to wrap her legs around him and ease the emptiness growing there. She wanted to feel his hands on her breasts and legs...everywhere. His body was like a furnace, his breath hot against her cheek, and the feel of it spiraled her desire.

His mouth left hers, and she almost sobbed at the loss. Then his lips were trailing like fire down the column of her throat, caressing her like velvet as he nipped gently with his teeth. His hand slid up the front of her, between their bodies, and cupped her breast, shocking and arousing her. His thumb rubbed over her nipple through the material, hardening the little bud and sending a sizzle of desire through her so intense that she groaned aloud.

It was the sound of her own voice, uncontrolled and strange to her, that shocked her out of the trance of desire in which Ravenscar had locked her. She realized with a rush of shame where they were and what she was doing. She had planned to show up the arrogant earl, and instead he had seduced her as easily as the lowest tavern wench, making her hot and panting with desire for him, eager to feel his touch, his kiss...and so much more that it made her blush just to think of it.

''No!'' She pulled away from him, and, startled, he

let her go. He stood watching her, his arms shockingly empty, fire coursing, unfulfilled, through his veins.

Miranda smoothed down her dress and reached up to push a strand of disheveled hair back into place. "Really, Lord Ravenscar," she said, forcing all the cool calm she could muster into her voice. *She must not let him see how easily he could shake her; it would be too humiliating.* "This is scarcely the time or place. Anyone could come upon us at any moment."

"They won't." His voice was low and, it startled him to find, almost shaking with the intensity of his desire. "We can go farther back. I know a place—" Devin stopped abruptly, realizing with horror that he was almost begging.

A saving anger pierced Miranda at the thought that he knew the best place to seduce a woman in his sister's garden. "Yes," she said icily, "I am sure that you have had ample experience there. However, I do not intend to be one of your doxies."

She turned to face him, her gray eyes shining silver with anger. "There really is no need for this charade, my lord. We both know what you want of me, and it is silly to pretend to a passion that neither one of us feels." Her smile was chilly. "You will not seduce me into marriage."

Her words were like salt on the raw sore of his sexual frustration. *He had damn well felt passion—an alarming amount of it, in fact—in obvious contrast to her icy lack of it.* It irritated him profoundly that he, who had set out to seduce her, had been the one to succumb to desire, while she stood there, cool and contemptuous.

"I do not intend to marry you. I never did, even before your tasteless proposal," Miranda went on, feeling once again in control. It was frightening how easily she had almost lost that control. *To think she had come so close to falling like a naive girl for this cad's false seduction!* "I am not interested in an arranged marriage—although, of course, I can see the advantages of one."

"Indeed." Devin folded his arms across his chest, regarding Miranda sourly.

"Oh, yes, indeed. For you, of course, there is my money. For me, well...I would be able to introduce my sister Veronica into London society in the way that my stepmother wishes. That would please both Veronica and my stepmother, who are both quite dear to me. And your name, of course, is an old and respected one, despite the fact that you have tarnished it with your dissipated ways."

"What!" His eyes widened, and his hands dropped to his sides, balling into fists. "How dare you?"

Miranda looked back at him innocently. "I beg your pardon. Is that not true? It is what I have heard. But perhaps you have been wronged by the gossips. Have you not wasted all your fortune? Do you not keep loose company and spend your time in gambling hells and houses of ill repute?"

He pressed his lips together tightly, a flush rising along his stark cheekbones.

"Well?" Miranda prodded. "Is it a false rumor?"

"You should not even know of such things, let alone speak of them," he snapped. "It's unseemly."

"Unseemly for me to speak of them but not for you

to do them? Really, Lord Ravenscar, I am not a fool, whatever you may think of those of us who live beyond the hallowed shores of England. Nor am I deaf. Did you not think that I would hear the rumors? Why, just tonight as I walked around the hall, I heard that you had shamed your father, wasted—''

"Shut up! You don't know what you're talking about.''

"Oh, but I am afraid I do. Promiscuity, profligacy, drunkenness—these are the sorts of things that are always grist for the rumor mill. Everyone talks about them. I'm sure that none of the people inside care if a paltry American woman should have the bad fortune to marry a man with your reputation. But it is definitely a point against you as far as I am concerned. And obviously none of your peers are going to let you marry one of their daughters. Aside, of course, from the natural affection that they feel for their daughters, none of them would wish to align their name with one so besmirched by scandal. That is why you must settle for an heiress who isn't of the nobility—even one who is not British. Your reputation must be very low indeed.''

His face was stony as he looked at her, his eyes cold, hard marbles. She knew that he would have liked to rage at her but was hampered by the fact that everything she had said had been the truth.

"Of course, the blot on your name would not bother us Americans as much. My fellow countrymen seem to be oddly enamored of titles. I suppose it is because we got rid of such meaningless things long ago. It has created a definite void for those who are very proud, you know. So I know some wealthy Americans have bought aristocratic husbands for their daughters so that they can have a title in the family. I, however, have little longing to be 'Lady' Ravenscar. It seems an empty title, and I rather like my own name, frankly. Although,'' she added, looking thoughtful, ''the idea of restoring your estate does have a certain appeal. I do like to put things into good running order, and I am sure it has been sorely neglected. I am quite attracted to old houses, and Elizabethan architecture is one of my favorites, as it is Papa's. I understand that Darkwater is an outstanding example of an early Elizabethan mansion. And, of course, the history of it is intriguing. The curse and all that. Is it true that Darkwater was built of stones taken—''

''Bugger Darkwater!'' Ravenscar exploded. ''The damned place can rot for all I care. This is one English peer who is not for sale to you or any other rich American. I would rather the whole house crumble about my ears. I'd rather die in poverty than marry a common, bloodless witch like you! Good night, Miss Upshaw. And goodbye.''

Devin shouldered past her and strode off.

6

"**Well!**" Miranda watched Ravenscar's figure disappear down one of the garden paths. "That was interesting."

She had intended to provoke a response in the man, but his explosion had been something different from what she had expected. Irritation, swallowed bile, frustration and dislike—those had been what she hoped to engender in the earl. But the hot fury and wounded pride that had glittered in his eyes had been more than she had bargained for. So had the blunt pronouncement that he was not for sale. *It was enough to make one think that perhaps there was more to the man, after all.*

Miranda walked over to a stone bench, placed to admire a plot of flowers, and sat down on it. Her knees, frankly, were feeling a trifle watery. The evening had been...well, tumultuous. Devin Aincourt had surprised her more than once this evening, and that intrigued her. His kisses had melted her. She was too honest to try to pretend otherwise. No other man had ever sparked such feelings in her, and—to continue in the same honest vein—she would like to experience them again. *Why did the one man who had ever made her feel this delightful, tingly, slightly scary way have to be a man of so little character? Why couldn't it have been someone forthright and honest? Why was it this man whose kisses were so sweet, whose lips could make her feel as if the world had dropped away, whose eyes were as green as a new leaf and whose hands were...*

Miranda shook her head to clear it. It was foolish to sit here thinking about someone as clearly unsuitable as the Earl of Ravenscar. And yet...had it not said something about the man that he had so forcefully rejected the idea of selling himself as a husband? Ravenscar had pride—and not just the vain pride of many aristocrats, but a deeper belief in himself. She had seen it in his eyes as he had lashed out at her. There had been hurt there and a certain disgust with himself. He had been angry, not just at her, but at himself for doing what he felt he must. Money had not been worth giving up his pride, and she liked that. Perhaps, she thought, she just might want to see the Earl of Ravenscar again.

She rose and strolled back to the terrace, her head bowed in thought.

"Miss Upshaw?"

Miranda raised her head to see Lady Westhampton standing on the terrace, her hands knotted around the ends of the shawl that she had wrapped around her shoulders, her face creased with anxiety.

Miranda smiled. "Hello, Lady Westhampton."

Rachel visibly relaxed at Miranda's easy greeting.

She had seen her brother storm through the ballroom a few minutes earlier, and she had been worried that something bad had happened between him and Miranda. But Miranda clearly looked as if nothing were bothering her. Rachel wondered if it was only her brother who was upset, or if Miss Upshaw was simply better at hiding it.

"I hope you have enjoyed the party," Rachel began tentatively.

"Yes, it has been quite entertaining."

"Really?" Rachel eyed Miranda a trifle uneasily. "I, ah, I hope that nothing happened...I mean, that my brother did not, well, *offend* you."

A mischievous grin flashed across Miranda's face. "No. Actually, I think it was the other way around. I offended Lord Ravenscar."

Rachel chuckled. "I cannot imagine that, Miss Upshaw. Devin is not easily offended."

"Is he not? Really? I had a different impression of him. It seems to me that he is quite proud and easily offended."

"Oh, dear." Rachel's heart sank. "He did do something, didn't he? Or say something?"

"Well, he did say he would rather Darkwater crumble about his ears than marry me. But, you see," Miranda added honestly, "I had been rather blunt and, well, even a bit mean."

"Oh." Rachel looked at her blankly. "*You* were mean to Devin?"

"Yes. I can be, you see. There are some men in New York who are quite terrified of me."

Rachel chuckled, then glanced at her uncertainly. "You are joking, aren't you?"

"Not entirely," Miranda admitted. "I cannot abide dishonesty. And I have been rather abrupt with one or two men who thought they could get the better of me with trickery. Anyway, I was irritated with Lord Ravenscar because he was being dishonest."

"Devin? He is usually just the opposite—blunt to the point of being rude."

"Really? I prefer that, actually. Offensive as he was the other day, when he proposed to me, I think that it was preferable. He was arrogant and rude, but at least he was honest. Tonight he tried to seduce me into marrying him."

"Oh, dear," Rachel said in a faint voice.

Miranda glanced at her and saw the color in the other woman's cheeks. "I'm sorry. Now I have embarrassed you. I almost forgot that he is your brother. You cannot like to hear him spoken of this way."

"No," Rachel agreed honestly. "But I have heard many bad things about Dev over the years, unfortunately."

"Well, I would rather have him tell me the truth— that he hates the idea of marrying me but will do it for the money—than to have him pretend an interest that he does not feel."

Miranda hesitated, realizing even as she spoke that she herself was not telling the entire truth. She did not really think that Ravenscar had felt none of the desire he expressed. She had felt the heat of his body and the other unmistakable hallmarks of passion in a man. The problem was that he had engineered the situation to try to trick her into saying yes. And, she was honest enough to admit, a great deal of her anger had been because she was afraid that he had not felt desire to the amazing degree that she had felt it. However, she could hardly explain such things to the man's sister, so she skimmed over the truth.

"So I pointed out some of the drawbacks to marrying him—the rumors and such. It made him angry, I'm afraid."

"Oh dear," Rachel said in a small, sad voice. "I had hoped you would not have heard those rumors."

"I heard most of them tonight. People are very fond of gossip."

"And Dev makes gossiping easy." Rachel's voice was tinged with bitterness. "I love him, Miss Upshaw. I truly do. But sometimes it seems as if he delights in making it difficult to do so. What did you hear?"

Miranda looked at the other woman. Lady Westhampton looked so pale and unhappy that she could not bring herself to repeat the things she had heard. "Nothing that you haven't heard already, I am sure," she said gently. On impulse, she reached out and took Rachel's hand. "Please, don't be so sad. You cannot make your brother's life right, you know. Only he can do that."

"It has not been easy for him," Rachel said. She looked at Miranda with a plea in her eyes. "Please don't judge him by what other people say about him. I mean, yes, most of those things they say are probably true, but that's not what Dev is, really. He is a good man inside. I know it. He was always good to Caroline and me, growing up, and—"

She broke off and sighed. "Sometimes I think that curse is true. The Aincourts are doomed to misery. None of our ancestors were ever very good at hanging on to our money. We have wasted it and lost it on foolish ventures. The family would have been penniless long ago except that we also had a talent for making good marriages—*profitable* marriages, I should say. The Aincourts have had looks—and often charm. We attracted wealthy spouses, but the marriages have rarely been happy."

They had been strolling along the terrace as they talked, and Miranda quietly steered Rachel away from the other people and the ballroom.

"My sister and I married as we were supposed to," Rachel went on. "Caroline seemed lucky. Her husband was a spectacular catch, a duke, no less, and he loved her very much. They were happy. They had a daughter. Then, four years ago, she and her daughter died in a carriage accident. Richard tried to save them, but he could not."

"I'm so sorry." They had rounded a corner, out of sight of the rest of the party, and Miranda led Rachel to a stone bench and sat down.

"Thank you." Rachel offered her a wan smile. "I was the other dutiful daughter. I married the man my father picked out. He is a good man, a kind man. But—" she sighed, then went on "—but I did not love him. I loved another. I thought Michael knew that, accepted it, that he expected a marriage that was a business relationship and nothing more. I found out later that he did not. When he found out that I loved another, he thought I had deceived him purposefully.

He—well, we live apart. He gives me everything I need—he is a generous man. He and Richard support my mother, too. But none of us are happy.''

"I'm sorry."

"It is too late for me or Caroline. But Dev—Dev could still find happiness. That is why I wanted you to marry him. I think he could change his life with the right woman. He's…deep down he is a good man, a man of honor. But he and my father could not get along. Dev could never do anything right in our father's eyes. Dev was not like him at all. And he wasn't quiet and dutiful, as Caroline and I were. He argued with Father, and it made Father furious. My father was a hard man. He was very religious, and he hated it when Dev gambled and drank and—other things. I always thought that was why Dev came to be so wild. He went in that direction because it made our father so enraged. Father hated Dev's painting, too. He said it was not a fit thing for a nobleman, that Dev acted as if he had peasant blood in him, wanting to scratch about with paints. He thought it was useless and beneath him, but Devin loved it. So they fought over that, as well. Then, when Devin was eighteen, he went to London, as most young men do. And everything got worse there. He had freedom at last, you see, and he did just as he pleased. He worked on his art, and he met other artists, and Father thought they were a bad influence on him. But they were not the worst. He fell in with a set of people who were, well…not good people. They encouraged him to live the worst sort of life he could.''

"What did your father do?"

"He was so angry. He kept writing to Dev and telling him that he had to abandon his wicked ways and come home, and of course that just made Devin more stubborn. Father threatened to cut him off, and then, one time there was a scandal, worse than the others, and Father did cut him off. He would have disinherited him, but he could not. The estate is entailed, and he didn't have the power. But he stopped his allowance. I'm not sure how Dev even lived then. I am sure that Michael and Richard and others gave him money. He can be quite charming, and—well, we love him. I slipped him as much money as I could. Richard told me once that Dev made money playing cards, and I suppose he helped to support himself that way. He and Father never reconciled. Just before Father died, Mother wrote to us that he was very ill, and I went back. I got Dev to go with me, but when we got there, Father refused to see him. He wouldn't even let him in the room. Dev took one of the horses and rode back to London. He refused to go to Father's funeral. I don't know if he has been back to Darkwater since then."

She stopped and sighed. "He wouldn't have been like this if Father hadn't been so hard on him." Her voice hardened. "And if it were not for his...friends. I just know that if he could be taken away from their influence, if he could have some peace and happiness in life, that he would be a different man. I want that for him. That's why I was hoping that...you know, that you would marry him."

"I'm not at all sure that marrying me would make

Ravenscar happy,'' Miranda pointed out dryly. "We don't get along very well, you know.''

"I know. But...insipid females don't hold his interest. I thought someone strong like you, someone good, could make his life different.''

They were silent for a moment. Miranda looked thoughtfully at her hands. "You mentioned his painting.... He is an artist?''

"Oh, yes! He's terribly good. Would you like to see some of his work?''

"Yes. I would.''

Intrigued, Miranda rose and followed Lady Westhampton as she went into the house through a back door and ascended a narrow staircase that she presumed must be the servants' staircase. They walked down a hall to the front gallery, which ran the width of the house.

"You can't see them too well, unfortunately,'' Rachel said and gestured toward the outside wall, which was lined with long windows. "In the daytime, there's plenty of light, but at night...''

All the sconces along the wall opposite the windows were lit, for the whole house was ablaze with light for the party, but even so, there were shadows.

"I can see well enough,'' Miranda said, going closer to look at the first picture. "Are all these Ravenscar's?''

"These first three are. There are more on the other side.'' She smiled faintly. "I had to allow a few of the Westhampton ancestors.''

The first painting was a portrait of Rachel herself. She was standing beside a high pedestal, her forearm resting on it, and she looked out at the observer, a faint smile lingering on her lips. It was a younger and happier Rachel. The colors were muted greens and tans, against which the raven-haired Rachel in her simple white dress stood out vividly. The green eyes laughed; she seemed on the verge of revealing an amusing secret. And it had been painted, Miranda thought to herself, by an expert. The woman in the portrait had life; more than simply a physical likeness, her personality shone out, warm and inviting.

"It's beautiful," Miranda said honestly.

"I was seventeen when he painted it," Rachel said quietly. "He gave it to Michael when we were married." She walked on. "And this is Caroline. It's a few years earlier. Dev was about, oh, seventeen or eighteen. Caroline must have been fifteen."

Miranda looked with interest at the young girl, a dreamy sort with huge blue eyes and the thick black Aincourt hair tied back with a ribbon and cascading down her shoulders. She wore a blue cloak over her white dress, one side of it flung back over her shoulder, and she carried a cat in the crook of her arm. Every detail was rich and luminous. Miranda's hands curled inward, fingers digging into her palms to contain the excitement that filled her on looking at the paintings. She moved on to the next, this one a landscape of a barren, rock-strewn countryside, beautifully stark and drenched in sunlight. She could almost feel the warmth.

"These are beautiful!" Miranda turned to Rachel, barely able to contain the pleasure that rose up in her. She had been enchanted with the museums and galleries that she had encountered in Europe. Looking at much of the splendid, often old, art, she had been seized with the same sort of excitement, even joy, that filled her now. "He is a wonderful artist! You say you have more?"

Rachel nodded, smiling. "At the other end of the hall, and in my bedroom and sitting room."

Rachel took her along the gallery, where she showed her four more paintings that her brother had done, and then down the hall to a large, well-appointed sitting room. Here and in the bedroom beyond it hung another six paintings. One of the paintings was of a pale stone house, formidably large but graceful, built in the shape of an E.

"Is this Darkwater?" she ventured, and Rachel nodded. "Somehow I assumed it would be dark and brooding. The illustration in the book looked darker."

"Oh, no, the name comes from the tarn near there. The tarn is black as coal. But the house is beautiful and light. At least from a distance. Up close, it's rather falling to ruin. But gracefully. It's limestone. When the sun hits it like this, it does look golden."

That was the way Devin had painted it, with rich golden light cascading over the stones almost like water, the windows of diamond-shaped panes glittering.

"He painted that from memory," Rachel went on. "He did it after he left home. This is one of the tarn."

She pointed to another, smaller, picture, this one of an inky black pool set in the midst of outcropping gray rocks. It was a darker picture, shadowed and cloudy, with a single shaft of sunlight shooting down from the sky like a sword, its light swallowed up in the blackness of the pond. Miranda shivered involuntarily. It was as vivid in its own way as the lighter paintings, but its richness created an almost eerie scene, quiet and brooding, the piercing sunlight at war with the landscape. The other paintings were starker, too, one of a dark four-poster bed beside a window, the tangled white sheets a backdrop for a vivid red velvet dress tossed upon it, and another of a white washing bowl and pitcher upon a dark wood dresser, a bloodred rose lying wilting beside it in a splash of color. But in all of them there was the same richness of texture and color, the same expert hand in the details.

"May I see them sometime in the day?" Miranda asked, turning to Rachel, her eagerness showing. "I'd love to look at them in better light."

"Of course. You like them?"

"I think they're magnificent. I—" She came back to the painting of the bed with the bright red dress lying carelessly across the rumpled sheets. The painting was deeply sensual, almost erotic, and it stirred Miranda in a primitive, essential way. "I don't know what to say. Are these recent?"

Rachel's face clouded. "They are more recent than the ones in the gallery. But he doesn't paint anymore. He hasn't for several years."

"He doesn't!" Miranda gaped at her in almost comical shock. "You mean he stopped? He doesn't paint at all? Or draw?"

Rachel shook her head. "Nothing."

"But why?"

"I don't know. I asked him once or twice, but he always shrugs it off. He just says he got tired of it, or that it began to seem foolish. It's all part of the way he lives." Again bitterness crept into her voice. "His friends...the drinking and gambling and..." Her voice trailed off, and she shrugged expressively.

"I can't believe it. That's a sin!" Miranda's eyes turned back to the paintings.

"I know." Tears sparkled in Rachel's eyes. "I only wish Dev realized what a gift he has, what talent. He doesn't see the beauty he has inside him."

Miranda frowned as she followed Rachel out of the room and down the stairs to the ballroom. She and her father left soon after, and she was subdued all the way home in the carriage. Was it possible, she wondered, to fall in love with a man over soul-stirring artwork and a few equally stirring—albeit in a different area—kisses? It seemed absurd. Yet Miranda could not deny that there was a new and wonderful feeling inside her.

However, she was smart enough to keep her thoughts to herself. She knew that if she told her father that she was considering even the faintest possibility of marrying the Earl of Ravenscar, he would plague her to death, and she did not want to have to deal with his arguments while she was still tussling over the subject in her own mind.

She allowed her father to show her the papers he had acquired since he had first got wind of the Earl of Ravenscar's eligibility. These included an accounting of the sorry state of his finances, sent over by the trustee, Ravenscar's uncle, Rupert, as well as a description supplied by the estate manager of all the myriad problems of the estate and a long list of repairs needed to bring the house itself into good condition.

It was a depressing recitation of woes that would have daunted most people; Joseph knew his daughter well enough to know that such a financial mess would only set Miranda's fingers itching to fix it. Miranda knew his purpose, and she allowed that it was a tempting situation. However, while it was reassuring to think that she would have plenty to keep herself busy if she did indeed marry Ravenscar, it was not enough to impel her to take that plunge.

Nor was the beauty of the art the man had produced enough, though it filled her with awe and a swelling joy all over again when she called on Rachel the following morning to view Devin's paintings in the bright light of the day. His artwork was, if anything, even more beautiful in full light, for it allowed one to see the full power of his work. Rachel wisely left her alone and free to peruse the paintings as much as she wanted. Miranda sat on a velvet-cushioned bench in front of the paintings in the gallery and wondered with a certain sad amazement how the man who had painted these could have given it up. And though she felt almost as if she were looking into his otherwise well-hidden soul when she gazed at his art, Miranda knew that it, too, was not alone the source of that joyful, slightly scary new feeling in her chest.

That feeling had a great deal to do with those torrid kisses in the dimly lit garden and, perhaps even more so, with the strange, almost dizzy sensation she felt when she looked into his eyes, as though she were standing on the edge of a high precipice—and wanted to throw herself headlong into the void.

Miranda was a woman who was used to trusting her

instincts. Quickwitted and intuitive, her first reaction was usually the right one, and she was confident in her decisions. However, this was an arena in which she was not familiar. Miranda had never been in love. She had not passed through that giggling, moon-eyed stage when it seemed that she was falling in love every few weeks, as many other women of her acquaintance had when they were young. She had been busy at the time buying up real estate on Manhattan Island.

It was not that she had had no experience with men. She had a full social life in New York. She flirted with men, danced with them, even allowed a few to pay court to her. But she had never found herself in love with any of them. *Did this funny ache in her chest when she thought of Devin Aincourt signify that she was in love? Did the fact that she could not stop thinking about him mean that she should attach herself to him for life?*

Whatever it meant, she knew that she was enjoying it. And she knew that she wanted to see Ravenscar again.

Her first opportunity came two nights later at the opera. Her father had rented a box for the season, since they had planned to stay in London several weeks, but this was the first opportunity they had had to attend. Elizabeth was flushed with excitement as they took their seats in the lavish box, and even Hiram, her father's assistant, who usually wore only one stoic expression, looked happy to be there. Miranda, seated beside Hiram and armed with a set of opera glasses, scanned the audience. She found Devin's mother, seated in a box with Rachel and two other women of

Lady Ravenscar's age, as well as a couple of faintly bored-looking men. However, there was no sign of Ravenscar himself. Miranda wondered if the opera was something Ravenscar shunned; he did not seem the sort to attend simply because his mother or sister pressed him to do so.

Rachel caught sight of Miranda watching them, and she smiled and bowed in the direction of their box. Miranda smiled back, lowering her glasses. She cast another look around the rows of boxes. Across from her, and closer to the stage, a new party entered one of the empty boxes. There was a woman dressed in emerald green, and three men in black-and-white evening dress came in with her. Miranda drew in her breath sharply. Even from the back, she recognized one of the men as Devin.

Almost as if he had heard her, the man turned and glanced around the opera hall. His eyes stopped at Miranda's box, and he looked straight at her. He made no bow, merely raised his eyebrows a trifle, then turned away. Miranda smiled to herself. His haughty dismissal did not bother her. It only showed how well she had gotten to him the other evening, and she liked the fact that he rebelled against marrying for money.

But who was the woman with him? For the first time in her life, Miranda felt the sting of jealousy. Scooting her chair to the side of the box and a little farther back, where she was hidden in the shadows, she raised her opera glasses again and studied the woman in the box with Devin.

She was beautiful. Miranda's chest tightened, and she clenched the opera glasses tightly. The woman was golden—her hair a deep honey blond and her large, round eyes a startling golden brown. Even her pale skin was not so much white as the very faintest shade of gold. She was dressed in the first stare of fashion— perhaps beyond the first stare, Miranda decided, as she took in the full effect of the gown. It was the lowest cut neckline Miranda had ever seen, dipping perilously close to the woman's nipples. She had full, lush breasts, certainly worthy of showing off, and they threatened to spill out of the top of her gown at any moment. Emeralds sparkled at her ears and wrist, and a matching pendant dangled from her neck, drawing the eye to where it brushed the tops of her breasts. Her hair was pulled back to the crown of her head by a wide green satin ribbon, and from there it cascaded down in a tangle of rich, thick curls. Her features came close to perfection, marred only by a rather short upper lip—but even that flaw seemed to add to her looks, for it gave her a decidedly sensual look.

As Miranda watched, the woman turned and looked up at Ravenscar and smiled. It was a secret, tempting smile, and with that one look, Miranda knew that this woman was more to Devin than just an acquaintance whom he had escorted to the opera. *Was she his mistress? Did he love her?* The questions burned in Miranda, and as the opera started, she found herself studying their box as much as she watched the show unfolding onstage.

They were visited at intermission by Lady Ravenscar and her brother, Sir Rupert Dalrymple. Miranda had met him briefly at Lady Ravenscar's failed dinner party, and she found him a pleasant and entertaining enough conversationalist, but tonight she had difficulty keeping her attention on anything he said. There was only one person she was interested in seeing here, and she could not keep from glancing now and again at their open box door, hoping that she would see him there.

When she finally did look up to see Lady Westhampton coming through the door, followed by her brother, her stomach did a crazy flip, and she dropped her fan.

"Hallo, Mother. Uncle Rupert." Ravenscar's eyes slid to Miranda, then over to Hiram, without acknowledging either one of them. Miranda suppressed a smile, knowing that he had again, without speaking, given away the fact that seeing her disturbed him.

He went on to greet her father, who in turn introduced him to Mrs. Upshaw. Elizabeth colored slightly and whipped open her fan, bringing it up to cover the silly giggle that escaped her. Despite her protestations against him, Miranda thought, slightly irritated, her stepmother was no more immune to his good looks than any other female.

Ravenscar bowed to her, then turned toward Hiram, his brows raised faintly in question. Miranda's father said quickly, "Oh, this is my assistant, Hiram Baldwin. You met him at my house the day that you, well, ah..." Joseph's voice trailed off as he realized, belatedly, that Ravenscar's memories of the day Miranda turned down his proposal might be less than pleasant.

"Oh, I am sure that Lord Ravenscar does not remember, Papa. He barely saw anyone that day," Miranda stuck in.

Ravenscar turned toward her. "Miss Upshaw. Certainly I remember you."

"I had wondered, since you did not greet me when you entered," Miranda said pleasantly.

"Boy has no manners," Ravenscar's uncle interjected with a jovial laugh. "You must forgive him, Miss Upshaw."

"Must I?" Miranda replied lightly, and though she spoke to his uncle, her gaze was on Ravenscar. His eyes remained equally fixed on her.

"I am sure Miss Upshaw is not surprised, Uncle," Ravenscar drawled in his most irritatingly upper-crust voice. "She is well aware of what a barbarian I am."

Miranda smiled at him with false sweetness, and he swung abruptly away. "I must take my leave now. Mr. Upshaw, Mrs. Upshaw, pleased to meet you. Baldwin. Miss Upshaw." He pronounced her name with great precision, turning back toward her and adding a bow so courtly it was a sarcastic statement on its own.

"My lord. So pleasant to see you, as always." Miranda returned his gesture with an equally grand curtsey.

Devin's jaw clenched so hard that she could see the muscle in it jump. Then he turned on his heel and strode out of the room, ignoring the protesting look shot him by his sister.

Rachel turned and went to Miranda, saying in a low voice, "I am so sorry. I don't know what's the matter with Devin tonight. He has been excessively sour from the moment he came into Mother's box this evening. He was the one who suggested he escort me to your box. I didn't even think about it, because he was looking so glum and glowery. Then he comes here and acts perfectly rudely.''

"Don't worry, it doesn't bother me,'' Miranda responded with absolute candor.

The truth was, the exchange with Ravenscar had left her feeling rather invigorated, and Rachel's revelation that it was he who had wanted to come visit their box was even more encouraging. There had been something in his eye when he turned to face Hiram that in anyone else Miranda would have identified as jealousy, and it made her smile inside to think that perhaps Ravenscar had wanted to come to their box to discover exactly who the man was who was sitting beside her.

"I was wanting to talk to you, Lady Westhampton,'' she said, linking her arm through Rachel's.

"Rachel.''

"All right, Rachel. Why don't we take a stroll out in the gallery?''

"Of course.''

Rachel went with her readily, her curiosity obviously aroused. Once out in the grand hallway, Miranda glanced around and led Rachel toward the least populated area she could find, lowering her voice and bringing her head close to Rachel's.

"Now,'' Miranda said, "tell me about the woman who came to the opera with Ravenscar.''

7

The face Rachel turned to Miranda was almost comical in its dismay. "Who?"

"The woman with whom your brother came, the blond beauty."

"Oh. Oh, well, she's no one really. Lady Vesey is her name."

"Is she Ravenscar's mistress?"

Rachel drew in her breath in a gasp. "Miranda!"

"Well?" Miranda fixed the other woman with a pleasant but determined gaze. "You don't know me well, so I will tell you that I will eventually worm out of you everything you know about her. So you might as well go ahead and tell me all about her now."

Rachel looked at her uneasily. "I really—you shouldn't—"

"If you think that telling me about her will ruin the possibility of my marrying your brother, let me assure you that it will make absolutely no difference. Well, no, that is not true. You see, I believe in knowing everything I possibly can about a venture before I enter into it, whether it is buying a piece of real estate or having a dress made—or getting married. I want to know everything—good, bad and all the variations in between. Without all the details, I cannot make an informed decision. So I think that it is highly unlikely that I could marry your brother until I have discovered precisely what his relationship to Lady Vesey is.''

Rachel let out a groan.

"I promise you, I am not naive," Miranda went on. "I know that people here like to think of Americans as unsophisticated, and perhaps in some things we are. But when it comes to matters of scandal, I will wager that we are as up-to-date as Europeans. I know that men frequently have mistresses. I would not expect a man, especially one such as your brother, not to have had, well, shall we say, affairs of the heart? But I have to know what I'm dealing with. What is Lady Vesey to him? Does he love her? It is scarcely fair to me, you must admit, to expect me to go into something like marriage blindfolded.''

Her companion cast her an agonized look. "No, you are right. It is terribly unfair of me to not want you to know. But I am afraid—oh, please, do not hold it against Dev. He was very young when he met her, and—and the woman is a witch! A harpy! She sank her claws into him, and she's never let go.''

Rachel stopped and sighed, then began again, her voice calmer. "Her name is Leona, and she has been considered one of the greatest beauties of the *Ton* since she came to London—many, many years ago,'' she added cattily. Rachel smiled self-deprecatingly. "Well, I don't know how old she is, exactly, but I am sure she is several years older than Dev. She was already an established beauty and Lord Vesey's wife before Dev came to London. When he came here, he associated with artists and other young men of whom my father disapproved, young men whose lifestyle was very free and easy. He did gamble and drink and womanize, I'm sure. He had done the same sort of things even at home, and every time it brought about a major battle with Father. I almost think that is why Dev did them—to antagonize our father. I think I told you that in London he became even wilder, but, still, I think he was not much worse than most young men.''

"They are apt to sow their wild oats," Miranda said encouragingly.

"Yes, you know how it is," Rachel said, grateful for her understanding. "He had actually met Leona at home at Darkwater. Her husband's estate is not far from ours, and he saw her there. Of course, nothing would have come of it, because Leona rarely visits Vesey Park. But then Devin came to London. And he saw Leona again. Well, you know what she looks like. You can imagine how pretty she was then, in her youth. Dev fell in love with her—hopelessly, helplessly in love. A better woman would have discouraged him. A kinder one would have sent him on his way after a brief affair. But Leona is neither good nor kind. She is wicked, and she led Dev into all the same wicked pursuits she followed."

"Was it over Leona that your father disowned him?"

"No. At least, I don't think so. Father heard about his pursuing Leona and he disliked it intensely, but I—I think it was something else. I don't think he was, well, really...involved with Leona yet when he and Father had that great fight. I was still young at the time, only fourteen, and neither Father nor Mother would speak to us about it. I only know that it was something terribly scandalous. But after that scandal, whatever it was, Dev became completely enmeshed in Leona's group. I don't even know everything they have done. People have tried to protect me, you see.'' She offered Miranda a small smile. "I confess that I have not really wanted to know. I am not as brave as you.''

"I would probably feel the same as you if it were my brother we were talking about,'' Miranda lied kindly. She knew that the truth was that if it had been her brother in a wicked woman's clutches and fast sinking into sin, she would not only have found out everything she could about it but would also have set forth to try to stop it. But then, she also knew that she would not have had to do anything about it, because her father would have seen to it already; he would have pulled his son out of the muck, not disowned him, as Devin's father had.

"I think he loves her,'' Rachel admitted in a soft, sad voice. "At least, he has remained faithful to her all these years—in his own way. People dismiss the good things about him, but he is a very loyal person. He would do anything for me or someone else he loved, and I know he feels the pull of his duty. I think sometimes that he hates himself for the life he has led. There are people so cruel that they blame him for our father's death—and it was not his fault! He had nothing to do with it. Father had not even spoken to him for years. But the word got out that Father would not see him even on his deathbed, and the rumors grew. But Dev's loyalty to Leona hurts him. She has dragged him down into the muck.

"By the time I married and came to London, he had become quite steeped in sin. Neither he nor Leona were received by any but the most racy sets. I was appalled and hurt when I gave parties and so few of the most proper matrons came—when they were invariably pleasant to me at other parties. But then Michael told me, as gently as he could, that they would not come because Dev attended my parties—sometimes with Leona and her brother Stuart and their friends. I told Michael that I would never exclude my own brother from my parties, and I didn't, but I think Michael must have talked to Dev, because after that Devin stopped coming to my parties. And then the more proper matrons were willing to attend and bring their daughters."

"That must have been very hard for you," Miranda said sympathetically.

Rachel nodded, tears glimmering in her eyes. She dashed them away impatiently. "It was. I would rather have had Dev there than all the others. I was quite angry with Michael for interfering. But he knew, and so did Dev, that if I continued that way, before too much longer I would be considered part of their set and excluded from the rest of the *Ton* just as they were. Dev didn't want that to happen to me, so he stopped coming, except in the afternoons and such. Even the crustiest of old biddies could hardly expect me not to allow my brother to call on me."

She added with the glimmer of a smile, "Of course, it could be that Dev just grew rather bored with my parties. I am sure he was accustomed to far livelier entertainments."

They turned and started to stroll back toward the Upshaws' box. Rachel was silent for a moment, then said, "Leona is an evil woman. I think she bound Dev to her with her wiles, and that and his strong loyalty have kept him with her. She has encouraged him in the wicked things he's done. I know it was she who influenced him to stop painting. She wouldn't like anything that held his interest and devotion the way painting did. If you had ever met her, you would have seen what sort of person she is—sly and deceptive and—"

"Perhaps I should meet her," Miranda suggested.

"No! Oh, no, don't even think such a thing!" Rachel turned a horrified face toward Miranda. "I am sure she would do something to hurt you. She is bound to be afraid of losing Dev if he marries you—unless her pride has grown so huge that she dismisses the idea of his ever falling in love with someone else."

"Well, I am, after all, only an American heiress," Miranda pointed out with a smile.

Rachel returned a small smile. "I only hope that is the way she feels. Otherwise...if she felt threatened, well, I wouldn't put anything past her."

"Don't worry. I think that Lady Vesey might find me a more formidable opponent than she expects. If I were to marry your brother, that is."

Rachel looked at her with barely restrained eagerness. "Are you? Going to marry Dev, I mean?"

Miranda shrugged. "I have been considering it."

"Oh, Miranda!" Rachel's eyes shone. "Please, please consider it very well. The more I am around you, the more I feel that you would be able to change Dev's life. That is why I urged him to offer for you. I thought if he had a wife, someone he could fall in love with, give his devotion to, then maybe he would be able to break free of Leona's influence. If only he could be taken away from that evil woman, I know that he would be different. Better. At least happier. She doesn't make him happy, I know that. She keeps him fretting and uncertain. It is part of her hold on him. But you...if he were married to you, well, he might change. He might realize that happiness could be his. It is what I want so much for him."

"I know."

"I must seem very selfish to you. But I think Dev could make you happy, too. If he had a home and family, he could be a different man."

"The man he is, is rather charming," Miranda confessed.

Rachel chuckled. "Yes, he is, isn't he?"

"But you must not tell him I said so."

"Oh, no," Rachel promised with a smile. "I would not. Trust me. But I am awfully glad you find him so."

Devin returned to Leona's opera box with a scowl on his face. He felt faintly as if the Upshaw girl had been laughing at him, and he did not like the feeling at all. In fact, he had not liked the way he had felt the whole evening. He had not wanted to go to the opera in the first place. He had been in a bad mood for several days, ever since Miranda Upshaw had so casually pointed out that he was for sale, like a horse or a piece of furniture. He had spent the time since then telling himself that he would be damned before he married that American upstart—all the time, that is, when he wasn't thinking about the way she had felt in his arms, her lips yielding under his, and wondering what it would have felt like to have taken the moment further, to have peeled the clothes from her sweetly curved body and explored it inch by delicious inch.

Not, of course, that he liked the baggage or was interested in her—especially not in marrying her. But it would have been satisfying to have bent her to his will, to have caressed and kissed her until she was panting for him, begging him to take her, which he would, of course, do, but not until after he had made her ache for him as she never would for any other man. Every time he thought about that imagined ending to the evening—instead of the reality of his storming out of his sister's house in a black fury—he had grown hot and stiff, and it had been only he who had ended up aching. That fact had only made him dislike the American more. He hated even to say her name. Miranda. What a foolish conceit, as if she were Shakespeare's enchanting heroine, a role in which he could imagine no one less likely than she.

So he had been in a foul mood when he received Leona's note telling him to call on her this evening, and the peremptory tone of the missive had set his teeth further on edge. When he got there, Leona had demanded all the details of the progress of his engagement with the American heiress, and when he told her that there was no engagement and never would be, she had stormed and pouted and wheedled. Finally, just to make her stop, he had agreed to escort her to the opera tonight, even though he had known she intended to use the time to try her powers of persuasion on him again.

He had been rather clever, he thought, in talking Stuart and another friend into attending the opera with them, promising that there was a fetching opera dancer who would catch their eye. While he had been congratulating himself on his cleverness, he had glanced around the opera house and his eyes had fallen on Miranda. He had felt as if a load of bricks had fallen on him. He had stood for a moment, stunned, unable to look away, cursing his bad luck that she should be there while he was with Leona. He reminded himself that he had no reason to feel guilty because he was with Leona. He wasn't engaged to Miranda and didn't intend to be, after all. There was no obligation.

Then he saw the man sitting next to her, and something twisted sourly inside him. *Had the witch moved on to her next victim?* He had turned away and sat down, pointedly ignoring her, but his brain would not do so. Throughout the first act, he kept thinking about the man and wondering who he was. He thought he would have at least recognized most of the peers the man's age—unless, of course, he was Cavendish's son, but everyone said the reason no one ever saw the man was that he was mentally deficient. He began to wonder if perhaps the man was not an aristocrat at all but merely some clever fortune hunter pretending to be Lord Somebody. *That would serve the wretched girl right!*

At the intermission, curiosity had driven him to find out who the fellow was, so he hastily excused himself, ignoring Leona's startled glance, and made his way to his mother's box. Rachel had been more than willing to let him escort her to the Upshaws' box, but when they got there, he had felt ten times the fool. As soon as Miranda looked at him with those penetrating gray eyes, he had been certain she assumed he had come to see her. *Which, of course, was not the truth. Or not exactly.* Then, when he had discovered that the man was no one but Upshaw's secretary, he had been swept with relief, which was an even more foolish reaction than his initial one. It was almost as if he had been jealous, he realized, and that, of course, was completely absurd. *He wanted nothing to do with Miranda Upshaw, and it mattered not a jot to him whom she wed.*

He had appeared, he felt sure, foolish and inarticulate. *She,* of course, had been as cool as a cucumber, sitting there looking at him in that faintly amused, superior way. It made him grind his teeth all the way back to Leona's box.

Then, as soon as he sat down, Leona started in.

"Ravenscar..." she said, smiling in her catlike way. "Mr. Wyndham tells me that that is the American heiress's box you just went to. Is that true?"

"Yes. Rachel insisted I accompany her."

"And here I was being proud of you. I thought you were making a push with her." Leona picked up her opera glasses and peered through them at the box in

question, as she had done every few seconds since
Wyndham had told her that the Upshaws were sitting
there.

"Don't be absurd."

"Damn! I cannot see her. She is sitting in the shadows. Why doesn't she move up some? Oh, bloody
hell. Now they're turning down the lights."

Devin was relieved, but the start of the second act
of the opera did not deter Leona. She moved her chair
closer to Ravenscar's and leaned into him, whispering
behind her fan, "You know, you should have seized
the opportunity, Dev. Why else would you have gone
over there?"

"Hush. The music's starting."

"Oh, piffle. As if you or anyone else here cares
about the music. One only comes to the opera to see
and be seen, you know. All this in between is nothing
but a nuisance. Unless, of course, you play some interesting games." She smiled in the dark and moved
so that her leg lay against Devin's.

He twitched his leg away impatiently. "Don't,
Leona."

"Why are you in such a foul mood?" she asked
crossly. "Is it because the heiress has escaped you?
Even if she did, you know that you can get her back.
Use your charm."

"I don't want her back!" he snapped.

"Oh, Dev...for me?" Leona pouted prettily.

"If you had met this woman, you wouldn't be so
insistent," he growled.

"Really...are you saying that I should be jealous of
this colonial golden goose?" Leona's laugh was rich

and confident. "I think I can stand the competition."
She placed her hand on his thigh. Her fingers began
to walk up his leg. "Wouldn't it be pleasant to have
all that money? We could do whatever we please."
Her creeping hand moved ever closer to the joinder of
his legs.

"Dammit all to hell!" Devin jumped to his feet and
strode out of the box, leaving the other occupants staring after him in amazement.

Miranda saw Ravenscar abruptly leave Lady
Vesey's opera box. Intrigued, she rose and slipped quietly out of their own box. She saw him trotting down
the stairs at the far end of the corridor, so she followed
silently, catching sight of him just as he pushed open
one of the great outer doors and strode into the night.
She was not sure exactly what impelled her, but she
followed to the door and pushed it open. Something
inside her wanted to call out to him, to bring him back
to her, but she managed to clamp her lips shut on the
impulse.

As she watched him, Dev paused a few steps above
a young girl who was sitting on the bottom steps outside, two large baskets of flowers on either side of her.
She was a flower girl, come to ply her trade at the
closing of the opera, hoping to interest a few gentlemen in buying nosegays for their ladies. She was
young, no more than ten or twelve, Miranda would
guess, and she was pitifully thin, her hair straggling
lankly down beside her face, skinny ankles sticking
out from beneath her dress. Miranda felt a tug of pity

for her, as she always did for the flower and food vendors.

Dev dug into his pocket and pulled out a few coins, and Miranda wondered, with a spurt of jealousy, if he intended to purchase a bunch of flowers to take back inside to Lady Vesey. However, he only tossed the coins into the girl's basket and started on his way past her. Miranda smiled to herself, pleased that he had taken pity on the girl.

At that moment, another man, well-dressed and obviously inebriated, came slanting down the opera house steps on a path that would cross Dev's. As he neared the flower girl, he stumbled and knocked into the girl's basket, sending all the flowers in it flying across the steps. The girl cried out in consternation at the scattering of her livelihood. The drunken patron paid no attention, merely crunched on through the scattered flowers, demolishing most of them.

Outrage rose in Miranda at the man's careless destruction of the girl's flowers, and she started out the door, about to yell at him. But then she saw Dev cross the few feet to the man and catch him by the collar of his jacket. He spun the man around, and though Miranda could not hear, she saw him deliver a terse message to the man, nodding back toward the flower girl's crushed posies. The man looked at the mess he had created and sneered.

Ravenscar delivered a short jab straight to the other man's solar plexus, and the man doubled over. Devin jerked him back upright by his collar and spoke again. This time the man dug in his pocket, pulled out a bill and handed it to the girl. Dev gave him a nod and released him. The man continued on his way. The girl took the bill and tucked it quickly into her pocket, gratefully spewing out thanks to Ravenscar. Devin merely gave her a smile and went on his way.

Miranda watched his retreating figure until he was out of sight, her eyes alight and a smile curving her lips. Then she turned and rejoined her family inside their opera box.

8

Irritation sent Dev several blocks away from the opera house before he even thought of where he was going. He certainly did not want to return to his house. Stuart and one of his friends were back at the opera with Leona—*Good God, there would be hell to pay for walking out on her like that*—and even if they had been free, he didn't feel like seeing them. Nor did the thought of any of his usual haunts—taverns, gambling dens, bordellos—appeal to him. He simply was not in the mood for entertainment. He wanted...he wasn't sure what. To be free from the demons that haunted him, he supposed. The specter of poverty and ruin, the threat of a loveless marriage to a woman who held him in contempt, the prospect of treading this useless path of his life forever...

Perhaps it was the gloom of his thoughts that turned his feet in the direction of his brother-in-law's palatial home. He soon reached the gate of the mansion, which, in its parklike grounds with a high stone wall all around, took up a large chunk of the fashionable area of London.

Once, hundreds of years ago, this wall and gate had been guarded by the Duke of Cleybourne's soldiers. Now it was merely a footman who stepped out of the small sentry box inside the gate and peered through the iron bars at him. "Oh! My lord. Been a while since we've seen you here. Just a tick, sir."

The man bustled out with a ring of keys and opened the lock, pushing the wide gate back far enough that Devin could step through. "His Grace will be that happy to see you, my lord," the servant said chattily. Richard's servants were notoriously fond of their employer and loyal to him. Devin's mother deplored their familiarity, but Devin found it rather pleasant. It was a trifle odd that Richard, whose title was one of the oldest and highest in the land, was the least high in the instep of any peer Devin knew.

The footman who answered the front door to Devin's knock also knew him and greeted him with even more delight, escorting him immediately to Richard's study. Devin found Richard seated beside the fire, gazing into the flames. There was no other light in the room, and the firelight lit Richard's face oddly, casting deep shadows across his cheeks, giving him an even more saturnine appearance than usual.

At the sound of Devin's footsteps, he turned, saying gruffly, "What the devil do—" He stopped when he saw Devin, and a smile creased his face. "Dev! Come in, come in." He stood up, motioning to the footman. "Light some of the lamps, Harper."

"Yes, Your Grace," Harper replied happily, going around to light the wall sconces, as well as the oil lamp on the small table beside the Duke's chair.

Devin now understood the reason for the servant's delight in seeing him; obviously Richard had been sunk in one of his glooms this evening, and the footman hoped that Devin's visit would bring him out of it. Richard had once been a man who enjoyed life— of a more serious nature than Devin, of course, but still a man who enjoyed a party or a night spent touring the taverns with his friends. However, ever since the death of his wife four years ago, he had become something of a recluse. He shunned his country estate, where the fatal accident had occurred, and lived in the London ducal mansion, but despite being in a thriving city, he rarely went anywhere or saw anyone, except for the times when some friend or in-law ventured in to see him. Sometimes he even refused to receive visitors, which worried his loving servants terribly.

Dev remembered a little guiltily that he had not been to call on Richard in several weeks. He recalled now that Rachel had said, frowning, that Richard seemed to be getting worse, not better, as the months and years passed. Richard, like most men of Devin's acquaintance, was not the sort to talk about his grief. Consequently, he and Devin rarely broached the subject of Caroline's death, though they had been the two men who loved her most on earth.

Devin glanced involuntarily now at her portrait. It was one he had painted himself a few weeks before Caroline's marriage to Richard. She had asked him to do it, wanting it as a present for her future husband. It had hung over the fireplace in the great room of their estate house, but Richard had brought it here, where it dominated one wall of the study. In the painting, Caroline was smiling in that dreamy, almost sleepy way she had, a young woman on the verge of her adult life and expecting to enjoy it to the fullest. She was dressed in the elegant satin gown she would wear at the wedding, and she wore the famous parure of Cleybourne emeralds: a circle of emeralds and diamonds that clung to her throat, dangling a pendant of a single huge emerald; earrings of perfectly matching emeralds centered in tiny diamonds; a bracelet of linked emeralds; and even a dainty diamond tiara decorated with five exquisite emeralds. It seemed to be an extravagance of jewels that would have overwhelmed the young girl wearing it, but Caroline was tall, like most of the Aincourts, and possessed of a vivid beauty. Nestled in her raven hair and caressing her pure white skin, complementing the brilliant blue of her eyes, the jewels looked magnificent and correct.

Devin had captured her happiness and even that hint of smugness in her smile and eyes that indicated that she knew she was making a splendid marriage to a man who loved her above all else. Her skin gleamed in the pale light that poured over her through the window beside her, and her eyes were so alive one almost expected to hear the girlish giggle that was her trademark.

"It is the most beautiful portrait I have of her," Richard said, following Devin's gaze. "That's why I have it here, where I can see it the most." He looked on past the portrait to the smaller one of a young girl beside it. "I only wish I had had you draw one of Alana. The artist couldn't do her justice—she was always moving about, you know."

Devin looked, too, at the portrait of his niece. She was about four; it must have been done not long before the accident. Richard was right. The artist had gotten her features correct, but the sparkle that animated the child was not there, nor was the smile that lit up any room she entered. Devin would have painted her outside, washed in sunshine, laughing and playing with one of the cats or dogs. But then, by that time, he had given up painting.

"Have you ever thought of taking it up again?" Richard asked.

"Painting?" Devin looked at him in surprise. "No. I'm past that. It was nothing but a hobby. Something I liked when I was young."

"Really? Care for some port?" Richard turned toward the hallway and raised his voice slightly. "Harper! I presume you're still lurking out there in the hall. Bring us a bottle of port and two glasses."

Richard turned back to Devin and gestured toward the two chairs in front of the fireplace. "I would have thought you would sometimes want to draw a particularly interesting face, or that you would see some scene that struck you so you had to paint it."

Devin shrugged, his thoughts going, strangely, to Miranda Upshaw's face—too strong a jaw and wide a mouth for beauty, but with those arresting gray eyes and such a determined set to her chin that one could not help but notice her. *It would be difficult, if not impossible, to get those eyes right.*

"I'm afraid I lost the interest," Devin said dismissively. "No doubt the skill, too, by this time. As Fa-

ther used to say, scarcely the occupation for a gentleman.''

''Ah, I see. In the way drinking and gambling are.''

Devin glanced at him sharply. Richard was watching him, a faint smile on his lips, and Devin had to
chuckle.

''You know me well. And, no, I don't think my
father ever regarded those as fit occupations for a gentleman, either. His idea of a proper life was prayer,
morning, noon and night, with a little chastising of
sinners and three good meals in between. He was, if
you remember, a man who liked his food, which is
why he rarely addressed his Maker on his knees. It
took two servants to haul him up afterward if he did.''

''Yes. I remember the old tyrant. He once told me
I was too worldly to marry his daughter, but fortunately my father's illness meant that I would come into
the title soon, and that apparently made up for my
sins.''

''I am sure it did. And your well-stocked coffers
even more so.''

At that moment Harper came back into the room,
carrying the tray of port and glasses. He set the tray
down on the small table beside the Duke and started
out of the room.

''Oh, and, Harper…close the door behind you, and
then you can go to bed. There's no need to stand watch
out in the hall. I assure you that I do not plan to put
a period to my existence, at least not while Ravenscar
is here.''

''I am relieved to hear that, Your Grace,'' Harper

replied with little indication of chagrin, and bowed out of the room, closing the door.

Devin looked at Cleybourne, his eyebrows raised. "Are they expecting you to end your life soon?"

Richard grimaced and reached over to pour the port. "They have too much time on their hands, and they use it to come up with absurd fears. Unfortunately, now they have planted that seed in your sister's head. Rachel has paid a call on me three times in the past two weeks, usually with no purpose. I suspect that Baldock—my butler—decided to confide his fears in her."

Devin was silent for a moment, taking a sip of his drink. Finally he said, his voice carefully indifferent, "And are you planning your imminent demise? Attending a funeral would put rather a crimp in my plans, I must warn you."

Richard smiled faintly. "No. I shan't put you out like that."

"Good."

They finished off their glasses, and Richard refilled them. He raised his glass toward Devin. "I forgot—congratulations, Dev. We should drink a toast to your impending marriage."

"My im—" Devin stared at him, glass halfway to his mouth. "How the devil did you hear about that? Oh—Rachel, of course."

"Of course. She was here Monday and told me all about the estimable Miss Upshaw."

"Well, there is to be no marriage, so you may save your toast."

"Indeed? Rachel sounded very hopeful."

"She is. So is my mother. But I fear both of them are doomed to disappointment."

"Why? It sounded a good thing for you. I mean, she is an American, no name and all that, but..."

"I know. In my position, one cannot afford to be too choosy. Money overcometh all."

"Actually, I was going to say that Miss Upshaw sounded as though she would make you an excellent wife."

"Hmm. If I cared to be shackled to a shrew."

"My. That scarcely resembles Rachel's description of the woman."

"Rachel doesn't face marrying the wench. Miss Upshaw is hard, manipulative and entirely without feeling."

"Indeed?" Richard took a sip of his drink, watching Devin with interest over the glass. "It sounds as though she has made a rather bad impression on you."

"She accused me of selling myself to the highest bidder. Well, not accused, exactly, because she seemed to have no problem with my doing it. As if it were a matter of course for a British peer to go on the block. 'Several Americans are purchasing nobles for their daughters to marry. My fellow countrymen seem to be peculiarly fond of titles,'" he mimicked savagely. "That's when I told her that this British peer was not for sale." He sighed, looking down darkly into his glass. "Of course, it is all the more infuriating because I *am* for sale. One title, man attached, for the price of enough money to live as I am accustomed to."

"And save Darkwater," Richard pointed out. "That is scarcely a small matter. Your estate is in desperate shape, from what I've heard, and not just the house itself. There are a number of people who depend upon you and your family. I am afraid that Americans find it hard to understand the concept of duty to one's family and to the people who have depended on the family for years. There is a feudal quality to it that escapes them."

"I'm not a saint, Richard. You know that." Devin downed the remainder of his drink and got up to pour another one. "If I married her, it would be because I can't fancy myself in debtor's prison."

"I can't say that I would, either. You know, Dev, if you need some funds..."

"I know. You're a generous man. But I have reached *point non plus.* A temporarily plump purse will not suffice." He sighed. "Uncle Rupert assures me that the estate is tapped out. It isn't making money anymore, it's losing it. And it would need massive infusions of cash to make it profitable for future generations. The house is falling down about their ears, and the grounds are choked with weeds and brambles."

"Ah. Thus speaks the man who is concerned only with the state of his own pocket."

Devin grimaced. "I don't give a damn about Darkwater. But Mother will plague me to death about it."

"Then why not marry the girl? You will have your money, and Lady Ravenscar will cease to plague you. There is no one else you've a mind to wed, is there?"

"No. And you needn't tell me that no one of good family will marry me, anyway. Everyone delights in pointing that out to me."

"Rachel tells me the American girl is attractive and charming."

"Attractive, she is. Charming? I wouldn't say that. She is blunt, aggravating and completely impossible."

Richard's eyebrows lifted, and he hastily took a sip to cover the smile that came to his lips. "Indeed? Well, obviously she would make your life miserable."

Devin shrugged. "I can pack her away to Darkwater. That is what they all tell me."

"All who?"

"Leona, Stuart, even Uncle Rupert. But..."

"But what? It goes against your conscience to take the woman's money, then immure her in Darkwater alone?"

"A little," Devin admitted. "And I would have to, because I know I could not live with the witch."

"Why is that? What does she do?"

Devin shifted uncomfortably, then burst out, "Dammit, I don't know, Richard! She just makes me feel...she looks at me with contempt. She says things that no one in polite company would say. She is utterly cold."

"Well, you would not have to occupy her bed frequently," Richard stated.

Devin scowled, his loins tightening involuntarily at his brother-in-law's words. "She's not cold in that way. In fact, she's quite—" He shook his head as if to clear it. "She confuses me. She plagues me. I keep thinking about her. Tonight I saw her at the opera, and she looked at me in such a way—as though she found me amusing. She has eyes that can look right into you. And she's utterly maddening. I am sure we would fight constantly. We have fought every time I've been around her. She turned me down, you know. I proposed to her, and she just looked at me and said in that flat way, 'No.' Then the next time she told me that she saw the advantages of marrying someone with my name—there was Darkwater to restore and the title, though she doesn't care that much about it, and then, of course, the most important thing, she could bring out her sister into London society. Of course, she also told me, I couldn't hope for anything better than a nameless American, being such a profligate and drunkard and womanizer.''

Richard choked on his drink and began to cough. ''Did she actually say that?''

''Of course. I told you, she says anything that comes into her head. She would send my mother into a swoon, no doubt.'' He grinned. ''Although it might be worth it just to see that.''

''Hmm. You might want to latch on to this girl. Think of the dustup she could cause at Almack's.''

Devin chuckled, and they were silent for a moment, drinking, absorbed in their own thoughts.

''You know, Dev,'' Cleybourne said finally, ''marriage might not be such a terrible thing, even to Miss Upshaw.''

''Are you hoping it will make a decent man of me? That is what Rachel thinks—though she tries to express it more tactfully, of course.''

''No,'' Richard replied quietly. ''I think you are a decent man, no matter how much you try to convince people otherwise. But you might find that life would be more...interesting with a wife like Miss Upshaw.''

"Then you think I should marry her, too?"

"I think you should do what is best for you." Richard shrugged. "Of course, in this situation, I don't see that you really have any choice in the matter. She turned you down, after all."

Devin shot him a sideways glance. "I could change that any time I wanted."

Richard let out a short burst of laughter. "Damme, you probably could."

"Enough of such somber things," Devin said, downing the remainder of his glass. "Drink up, and I shall challenge you to a game of Ecarte."

"Ah, you will soon be out of debt, then, as you will doubtless beggar me. Let us remove ourselves to the game room." Cleybourne stood, wrapping his hand around the bottle, and they left the room to settle down to a long night of drinking and card playing.

To her surprise, Miranda found that her stepsister was curled up in a chair in Miranda's room, sound asleep, when Miranda returned from the opera that night.

"What are you doing here at this hour?" she asked playfully, touching Veronica's shoulder to bring her awake.

Veronica jumped a little, startled, and looked up at Miranda, blinking. "Oh! I was waiting up for you. I wanted to hear all about the opera." She stretched, rubbing her neck. "I don't get to do anything fun! Mama says I cannot go to the opera until I make my coming out."

"I am sure your mother knows all about such things better than I."

"But I didn't get to go to the ball, either. Do you know that I've never even seen this Ravenscar fellow? And you didn't tell me about the ball. So I decided I would wait up for you and get all the latest information. Only I fell asleep."

"All right," Miranda said with a smile. "You be my maid, and then we won't have to awaken Rosie. And I'll tell you all about the opera."

"And the ball."

"And the ball."

Veronica jumped up to undo the long row of buttons down the back of Miranda's dress. Miranda described the opera house and the music, the glittering array of jewels and dresses on all the women attending. She also did her best to recall the details of the ball—the arrangements of flowers, the dresses, the lights blazing from every possible place, the music that had played. Veronica listened avidly, her eyes lighting up as she imagined all that Miranda described.

"What about the Earl?" she asked when Miranda paused, seemingly done. "Don't stop there. Tell me about the Earl of Ravenscar. Did you see him tonight? Did you dance with him at the ball?"

"Yes, and yes."

"Don't stop there!" Veronica cried.

"What do you want to know? He's a passably handsome man."

"You can do better than that."

"All right. He has eyes as green as glass in the sunlight, and his hair is black as coal. There is a little scar here on his cheekbone, close to his eye. He's tall and broad-shouldered and wickedly handsome, and not at all the sort of person young girls like you should be daydreaming about.''

''But are you going to marry him?'' Veronica pressed.

Miranda paused, looking off into space for a moment, then back to her stepsister. ''You know...I think I just might.''

9

"My lord...my lord..." The soft repeated words finally brought Devin awake.

He opened one eye and looked up to see his butler looming over him, wringing his hands and frowning. Devin growled something unintelligible and sat up.

He realized two things simultaneously as he did so: one was that he was incredibly stiff, particularly his neck; and the other was that his head was pounding furiously. The reason for the latter, he knew without even having to think. His head felt as it always did when he had consumed an excessively large amount of alcohol the night before—swollen and tender and as if a thousand tiny elves were going at it with hammers from the inside.

It took a moment to realize the reason for his unusual stiffness. He was seated at his desk in his study, not lying in bed, and he had fallen asleep on the desk, his head cradled on one arm, with the result that his neck felt permanently crooked, and his hand and arm were numb and useless.

He blinked against the light and groaned, trying to

remember what he had been doing in his study and why he had fallen asleep there.

"My lord," his butler began again, but Devin raised an admonitory hand.

"No."

The butler stopped, shifting nervously from one foot to another, looking at his employer, then at the door, then back at Devin.

"Give me a minute to make sure I'm alive," Devin went on. "I think I may be in one of the circles of purgatory."

"I beg your pardon?" The butler added confusion to his expression of anxiety. He was not the man who had buttled for Devin for years, that good chap having been offered better pay elsewhere. This man had worked in the Earl's household for only two months, and he had found it both undemanding and unsettling. He still had not decided whether the easygoing manner of his employer was worth the strange hours he kept and the less than genteel folks who came and went there.

"Never mind. I need a glass of water. No, wait, coffee. Perhaps both."

"Yes, my lord. But first, there is the matter—"

Devin let out a groan. His memory was coming back to him by degrees. He recalled the opera the night before and leaving Leona in a huff, then going to Richard's house. They had played cards, finished off the bottle of port and opened another before he had finally left. It had been very early in the morning, he remembered, as he made his unsteady way home, for the sky had definitely shown signs of lightening in the east. A man of sense, he knew, would have gone straight to bed at that point, but he had not. He had been carrying their second bottle of port, which still contained some liquid, and he had taken the bottle into his study and continued to drink.

He had also, he regretted to remember, decided to try out his drawing skills. Richard's words had somehow implanted in him an urge to draw, to see if he was still capable of rendering a human face on paper. It had been an utterly useless thing to do, of course, but then, he frequently embarked on utterly useless courses of action when he was in the grip of drink. So he had dug out paper and pencil and had wasted an hour or two trying to draw faces—well, one face in particular. He had been unable to get Miss Upshaw's countenance out of his mind, and he had tried to exorcise it by recreating it. He had been singularly unsuccessful, a fact which was attested to by the number of balled-up sheets of paper in the waste bin and scattered around it. However hard he had tried, he had not been able to capture the exact look of penetrating intelligence and inner amusement that marked Miranda's face.

Somewhere along the line, obviously, he had fallen asleep. He leaned back against his chair now and fixed his butler with a deadly gaze. "I said coffee. Forget everything else."

"But it is the lady, sir—I don't know what to do."

"The lady?" Devin sank his fragile head onto his hands. "What lady?"

"The lady outside, my lord. She insists on seeing you, and she seems most determined. I told her you were unavailable, but she refused to believe me, sir. I—I didn't know what to do.''

"Send the baggage packing.''

"I would have, sir, but she—well, I recognized the unmistakable lines of Madame Ferrier in her dress and pelisse, sir, and her speech, her manner, well—'' He lowered his voice, almost as if he were revealing a secret. "She appears to be a lady.''

"You're daft.''

"No, he's not,'' said a clear voice from the doorway.

Both Devin and the butler whipped around to look at the doorway, a movement that caused Devin's stomach to lurch dangerously.

"Miss Upshaw!'' the butler exclaimed, obviously shocked.

Devin groaned and let his head sink into his hands. "I should have known.''

"I am sorry,'' Miranda said, addressing the butler rather than Devin. "But I was getting rather bored cooling my heels out in the entry, and frankly, I was afraid that you might not have the nerve to awaken Lord Ravenscar. I thought you might need my help.''

"Good God,'' Devin groaned, "am I to be plagued by you everywhere, even in my own house?''

"Rough night, eh?'' Miranda said, not without sympathy, coming farther into the room. She turned to the butler. "He needs coffee, I imagine, Mr....what is your name?''

"Simmons, Miss. Just Simmons.''

"All right, Simmons. Bring a pot of coffee as quickly as you can, and I think it would benefit the man greatly if you would also make a glass of my remedy. It works like a charm. Mr. Hoskins, Papa's trade representative in the Northwest Territory, used to swear by it. Poor man, he was given to drink, and whenever we arrived there, we were as likely as not to find him sunk in a hangover. It was the loneliness and snow, you know—drove him to drink. I always made him a glass of remedy, and it made him better in minutes. First you take a raw egg, then you add a pinch of crushed black pepper, a—''

Devin let out a pitiful moan. "No, please, I beg of you, no more description. I am sure that the cook would leave me if called upon to make such a concoction. Simmons, fetch the coffee. I shall deal with Miss Upshaw.''

Devin rose to his feet, using the desk as a brace, and faced Miranda. He smoothed back his hair and unrolled his shirtsleeves, only then realizing that he was without coat or even waistcoat, both of which he had thrown over one of the chairs early this morning. His ascot was with them, leaving him in a thoroughly disheveled and improper state—shirttails out, the top button undone—to be receiving a visitor, much less a female one.

"Miss Upshaw, I am afraid this is highly improper,'' he began. "I don't know what you do in America, but in London, a lady simply does not enter a bachelor's quarters unescorted, unless she is a rel—'' His voice died as his eyes fell on the pile of wadded-up papers beside the wastebin. Hastily, he kicked a number of them under his desk.

"It would be improper in the United States, as well,

Lord Ravenscar,'' Miranda assured him, her eyes following his to the balls of paper in and around the trash can. The nervous, almost guilty look on his face intrigued her, and she wondered what the papers contained. "However, I had something I needed to talk to you about, and I saw no sense in sitting around hoping you would show up at my doorstep again, or that I would run into you at the opera or the theater or some party.''

"You could have sent me a note requesting me to call on you.''

"And you would have come?'' Miranda quirked one eyebrow in disbelief. "Anyway, I dislike waiting. I like to take charge of my own destiny, not put it in the hands of others. So I decided to call on you myself. I suspect it is a trifle early in the day for you, since it is only half-past noon, but I wanted to be sure to catch you before you left.''

"Left? For where?''

"I don't know. Anywhere. Left for the day, I mean. Really, my lord, are you sure you don't want me to pop into the kitchen and make you that remedy? You do seem to be having some difficulty keeping up with the conversation.''

Devin regarded her balefully.

Miranda gazed back at him, never changing her pleasant expression. The man looked like hell, she thought. *It was almost enough to make one change one's mind.* But Miranda was not the sort who changed her mind easily. Once she had made a decision, as she had this morning after a nearly sleepless night of thinking about it, she was not likely to second-guess it. She was confident and ready to go forward. That was why she had decided to go directly to the Earl's house and get the thing started.

She knew what she wanted, and why. The only problem now was bringing it about. But Miranda was confident that she would be able to turn Ravenscar around.

"Miss Upshaw, let me be as blunt as you seem to like to be."

"Please do."

"What are you doing here?"

"That is quite simple. I have come to tell you that I have decided to accept your proposal. I will marry you."

Devin said nothing. He simply stood there staring at her. It occurred to him that perhaps his ears were playing tricks on him. He had, after all, had a great deal to drink the night before.

"I beg your pardon?"

"I said that I have changed my mind about marrying you. I accept your proposal."

"You can't do that," he protested. "I told you, I wouldn't marry you even if it would save me from debtors' prison."

"You offered for me."

"You refused my offer."

"A woman has the prerogative of changing her mind," Miranda pointed out. "Besides, you can't take back your offer. It would be ungentlemanly in the extreme."

"No, no, no," Devin said, coming around the desk

toward her. "One offer, one chance. That's it. You refuse, and the offer is gone."

The butler reentered the room at that moment and almost backed out again after one glance at the wild look on his employer's face. But Miranda stopped him with a look and a gesture.

"Ah, the coffee. Set it on the desk, Simmons. Would you like for me to pour?"

"No!" Devin fixed the butler with a glare. "Put the tray on the table by the couch, Simmons. I'll pour."

"Yes, my lord." Simmons quickly did as Devin directed and beat a hasty retreat, skillfully managing to leave the door open a crack when he closed it.

Miranda followed him to the door and closed it. Devin turned to the table and poured himself a cup of hot coffee. Miranda seized the opportunity to walk softly to his desk and reach under it with one toe, nudging out one of the balls of paper that Devin had been at such pains to hide. While his back was turned, she reached down quickly and picked it up, stuffing it into her pocket. When he turned back around, she was regarding him placidly, her hands folded together in front of her.

"May I offer you a cup of coffee, Miss Upshaw?"

"No, thank you. I am sure you will benefit from it far more than I."

Devin took a sip of coffee and waited for a moment. When his stomach did not rebel, he took another drink. When he had downed the entire cup, he thought perhaps he was ready to deal with Miranda.

"Now…" Devin tried to fix a pleasant smile upon his face, despite the fact that his head was still pounding like thunder. "Miss Upshaw. I am not sure what has brought you to this turnaround, but if you think about it for a moment, you will realize that it is completely unworkable. You and I could never get along. We can't stay in the same room longer than five minutes without getting into some sort of wrangle. We could not possibly be married."

"You must know a very different sort of married couple to think that getting along is a requirement of marriage."

"You despise me!"

"Now that is a trifle harsh. I never said that I despised you," Miranda said thoughtfully. "I found you arrogant and rather unlikeable, I will admit, but it isn't a prerequisite of marriage to actually *like* one's spouse. I am sure that your feelings toward me are much the same as mine toward you."

"If that is the case, then one or the other of us will probably be dead before the end of our honeymoon," Devin commented dryly.

Miranda smiled faintly. "I assure you, my lord, that I am not homicidal. I am also well able to take care of myself."

"This is absurd." Devin set aside his empty coffee cup.

"No. I assure you it is not. It is well thought out. I spent all last night going over it. And I can tell you that I rarely come to the wrong conclusion."

"Speaking of arrogance..." Devin murmured. He settled himself against the edge of his desk, stretching his long legs out in front of him and crossing his arms over his chest, and regarded Miranda with a patient, if somewhat bloodshot, gaze. "All right. Let me hear these well thought-out reasons."

"As I told you the other night," Miranda began, "I had begun to realize the advantages of the sort of arranged marriage you offered me. It was not what I had expected in life, so it took a bit to grow accustomed to it. For you, the choice is obvious, however much you may dislike it. I have seen your financial statements, you know, and it is quite clear that you are teetering on the edge of ruin."

"You have seen my financial statements?" he asked, amazed.

"Your uncle was kind enough to send them to us."

"How nice of him."

"Yes, I thought so. At any rate, if you hope to survive, certainly if you want to save your family's estate, you need to marry into money—and soon. I am your best opportunity. Even a colonial nobody is better than living out your days in debtors' prison."

"I won't go to debtors' prison."

"Oh, no, that's right. You have a sister and mother off whom you can leech." Miranda ignored Ravenscar's furious glare. "Still, I scarcely think they can give you the lifestyle you are accustomed to out of their clothes allowance. Do you?"

"There are other options."

"What? Gambling? Or perhaps you intend to get paid for leading flats into gambling hells? No, I think marriage is the only way to gain the amount you will need. And you have burned your bridges here in England. A wealthy peer has no interest in allying himself to scandal. Isn't that true? Do you have any other heiresses to choose from?''

''You know I do not.''

''I would say that makes me not only your best hope but your only one.''

''You have such a tactful way of expressing yourself.''

''I thought that you would appreciate blunt speaking. We are, after all, discussing a business arrangement. Isn't that right? Papa and I would settle a lump sum of money on you—not too great a one, I'm afraid, because of your well-known propensities to, well, spend it quickly. We will pay your outstanding debts, and, of course, you will also have a generous monthly allowance. I will pay for the upkeep of the houses, and Papa and I will take care of the restoration of Darkwater. I understand that the estate is in poor shape, also, and I will, of course, undertake to bring that back into some semblance of repair. I would not be surprised if it actually began to make a profit before too long. I am rather good at that sort of thing, you know.''

''Miss Upshaw.'' Devin rose, his eyes narrowed. ''While you are making plans for my future, might I remind you that you will not be in control of all this once we are married? When we marry, all your money will be mine. You will not even have the right to hold property. I will be the one to decide about allowances and lump sums. You, my dear, will be in my power.'' He moved closer, looming over her, his face grim. ''The husband rules in England, and you will do as I say. Had you thought of that in all your little plans? I could lock you up in Darkwater and take off for London to enjoy spending your money.''

His eyes were fierce, his posture menacing, but Miranda held her ground. "Lord Ravenscar, I must tell you that once when I was with Papa buying furs in the wilds, I was face-to-face with a rather large black bear. Your attempt at intimidation pales by comparison." She sidestepped him and moved away.

"Whatever you may think," she said calmly, turning around to face him from several feet away, "I am not stupid. Nor is my father. First of all, the bulk of the family fortune belongs to my father. He will pay for *what* he sees fit *as* he sees fit. He will pay your debts and restore Darkwater. I can assure you that he will do exactly as he pleases in that regard. You seem to have a misconception that Americans are stupid. Or perhaps it is his friendly manner that fools you. But, believe me, you will never get a penny out of my father other than what he wants to give you. As for my personal fortune, if you think that I would give up the money I have worked to accumulate over the past ten years just for the pleasure of marrying you, you are very much mistaken. Before I marry, my money will be placed in a trust, the trustees of which will be my father, my attorney and Hiram Baldwin. As you might suppose, they will invest it as I order and distribute it as I order. Should you be so foolish as to try to lock me up anywhere—or so lucky as to be able to do so—I think you would shortly find yourself without funds.''

Ravenscar's eyes flashed, and his body went rigid with fury. "Do you think that you can control me this way? That you can make me dance to your tune because you have money?''

He crossed the space separating them in two quick strides, and his hands clamped around her arms. His eyes blazed down into hers, and he was so close she could feel the heat of his body. His breath rasped in his throat. His intensity and fury were like a tangible force. ''No one owns me, least of all you.''

A thrill ran down through Miranda. The truth was, she generally frightened men; there was something exhilarating about facing a man who had no fear of her. She returned his gaze, glare for glare, her body taut.

''You think you are safe because you can set up trusts?'' he went on. ''Because your father and every other man you know jumps to do as you say? I am not one of them. Perhaps no one bothered to mention that, amid all my faults, there are a few things at which I am skilled. I am a crack shot, Miss Upshaw.''

Miranda gazed back at him levelly. ''Are you threatening me, Lord Ravenscar? Perhaps someday we should have a contest. When I accompanied my father on trading expeditions, we went to some of the wildest places on the continent of North America, places where there was no law and never had been. I learned how to use a gun at an early age. In fact, I was taught by one of the best backwoodsmen in the country.''

Devin stared at her, then, unexpectedly, began to laugh. He dropped her arms and moved away, saying, ''I am sure you were, Miss Upshaw. Anything else would be uncharacteristic. Next you will tell me that you know the art of fisticuffs, as well.''

''No. That I do not. My size and strength generally

kept me at a handicap. However, I was taught by trappers how to use a knife to slice and skin and kill, as well.'' She gazed back at him blandly.

''Touché.'' He shook his head. ''You are without a doubt the most unusual woman I have ever known.''

''I shall take that as a compliment,'' Miranda said briskly. Her breathing was still a little uneven. It unnerved her that he could affect her so, but she was not about to let him see that. ''I think perhaps you misunderstand me. The truth is, I have no wish to control you. My only limit is on your spending my money, and I think you will find that limit not an onerous one. I do not force people to do what I want. I generally find I am able to accomplish that with reasoning.''

He chuckled. ''Still, you get your way.''

''I often do,'' Miranda admitted. ''I do not insist upon it, however, certainly not in a marriage. However, I have as little desire as you to be ruled by another, so I have taken steps to prevent it. That is all.''

''I see.'' Devin nodded.

''Does that offend you?''

''Of course.'' A glint of humor flashed in his eyes. ''Actually, once the slap in the face is over, I think I feel…relieved. I am, as you may have guessed, terrible with money. Witness my present predicament.''

''That is understandable. You are an artist.''

Devin let out a derisive snort. ''Hardly that. No, I fear that I am just a gentleman of leisure, and I am not terribly good at anything except a number of 'gentlemanly' pursuits. Riding, hunting, card playing.''

''Oh, there are places where you might find those things would stand you in good stead,'' Miranda remarked. "So, my lord Ravenscar, do you wish to rescind your offer? Or will you accept this marriage 'contract'?"

He thought with amusement of what Leona would think once she found out what her 'mouse of an heiress' was really like.

"No domination by either of us, eh?" he said thoughtfully.

"That is correct."

"I think I would be agreeable to that." It was, he told himself, the only sensible thing to do. His reluctance stemmed from nothing but a pride that was, frankly, too large for his present circumstances. He had to marry, and irritating as Miss Upshaw was, well, as Richard had pointed out, at least life with her would not be dull. *And getting an heir with her would be anything but an onerous duty.*

"Good. I would hate to have to make another search for a suitable spouse," Miranda said.

"That won't be necessary," Devin replied curtly, a little surprised to find how much the idea of her marrying someone else displeased him. "My offer still stands. Will you marry me, Miss Upshaw?"

"Yes, my lord, I will," Miranda replied promptly, then went on, "I think we should do it quickly, don't you? There is little point in waiting. We need to start clearing up the debts and restoring the estate. I think a short engagement is preferable."

"That's fine." He felt a trifle dazed by her brisk, businesslike manner. It seemed that an engagement should entail something more—some celebration, a kiss, at least....

He reached for her, but Miranda neatly turned and walked away, saying, "Now, as to the details...I think a wedding away from London, don't you? There will doubtless be enough gossip as it is, without giving them weeks and weeks to build it up."

Devin resumed his position at the desk and watched her thoughtfully. *Had she seen the kiss coming and skillfully eluded it, or had she not realized what he was about to do?* "You know, Miss Upshaw," he began, "one has to wonder. This is all very well for me. The advantages of marrying you are clear. But why do you wish to marry me? Given the fact, after all, that you find me arrogant and—what was the other quality? Unlikeable?"

"It is more the idea of an arranged marriage that appeals," Miranda explained calmly, sitting down in a chair facing him. "At first I did not like the idea, as you know. But then, as I began to think about it, I could see the wisdom of marrying not for love or passion, but for practical reasons. As I mentioned the other night, I would like to restore your estate. The house and the lands. I enjoy dealing in real estate. There's nothing quite as much fun as taking a piece of land and making it turn a profit."

"Indeed?" He looked doubtful.

Miranda chuckled. "It appeals to me. I would like to restore Darkwater to its former beauty. And I would like to see what can be done to turn your estate around, modernize it, whatever it takes to make it begin to produce again."

"Odd reasons to marry. One would suppose you could simply buy an old house and restore it."

"Ah, but then it would not be one's own. I would have no real, personal connection to it. That makes it much more special. Besides, there is the allure of your social standing. My stepmother would greatly enjoy seeing Veronica have her debut here in London. It would be nice to be able to do that for her. Veronica will enjoy that kind of thing."

"So you are marrying in order to bring out your sister in a few years, thereby making your stepmother happy, and to restore Darkwater."

"Partly. But as I told you before, those things were not enough to make me willing to marry you. But as I thought about it, I realized how freeing the whole arrangement is."

"Freeing?" He looked puzzled.

"Yes. You see, I have been plagued by fortune hunters, both here and at home. I never know whether a man truly likes me or just wants to get his hands on my money. With an arranged marriage, there is no uncertainty. I know you do not care for me—indeed, I think we have established that you find me odd and off-putting. That makes it much easier than hearing honey-sweet words and wondering constantly if they are false. I much prefer plain dealing."

"You prefer to be without love?"

"I prefer to know where I stand. I despise lies. I hate people trying to fool me, deceive me. An honest emotion is always better than deception, I think, even if the emotion itself is not the most pleasant. At least one knows how to deal with it, how to act. And one doesn't feel a fool afterward when one learns the truth. Besides, I have no intention of being without love. It is simply that in such circumstances, love, if one finds it, comes outside of marriage.''

''I beg your pardon?''

''I said that love is separate from marriage when the marriage is an arranged one, and that is really much easier, don't you think? Once I thought about it, I saw that the European way is much more practical. You and I marry for our own practical reasons, and then, in our daily lives, we simply go our separate ways. You will do what you want, live as you want, and so shall I. Then you have none of the jealousy and petty feelings that can infect a marriage made for love. You will have your lovers, I will have mine. You will—''

''What!'' Devin bounded up from his easy, relaxed pose, his face drawn into a scowl. ''What do you mean, you will have lovers?''

''Why, simply what I said. Is something the matter? I was talking about the business sort of marriage that we are entering into. Isn't that what you had planned? That you would marry me for money but keep a mistress for pleasure? Or love?''

''Well, yes, I would,'' he retorted, then stopped short, realizing how his statement sounded.

Miranda raised one eyebrow. ''You expect different behavior from me than from yourself?''

''Well, yes,'' he admitted, looking a little uncomfortable. ''It's one thing for a man, but for a woman—''

''Yes?''

''Well, women just don't go around having affairs outside of their marriages.''

"They do not? But I had heard that Lady Vesey was married."

"Leona? Leona has nothing to do with this."

"But I understood that she was your mistress."

"What?" He looked stunned. "How do you— Where did you hear that?"

"From Lady Westhampton."

"Rachel?" He gaped at her. "My sister? What possessed her to tell you—"

"Oh, she didn't volunteer the information. I asked. When I saw you together with Lady Vesey, I suspected that was the case, so I asked your sister. She could scarcely deny it."

"I don't see why not!" Devin retorted. "Rachel should know how to act in polite circles."

Miranda's brows rose again. "Meaning that I do not?"

"No, not if you go about asking people such questions. Particularly of a chap's own sister. My Lord, you shouldn't be talking about such things with *me,* let alone Rachel."

"Why not?"

"It simply isn't done."

"Oh, pooh." Miranda waved away his objection. "What nonsense. I thought we were to be open and honest with each other. Partners in a business, so to speak. Surely we are above pretending that what everyone knows to be true is not."

"That is not the point," Devin growled.

"Then what is the point?" Miranda asked calmly.

"You cannot go about having affairs! I will not have the Aincourt name besmirched," Devin snapped.

"Lady Ravenscar does not engage in affairs. My wife's name will not be bandied about by every gossip in London."

"I meant that I would be discreet, of course," Miranda assured him. "I would not do anything that might hurt the Aincourt name, which you have guarded so carefully these many years."

"All right, sneer if you like. I admit that I have not been a model of propriety. I have hurt my family's name and reputation. But it is different!"

"Because it's you?"

"Because I am a man," he said through clenched teeth. "It is an entirely different matter for a woman."

"Why?"

"Why? How can you even ask? Everyone knows."

"Knows what?"

"That women are—that they—"

"Are more moral than men? Have a higher standard?"

He pressed his lips together for a moment, frustrated, then finally burst out, "No one cares if a man has a by-blow or two, but a woman's unfaithfulness jeopardizes the succession."

"The succession?" Miranda giggled. "You sound as if you are talking about the kingdom."

"You know what I mean. One could never be certain if an heir were truly an heir if—"

"I told you I would be perfectly discreet. I would be careful, as well. You would not have to worry."

"I would worry a great deal if I had to be calling men out to save your honor!"

"What nonsense. There would be no reason to call

anyone out. I cannot imagine why you are making a fuss about it. I mean, it isn't as if you cared about me.''

"I certainly do not."

"Then why should it matter what I do? I know you are too fair a man to expect me to live differently than you or Lady Vesey."

"Would you stop throwing her name into this?"

Miranda shrugged and plowed ahead. "And surely you do not expect us to remain celibate after we marry."

"Celibate! God, no. Where did you get that idea?"

"Well, I mean, in a marriage such as ours, where there is no conjugal love—no real liking, actually, when you come right down to it— if we did not seek pleasure elsewhere, then we would have to be celibate. I know you don't intend that."

"Of course I don't intend that. I haven't intended *anything* yet. I have no earthly idea how you have come up with any of what you are saying." Devin shoved his fingers back through his hair, disarranging it even further, and looked at her wildly.

"No doubt you need some time to think about it," Miranda told him kindly.

"It will take more than time. Are you saying that you and I are not—that we will not—"

"Share a marital bed?" Miranda offered. "That's right. That is part of the appeal of this sort of marriage. We do not have to consummate it. If you had to pretend to love me and woo me, then you would have to follow through, and that must be a very difficult thing when one does not love a person, I would think. But this way, when you go into it honestly, without all the trappings and lies, when it is merely a business arrangement, pure and simple, neither of us will have to pretend that we want to consummate the marriage. I am sure the thought of that appeals as little to you as it does to me.''

He looked at her, dazed, and finally murmured, ''Yes, of course.''

''There you are. That is one of the reasons why I realized what an excellent arrangement this is. We will have separate beds, separate lives.''

''But—but what about heirs?'' Devin brightened. ''After all, that is one of my primary duties as the Earl of Ravenscar, making sure that the title has an heir.''

''Well, in time, I suppose, if that is so important, then we will have to deal with it,'' Miranda said, considering the idea. ''We will make some sort of arrangement. But that is a long way away. There is no need to worry about it now.''

''Of course not.'' Devin walked around his desk and sank down in the chair behind it. He felt rather as though he had just been through a whirlwind. No, it was more the feeling that he had been swindled by some mountebank, but so skillfully that he could not even put his finger on exactly when and how it had occurred.

''Good, then it's all settled,'' Miranda said briskly, rising to her feet. ''My father will be delighted, as will your mother, I am sure. We shall set the proceedings into motion. You will find them quite painless and quick. Now perhaps you ought to lie down with a rag soaked in lavender on your forehead. You look a trifle under the weather.''

Miranda swept out of the room, leaving Devin behind her, looking faintly stunned. She walked out of the house and down the steps to her waiting carriage, and only after she had climbed up into it and settled down in the plush seat did she allow a grin to break across her face.

She had told a tremendous pack of lies back there, she thought, but the idea seemed to cause her little remorse. Last night, as she had lain awake, thinking, she had come to an important conclusion: against all reason and logic, Devin Aincourt was the man she wanted. Once she was certain of that, everything else had fallen naturally into place. Miranda was not one to distrust her instincts. She would marry him, and she had no intention of sharing him with Lady Vesey or anyone else. She knew that he wanted her; she had felt it in his kisses, his embrace. She was also sure that he would marry her. Beyond that, it would be up to her to bring him to love her.

It was to that end that she had spent the rest of the night planning her campaign. So far, everything had gone exactly according to plan. She had left Devin confused, vaguely jealous and definitely frustrated. It was, she thought, a good beginning. The next step would be whisking him off to Darkwater for the wedding, away from London and the clutches of Lady Vesey. She knew she could rely on her father and the eager Lady Ravenscar to make that happen as soon as possible.

Reaching into her pocket, she brought out the crumpled piece of paper that Devin had been at such pains to hide under the desk when she walked in. She had been curious about it the entire time they had been talking. Now she took it out and opened it, carefully smoothing out the wrinkled page. It was, she saw, a drawing of her face, only half-done, but easily recognizable.

She looked at it for a long moment. Devin had fallen asleep at his desk last night because he had been trying to draw her face. She remembered the pile of crumpled papers he had kicked under the desk. The waste bin had been full of them, as well. She smiled with satisfaction and leaned her head back against the cushion. *It was all going even better than planned.*

10

Miranda's father was predictably pleased with her announcement that she had decided to marry the Earl of Ravenscar. Veronica, too, found the news tremendously exciting. Miranda's stepmother, however, looked less pleased. Though Elizabeth wished Miranda every happiness, as was polite, her face was marred by a small frown, and she took Miranda's hand, looking into her eyes and asking earnestly, "Are you sure that this is what you wish to do? Joseph can find another house, another aristocrat, I'm sure."

"No. I have decided that this is the aristocrat I want," Miranda replied, with a small, secret smile. "Don't worry about me, Elizabeth. It is very sweet of you to be concerned for my happiness, but, truly, I am quite certain that this is what I want to do. Have you ever known me to vacillate?"

"No," Elizabeth replied honestly. "You are always quite confident. But sometimes…well, the Earl of Ravenscar is much more…ah…sophisticated than you. He is older, and he has lived a wicked life. I am very afraid that he has deceived you, that you believe

him to be other than what he is. I am afraid you will
be hurt.''

Miranda smiled at the older woman fondly and
reached out to hug her. ''Dear Elizabeth...I think that
I have an accurate understanding of what the Earl of
Ravenscar is like. I am not going into this marriage
blindly. Nor am I doing it for Papa's sake. This is what
I want. Trust me, and don't worry.''

Her stepmother acquiesced, still looking faintly
troubled.

As she had known he would, Joseph immediately
swung into action, calling on his London attorney and
setting up a meeting with Devin's attorney. Miranda
left the business dealings to her father, because she
was far too busy with the myriad of tasks attendant
upon a wedding, even the small family sort that she
had requested. Primary among them was getting a
wedding dress and trousseau made in the short amount
of time before the ceremony. Looking the absolute
best she could at her wedding and for the first few
days of her marriage was essential. Though she had
already bought several new dresses when she came to
London—and before that had visited the best coutu-
riers in Paris—she did not have something suitably
fashionable and lovely for every moment of the day
for two or three weeks.

Rachel was more than happy to help her with this
task, and so were Veronica and her stepmother, who
set aside her reservations about the marriage in the fun
of choosing beautiful new clothes. There were also
dresses to be made for each of them for the event.
They spent hours at Madame Ferrier's, poring over the

fashion plates in her books and discussing fabrics and colors. Madame Ferrier grew so excited about the opportunity to create so many dresses for a client who paid promptly and well that on several occasions her French accent slipped into pure Yorkshire. Once the dresses were chosen and Madame Ferrier could set about harrying her seamstresses to have them done on time, they had to find all the necessary accessories— reticules, shawls, ribbons, shoes, hats, parasols...the list seemed endless.

Two days after Miranda told Devin that she intended to marry him, Lady Ravenscar held a party to announce the engagement. It was, perforce, a small celebration, partly because she hadn't the time to prepare a large party and partly because she hoped that a gathering of only those closest to her would help to hold down the gossip. It would be impossible to expect the *Ton* not to talk about the wedding, of course, but she did hope to keep the talking to a minimum.

Therefore the party was small, elegant and thoroughly boring. Miranda, sandwiched between Lady Ravenscar and her son, who looked even more bored than Miranda felt, politely smiled and greeted the people to whom Lady Ravenscar introduced her and wished she were somewhere else. By the time the guests had stopped arriving and Lady Ravenscar allowed them to break from the receiving line, Miranda had come up with an idea.

Turning to Devin, she raised her fan to cover her mouth and whispered, "Do you think anyone would miss us if we left?"

Devin looked at her, his brows rising in the first

look of interest on his face that she had seen all evening. "They will assume we have expired from boredom, I imagine. Why? Did you have something in mind?"

"I have heard much about Vauxhall Gardens since I came here," Miranda began, tucking her hand into Devin's arm. They began to stroll away from the others. "It is said that one should not miss it, but that a lady cannot go there unescorted."

"Good God, no," Devin agreed. "It is acceptable, of course, if one is accompanied by a male relative or, say, a fiancé."

"That is what I thought." Miranda looked up at him, her eyes smiling.

Devin cast a look back around the room. No one seemed to be paying the slightest attention to the two of them. Most of Lady Ravenscar's friends were clustered around her.

Devin whisked Miranda out of the room and down the hall to the front door. An impassive footman, long accustomed to such behavior from Lady Ravenscar's son, opened the front door for them. Laughing like children escaping their studies, Devin and Miranda trotted down the steps to the street, where Devin hailed a passing hansom.

"You have to have a domino and mask," Devin told her, but those necessities were easily provided by a stop at his lodgings before they continued to the Gardens.

Vauxhall was everything Miranda had heard it was—tawdry, exciting and colorful. Boxes lined the wide walkway, filled with partygoers, most of them

masked, as Miranda and Devin were. Women of a sort
that Miranda assumed was less than virtuous strolled
along, being ogled by young men in the boxes and
returning their catcalls with giggles, winks and waves.
Miranda saw more than one such miss lured over to a
box and boldly kissed.

Miranda watched it all with fascination. Couples
slipped off down other, darker, less-traveled walkways
for purposes Miranda had no trouble guessing at.
Vauxhall Gardens was clearly rife with assignations.

Devin procured them a box from which to observe
the passing parade and the midnight fireworks. Miranda asked him questions about the people they saw
and the things they were doing, many of which made
him laugh at their bluntness.

He turned and looked at her at one point, saying,
"You surprise me, Miss Upshaw."

"Please, call me Miranda. It seems only fitting,
given that we are to be married, don't you think?"

"All right. Miranda. You surprised me this evening."

"Why? By wanting to leave the engagement
party?"

He nodded. "I thought that it was precisely the sort
of thing you were marrying me for."

Miranda chuckled. "Hardly. I can find any number
of boring social occasions on my own in New York.
I told you, it is the freedom that marriage offers that
interests me."

He looked at her consideringly, then leaned over
and kissed her. "And what about this? Does that figure
into your consideration of marriage?"

Miranda managed a breezy smile, determined not to let him know that his kiss had sent tingles running all through her. "Should it?" she countered and rose to her feet. "I fancy another promenade. Shall we?"

"Of course." He rose, saying nothing about the quick way she had cut off the romantic scene.

They strolled once more down the wide corridor between the boxes. This time, as they reached the end and were about to turn to walk back, a man came toward them out of the dark. He was not masked, and Miranda saw his face clearly in the light that spilled from the promenade. But it was what he held in his hand as he rushed toward them that drew a startled gasp from her—a short-bladed knife that glittered in the glow of the lanterns.

Devin saw the knife at the same time she did, and he twisted away from the man, jerking Miranda around behind him as he did so. The man's knife sliced harmlessly through the extra folds of Devin's domino. Devin let go of Miranda's hand and grabbed for the man, seizing his wrist. But the fellow twisted away and took to his heels.

Devin started after him, then glanced back at Miranda and stopped, his face a study in frustration. Miranda knew he longed to chase the miscreant down and punish him, but he could scarcely leave her alone in such a place.

"I think it is time we returned," Devin said tersely as he took her hand and led her out of the Gardens.

"Does this sort of thing happen to you often?" Miranda asked mildly as they settled into the hansom Devin hailed.

He glanced at her, then let out a chuckle, shaking his head. "Any other woman of my acquaintance would be having hysterics right now."

"Would you like me to?" Miranda asked politely.

"I suppose I could."

"No. This is far preferable, believe me."

"You did not answer my question," Miranda pointed out. "Do you make a habit of being set upon by thieves?"

"Not usually. Perhaps it is something to do with you."

Miranda quirked one eyebrow at him. "I don't think you can get out of it that easily. Is it one of your creditors, do you think? We might tell Papa to pay that one off first."

Devin burst out laughing at her calm remarks. "It would have been more helpful, then, if he had told us who he represented. As it is, I haven't a clue."

"Then I suppose it is a good thing that you are going up to Darkwater in a few days."

"Yes." He looked at her. "Do you think that you can keep yourself out of trouble while I am gone?"

"My dear sir, I believe so, since it seems that you are the one who leads me into it."

The Aincourts left two days later for Darkwater. Rachel and her mother had to make sure that the house was put in the best order that it could be for the upcoming nuptials, and a hint dropped in Rachel's ear made sure that Devin accompanied them. It was part of Miranda's plan to get him as far away from London and Leona as she could, and the family estate in Derbyshire answered her needs perfectly. Besides, Devin was far too distracting. She needed all her wits about her when she dealt with him, and that was difficult when she had so many things to do. As it was, the fact that thoughts of him kept popping into her mind at times when she should have been concentrating on other things caused her enough problems.

The two weeks that she and her family stayed in London after the Aincourts left sped by. Aside from the time-consuming fittings for her wedding clothes and the numerous shopping expeditions for accessories, there were also her normal business activities to pursue—letters to write, accounts to be gone over—and though Hiram did much of the work, there were things that required her personal attention, especially since her father was often embroiled in conferences with the attorneys over the wedding settlement. Miranda also had to oversee the task of packing up her entire family for their trip to Darkwater, and shop for wedding presents for her soon-to-be husband, both the formal, somewhat impersonal present that was expected, as well as a more personal one that she had in mind.

Two days before they were to leave for Darkwater, Miranda was seated at her desk in the study, going over the final packing list with the butler, when one of the footmen entered and gave her a card on a small salver, saying that there was a gentleman there to see her.

"Who is he?" Miranda asked, frowning down at the card. "Cannot Elizabeth or Father take care of him?"

"No, miss. Mr. Upshaw is out, sir, and Mrs. Upshaw is upstairs taking a nap. She is feeling poorly today.'' The young man paused, then added, ''He said it was important, miss. I told him you were busy, and he said he would wait all afternoon if he had to. He looks determined, miss.''

''Oh, bother. All right. Show him into the drawing room.''

She walked down the hall to the formal dining room, rolling down her sleeves and fastening the cuff buttons. She had barely walked into the room when the footman appeared again, with another man behind him.

''Mr. Caulfield,'' he intoned and backed out of the room, leaving Miranda alone with the stranger.

The two of them stood silently for a moment, studying each other. Her visitor was a man well up in years, with a shock of white hair and hands that trembled. He was dressed well, in the style of an old-fashioned gentleman, and he carried himself ramrod straight, his hat and a gold-tipped cane in his hand. His eyes were blue, and there was a fierce light to them that made Miranda a trifle uneasy.

''Miss Upshaw,'' he began, his voice surprisingly firm for his years. ''I have come to warn you.''

''Warn me? About what? I am sorry, Mr. Caulfield, but I am afraid that I don't even know you.''

''You do not,'' he agreed, advancing toward her. ''It is forward of me to show up on your doorstep like this, I know, but I had to warn you. I could not let you marry that devil.''

''I beg your pardon?''

''Lord Ravenscar. I heard you were to marry him.

Gossip travels, even as far as Brighton, especially when it's about the Earl of Ravenscar. I could not let you do it. I could not let another innocent young girl be sacrificed.''

''Mr. Caulfield,'' Miranda's voice was chilly, ''I appreciate your concern, but I cannot stand here and allow you to slander my future husband. I think it would be best if you left now.''

''Not until I say what I came to say!'' he burst out, and his bright blue eyes took on an even wilder look. He tapped his cane hard upon the floor for emphasis. ''The man is a murderer!''

Miranda stared at him. Her knees felt suddenly weak, and she sat down in the nearest chair. For a moment she could not seem to find the breath to speak.

''Aha! I see that got your attention, right enough,'' the old man said with a touch of glee.

''Excuse me.'' Miranda found her voice again, a rising indignation giving her strength. ''That is a serious accusation you make about Lord Ravenscar. You are alleging that he killed someone?''

The old man sneered. ''Oh, he didn't dirty his hands with it, no. It's nothing the authorities would do anything about. But he killed my granddaughter just the same, killed her as if he'd thrown her into the ocean himself.''

''Mr. Caulfield,'' Miranda said crisply, rising to her feet, ''I will not sit here and allow you to talk about my fiancé in this manner. You say he is a murderer, but he didn't actually kill anyone. Exactly what is it you're talking about? What are you accusing him of?''

''He seduced her, that's what! And she couldn't

bear the shame. She threw herself into the ocean. Because of him!'' Caulfield's eyes glittered with fury, and he shook his fist in the air. ''I called the coward out, and he didn't even answer me.''

Pity stabbed through Miranda. ''Mr. Caulfield, I am very sorry for your loss. But it sounds as though your granddaughter killed herself.'' She wondered how much of the old man's story was true and how much of it he had concocted in his mind to assuage his own grief and guilt. She knew that if the old man had indeed sent a challenge to Devin, it was pity, not cowardice, that had made Devin refuse to answer it.

''Because of him! He drove her to it. She was a good girl until she met him. He led her astray.''

Miranda did not know what to say. She had little understanding of someone who, when faced with a crisis, would choose to escape the matter in death, leaving her loved ones to suffer as this man obviously had. Instinctively, she could not believe that Devin had seduced a virtuous young maiden and then had refused to marry her when she got pregnant—for, reading between the lines of Caulfield's story, that would have had to be the case for anyone to kill herself. Even a foolish young girl would not choose to die simply because she had made an all too human mistake unless her shame was going to be exposed to her grandfather and the world. She knew that, as Rachel had said, deep inside Devin was a loyal and honorable man despite his apparent wildness. He was not the sort of man who would turn away a woman carrying his child, let alone a young girl who had been untouched until she met him. Nor, quite frankly, did Devin seem to be the sort who went about seducing virtuous young women. By all accounts, he had spent his time with sophisticated, knowing women like Leona Vesey, not blushing young maidens.

She had to think that Mr. Caulfield's granddaughter had not been the virtuous maiden he liked to believe she was. However, she could scarcely tell the man that, any more than she could point out that she doubted the girl would have killed herself if she had believed her grandfather to be a kind and forgiving man.

"And now, young lady," the old man went on, raising his forefinger and waving it warningly at her, "he's gone after you. Because you're an heiress. He wants to get his hands on your money. And what do you think will happen after that's done? Eh? He won't have any need for you any longer. You'll be lucky if he just leaves you and goes back to his fancy ladies in London. Because he just might decide he doesn't want to have to put up with the bother of a wife at all!"

A fierce anger seized Miranda. "That is quite enough, Mr. Caulfield. I have tried to be considerate of you because you are obviously somewhat unhinged by your grief. But you go too far now. Lord Ravenscar has no deadly designs on me. I am positive of that. And you have no right to come here and try to frighten me with your nonsense."

"I am trying to help you!" he shouted, slamming his cane down on the floor again, his face turning an alarming shade of crimson.

"No. You are trying to hurt Ravenscar. There is a

difference. Now, please, you had better go before you do damage to yourself. You are very overwrought.''

She marched over to the bell cord and pulled it sharply, summoning a servant. Behind her Caulfield began to rant and rave almost unintelligibly, spewing out hatred of Ravenscar and dire warnings of what would happen to her if she married him.

The footman who had shown Caulfield in soon appeared at the door, and his eyes widened with alarm when he saw the raging old man.

''Please see Mr. Caulfield to the door,'' Miranda instructed him crisply.

''Of course, miss. I'm terribly sorry, miss, I would never have let him in if I had realized....''

''Of course not. You couldn't know.''

Relieved, the servant took the old man by the arm and firmly led him from the room. Miranda followed them into the entryway to make sure both that the wild old man was gone and that the footman did not handle him too roughly. She watched as he firmly set the man outside the door and closed it behind him. She turned to go back to the study, although she felt little like continuing with the packing list. The old man had upset her. She was certain that what he had said could not be the truth, but she could not entirely dismiss it, either, given Devin's reputation, and the turmoil of feelings left her a trifle queasy.

She looked up and caught sight of her stepmother standing at the railing at the top of the stairs, her eyes wide and her face pale. ''Who was that?'' Elizabeth asked in a horrified tone.

''An old man who was, well, distraught. But he's

gone now. There's nothing for you to worry about.'' Miranda went up the stairs to her.

"But why was he here? What did he say?'' Elizabeth questioned, reaching out and taking Miranda's arm in an almost painful grip. "He looked quite mad.''

Miranda patted her stepmother's arm soothingly. She could scarcely tell Elizabeth what the old man had said about Devin; she was already too doubtful about Miranda's marrying him. Mr. Caulfield's accusations would doubtless send her into a frenzy of worry.

"It was nothing, really. I think perhaps he is a trifle unbalanced. I really didn't understand what he was talking about. But there is no need to worry. I can assure you that the servants will not let him in again.'' She smiled. "Now, I need your advice. They delivered the rest of the dresses today from Madame Ferrier's, and I'm not sure that the ribbon we bought really goes with the green cambric day dress.''

"The green? Oh, no, they were very complementary shades, my dear. Show me.'' Elizabeth seemed relieved, almost glad to be distracted, and the two of them walked away down the hall toward Miranda's bedroom.

It was a three-day journey from London to Darkwater, for they traveled with a wagon of luggage as well as the post chaise in which they rode, and Elizabeth had a tendency toward travel sickness, which meant that they stopped frequently and moved at a slow pace to avoid jarring her. Joseph spent most of his time riding on a horse alongside the carriage, and since he had purchased another mount, as well, Veronica or Miranda often joined him, which made the journey easier to bear. Even so, the trip was far too long for Miranda's impatient nerves. It had been almost two weeks since she had seen Devin, and she was eager to be with him again. However, this was a feeling she could not reveal to the others; a careless word about her eagerness from anyone in her family to Devin would set her plans back. So she had to contain her feelings and pretend to a calm and relaxation she did not feel, a pretense that only made her more frustrated.

It was a great relief when the post chaise rattled down the lane approaching Darkwater. Miranda leaned out of the window to catch sight of the grand old house. They rounded a curve, and there the house was before them, on a slight rise, most of the trees cleared out of the way years ago to present the house in all its glory.

Miranda drew in her breath when she saw it. Her father pulled his mount to a halt and simply sat there, looking at it. The setting sun cast a golden glow over its limestone block walls, turning the stone itself to a warm, honeyed hue and glittering upon the small diamond-shaped panes of glass in the mullioned windows. It was a house of graceful symmetry despite its size, built in the shape of an E, a popular conceit during the years of Queen Elizabeth's reign, and ornamented with parapets, oriel windows and elaborate chimneys. It was lovely, Miranda thought, immediately losing her heart to it. At this distance and in this kind light, the problems of the house were not obvious. It simply looked old and magnificent.

"Have you ever seen anything like it, Miranda?" Joseph appeared at the window of the post chaise, his face filled with awe and pleasure. "Isn't it grand?"

"It is indeed, Papa. It's beautiful." It struck her, with a pang of pride and pleasure that she had not expected to feel, that this beautiful old house was now her home, and the fairly detached interest she had felt in restoring the place was suddenly a hunger within her.

Veronica, who was also riding outside the carriage, came back to join them. "It's a castle! Are we really going to live there? Mama, look!"

Elizabeth, who was sitting beside Miranda, pushed aside the curtain on the other side of the carriage and looked out. Her eyes widened, and a little color came into her cheeks. "Oh, my," she breathed. "I never realized..."

"Isn't it grand?" Veronica went on merrily. "Doesn't it look like someplace a king would live?"

Elizabeth nodded. "Yes. It does."

"I can't wait to see my room," Veronica continued. "Miranda, may I choose which one is to be my room?"

"Yes, I suppose so—though to be polite, you must stay at least tonight where Lady Ravenscar has put you. After that, I don't see why you cannot choose which one you prefer."

"I want windows that look out this way. I want to see whoever comes up the road. That way, when you have parties—before I'm old enough to attend them, I mean—I can watch everybody arrive from my window. Will you give lots and lots of balls? It must have a ballroom, don't you think?''

''I am sure it does. However, I don't know how many people there are out here to attend 'lots and lots' of balls,'' Miranda responded, smiling indulgently at her stepsister.

''I will get to go to some parties here, won't I? Mama said that when she lived in the country, girls could attend small parties now and then, even before they made their debut.''

''I don't see why not,'' Miranda agreed. ''I am sure your mother is much more of an expert on that subject than I am.'' Since she herself had been hostessing her father's parties when she was fifteen, Miranda could hardly be said to have lived her life according to the proper social rules.

Veronica dropped back and came up on the other side of the carriage beside her mother to pursue this interesting subject, and Miranda was left to her own thoughts as she gazed at the house as the carriage rolled up to its door. Those thoughts soon turned from the house to her future husband. He had been on her mind the whole trip from London, and now that she was about to see him again, an almost unbearable excitement welled up inside her. She would have given a great deal to know whether he had thought of her, too—and whether he had been waiting for her the past few days, wondering impatiently when she would arrive. It was too much to hope for, she told herself; she had to take this slowly. But she could not keep her heart from hoping anyway.

Their post chaise pulled up in front of the house,

and a footman hurried out to open the door and help them down. As Miranda climbed down the carriage step to the ground, she glanced off to the left. A horse and rider sailed over a low hedge and thundered on toward them. Miranda's heart began to pound as she recognized Devin's broad-shouldered form. He slowed down, skirting the front garden, and came to a halt a few yards from them.

"Miranda!" Fluidly, he dismounted, tossing his reins to the footman. "I mean, Miss Upshaw."

He strode toward them, his eyes on Miranda. Miranda's pulse was hammering in her ears so hard that she could barely hear. Here, in the sunlight, fresh from physical exertion, his green eyes alight, he was even more handsome than she remembered. It made her feel a trifle weak in the knees.

"Lord Ravenscar," she returned, pleased that her voice came out evenly. Surely his riding hell-bent-for-leather to meet them was a good sign.

"I saw your carriage approaching, so I tried to catch you." He came to a halt in front of her and looked down at her for a long moment. This close, in the bright light of day, she could see that his green eyes had a small ring of gold around the pupil, like a sunburst, and she found the small detail captivating. Stripping off his riding gloves, he reached out, and Miranda managed to recover enough presence of mind to extend her hand to him. He took her hand and raised it to his lips, brushing a kiss on the back of it. "Welcome to Darkwater. We've been wondering when you would come. Mother was expecting you yesterday.

Rachel was worried you wouldn't even make it in time for the wedding.''

"And you?"

His engaging grin flashed. ''I knew that you would arrive exactly when you should, neither too early nor too late, since you were managing it.''

Miranda chuckled. He continued to hold her hand far longer than was polite, but she had no desire for him to let go. "Your faith in me is touching, my lord.''

"It's knowledge, Miss Upshaw, not mere faith.'' With a final squeeze of her hand, he let it go and turned to the rest of the party. "Mrs. Upshaw. Mr. Upshaw. Welcome to Darkwater.'' His eyes went past them to Veronica, who was still seated on her horse. "And who is this lovely young lady?''

"I am Veronica,'' she answered pertly. "I'm the one you never see because I'm too young.''

"Too beautiful,'' he corrected with a grin, and stepped forward to help her dismount. "Your parents are doubtless afraid someone will snap you up far too soon.''

Veronica giggled. Miranda knew that Ravenscar had earned himself a permanent place in Veronica's good books by paying attention to her, as few adults did. And, Miranda had to admit, it had raised him in her estimation, too. She had been afraid that he would play the haughty aristocrat with her family, as he had before with her, and she was particularly anxious about Veronica's easily hurt adolescent feelings. But Ravenscar had handled her with just the right tone of flattery and friendliness.

"I'm surprised to see you riding instead of in the carriage," he told Veronica.

"Oh, I love to ride," Veronica said eagerly. "And it's too beautiful to be cooped up inside some stuffy post chaise."

"You are right about that," Ravenscar agreed. "If you like to ride, you will be happy here. Lots of room and, at the risk of sounding arrogant—" he cut his eyes humorously toward Miranda "—our stable is one of the best in the country, I warrant."

"Oh! Can I see the horses?" Veronica asked eagerly.

"Of course. I shall take you on a personal tour tomorrow."

Grooms had arrived to take care of the horses, and the footman was waiting to open the door, so Devin led the group into the house. They stepped inside to find an imposing line of servants, all uniformed and starched, stretching down the entry hall.

Devin leaned down to whisper in Miranda's ear, "Eager to meet the new mistress. They are wondering how hard a taskmaster you shall be. I didn't want to break it to them that you are a tyrant."

Miranda looked up at him indignantly. "I'm not—"

She broke off, seeing the twinkle in his eyes. "I am very kind to servants," she whispered back primly. "It is those in a higher position whom I am likely to take to task."

"I am trembling in my boots." His grin belied any truth in his words.

He turned toward the first man in line. "Cummings.

Miss Upshaw, allow me to introduce you to the staff. This is Cummings, our estimable butler. And Mrs. Watkins, the housekeeper.''

He went down the line of servants, introducing each of them. Miranda was surprised and impressed to find that Devin knew the names of almost all of them, drawing a blank on only the newest and youngest of the group. Miranda would have expected a man like him to have known no one lower than the butler and housekeeper, especially given the fact that he had been in residence there so rarely the last few years. She commented on the fact as they were walking away, having introduced the rest of the family, as well.

"You mean you think I am too arrogant to know the names of the people I grew up with? You have an odd opinion of me, Miss Upshaw."

"I am pleased to find that it is an incorrect one."

He shrugged. "My relationships with the servants was never considered a very sterling quality, I'm afraid. Father always thought it was another manifestation of my basically low character. I spent more time with the head groom and the gamesman and his children growing up than I did with the suffocatingly dull sons and daughters of the local gentry."

"That sounds reasonable."

"Not to my father, it didn't."

Devin's mother and sister were waiting for them in the formal drawing room, a large room decorated in the white-and-gilt style of the century before. It was an elegant room, and it took a second or third glance to notice that the heavy blue draperies and the blue velvet cushions of the chairs and sofa were becoming threadbare, and that the Persian carpet beneath their feet was almost worn through in places.

The occupants of the room rose to their feet politely when Miranda and her family entered. Rachel came forward to greet Miranda warmly, and she, like her brother, gave Veronica a special bit of attention. Lady Ravenscar was formal but polite, as she had been every time Miranda was around her, and she paid only scant attention to Elizabeth and Veronica. Miranda could not help but feel that the woman was making an effort to treat them well because they were going to rescue her from poverty rather than out of any real liking for them. She doubted that she would ever feel really close to Lady Ravenscar.

There was a third person in the room, a tall, slender man with blond hair and gray eyes, handsome in a quiet, subtle way. He smiled now and came forward as Devin said, "Miss Upshaw, allow me to introduce you to my brother-in-law, Lord Westhampton."

"How do you do?" Miranda asked, intrigued. This was Rachel's husband, the one with whom she maintained a formal, separated marriage.

"Very well, thank you. It is a pleasure to meet you, Miss Upshaw." He smiled down at her kindly. "Lady Westhampton speaks highly of you."

"Thank you."

"I am sure that you must all be wanting to freshen up after your long journey, perhaps take a rest before supper," Lady Ravenscar said. "Rachel, why don't you show the Upshaws to their rooms?"

"Of course."

"I'll take Miss Upshaw," Devin told his sister casually, offering Miranda his arm.

Rachel led the others from the room and up the stairs to the chambers they had set aside for them, and Devin and Miranda brought up the rear. It was hard to take in all the details of the magnificent house, especially with the distraction of Devin's presence so close to her. It was difficult enough to maintain the cool, insouciant attitude that she wanted.

At the top of the stairs, Rachel turned to the right to take Veronica and the others to their rooms, but Devin went in the opposite direction. "Your room is this way. Since the wedding is only a few days away, there seemed little point in making you change rooms." He stopped at the doorway of a spacious room. "This is the Countess's chambers."

Miranda looked in, puzzled. "You mean, your mother's room?"

He smiled at her in a way that made her pulse beat a little faster. "No, my dear Miss Upshaw. I mean the room which connects to mine."

Miranda could feel a blush spreading across her cheeks. "Oh." She walked past him into the room to conceal her reaction.

It was a large room, with two tall windows that looked down on the rear gardens. There was a sitting area with sofa and chair in one quadrant of the room, and further along that wall stood a fireplace with an ornate marble mantel. Between the two stood a door. The room was furnished with heavy mahogany pieces, the most dominant of which was a large tester bed hung with dark-green velvet curtains. A large fading medieval tapestry hung on one wall. It was an impressive, formal room, one befitting a Countess and one in which Miranda could well imagine Lady Ravenscar having lived. It was not one that appealed overmuch to her.

"Of course, I expect you will want to change things," Devin went on, coming into the room after her and closing the door behind him.

Miranda nodded faintly. It seemed odd to think that she was going to be living in this room from now on, except when they traveled to London or somewhere else. There was a permanence, a gravity, to the idea that almost took her breath away. She glanced over at Devin. She hardly knew him, she thought. She would be living in a strange house in a strange land. She wondered if all brides felt this same little spurt of panic, or if it was because of the businesslike circumstances of their marriage.

Partly to hide her sudden, unaccustomed fit of nerves, she wandered about the room, looking into the wardrobe and dressers. She opened the door that stood in the wall beside the fireplace. Beyond it lay another room, even larger than this one and obviously occupied by a man.

"My chamber," Devin said, coming up behind her.

Miranda jumped, startled, and quickly shut the door. "Of course."

She would have moved away then, but Devin was standing in front of her. He braced his hand on the door behind her, blocking off that direction, too, and leaned closer to her.

"I have been thinking the last two weeks. I've had

a great deal of time to do so, you know. And it seems absurd for this to be a sham marriage.''

''It is no sham, my lord. I regard it as something quite real. It is just not...romantic.''

''There is no need for that, either,'' he responded. ''I am attracted to you. And you cannot deny that you are attracted to me. I have felt the desire in you. So why deny what we both feel?''

His face loomed closer. Miranda found it difficult to breathe—or even think coherently. His lips brushed across hers gently, sending a delightful tingle all through her.

''We have a connecting door,'' he murmured. ''It seems to me that we might as well make use of it.''

For an instant his mouth hovered over hers. She could feel his breath against her face, the warmth of his body. Her skin prickled. All she could think of, all she wanted, was his kiss.

Just before his lips touched hers, she jumped to the side. Her heart was racing so hard it was a wonder he couldn't hear it, she thought, and her hands were trembling. But she managed to put on a calm face as she said, ''I think not, my lord. It would seem foolish to introduce emotions into our arrangement. It will work so perfectly as it is.''

She gave him a perfunctory smile and reached back with one hand to turn the lock of the connecting door. ''There. This room will do fine.''

11

Devin walked into the study and closed the door behind him with a resounding thud. Across the room Michael, Lord Westhampton, raised his eyes from the book he was reading and looked at Devin with a mildly questioning face.

"Bad day?"

Devin grimaced. "Oh. Hullo, Michael. Didn't know you were here. I thought everyone else had gone to bed."

It was almost midnight, and the house was dark. Devin, lying in his bedroom thinking about the locked door into Miranda's room, had been unable to sleep and had gone prowling.

"Just a bit of reading before sleep," Michael replied. "Sorry. Didn't mean to invade your study. Shall I leave? Or does that look on your face mean you would prefer to have a listening ear?"

"I would prefer to change my life," Devin said, disgruntled. He walked over to the teak cabinet beneath the windows and opened the door. "Whiskey? I have brandy if you'd prefer."

"Whiskey's fine," Michael replied. "And what exactly would you change about your life?"

"Living it. I don't know. Oh, Christ." He poured two drinks into fine crystal glasses and handed his brother-in-law one, then drank half the other one in a single gulp. He sighed. "What am I doing marrying that woman? I must have been out of my mind to agree to it."

"I was rather under the impression that you had no other choice," Michael pointed out mildly. "Besides, I rather liked your bride-to-be. She's quite...different."

Devin grimaced. "That's one way to put it."

"Her theories about education for women certainly made for stimulating dinner conversation."

A smile cracked Devin's face as he remembered the look on his mother's face at supper tonight when Miranda had advocated that women be allowed to attend university. "It was a livelier dinner than usual," he admitted. "But you see my point—she has been here since four o'clock, not even half a day, and already she has stirred everything up. The woman is a menace."

"If you feel that strongly about it, perhaps you should cry off."

"Cry off! Are you mad? The wedding is in two days. Besides, a gentleman can't back out of it, and you know it."

Michael raised his eyebrows. "Yes, I can see how it would damage your reputation."

Devin shot him a disgusted look. "Oh, hell, Michael, you know I can't. I need the money. The Aincourts have never had the luxury of marrying for love.''

"Yes, I know,'' Michael replied quietly.

"Of course you do. I mean, you and Rachel—you had the same sort of arrangement. But it's different for you. The two of you are rational, civilized sorts. You can live in harmony—do what you want, live separate lives.''

"Yes. We do.''

"But Miranda! She's an odd creature. She has strange ideas about things.''

Michael nodded, waiting.

Devin downed the rest of his whiskey and set his glass down with a crack. "Dammit, she wants a platonic marriage!''

Michael blinked. "I beg your pardon?''

"Have you ever heard of such a thing? She says we don't love each other, so we shall go our separate ways, do what we want.''

Michael hesitated, then said, "I would think that such an accommodating wife would appeal to you.''

"Accommodating? I have never met anyone less accommodating than Miranda. She thinks we should go out and have affairs with other people.''

"I see. And you are against that?''

"The Countess of Ravenscar, having affairs with God knows who? Of course I am against it.''

"Then you are in favor of the two of you having a true marriage—fidelity and—''

Devin fixed him with a piercing look. "Don't mock me, Michael. You know I never had any intention of being faithful to her. Of course I want to do what I want, have affairs. I just—well, I didn't expect her to want them, too. She's as bold and brassy as any bird of paradise.''

''Really? I thought she seemed refined. A bit outspoken, of course, but that was refreshing. Not at all coarse.''

''Of course she's not coarse. Good God, Michael, why would you think that?''

''Well... 'bold and brassy' as a lightskirt,'' Lord Westhampton reminded him.

''You know what I mean.'' Devin got up and poured himself another drink. ''She wants to restore the house. That is what she's interested in. She wants to put the estate back in running order. That's why she wants to marry me. I asked her where she wanted to go on the honeymoon—Paris? Vienna? Italy? Do you know what she said? 'Oh, I don't care much for a honeymoon, my lord,''' Devin said in a falsetto. '''I want to get right on the house. Papa and I have already scheduled an architect to come look at it.' Now, does that sound like any woman you know?''

''No,'' Michael admitted.

''Other women *want* honeymoons. They want babies and clothes and parties and such. She wants to fix things. It's not natural.''

Devin slumped back broodingly in his chair. Across from him, Lord Westhampton hid a smile.

''She locked the connecting door,'' Devin said suddenly.

''I beg your pardon.''

''Between our rooms. I didn't really believe her. I assumed she would come around.'' He shrugged and sipped at his drink, more slowly this time. "That's part of her 'going our separate ways' idea. She said it would be a perfect solution. We wouldn't have to pretend that we are in love. We wouldn't have to go to the trouble of consummating our marriage. We could just live entirely separate lives."

"And that is not what you want?"

"Well, what about heirs? There won't be any, will there?"

"No. And I know an heir is important to you."

Devin looked at him suspiciously. "Are you laughing at me?"

"No. Well, only a little. I don't understand, Dev. If you don't care for the woman—indeed, it seems to be exactly the opposite—then why do you mind if she doesn't grace your bed? I have never known you to worry about an heir before. As long as she is discreet..."

"But she doesn't even care! She hasn't a spark of jealousy in her whole body," Devin grumbled. "Now, I ask you, is that normal?"

Michael shrugged. "Some women aren't jealous."

"Yes, if they don't care."

Michael glanced away. "Do you want her to care for you?"

"Of course not." Devin made a face. "Oh, hell! I just don't want her turning me down."

"A point of pride. I see."

"It's damned frustrating. She is the most contrary female I have ever met. And she isn't even beautiful."

"No," Michael agreed.

Devin cast him a sharp look. "Do you think she's not pretty?"

Michael pressed his lips together for a moment, then cleared his throat and said, "Yes, I think she is quite pretty. But not a beauty."

"But there is something about her eyes. Did you notice? They're gray and...and penetrating. Sometimes, when she looks at me, it's as if she can see right into my soul."

"Disconcerting."

"Yes, but..."

"But what?"

"Intriguing, as well, don't you think? And her hair is a nice color."

"Yes. Sort of chestnut. Very nice."

"Did I tell you that the first time I met her, she came to my rescue?"

Michael swallowed his drink the wrong way and began to cough. After a few minutes, his coughing fit died, and he asked weakly, "What did you say?"

"Three men attacked me. She was driving by in her carriage and saw it. So she made her driver stop and came running to help me. Whacked one fellow with an umbrella."

"Indeed."

"I've never met a woman like her."

"No, I should think not."

"The thing is, she...appeals to me." Dev looked at his brother-in-law. "You'd think I would be relieved not to have to bed the woman I married only for money. But I—I can't stop thinking about her. These two weeks up here, I kept thinking about her. I mean,

it's understandable. It's devilishly boring here. But...
well, what I mean is, why her? And it seems like the
more I know I don't have to take her, the more I want
to. Does that make sense?''

"Sad to say, yes, it does.''

"I didn't think it would last. I didn't think she
would stick to that idea.''

"Until she locked the door.''

"Right.''

"No doubt you figured you could charm her into
it.''

"Well, yes. I mean, it's not as if I'm an ogre.
Women like me.''

"So we're talking about a bit of hurt pride.''

Devin hesitated. "Yes...I suppose so. I mean, it
couldn't really be anything else.''

"I'm sure not.'' Michael took a quick drink to hide
his smile. "You know, Dev, I think this is going to
be a very interesting marriage.''

"That's one way to describe it. Hellish is more like
it.''

"I was going to go back home as soon as the wedding was over,'' Michael went on musingly. "But you
know, I think I may just stay awhile now.''

Lord Westhampton was the only person in the dining room when Miranda walked in the following
morning. He looked up at her and smiled. "Miss Upshaw. So, you are an early riser?''

"A lamentable habit,'' Miranda said with a smile.
"I am afraid I cannot seem to shake it. Good morning,
Lord Westhampton.''

He got up and came around the table to pull her chair out for her, "There is food on the sideboard. And a pot of tea. Shall I ring for a servant to bring you coffee? I understand many Americans thrive on it."

"Yes, and I am one. It would be kind of you to ring." Miranda got up and walked along the elegant dark sideboard, investigating the various dishes. "If I ate like this every morning, pretty soon you would have to roll me down the hallway."

She picked up a small sampling of the various dishes, leaving the kidneys, which she could not work up a taste for. She brought her plate back to the table and sat down just as a footman entered with a rack of toast. He set it down beside Miranda and went back for the pot of coffee.

"Tomorrow you can be sure that the coffee will be ready and waiting for you," Michael told her. "Cummings runs a tight ship. It has pained him these many years, I'm sure, to be unable to staff the house properly."

"Yes. I shall have to talk to him later. There are so many things to do—repairs to the house, the gardens, the estate." Miranda smiled, seemingly not at all daunted by the task before her.

"Ravenscar tells me you are very interested in restoring the estate."

"Oh, yes. Papa is, too, probably even more than I."

"If I can be of any assistance to you, please feel free to ask. I have had to do quite a few repairs to my own house over the years."

"How kind of you. But I warn you, if you tell Papa that, he will bend your ear for hours."

"I wouldn't mind. It's rare that I can find anyone who has any interest in the matter.''

They talked for a few minutes about the problems of very old houses. The footman reappeared with a pot of coffee for Miranda, and after he left, there was a short silence.

Then Michael said, "You know, Miss Upshaw... Lord Ravenscar is, well, he isn't exactly what he seems to be.''

"Really?'' Miranda looked at the man with great innocence.

"No, he...well, he is a much nicer person than most people think. I am very fond of him, and I should hate to think that he might get hurt.''

Miranda gazed at him levelly. "You know, Lord Westhampton, any observer of our wedding, seeing the two of us, would generally not worry that Lord Ravenscar is going to get hurt.''

"Yes, you're right, of course. Devin is not naive or innocent by any means. But neither is he a scoundrel. He has a heart, which he does his best to keep hidden, and he can be wounded. On the other hand, with the right woman, he could be very happy.''

"Well, that is fortunate, isn't it? Some people, I understand, can never be happy no matter what the circumstances.'' Miranda set down her fork. "I am not sure what you are driving at, Lord Westhampton. If you think I am not the right woman for Lord Ravenscar, then I am sorry you feel that way, because you really have nothing to say in the matter. On the other hand, if you are trying to ascertain whether I am the right woman for him, I can only say I do not know. I have found in life that we must wait and see what happens. I am not accustomed to turning aside from something because there are risks. I suppose there is a third thing you might be trying to say—that I must change if I am hoping to make Devin happy. That is not likely to happen. He is as he is, and I am as I am. Have I answered your concerns, my lord?''

Michael smiled. ''Yes, Miss Upshaw. I would say that you have answered my concerns more than adequately. I always thought it would take a very special woman to match Devin. I think perhaps he has found her.''

Miranda smiled back. ''I would like to think so.''

After that, they fell to talking of other things. Miranda found Lord Westhampton to be a very intelligent and well-read man, with a great deal of knowledge on a wide array of subjects. He was possessed of a dry and ironic wit, sometimes so subtle that it took a moment or two to realize exactly how well he had skewered a topic.

He was in the middle of describing how he had attacked the woodworm that had eaten into most of the railings and balustrades in his house when he looked up and suddenly broke off. Something flashed across his face, too quickly for Miranda to tell what it was.

''My dear,'' he said and rose to his feet, his manner a trifle stiff and formal. ''Good morning. Won't you join us?''

Miranda turned and saw Rachel framed in the doorway. She looked, Miranda thought, especially pretty this morning. She was wearing a simple green morning dress that brought out the color of her eyes, and there was a touch of pink in her cheeks. Miranda wasn't sure whether the country air was simply good for her, if the cause of her good looks was her happiness at her brother's marrying, or if there were another reason altogether.

"Hello," Rachel replied, her voice equally formal. "I hope I am not disturbing you."

"No, of course not. Lord Westhampton and I were just chatting about restoring old houses. I found it quite interesting, but he, I am sure, would appreciate being rescued," Miranda said cheerfully.

"I'm sure that isn't true." Rachel smiled at Miranda, then glanced at her husband.

"Oh, no," Lord Westhampton protested, and the smile that had been so relaxed and friendly a few moments ago now seemed forced. "Lady Westhampton can attest to the fact that I am quite fond of much that most people would consider boring. It was kind of you to let me rattle on so."

It seemed very strange, Miranda thought, that two such likeable people should be married—for several years, as she understood it—and still be so uncomfortable around one another. She wondered if Rachel had told her the whole story when she had described the separated state of their marriage.

Michael went around to hold Rachel's chair for her, then said, "Well, I shall leave you ladies to talk. Good day, Miss Upshaw. Rachel." He gave them a slight bow and walked out the door.

"Your husband is very nice," Miranda said. "I enjoyed talking to him."

Rachel gave her a small smile. "Yes. He is. One can always rely on Michael." She got back up and went to fill her plate, saying, "I trust you slept well last night?"

"Yes, thank you." Miranda accepted the change of subject.

"Would you like to go over the preparations for the wedding?" Rachel asked. "Or we could go to the church if you wanted to see it."

Neither idea particularly appealed to Miranda. "I am sure that whatever you and your mother have decided will be fine." Rachel looked at her oddly, and Miranda went on, "Not that I'm not interested. Of course I would love to go over them. But maybe later. I think Devin plans to show Papa and me around the house this morning."

"This morning?" Rachel looked surprised.

"Why, yes, I believe so."

"My, my. Already you've had a good effect on him."

Miranda chuckled. "Actually, I think it's boredom. He told me he had taken to keeping country hours because there was so little to do."

"Well, I hadn't noticed him up and about before noon since we've been here."

Miranda privately thought that it was also quite possible that he simply would not show up. But before Rachel finished her breakfast, Devin strolled into the room. There was a faintly glazed look to his eyes, it was true, and he said in an amazed tone, "Is this your usual hour to rise?" But he was there when he had said he would be.

"Actually, I am usually at work by now," Miranda answered with a chuckle. "I have been talking to Lord and Lady Westhampton for almost an hour."

"Good God." He looked appalled at the idea and went to pour himself a cup of tea.

After breakfast and two or three cups of tea, he seemed more alert, and they went in search of Miranda's father, Rachel having quickly excused herself from an exploration of the old house.

Miranda opted to meet with the estate manager before they began the tour, so their first stop was at his office, which lay across the sideyard and was in the front of the small stone house in which he lived.

"Lord Ravenscar!" he said, looking surprised, when Devin knocked on the door and walked in.

"Hallo, Strong." Devin glanced around the office.

"If you had sent me a note, I would have been happy to call on you in the main house, my lord," the estate manager went on nervously, scurrying around and moving files out of one chair and dragging another closer. He was a short, stocky man, balding at the back of his head, so that he looked as if he wore a monk's tonsure.

"Miss Upshaw had a fancy to see your office," Devin explained. "Miss Upshaw, this Mr. Strong, the estate manager. Strong, the future Lady Ravenscar, Miss Upshaw."

"How do you do, miss? It's a pleasure to meet you." Strong quickly covered up his first look of surprise and smiled at her, whipping out his handkerchief to dust off the seat of the straight-backed chair for her.

"Thank you." Miranda reached out and shook his

hand. "And this is my father, Joseph Upshaw." She sat down in the chair while her father pumped the man's hand.

Strong retreated behind his desk, casting a look at Devin. Miranda suspected he was not used to dealing with countesses who shook estate manager's hands. "Congratulations on your marriage, my lord," he said obsequiously. "I wish you very happy, ma'am."

"Thank you. I am sure I will be," Miranda said crisply. "I would like to talk to you this afternoon about the estate, after we finish the tour of the house. Just to get a general idea of what the problem areas are and what it will take to bring it back to a profitable working order. After the wedding, I shall get into it more deeply, of course."

Strong gazed back at her blankly. He blinked. Finally he said, "You—you want to talk to me, Miss Upshaw?"

"Yes." Miranda wondered if the man was a trifle dim. If so, it was no wonder that the estate had gone downhill the last few years. "About the state of Lord Ravenscar's holdings."

"But...but..." he sputtered, looking toward Devin for help.

"They are going to fix the place up," Devin explained. "Didn't anyone tell you that?"

"Well, yes, your uncle wrote me. I mean, I understood that there would be, uh..." His eyes rolled back toward Miranda, and he paused uncertainly.

"An infusion of cash?" Miranda asked politely.

"Yes, there will be. But first we will have to see what needs to be done, won't we?"

"I—I—but surely Mr. Dalrymple is the one you need to talk to about that. I mean, him being the trustee and all, he'll be the one handling the money. He'll be arriving this evening, won't he?"

Miranda cast a look at Devin, who said, "Yes, he is due in this evening. But the fact is, Strong, Uncle Rupert won't be the one you will be dealing with anymore. From now on, it will be Miss Upshaw. Or, rather, Lady Ravenscar, as she will be."

The estate manager's mouth dropped open, and he stared at Miranda as if she had suddenly grown two heads.

"We shall start off slowly," Miranda assured the man, thinking that she would probably have to bring in Hiram Baldwin to help Strong, at least temporarily. The man looked as if he might faint. "This afternoon I just want to go over things in general. I won't need to look at the figures just yet. But I really know nothing about the estate. What sort of land it is, how it's being used, whether it's being put to the best use. Later we can get into it in more detail. Then I'll need maps and records for the past few years. We may have to go back even further than that. And, of course, I'll want to ride around the estate and see everything first-hand."

"The whole estate?" He goggled at her.

"Well, not at one time, of course," Miranda said in what she hoped was a soothing tone. "First, of course, we are going to go over the house and grounds. Devin is going to show us around them now."

"Lord Ravenscar?" Strong looked almost as doubtful as he had when he had heard that Miranda intended to run the estate.

Miranda smothered a smile as Devin said, "I do remember where everything is, you know."

"Oh, of course, my lord, I didn't mean to imply..." Strong began to rub his hands together anxiously. "I am sure you will do an excellent job of it."

The three of them rose and left the office. Miranda suspected that as soon as the door was closed behind them, Mr. Strong had run to pour himself a stiff drink.

She turned to Devin, saying thoughtfully, "Is Mr. Strong a trifle slow? He seemed to have a deal of trouble understanding what I wanted."

Devin smothered a smile. "I think you are a bit...shall we say, intimidating...for the ordinary man, Miranda. He is not accustomed to a countess walking in and saying she would like to see the books. I am sure he'll be fine once he gets used to you. Give him a little time to recover from the shock. Maybe he will be better after he talks to Uncle Rupert."

They went first around the outside of the house, exploring the neglected grounds and examining the exterior of the mansion. Devin pointed out where the herb garden on the kitchen side of the house had stood, as well as the elegant formal gardens on the terrace behind the house. Flowers still grew there, the roses in a wild tangle, the vines of the arbor running over and dripping down into the doorway. There was a kind of shaggy, careless beauty about the flower gardens, but the unpruned hedges at the bottom of the terrace simply looked like thickets of wild bushes, and the graveled paths were muddy and pocked with holes.

"There's been only old Mr. Pettigrew and his grandson for a few years now, and they cannot take care of it all. I have even seen Cummings out in the roses a time or two, trying to cut back the weeds so he can still have roses for the vases," Devin said. "When I was a boy, I can remember there was a maze down on that side of the terrace." He pointed toward an area that was overgrown with grass now. "It had to be carefully pruned, and over the last generation it had become completely overgrown. Father had them cut it to the ground and uproot it. He was afraid one of us children would manage to crawl into it and become hopelessly trapped."

"I read that the landscaping was done by Capability Brown," Joseph said. "Is that true?"

"As far as I know. The alternating elms and beeches as you come up the lane are ones he had planted. And over there—" he pointed in the other direction from the maze, where trees encroached upon the grounds "—those were once a very neat orchard, or so my father told me. Fruit trees all in military rows, planted by his grandfather. In the spring it's beautiful, a thick blanket of pink and white flowers."

"I have a landscaper coming next week," Joseph said with satisfaction. "We'll soon set it to rights. I don't suppose you have the original plans?"

Devin shrugged. "I don't know. I suppose they might be in the library or my study. I shall look for them." He turned and looked back at the house, shading his eyes against the sun. "The exterior stone is in pretty good shape, just nicks and chinks here and there, some stone carvings that have fallen off. The roof needs repair badly, I know that. The west wing is entirely closed off because of the water damage. Most of the chimneys don't draw properly. There's woodworm in most of the banisters and railings. Dry rot. Wet rot. There are some floors in the west wing that I am not even sure are safe.''

He looked from Joseph to Miranda and back again. "Still game for repairing the old pile?"

"You must be joking. You've only whetted Papa's appetite," Miranda said with a chuckle. "Lead on."

They went inside and walked through the house, taking what Miranda termed a short overview. The original old great hall of the center wing had been turned into the large entry of the house, the centerpiece of which was an elegant staircase that rose to the landing, then curved in both directions up to the second floor. The steps were marble, as was the floor of the entry, and the banisters were made of English oak. Miranda had already noticed on her way downstairs this morning that the railing was pricked with hundreds of tiny holes, indicating the presence of woodworm.

"At least we don't have deathwatch beetles," Devin said as they started making their way around the stairs. "Or at least we haven't heard them knocking." The larger beetle, which was even more voraciously destructive than the woodworm, was known by the tapping sound it made inside the wood.

"That's good."

"Those are the best tapestries." Devin pointed to the huge, faded hangings that decorated the walls of the large room, along with several enormous portraits of ancestors, many of them darkened with time. "Mother had the best ones taken from all the rooms and moved down here, where they would be seen first."

He led them next to the vast kitchens and the warren of small larder rooms and servants' quarters, then took them into the main ballroom, a huge expanse of marble floor that took up most of the central wing of the bottom floor. Then they climbed up the stairs and started from the top, opening the windows in the attic to look out upon the slate tiles of the roof, many of which were broken or displaced, and examining the water damage. They made their way down, walking up and down the halls, poking into all the rooms, so that by the time they reached the second floor, where the main family rooms were, it was long past time for lunch, and they were hungry and dusty, as well.

However, Joseph and Miranda wanted to finish the tour, so Devin led them down the hall, looking into what he called the morning room, which had been paneled all in dark wine-red Cordovan leather with brass studs, now faded and cracked. Next came a music room, and across the hall was what he termed the small ballroom, a chamber about half the size of the main ballroom below. Beyond it lay the library, a large, gloomy room.

Devin crossed to the windows and pulled aside the heavy draperies, revealing a set of tall windows that faced south, letting in a pleasant light that revealed a room two stories high, filled with books.

"Oh, my..." Miranda breathed. "What a wonderful room!" Two tables and a number of well-cushioned chairs sat in the middle of the room, as well as a large globe on a stand and another stand containing a large, old, leather-bound Bible. Built-in bookcases eight feet high ran all around the room. The double bank of windows took up much of one side wall, and above the bookcases on two of the other walls were more hangings and portraits. But the fourth wall held a wooden walkway about four feet wide, reached by a wooden staircase, and that wall was also filled with bookcases.

Miranda walked all around the room, admiring everything, thinking of how she would refurbish the room and make it beautiful and comfortable. This, she knew, would be a room in which she spent much of her time. "I love it here."

She climbed the wooden staircase to the loft of the library, noting that the banister here, too, had the tiny pinholes that indicated woodworm. When she reached the upper level, she walked along, admiring the books.

"Oh, look!" she cried. "Here are books about the house. I can't quite see all the titles. I wonder if there is a map of the gardens in any of them." She stepped back to get a better angle of sight to the top shelves. "I'll need a stool."

She went up on tiptoe, straining to see better, and reached behind her to balance her hand on the rail. The balustrade gave way beneath her hand, and Miranda, off balance, felt herself falling helplessly backward into space.

12

Miranda shrieked, twisting and grabbing frantically as she fell. With one hand she managed to grab one of the slender railings, and she held on for dear life. Below her she could hear her father shout her name and the sound of feet running. Her arm felt as if it were about to tear out of its socket, and her fingers were slipping from the railing. She scrabbled desperately with her other hand for some purchase, but found nothing but slick wood floor. Then the rail snapped, and she plummeted toward the floor below.

But the seconds when she had clung to the railing had given Devin enough time to reach the spot below her, and he caught her as she fell, so that instead of crashing into the hard wood, she thudded against the solid flesh of his chest. He staggered back under the force of their collision, and they fell into a heap on the floor. For a moment they lay there, stunned. Devin's arms were clasped around Miranda so tightly she could scarcely breathe, and she realized an instant later that she was clinging to him equally hard. She closed her eyes, and a shiver ran through her. For an instant she had thought she was gone.

"Miranda! Are you all right? Jesus God, I thought you were dead!" Her father, who had run for the stairs to climb up to her, now hurried over to where they lay.

"I—I'm all right," Miranda said, her voice muffled by Devin's shirt.

Joseph reached down and grasped her arm, helping her up, and Devin released her. She stood up, brushing at her dress with her hands. She wanted to burst into tears, she realized, to throw herself back against Devin's firm chest and give way to hysterical sobs. But that was not her way. Besides, she told herself, Devin had just saved her life; she shouldn't repay him by turning into a sodden, clinging female.

She clasped her hands together to hide their trembling and turned to Devin. She tried to give him a smile, but it didn't work. "Thank you. You saved my life."

"You're welcome. I— You scared the very devil out of me."

"Me too," Miranda confessed, and this time a smile came out. "I should have been more careful. I know the whole place is infested with woodworm."

Devin nodded and glanced upward at the empty stretch of balcony where the railing had fallen. "I didn't realize it was that bad."

He looked at the balcony for a long moment, a frown starting on his forehead.

"I think a nice rest would be in order for you, my

dear," Joseph said, putting his arm around his daughter. "Come along, I'll take you up to your room."

"But I am supposed to see Mr. Strong after this," Miranda began to protest.

"Don't worry about Strong. He'll probably welcome the chance to recover from the shock of meeting you," Devin told her with a grin. "I'll send him a note telling him you will see him later. The place has been going to the devil for years. It won't matter if you take another day or two to whip it into shape."

Miranda's legs were beginning to tremble in the aftermath of her fear, and she was afraid that she would start to shake all over if she stayed there much longer, so she nodded and let her father lead her out of the room.

Devin stood where he was for a moment, looking at the open doorway. His heart was still pounding like a mad thing. He didn't think he would ever forget the sight of her tumbling off the loft. For an instant it had been as if the world had stopped.

He turned then and went up the staircase, walking along the loft until he got to the vacant spot where Miranda had fallen. He looked down at the break in the wood, first on one side, then on the other. They were the same—neatly sawed almost all the way through, only the bottom third torn and jagged. Someone had laid a trap, and Miranda had fallen into it.

Miranda refused to move back the wedding because of her fall. That evening, after a nap had restored her nerves, she was a little embarrassed by everyone's concern, and she assured them all that she was fine.

"My pride is bruised, mostly," she said with a smile. "There is no reason not to continue with the wedding as we had planned. The worst thing that's wrong with me is a slightly sprained wrist."

So the following afternoon Devin and Miranda were wed in the village church. The ceremony was simple and brief, as Miranda had requested, but the church was filled with the scent of the masses of white roses on either side of the altar, and the old stone church was cozy and bathed in the golden light of the fading afternoon sun. It was for Miranda a beautiful moment, sweet and profound, and the words the vicar spoke resonated through her. *This was what she wanted. This was what was meant to be.*

Devin's hand was warm and firm around hers. She glanced up at him. His face showed little expression, and she wondered what he was thinking, whether he was sad or happy, or scared at the prospect of losing his freedom. She wondered if he thought of Leona and wished that it was she instead of Miranda who stood beside him there. Fiercely, Miranda swore to herself that she would someday erase the thought of Leona from his mind.

They rode back to Darkwater in an open barouche, and along the way, the people of the village turned out to wave and smile and cry out good wishes and congratulations. There would be a large party for all of them in the side yard at Darkwater this evening, while the Aincourts' friends and family gathered to celebrate in the small ballroom.

She glanced over at Devin, who looked at her and winked. "All a bit medieval, isn't it?"

Miranda chuckled. "You read my mind. But I am sure Papa is wallowing in it."

"Pleasing your father must be very important to you."

"I love him. But I wouldn't do absolutely anything to please him."

"Yet you married to please him."

"I married to please myself." The words slipped out before Miranda really thought about them.

"Indeed?" Devin's eyes darkened. "Then I sincerely hope that I am able to accomplish that."

"Doing what *I* want will please me," Miranda explained. "I realized that life is much easier for a married woman than a single one, even one with as forward-thinking a father as mine. A married woman may go where she likes and with no one accompanying her, and no one thinks a thing of it. There are no silly restrictions about wearing whites and pastels and no bold colors. The world does not recoil in horror if she is alone with a man. And, of course, there are the other reasons I told you at the time we became engaged."

"I remember." Devin watched her for a moment. "You are an odd woman. Most women, when they speak about marriage, speak about love."

"Many women feel the need to make the best of a bad situation," Miranda replied crisply.

Devin was startled into laughter. "My dear Lady Ravenscar, you are hopelessly blunt."

"It is very odd to be called that," Miranda said softly.

"You had better get used to it."

"I suppose so."

He studied her thoughtful face. "Having regrets already?"

"No." She looked up and smiled. "Merely thinking. Wondering what our lives will be like."

"Unusual, I should think."

"You are probably right."

At the house, they moved up to the small ballroom, where a large repast had been laid out in celebration of the wedding. Family and friends were there, including all the people of the area who were considered of sufficient social standing to attend the country wedding of the Earl of Ravenscar. Miranda had been given to understand that a city wedding or one planned for months in advance would have been an entirely different thing. Invitations would have been much sought after, and many of the lesser gentry who would be here today would not have been part of the elite. Miranda had trouble understanding the ins and outs of who was suitable to be invited, the rules a seeming mishmash of considerations of money, family standing, proximity and social entanglements. Miranda had nodded when Lady Ravenscar tried to explain and told her gratefully that she would leave it all in that lady's hands.

Miranda and Devin stood in a receiving line just inside the ballroom, along with Devin's mother, Uncle Rupert, and Rachel and her husband, all lined up in an esoteric order that they all seemed to understand without question. Miranda's family brought up the end of the line, needless to say. Miranda was sandwiched between Devin and his mother, a fact for which she was grateful, as it eliminated the need for her to carry on much conversation. Devin would introduce her to whoever came up—or, if he could not remember, which was sometimes the case, his mother would smoothly come to the rescue and introduce the visitor to Miranda herself.

Miranda was saying a few words to the doctor when she felt Devin stiffen beside her. At almost the same moment, on the other side of her, Lady Ravenscar's arm twitched convulsively. Curious, Miranda glanced over at the newest arrivals. An old woman was standing there, smiling at Devin, and behind her stood the woman Miranda had seen with Devin at the opera. Devin's mistress had come to the wedding reception.

"Miss Vesey," Devin said in a constrained voice to the old lady, bending down a little to shake her hand. "How nice to see you again. It has been a long time."

"Yes. I don't get around much these days. I was so glad that Lady Vesey offered to accompany me. You know Lady Vesey, don't you, my nephew's wife?"

"Yes. I know Lady Vesey." Devin's voice was cold and controlled, but Miranda could sense the intense emotion radiating from his body. She wished she knew exactly what he was feeling.

She had no doubt what his mother was feeling. Lady Ravenscar was as taut as a violin string, and Miranda suspected that she would have liked to fly across the few feet separating them and slap Leona.

Leona, on the other hand, looked like the cat who had got into the cream. She was dressed beautifully, in a conservative silk dress of a muted green, nothing like the low-cut gown she had worn to the opera. However, it fit her so well and did such wonderful things for her eyes and hair that it drew one's attention almost as much as the evening gown had. She was stunning—hair, eyes, skin—and her beauty was just as dazzling close up as it had been at a distance. Miranda could not help but feel a frisson of uncertainty as she gazed at the other woman's perfectly modeled face. *How could she ever hope to compete with this woman for Devin's affections?*

"Ravenscar and I are old friends," Leona said now, looking up into Devin's face with laughing eyes. "Aren't we, my lord? I hope you won't mind my inviting myself along to the celebration. Vesey's aunt needed an escort, otherwise I would never have imposed."

"Of course not," Devin's mother said icily. "A lady would never do such a thing. Hello, Lady Vesey."

Leona's gaze slid over to Lady Ravenscar, and in doing so fell on Miranda. Her eyes widened a trifle, and Miranda thought she saw the woman stiffen before she smiled at her. It gave Miranda a wicked spurt of pleasure to think that the sight of her had discomfited the woman. Obviously Lady Vesey had expected a different sort of woman.

"Allow me to introduce you to Devin's wife," Lady Ravenscar went on. "Miranda, this is Lady Vesey. Her husband's estate lies not too far away from here. We see very little of them, however." She paused before adding, "They are almost always in London."

Miranda ignored her momentary flash of uncertainty

and held out her hand to the woman. "It's nice to meet you, Lady Vesey. I am enjoying meeting Lady Ravenscar's friends. If only we had known you were here, we would have sent you an invitation."

Leona bridled a little at the suggestion that she was of an age with Devin's mother, but there was no way that she could refute the statement. So she smiled, chalking the remark up to Miranda's naivete, Miranda felt sure. "Thank you. You look so nice, my dear. Lady Ravenscar must have enjoyed fitting you out with clothes."

Miranda chuckled. "You conjure up an interesting picture of me before I met Lady Ravenscar."

"I am afraid I didn't have enough time to accompany Miranda on her shopping expeditions," Devin's mother said, continuing the duel with Leona. "Fortunately, she has a wonderful sense of style and an understanding of what is appropriate and what is not."

Miranda enjoyed seeing the faint flush rise in Leona's cheeks. Lady Ravenscar had made a direct hit with her last statement. With great ingenuousness, Miranda went on, "You must come call on us, Lady Vesey. I would so love to talk to you again. I am sure that I will need all the advice I can get from ladies like you, who have been married a long time."

The same quiver of expression crossed Leona's face, a mixture of insult and uncertainty whether Miranda knew that she had been insulting or was simply too ignorant to realize what she had said.

"Yes. I would love to call on you."

"Won't that be delightful?" the old woman, Miss

Vesey, said happily, and Miranda smiled at her with true warmth.

"You must come, too, Miss Vesey."

"Of course, my dear. I wish you very happy, Lady Ravenscar."

Leona added, "Yes, of course. Very happy." She hesitated.

Miranda suspected that Leona had started to say her name as her elderly aunt had, but the words had stuck in her throat. Miranda thought that Leona had come because she had wanted to cause a stir, as well as get a glimpse of Miranda and remind Devin of who he really loved. But Miranda guessed that Lady Vesey had not thought through the whole idea of having to greet and congratulate her lover's wife.

"Thank you, Lady Vesey," Miranda replied, making it more difficult for her.

"Lady Ravenscar." The words grated out of her throat, and then Leona turned and followed her husband's aunt down the line.

Uncle Rupert said little to Leona, merely gave her a glance of horror, and Rachel favored the woman with a freezing look. Lord Westhampton was perfunctorily correct. To Miranda's amusement, however, her own father greeted Lady Vesey with the same unrestrained delight he had displaying all evening. He chatted with the aunt and pumped Leona's hand as he talked to her, chattering on in his amiable way about his daughter, Ravenscar and Darkwater.

Devin cast a sideways glance down at Miranda, gauging her reaction. He leaned closer to her and whispered, "I am sorry. I had no idea...."

"No. I am sure you did not," Miranda replied equably and gave him an unconcerned smile. She had no intention of giving vent to her jealousy, least of all in front of Devin.

There were not many more guests to greet after that, and when the line broke up, Devin took Miranda's hand and led her toward the floor. Every eye turned toward them expectantly, and the guests edged back to give them room. Devin nodded to the musicians at the end of the room, and they struck up a waltz. He turned to Miranda and offered her his hand, and she took it, moving into his arms as they began the steps of the dance.

She felt a trifle conspicuous, circling the floor, just the two of them, but it was a wonderful feeling as well, being in Devin's arms, feeling his hand pressing against the small of her back, following him as naturally as breathing. She thought with a wicked little rush of pleasure of Leona having to watch the dance. Leona, she hoped, had gotten something different from what she had expected when she decided to invade the wedding celebration tonight.

While everyone was watching the newlyweds gracefully circle the room, Lady Ravenscar turned to her daughter and pulled her aside, whispering, "Did you have any idea that woman was planning to come here tonight?"

"No!" Rachel looked appalled. "Of course not. I would have told the servants not to admit her. I didn't even know she was staying at Vesey Park."

"She can't have been here too long, then," Rachel's mother replied. "She usually creates a great stir when she does deign to visit the estate. She certainly did the first time she came.'' Her mouth tightened, as much of a grimace as Lady Ravenscar ever allowed herself.

Rachel knew she was referring to the first time Devin had met Leona, when he had been only a boy of seventeen and had fallen in love with her with all the heat and urgency of which only an adolescent boy is capable.

"Well, at least the girl doesn't know anything about her," Lady Ravenscar said. "I started to give that witch the cut direct, but I knew that would give Miranda a hint that something was up where Lady Vesey was concerned. It was an insult to Miranda, of course, but as long as she does not know it was an insult, it won't hurt her.''

Rachel, however, was well aware that Miranda did indeed know who Leona was and what significance she played in Devin's life, so as soon as the dance was over, Rachel moved toward Miranda.

The bride was engulfed by well-wishers as soon as she and Devin walked from the floor and he bowed to her, releasing her hand and turning her over to them. Miranda, coming back to normalcy with some difficulty after the romantic dance, struggled not to look after Devin's retreating figure to see if he went straight to his mistress. She conversed with the strangers as best she could, relieved when Rachel appeared and tucked her hand through her arm, smiling at the others and saying that she must steal her new sister away.

Rachel led her deftly out of the room to the hall beyond and over to a secluded alcove, which held an empty window seat. "I am terribly sorry," she told Miranda as soon as they were out of earshot of the other guests. "I had no idea she was even in the area. I wouldn't have dreamed that even Leona would have the gall to come here tonight!"

"It's all right," Miranda assured her with more calm than she felt. "I think it all went well enough." She smiled at her new sister-in-law. "And the dance was divine. I am too happy right now to worry about Lady Vesey."

"Are you?" Rachel asked delightedly. "Are you truly happy?"

"I am. Though not as happy as I hope to be in the future."

"You care for him, don't you?" Rachel said, laying her hand on Miranda's arm. "You didn't marry him for all this, did you?" She waved her hand in a broad gesture.

Miranda laughed pleasantly. "No. All this can be bought. A husband requires a great deal more than payment. I would not tie myself to someone for life to acquire a house, however grand it is."

"I knew it!" Rachel looked gleeful. "I am positive that you will make Devin happy."

"I cannot guarantee that," Miranda demurred, then added with a glint of a smile, "I will do my best, however."

Her husband was at that moment making his way through the room, doing his best to appear to be aimlessly chatting with his guests, all the while glancing around for Leona and plotting how best and most unobtrusively to separate her from the others and take her out of the room. Finally he spotted her at the other end of the room, standing close to one of the doors. She was watching him, and when their gazes met, she nodded her head toward the door and slipped out. Devin made a polite excuse to the vicar's cousin, who had stopped him to congratulate him, and followed Leona.

He wound his way through the crowd and out the same door. There was no sign of Leona, but the staircase just a few steps down the hall led to the back garden, so he followed his hunch that she had taken it. He hurried down the steps and out the back door. Sure enough, there was Leona, waiting for him, an alluring, mischievous smile on her face.

"What the devil do you think you're doing?" Devin burst out, his eyes flashing. He strode over to her and grabbed her wrist.

"What's the matter?" Leona asked with a pout. "Aren't you happy to see me?"

"It is my wedding day!" He glanced around, then pulled her behind one of the overgrown hedges that had grown up all over the yard. "Have you run mad? What are you doing here?"

"Oh, Dev, don't be angry with me." She smiled up at him, one hand coming up to his chest in a placating way. "I just wanted to see you."

When he did not respond with a smile but continued to stare at her in a stony way, Leona took a step back, one eyebrow going up and an angry light flaring in her eyes.

"How else was I supposed to see you except to

come here?'' she asked bitingly. ''You didn't even come to call on me before you left. You sent me a note!''

''You refused to see me when I came to call, if you will remember,'' Devin replied. ''I got turned away three times by your butler. It was tiresome.''

''What did you expect after you walked out on me at the opera?'' Leona pointed out. ''And with Stuart and Geoffrey there to witness it, too! It was humiliating.'' She paused, then added, ''You used to be more persistent. You know I would have given in eventually.''

''Yes, well, I had to leave for Darkwater, so I didn't have the time for games. That is why I sent you a note, telling you what I was doing. I never expected you to show up here.''

''What else was I to do? I wanted to see your bride. Besides, I thought you might enjoy a little...diversion after two weeks of being locked up in Darkwater. So I decided to take a few weeks' rest at Vesey's estate. It is where we met, you know. Do you remember that?'' She moved back to him, smiling in a beckoning way.

To Leona's surprise, Devin did not soften or smile back. He said only, ''Of course I do. But surely you must see how...how *wrong* it is to come here today. You were flaunting our relationship in everyone's face.''

''Since when did you and I worry about right and wrong?'' She went up on tiptoe and brushed her lips against his. ''Come, Devin, don't be angry. So I gave everyone a little something more to gossip about. We

have long done that, haven't we? And we could...
alleviate your boredom, if you'd like." She slid her
hand down his chest and into the waistband of his
trousers.

"Bloody hell, Leona!" Devin jerked away. "Are
you mad? Our house is full of wedding guests. Anyone
could come out here and find us. It's an insult to my
wife for you to even be here."

Leona's eyes narrowed. "My, my, aren't we pro-
tective of the little wife all of a sudden. When did you
become so provincial?"

"Good Lord, Leona, she is Lady Ravenscar now. I
cannot allow her to be insulted in my own home. What
did you expect? You are the one who wanted me to
marry her, if you'll remember."

"I didn't expect you to suddenly become a doting
husband!" Leona lashed back. "I didn't think you
would hare off to Darkwater, leaving me not knowing
when you would return. Or that you would stand there
smiling like a fool because you were introducing some
insipid little colonial as your wife. The idea was for
you to marry her, then return to me and our life in
London."

"I know. And that is what I am doing. I married
her, and after a decent stay here I will come back to
London." Devin realized even as he said the words
that the idea of leaving Miranda and returning to London left him strangely uncomfortable.

"Decent stay?" Leona repeated. "I cannot believe
what I am hearing! When did you start worrying about
what was decent or acceptable? When did you turn all
proper and respectable?"

"Proper? Respectable?" Devin had to chuckle. "Leona, my dear, I think you are being a trifle far-fetched. I did not want to get married. It was you who insisted on it. But now that I have done it, I have to go on with it. I couldn't exactly leave her at the church and hie off to London."

"Once you would have," Leona told him.

Devin said nothing. He knew that what Leona said was true. Years ago, even a few months ago, he could not have waited to get away from Darkwater. He would have spent the past two weeks dreaming about Leona and returning to London. The truth was, he had scarcely thought about either one of them; most of his thoughts had been occupied by the supremely irritating Miss Upshaw.

"You told me you hated this girl," Leona went on.

"She is the most annoying female I have ever met," he responded candidly, but his words were accompanied by a softening of his expression, and a faint smile played over his lips.

Leona frowned. "Whatever is the matter with you? Don't tell me you have developed a *tendre* for that insipid female!"

Devin chuckled again. "*Insipid* is the last word I would use to describe Miranda. Don't be ridiculous. I have not developed a *tendre* for her. I cannot be in the same room with her for two minutes without getting into an argument."

He thought it best not to mention the fact that he also could not go to sleep at night because he could not stop thinking about her sleeping just one door away from him, or that he went downstairs every morning eager for another encounter with Miranda. Leona had always been unconcerned about his sexual interest in other women. But somehow this time he thought she would not be so understanding.

His laughter soothed Leona. She knew the intensity of Devin's desire; she had been the object of it for fourteen years, after all. And she could not imagine him laughing about a woman who was the object of that fierce lust.

Leona gave one of her throaty chuckles, leaning her head back to look up at him. "Well, you know where I am...any time you grow tired of dancing attendance on your heiress."

"Yes. I know. Now...will you kindly collect your aunt and return to Vesey Park?"

Irritation flared up in Leona again. The entire evening had not gone at all as she had planned. The American had not been the mousy, retiring girl she had assumed she was. She was not beautiful, of course, as Leona herself was—but she seemed not at all intimidated by Leona, and she had looked thoroughly at home in her elegant gown, standing there at Devin's side. Then Devin had followed Leona outside, and instead of eagerly seizing her and exclaiming how glad he was that she was there, how much he wanted her, he had flown into a fury because she had dared to come to the wedding party and "insult" his odious wife.

"Yes, I will go," she snapped. "If this is the way you are going to act, I may just go all the way back to London. I am sure there are several men there who would be happy to keep me entertained while you are cooling your heels up here in the hinterlands!''

She turned and swept away, satisfied that she had roused enough simmering jealousy with her last remark that it would not be long before Devin decided to come to call at Vesey Park.

It would have filled her with gall if she had known that Devin's first thought was a hope that she would make good her threat instead of staying here to try to stir up trouble. He waited for a few minutes, then returned to the house and went to look for Miranda.

He was not sure what he expected Miranda to be like when he returned—but it certainly wasn't the laughing creature he found talking to Michael and his sister, the one who turned to him without the faintest hint of resentment or distrust and smiled, saying, ''Ah, there you are, Devin. I wondered where you had gotten to.''

The absence of jealousy and anger seemed so surreal that for an instant he wondered if perhaps Miranda really didn't know about Leona. But then he recalled that she had mentioned her during that bizarre proposal of hers, and he was even more puzzled by her lack of animosity. Most women, he was certain, would have been raving at the idea that their husband's mistress had showed up at their wedding. It was then that he realized she truly did not care whether he had affairs or even kept a mistress. The knowledge galled him.

He knew he should have been happy about it. He couldn't have asked for an arrangement better suited to him. What he felt, however, was closer to resentment than to happiness.

In point of fact, Miranda was quite relieved to see him—so much so that it overwhelmed any irritation or jealousy, making it easy to be pleasant and calm. She had been surreptitiously searching the ballroom for Devin ever since she and Rachel had returned; and his absence had set up a worry and fear in Miranda that she was not accustomed to feeling. She had been afraid that he had slipped away from the party with his lover, that he had been so overcome with desire and love for Leona that he had disappeared to some hideaway with her. That fear was heightened by the fact that she could not catch a glimpse of Leona, either. She knew that Rachel had been concerned about the same thing by the faintly pinched look around Rachel's eyes and the way she kept unobtrusively checking the room.

Now Devin was here, and Miranda could unclench her fists and let her shoulders relax. She would not be a satisfied bride tonight, but at least she would not be a publicly abandoned one.

Rachel's smile indicated how relieved she, too, was that Devin had reappeared. "Devin, there you are, and just in time. Don't you think it is getting to be time for the married couple to leave?"

"Already?" Miranda looked a little startled. "But the party is still quite lively."

"Yes, but the bride and groom always leave well before the end," Rachel said firmly.

"Oh." Miranda suspected that Rachel was doing her best to get Devin and Miranda as far away from

Lady Vesey's presence as possible. She would want to make sure that Miranda did not run into the woman a second time that night.

Miranda suspected that Leona, having accomplished her purpose, had already left. She also suspected that the reason she had been unable to locate Devin had been because he was seeing Leona off. However, she preferred not to think about that. He had not left with her, and that was all Miranda needed to know at present.

She did not mind leaving the party, in any case. Keeping up a cheerful, pleasant front the past few minutes had been something of an ordeal, and she was quite ready to get away from all the strangers and retreat to the comfort and safety of her room.

"Shall we go, then?" Devin turned to Miranda. "We can slip away without anyone knowing and avoid all the fuss."

"That sounds wonderful," Miranda replied honestly.

"I have nipped out of here many a time," Devin assured her. "It's easy. First, we shall go get a plate of food."

"All right."

They made their way through the crowd, smiling and nodding to well-wishers, but deftly avoiding coming to a full stop. At the buffet table, they loaded their plates and again wound through the crowd.

"Just act as if you're looking for an open space to sit and eat," Devin whispered. "Now we are almost to the door. Don't look around or act guilty—someone is sure to catch you then. Just walk as if we're heading toward those seats and now...out the door.''

Miranda slipped through the open doorway, with Devin right behind her.

"The back stairs are over here.'' He nodded toward them. "Come on, we'll have a picnic. I'm starving, and I haven't be able to get near the food all night. How about you?''

Miranda nodded agreement. "Where shall we go?''

"I know a place.'' He led the way up the stairs and along the hallway to a large room. Handing his plate to her, he lit a lamp in the room from one of the hallway sconces and ushered her inside. He made a sweeping gesture of the room. "Tables, chairs...''

"The nursery!''

"I grant you that they are a trifle miniature-size, but we can make do.'' He took the plates and laid them down on the table, then pulled out one of the small chairs in a grand gesture. "If my lady will sit.''

Miranda grinned. "I should be honored, my lord.''

She sat down, and Devin took his place opposite her. She smothered a giggle at the sight of him sitting with his knees almost up to his chin, and he gave her a mock frown. "I am the lord of the manor, I'll have you know. You mustn't make jest of me.''

"I would never do such a thing,'' Miranda assured him solemnly. Picking up her fork, she tucked into her food with enthusiasm. Her stomach had been too nervous for her to eat earlier, and now, she realized, she was ravenous.

While they ate, Devin entertained her with stories about his childhood, pointing out the cupboard where he had hidden as a little boy in order to jump out and scare his sisters, but had then fallen asleep and been presumed lost, with the whole household out looking for him.

"Only the first of many misadventures," he told her with a wry grin.

They talked and laughed, sitting there incongruously in their wedding finery, and it seemed to Miranda the happiest wedding dinner she could possibly have had.

Later they walked down to the medieval musicians' gallery, a small screened room that jutted out above the ballroom below. Through the latticework, they could look down on the party and hear the mingling of music, laughter and talk that rose from it.

"Rachel and Caro and I used to sneak in here after Nurse fell asleep and watch our parents' parties," Devin said. "They weren't terribly exciting, but they seemed so to us—mostly because they were forbidden."

"That always makes things much more fun," Miranda agreed.

He took her hand, and it seemed the most natural thing in the world, pleasant and warm, in keeping with the light, happy aura of their "picnic." But there was an underlying current of excitement in the touch, as well, a knowledge of his skin against hers, his warmth, his flesh, his smell—this man who was almost a stranger to her, yet her husband, as well.

They strolled along the hallway to her room, and Devin opened the door, stepping aside for her to enter.

She turned to say good-night, but he was already coming in the door, too.

"What—what are you doing?"

Devin closed the door behind him, and his eyes locked on hers. "Tonight is our wedding night." He took a step forward, and his hands went to her shoulders. "And I am your husband."

13

Miranda's breath locked in her throat, and she was unable to do anything except stare at Devin as he came closer. Then his hands were on her shoulders, and he turned her gently around, saying, ''Your maid will not come tonight. I will be your personal maid.''

His hands started on the row of buttons that marched down the back of her dress. His fingers brushed her skin as he did so, and it sent a shiver through her. Miranda struggled to collect her thoughts.

''I think that is hardly necessary. If I ring for the maid, I am sure she will come.''

''Most likely. Still...much easier if I do it.''

Miranda could feel the two sides of her dress parting and falling away from her back, exposing the bare flesh above her chemise. She clasped her hand to her chest to hold the dress up. His lips pressed against the bare skin of her upper back, velvety and warm. She felt the rush of his breath against her sensitive flesh.

''Devin...'' His name came out hoarsely, and she stopped to clear her throat. She straightened and stepped away from the pleasurable touch of his mouth. "No. Really. This is enough."

He slid his hands over her back, pushing her dress down onto her arms, caressed her shoulders, and it seemed as if everywhere he touched sprang to tingling life.

"It's not enough," he disputed her words, bending down to plant a trail of kisses across her collarbone and onto her shoulder. "It won't be enough until I have you. All of you."

"This is exactly what we agreed would not happen," she said, trying to inject censure into her voice, which came out far too breathless for her comfort.

"No. This is what *you* agreed would not happen. I never agreed upon it at all."

He slipped his hands in under the opened sides of her dress, gliding around her back and onto her stomach, nothing separating his skin from hers but the thin layer of her chemise. Miranda drew in her breath in a gasp. He made a soft noise and nuzzled her neck.

A long shudder ran down through her, and she could not suppress a moan.

"This is what's right. You can feel it," he murmured, his breath fluttering enticingly over her skin. "This is what it's meant to be like."

He moved his hands up to cup her breasts, kneading and caressing them as his mouth teased at her neck and ears. Desire flooded Miranda, almost frightening in its intensity, and she knew that she wanted nothing more than to spend the night in his bed, to be introduced to the delights of passion at his hands. It would be easy to give in, easy to taste the pleasure.

Easy, too, to lose the one thing she ultimately wanted.

"No." She made her voice firm, and she pulled away from him, turning to face him. "No. This is not part of our bargain."

His eyes were dark with passion, his face stamped with hunger. "Forget our bargain. We don't have to follow it. It doesn't matter."

"It does matter. It was the whole point of our getting married. To remain uninvolved...to be free to pursue our own—"

He cut off her words by pulling her into his arms and kissing her deeply. Miranda sagged against him, desire washing through her.

He broke off the kiss and began to trail his mouth down her neck, planting slow, heated kisses on the sensitive skin. "There is nothing wrong with having passion in marriage, as well," he murmured persuasively, his fingertips lightly brushing up her arms and back down. "Let me show you how good it can be. Let me...."

The very persuasiveness of his words and caresses suddenly struck Miranda, and she pulled back, her spine stiffening. "No, my lord, I think not. You are a practiced seducer, that is clear. But I am not so easily persuaded. I am not interested in a marriage of both intimacy and outside affairs. It would never work, at least not for me. I think it is better to keep the two things separate. Our marriage is a business arrangement, and we shall seek our pleasure elsewhere."

His face darkened. "Dammit! There is no reason—"

"There is every reason," Miranda responded crisply. "Your very reaction is reason enough. Already emotion has entered into it, and our marriage is not one of emotion."

"Not all of us are as cold and rational as you!"

"No, I fear not," Miranda replied, as if he had given her a compliment. "But I am sure that after you calm down and think about it, you will realize that I am right. With passion comes feeling, and with feeling come all sorts of entangling emotions—jealousy, hurt, anger. Well, it obviously would never do. It is much preferable to have that with a lover than with a husband."

A flame sparked to life in his eyes, and Devin clenched his fists. For a moment Miranda thought he was going to fly into a fury. But then he stepped back, his jaw clenched, and said, "Of course. If that is what you wish. I can see how you would prefer not to feel any emotion for your husband. It would be harder to make everyone dance to your bidding then, wouldn't it? Indeed, it is preferable to keep everything on a business basis. Employees cannot afford to complain too much."

"That isn't it at all!" Miranda cried.

"No?"

"Of course not. This is the marriage you wanted, too."

"It was you who—"

"I agreed to the kind of marriage you offered. You wanted to keep a mistress. You wanted to go your own way. You wanted not to be tied to a wife. Or has that all changed suddenly?"

"No, of course not."

"Well, that is what I want, too," Miranda countered. "I am simply talking about sticking to the arrangement we agreed upon—a marriage in name only."

"That does not mean we could not enjoy...certain aspects of marriage at the same time," Devin pointed out. "A marriage can provide pleasure and still remain a loose bond."

Miranda looked at him evenly. "Not for me. Marriage is either real or a sham. Ours belongs to the latter category. If you bring passion into it, it changes everything. I can no longer be objective. I am no longer beyond the realm of jealousy and pain. If I care, I care deeply. And I have no intention of spending my life wondering where you are and who you are with, while I sit at home bleeding from wounds only I can see. So you see, the only solution is not to care for you."

Devin stood looking at her for a long moment. Then he nodded once, briefly. "Good night, Miranda."

He turned and walked out the door.

Miranda spent a long, lonely night. More than once, she wished she had not turned Devin down; at one point she even considered getting up and going to the connecting door to tell him that she had made a mistake. But she managed to keep her resolve. What she had said to Devin was the truth—except that she had not revealed how much she already cared for him. There was more than strategy in her pledge not to consummate their marriage. She knew that to do so would tie her heart to him so irrevocably that she could not have a life without him.

When she awoke the next morning, her usual confidence and optimism had returned, and she went downstairs, ready to plunge into her plans. The landscape architect was due to arrive that afternoon, and the architect was coming the next day, so she decided to press ahead with working on the estate. She sent a note around to Mr. Strong, asking him to meet her in the library, where she had decided to set up office. Her father was there, and she invited Devin's uncle, as well, more out of courtesy than anything else. Devin was fond of his uncle, but given the condition of the Ravenscar estate, Miranda could not help but feel that neither Strong nor Uncle Rupert had been very skillful at management.

Somewhat to her surprise, Devin strolled in as the group was settling around the library table and took a seat beside her.

He saw her look of surprise and smiled a little. "I was bored," he explained in an aside as he sat down. "It was either this or needlepoint with Mother and Rachel in the sitting room."

"I'm glad to see you here," Miranda replied. "It is your estate, after all."

"Good day, my boy," Uncle Rupert said genially. "First time I've seen you volunteer to look at your finances." He winked. "Must be the lure of a female present."

"Makes it more pleasant than looking at you and Strong," Devin agreed placidly. "Now tell us, Miranda, what you plan to do."

"I had not expected to have so many people present," Miranda confessed. "I was merely going to go over the estate with Mr. Strong. Did you bring the information I requested?"

"I—I did my best, ma'am."

"I am sure, Ravenscar, that you and Mr. Dalrymple can add to my knowledge of the estate, as well," she went on, looking first at Devin, then his uncle.

"I will be happy to help you all I can, Miss—excuse me, Lady Ravenscar," Devin's uncle replied.

"Please, call me Miranda. We are related now."

"And you must call me Uncle Rupert, as Devin does," he responded, a twinkle in his eyes. "But, I confess, I am at somewhat of a loss. Exactly what are we doing? Strong came to me in a tizzy yesterday, saying that you were going to be running the estate? I told him it was a lot of nonsense, but—"

"Oh, I shall not see to the day-to-day running of it," Miranda assured him. "That would be far too time-consuming, and I am confident that Mr. Strong can make sure everything goes smoothly. I shall simply oversee it, of course."

Uncle Rupert stared at her in much the same way the estate manager had the day before. "You are going to oversee the estate?" he asked carefully, as though he had not heard correctly. "But—but you are a girl."

"Thank you. However, I have to admit that I am a good bit older than a girl."

"Miranda...I can assure you that money will help us to put the estate in good order. There is no need to worry about it. You should be enjoying yourself. It's not every day one gets to be a new bride. No doubt there are many things about the house that you will need to get acquainted with first.''

"Oh, I shall meet with Mrs. Watkins and Cummings, of course, but they seem to have things well in hand. If one has a good housekeeper and butler, the household takes little of one's time and energy, I find. It certainly won't keep me from getting the estate in order. Don't worry about me, Uncle Rupert. I am used to working. I have never run an estate of this sort before, of course, but I have had quite a bit of experience with other businesses. I feel sure I will be able to get the hang of it.''

"But—'' Rupert turned in confusion to his nephew "—Devin...I don't understand.'' He looked back at Miranda. "Perhaps you don't realize I am the trustee of Devin's estate. I will be happy, of course, to try to explain to you about it, but—''

"Well, no, sir, actually you are not the trustee,'' Miranda said as gently as she could. "I know that you have been running the estate for Devin for a long time now, and I am sure he appreciates it a great deal. But in point of fact, the trust for his property ended over five years ago. There *isn't* a trustee.''

It was just this sort of sloppy handling that she feared had helped the estate to its ultimate demise. Uncle Rupert seemed willing and good-natured, but she had seen little evidence yet of his acumen. It was a delicate situation, for Devin was quite fond of his uncle, but she did not see how she could allow the man to remain in charge of a job for which he was vastly unsuited.

"I suppose that that is technically true," Rupert admitted.

"It has been very kind of you to continue to do it for so long," Miranda went on. "But I feel sure that if the truth were known, you would prefer not to have the work and the responsibility. Wouldn't you?"

"Well, yes, of course, but duty called, you know." He coughed deprecatingly.

"If you will be so kind as to give me the benefit of your experience and advice, I would be very grateful. As I said, I have not had dealings with this particular sort of business. Most of what I have invested in has been raw land or city lots. And, of course, there was the canal venture that I entered into in Pennsylvania." At his blank look, she went on. "Connecting coal fields to their markets in Philadelphia and New York. It will revolutionize the industry. But that is neither here nor there."

"Ah..." Rupert looked faintly dazed. "I will of course be happy to lend you a hand, my dear. Indeed, now that I think of it, you are right. It will be a relief no longer to be responsible for the estate." His face brightened visibly as he thought about it. "It was rather a hard thing, seeing it sliding down like that year after year and not having the resources to stop it."

"I am sure it was," Miranda said sympathetically. "It is a rather large estate, is it not?"

"Almost ten thousand acres," Strong put in. "Of course, a lot of that is in the Roaches. It's rocky and pretty much useless."

"The Roaches?"

"Yes. A godforsaken landscape," Uncle Rupert said. "It's the tail end of the Pennine range. Hilly and rocky. Not useful for anything, as Strong said."

"It's attractive," Devin commented. "In its own strange way. We'll ride down there one day so you can see it if you'd like."

"Yes, I would." Miranda smiled at him. "I would like to ride around the whole estate. I want to see exactly what I'm dealing with. Meet your tenants."

"All right."

"I shall be happy to take you out on a ride, Miranda," Uncle Rupert said. "Why don't we all go? We can ride along the river, eh, Dev? It's a lovely spot. Have a picnic."

"Of course," Devin agreed.

"Excellent." Miranda favored Devin's uncle with a smile, then turned to the estate manager. "Now, Mr. Strong, I would like first to see maps of the estate. And you must tell me what the main product is. I assume it's agricultural."

"Yes, ma'am. Rents from tenants. They've been dropping steadily the past few years. The land just doesn't produce as many crops."

"I see. We shall have to see what we can do to bring it back. You know, Mr. Jefferson has written extensively on modern farming methods that he used at Monticello. I shall have to send for those—and I am sure there must be Englishmen who have been experimenting with the same sort of thing. Also, I should like to go over the books for the estate. I'll get our assistant Hiram Baldwin to help you there. We will need to see several years, I imagine, to pinpoint the problems. That should do for starters."

"Yes, ma'am," Strong agreed in a faint voice.

Uncle Rupert chuckled and turned to his nephew. "I say, Dev, your new bride is something of a whirlwind."

"Yes." Dev looked at her, and a smile played about his lips. "I would say that she is."

Miranda settled into her life at Darkwater with an ease that surprised even her. Both the architect and the landscape expert arrived, and there were meetings with them about restoring Darkwater. She was pleased that Devin often attended the meetings and even got involved on more than one occasion in the discussion of what should be done. When she expressed her surprise at his participation, he replied in his light way that he had been bored, but she could tell that he had more interest in the old house than he was willing to let on, and he certainly knew a great deal more about it than she would have guessed.

She also was examining the estate finances, though she quickly saw that she made poor Mr. Strong so nervous that she had Hiram Baldwin do much of the research and discuss his findings later with her. It was, apparently, a wearying succession of crop failure and depleted land, of failed tenants and unpaid rents.

But, despite her meetings, she had ample time left over to visit with Rachel, whom she was growing to like more and more every day, and to tramp about exploring with Veronica. Devin sometimes accompanied them, which always made the excursions more fun. He was good with Veronica, teasing her and making her laugh, and he could usually be counted on to come up with something interesting to do even when they were confronted with a wet, miserable day that kept them indoors the whole time.

He did not mention their sleeping arrangements or try again to seduce her, a fact that worried Miranda a little and often left her feeling restless and dissatisfied. Devin seemed to have accepted her decision too easily for her comfort, and sometimes she wondered if he felt so little desire for her that it did not bother him to stay away from her. And knowing that Leona was only a few miles away at Vesey Park, she also could not suppress the fear that Devin was seeking the fulfillment of his masculine needs elsewhere. Neither thought was encouraging.

However, sometimes she would glance over at Devin—in the music room after supper or on a walk in the afternoon, or even sitting across the dinner table from him—and she would catch a certain look in his eyes, a glimpse of a smoldering, banked fire that made her own loins tingle. At those moments the very air seemed to hum between them, and Miranda would be certain that he was not indifferent to her at all.

She would have felt better if she had known that Devin, far from being indifferent to her, was becoming daily more and more consumed by lust for her. At first he had decided to abide by her decision. He wanted to bed her, but, after all, he reminded himself, he had had many women and would doubtless have many more. *He did not need this particular one.* It was a trifle annoying that she was so easily able to turn him down, but he knew that she was right—he was not interested in any sort of marriage but the kind she described, where he was free to do as he chose and sleep with whomever he chose. After a time he would leave Darkwater and return to London and Leona and his life there. Darkwater and his new marriage had not yet started to bore him to tears, but he knew that they would, and when that happened, he would be gone. Bedding Miranda would be a diversion, but it was scarcely important, and the last thing he wanted was for her to become attached to him and turn into a lachrymose, clinging female who got upset every time he left.

Therefore, he had not attempted again to seduce her into his bed. But he had found, strangely, that staying away from her had been difficult. Thoughts of her occupied his head. He wanted to see her, to be with her. When she was not around, he thought about her, and more than once he sought out pen and paper, trying to sketch her face and finding with frustration that he could not quite get the look in her eyes that fascinated him so.

Nights were the worst times. He would lie awake in his bed, thinking about her, only a door away from him, and his thoughts would become more and more feverish, until he would often get out of bed and begin to pace the room, more than once ending up downstairs in his study, drinking away the thought of her. It annoyed him that he could not turn off his desire for her, that the more he tried *not* to think about her, the more he thought about her.

He sought her out frequently, joining her on her

walks or giving her a tour of the village or going to her meetings with the architect. He had even, much to his inner horror, found himself playing charades with her and her stepsister one evening, along with Michael and Rachel. He knew that if any of his usual companions had seen him, they would have laughed 'til they cried at the sight of him engaging in such prosaic and banal pursuits. But, somehow, as long as Miranda was there, none of the times seemed dull or prosaic. She always had an interesting thought or a humorous quip to brighten things up—and there was the physical pleasure of looking at her and remembering how she had felt in his arms. He could remember, too, the taste of her mouth, the smooth texture of her skin, the sweet rose-tinged smell of her—it was these thoughts that plagued him at night, impelling him to leave his bed and seek whatever surcease he could find in books or bottles of liquor.

The turmoil of feelings coursing through him was exacerbated by the faint but persistent sense of guilt that had been gnawing at him since he had told Leona to leave the wedding reception. He had had to do it, of course; he could not have allowed her to ruin Miranda's wedding day. The thing that bothered him was that he had wanted to send her away. He had been angry with her, which was not uncommon; there had been many times when she had irritated him beyond belief, and he had even raged at her. But always before in his anger there had been a thread of lust winding through it, a desire for Leona that thrummed in him. Indeed, the anger had usually been brought about by a desire that she had frustrated in some way, or by the jealousy he felt when he saw her with her husband or witnessed her flirting with another man. Whatever emotion he felt around her, passion was always part of it.

But the other night, he had not wanted her. Even when she had acted seductively toward him, he had been left cold. His anger had been hard and cold, and he had felt not desire for Leona but only a need to protect Miranda from the insult Leona represented. For the first time he could remember, he had put another woman before Leona, and even though Miranda was his wife, he felt guilty about his decision. *It did not mean that he did not love Leona, of course.* He had loved her for years; he could not imagine not loving her.

What he felt for Miranda was a momentary obsession, one that would go away if he slept with her. He had felt such things before for other women, and that had always been the case. He saw a woman; she intrigued him; he pursued and won her. And then it was over. It had never changed how he felt for Leona or even altered the desire that always lay in him for her.

The difference, the odd thing about his obsession with Miranda, was not only that it was deeper and more intense than what he usually felt, but also that it seemed to somehow mask his feelings for Leona. He knew Leona expected him to visit her at Vesey Park, and he had had ample time to do so. No one would question him about where he went of an afternoon, least of all Miranda, who seemed aggravatingly unconcerned about what he did. Yet he did not go. He thought about it from time to time, but his overwhelming feeling when he did so was one of reluctance.

That fact bothered him—and it bothered him, too, that even though he still desired Miranda, he had held off from pursuing her because she had said she did not want him to. He was not the sort to force himself upon a woman, but he had certainly never stopped trying to seduce a female just because she seemed reluctant. But there had been something in Miranda's eyes the other night when she had looked up at him and said that when she cared, she cared deeply. He had glimpsed in her then the possibility of love and betrayal, and he had known that if he seduced her into loving him, he could hurt her deeply. And since then, even though the passion still burned in him, he had made it a point not to try to arouse the same passion in her.

He had not considered that idea with any other woman that he could remember. But when he thought of winning Miranda over and taking his pleasure in her, there was always the thought immediately after of what would happen when he tired of her and returned to Leona, as he knew he would. So he wound up, he thought, like a fool, wanting her and not having her, yet unable to completely give her up, either. There were times when he wondered if marriage had made his brain soft; he certainly was not acting like himself these days.

He told himself that the primary reason for this silly obsession with Miranda was boredom. There was almost nothing to do here at Darkwater except sit around and think. It was no wonder his thoughts turned so often to the lust Miranda incited in him, and the more he thought about her, the more serious the lust became. When he tried to take his mind off it by doing something, the something he wound up doing usually involved her, which did little to appease the desire coursing through him.

About a week after the wedding, his mother invited the vicar, his wife and the local doctor over for supper. In London his mother would have found such company as a doctor and a vicar poor pickings indeed, but in the country she had to make do. Devin was in a foul mood to begin with, and watching Miranda spend most of the evening in rapt conversation with Dr. Browning did little to make him happier.

Dr. Browning was the son of the doctor who had worked in the village when Devin was young. The old Dr. Browning had given his practice over to his son a few years ago and now spent most of his time tending his rose garden. The present Dr. Browning was about thirty years old and handsome in a sober way. He dressed without much regard to style; Devin knew his own valet would have blanched at the way the doctor's cravat was tied. He was a large man, and Devin assumed that some women found his blond-haired, blue-eyed, strong-jawed looks attractive. Certainly Miranda seemed to find nothing about him to displease her.

Dr. Browning was seated beside her at the dinner table, and they had begun to converse there. By the time dinner was over, they were so engrossed in their conversation that they continued it in the drawing room, where everyone retired after the meal.

Devin wondered what they could possibly be talking about that could interest Miranda so. It occurred to him that perhaps this doctor was exactly the sort of man Miranda would find attractive, a man who had dedicated his life to something, who was intelligent and well-read, who did something useful with this life. Dr. Browning obviously thought things, knew things, that she found fascinating. And his looks were above average. Nor would the fact that he was only a doctor, whereas she was now a countess, deter Miranda if she liked him. Like so many Americans, she really did not seem to understand class distinctions.

The doctor, in fact, might be exactly the sort of man Miranda would choose for one of those affairs that she seemed so set on having. Devin wondered if she was even now thinking the same thing. It seemed to him very wrong that a doctor should be either that young or that handsome. *Doctors should, by the very nature of things, be old men—well, at least middle-aged.*

He glared balefully at them through much of the evening, then rose abruptly and left the room.

Miranda saw Devin leave the room, and she wondered why he had departed so suddenly without offering even a goodbye. She was growing weary of talking to Dr. Browning—or, rather, listening, as he was a long-winded sort—and she had hoped that Devin might liven things up by suggesting a card game or something else a little more exciting than Dr. Browning's description of his village practice. She had made the mistake of making polite conversation with him at dinner, asking about his career, and he had latched on to the topic, telling her all about growing up admiring his father, then his schooling, and now the many diseases and conditions he encountered in the village.

It was a great relief when the vicar's wife said that they must excuse themselves, as the vicar had a sermon to work on, and the doctor, fortunately, realized that he too, had been there long enough. Michael, who was leaving the next morning, decided that he should retire early, and nearly everyone else agreed that they should do the same—bored, Miranda assumed, into sleepiness.

She went up to her room and let her maid help her change into her nightgown. She started to lie down, but she knew that she could not possibly go to sleep this early. So she put on her dressing gown and slippers and, picking up an oil lamp, made her way downstairs to the library. As she walked toward the library, she noticed that the door to Devin's study stood open, light slanting out onto the hallway carpet. Curious, she turned toward it instead of the library.

Devin was seated at his desk, a bottle of whiskey and a glass in front of him. He had discarded his coat and cravat, and his shirt was unbuttoned at the neck, the sleeves rolled up. He was idly tossing dice, first with one hand, then with the other. He took a healthy gulp from his glass while Miranda watched. Then he transferred the dice to the other hand and rolled.

"Damn," he muttered softly, glaring at his left hand. "You are a dead loss. A hundred and fifty yellow-boys behind already."

"Talking to yourself?" Miranda asked lightly, stepping into the room.

Devin glanced up, startled. "Miranda! What are you doing here?"

The sight of her standing there pierced him with a fresh, fierce lust. She wore a dressing gown, with the neck of her nightgown peeking above the lapels, white and softly feminine. Her hair was brushed out and lay tumbling down across her shoulders, long and silky, inviting his touch. He wanted her with a passion as hot as any he could remember.

"I just came down to the library to get a book," Miranda replied. "I saw your light was on, so I thought I would see what you were doing."

"Tossing one hand against the other. The left hand has abysmal luck." The way his eyes ran down her made Miranda suddenly aware of the fact that she wore only a dressing gown over her nightrail, a flimsy thing that the modiste in London had made for her honeymoon. "You are up late."

"Not so late. Everyone retired early, after the vicar and his wife left. The doctor, too, of course."

"I am sure you were reluctant to see the doctor go," Devin said sarcastically, downing the last of his drink and immediately reaching out to pour another one.

Miranda watched him pour. His hand was a trifle unsteady.

"Have you been sitting here drinking all this time?" she asked.

Devin shrugged. "More or less."

"Why? Why did you leave the party?"

"The party? Is that what you would call it? Seemed about as lively as an interment to me. Of course, I was not privy to the good doctor's fascinating conversation.''

Miranda stared at him in surprise. "I beg your pardon?''

"The doctor. I didn't have the pleasure of talking to him all evening as you did.''

"It was scarcely a pleasure,'' Miranda began, ready to vent her true feelings, but Devin's next words stopped her.

"It certainly seemed as if it was a pleasure.'' He looked at her, a fierce bright anger burning clearly in his eyes. "You were hanging on every word he said.''

Miranda's brows vaulted upward, but she said nothing to contradict him. Devin sounded jealous, and she found the idea not at all displeasing.

"He was telling me about his cases,'' she said, carefully telling the truth.

"Was that it? I thought perhaps you were making an assignation.''

"What? Now, really, Dev, that is going too far.''

"Oh, I don't think I have gone nearly far enough,'' Devin said in a silky voice that was somehow frightening. He rose slowly and leaned forward across his desk, bracing himself with his fists. "Tell me, is he to be your first fling? I must say, I would think the local doctor a trifle too close to home. Wouldn't you?''

"I hadn't really thought about it,'' Miranda returned truthfully.

"Is he what you like, Miranda?'' he went on in the same quiet, deadly voice. He pushed his chair back and came out from behind his desk. "A sober, industrious citizen? Someone who can fascinate you with tales of his good deeds?''

"He does spend his days in more fruitful pursuits than drinking and casting dice,'' Miranda retorted with some asperity. His closeness made her a little breathless, but she wasn't about to let him know that.

Devin chuckled without humor, "Ah, my dear wife. So you *have* chosen him for your first foray outside the marriage. Well, good luck with him. I'll lay you odds that he is as dull a stick in bed as he is out of it.''

"Indeed? Well, I suppose I shall find out, won't I?''

His hand lashed out and grasped her arm, digging in painfully. "No, you won't, my lady!''

"I beg your pardon? Are you telling me who I can and cannot see?''

"I am telling you that you will not bed down with that lump of a fellow right in front of me.'' His eyes flashed, bright green in their fury. "I will not be made a mockery of, madam. You may think you call the tune because of your fat purse, but I can tell you, you will *not* do this.''

Miranda could not help but thrill to the hot emotion in his eyes, even though she might bridle at his commanding tone. She had no intention, of course, of doing anything with Dr. Browning except fleeing to escape his conversation the next time she saw him, but she did not intend to let Devin know that.

"You are ordering me?''

"I am ordering you,'' Devin replied, reaching out and placing his hand across her throat. Her flesh was soft and silken beneath his palm, and the intensity of his lust shook him. "I will not let him touch you. Do you understand?"

Miranda's breath was ragged, her thoughts scattered. All her awareness was centered in that span of flesh where his hand lay, burning her with his intensity. "I understand that you are breaking our agreement."

"To hell with our agreement! Did you actually think I would allow you to sleep with other men? Did you think I was that low? That weak?"

"What am I supposed to do, then?" Miranda asked calmly.

"This," he answered, as his hand stole beneath the neck of her gown, and his mouth came down on hers.

14

His mouth was hot and hungry on hers, and his hand burned her skin as it grazed the top of her breast. The neckline of the gown impeded his progress. He curled his fingers around it and jerked down, and the flimsy material gave beneath him with a rending sound. He cupped her breast, exposed by the tear, and a soft groan escaped his lips. He changed the slant of his mouth on hers, burying his lips deeper into hers, his tongue taking her mouth. With a gentleness at odds with the fierce way his lips consumed her, he caressed her breast with his fingers, kneading and stroking, finding the bud of her nipple and teasing it with his fingertips until it hardened.

"Miranda…" He breathed her name as his lips left hers and began to trail across her cheek to her earlobe. "Let me…please, I can show you how good it could be." He took the lobe between his teeth and worried it, sending darts of heat shooting through her.

His mouth moved downward, and everywhere he touched her skin it was like fire. Miranda trembled, sagging against the support of his arm, hard as iron around her back. "Dev..."

Hearing his nickname in her mouth sent a tremor of desire through him. There was an intimacy there, a liking, that he had never believed Miranda felt for him. He untied the sash of her dressing gown and opened it, sliding his hands in underneath it, pulling her up into him. She was soft against him, her nipples hard points of desire. He ran his hands over her back and hips, digging this fingertips into her buttocks and pressing her up against his engorged staff.

Fire licked along their veins, radiating heat through them. Miranda moved her hips against him, aware only of a deep, primitive need to do so. His breath came out in a shudder, and he nipped gently at the juncture of her neck and shoulders, teasing with the sharpness, then laving it with his tongue.

He wrapped his arms around her, lifting her up and turning to carry her back to his desk. Instinctively, Miranda clamped her legs around him. He set her down on the desk, sweeping off the other contents onto the floor and bearing her back down on it. His body was deliciously hard and heavy on hers, the imprint of his passion burning into her abdomen. He curved his hands around her breasts, his thumbs caressing her nipples. He looked down at her face for a moment, taking in the way her eyes darkened with passion and her face turned soft and sweet as his hands caressed her.

Dev bent and kissed the nipple of one breast, then curled his tongue around it in a lazy, teasing circle. She arched up against him, moaning, and it shook his control almost to the breaking point. He paused for a moment, fighting back the rush of lust.

Looking straight into her eyes, he said, "Isn't this what you want? Isn't this enough for you?"

At this moment, it was, Miranda knew, but she managed to pull the scraps of her self-control together enough to answer, "Is it enough for you?"

He stiffened, his eyes still boring holes in her. "What?"

"Are you saying you want to be my husband in reality?"

"Yes."

"Both of us entirely faithful to each other?"

He almost said yes, but he thought of Leona, and his face changed subtly. Miranda let out her breath in a sigh.

"Ah. I see. *I* would be faithful. *You* would not."

She sat up, and he stepped back, not stopping her, although he ached to shove her back to the desk and take her right there. Miranda pulled the sides of her dressing gown around her and belted the sash tightly.

"I think we shall stay with our present arrangement," she said and walked from the room, taking care not to give in and run.

The following morning Uncle Rupert came down to breakfast earlier than normal for him and announced that it was time he gave Miranda the tour he had promised.

"You have been here over a week, and you've scarcely seen anything of the estate, just the village and a few farms around the house. I thought we would ride along the river," he said. "Beautiful spot, don't you think, Dev? After our stultifying evening yesterday, we deserve a treat."

"That sounds splendid," Miranda said. She would rather have stayed and worked on some of the multitude of tasks she had to do, but she felt that she ought to make a special effort with Devin's uncle, whose feelings, she suspected, had been a little hurt by his being removed from management of the estate.

"What do you say, Joseph?" he went on, turning to Mr. Upshaw. "And you, Dev? And, of course, anyone else who would care to come..."

Michael and Elizabeth, who were also there, shook their heads, but Joseph was eager to go, and Devin was almost as quick to agree.

"I'll tell Cook to fix us up a light luncheon basket," Rupert went on. "We can rest at Chasenford. It's pretty there."

They arranged to meet at a little before eleven, at which time they set out from the stable yard for the river with the quaint name of Dove. Much of what Miranda had seen of the area consisted of magnificent vistas of moors or rolling hills, grand and green and almost barren of trees. She was unprepared for the sight of the river when they wound their way down to it, meandering in a shallow, lazy fashion at the base of high white limestone cliffs. The cliffs rose up in a sheer expanse, scarred here and there with holes that Dev explained were the entrances to caves that wandered through the porous rock. The narrow river was lined with grassy banks, dotted with large chunks of limestone rock. Slender, graceful ash and alder trees grew along its edge, casting shadows across the dark-green water. It was a lovely, peaceful place, undisturbed except for their presence.

The banks were narrow, and they broke up into pairs to ride alongside it. Dev moved forward to chat with his uncle, and Joseph rode beside Miranda, enthusiastically pointing out all the beauties they saw. They gradually fell somewhat behind the other two.

Miranda was watching Devin, not really paying much attention to what her father was saying. Joseph turned to look up at the limestone cliff towering above them, and suddenly his expression turned to one of horror.

"Watch out!" he screamed, spurring his horse forward and reaching out to slap the flank of Miranda's horse.

Miranda turned in surprise even as the horse leapt forward. An instant later, so close she felt the breeze of it falling, a large chunk of limestone crashed onto the ground behind her. The noise sent her mount into a panic, and the mare took off running, unseating Miranda and sending her falling flat on her back, knocking the wind out of her.

She lay on the ground, staring up at the sky, struggling to breathe, trying to assimilate what had just happened. There were shouts from in front of them, then the sound of horses running. A moment later Devin was looming above her.

He dropped down onto his knees beside her, his face creased with fear. "Miranda! My God, what happened? Are you all right?" He swept her up into his arms, holding her against his chest. She could feel the trembling of his body.

Finally, blessedly, her lungs relaxed and air came rushing back in. She nodded a little uncertainly, whispering, "I think so."

"That rock almost killed you. If you had been a second slower... "

"Papa...?"

"He's fine. Just getting his horse under control. Uncle Rupert's gone after your mare." He rubbed his hand up and down her back. "Bloody hell! You could have been killed."

"Miranda!" She turned her head to see her father trotting along the bank toward them, leading his horse. "Are you all right? Sweet Jesus in heaven, when I looked up and saw that rock tumbling off..." He, too, went down on his knees, not quite so agilely, beside her.

"You saved my life."

Devin's arms tightened around her, and she felt his lips press against her hair. Miranda was shaking from the experience, and she clung to Devin.

Uncle Rupert rode up, leading Miranda's mare, and dismounted quickly, coming over to join the group. "Is she all right?" His gaze went from her to the large rock now sitting on the flat bank behind them, split in two from the force of its fall.

"Good Lord! Is that what almost hit you? It's a wonder you weren't killed! That's the thing with limestone—it breaks off and falls. But usually it's after a lot of rain. I never would have thought—I beg your pardon. I am deeply sorry. I never should have brought you this way."

"There is no way you could have known," Joseph said, rising creakily. "Thank God Elizabeth wasn't with us. She would be hysterical by now."

"I think I am close to it," Miranda said, trying a smile.

Devin made a rude noise. "You wouldn't know hysteria if you met it. My heart's about to pound right out of my chest, and you're cool as a cucumber."

"Well, I'm alive. Let's see if I can stand up."

Devin rose, setting her on her feet, his arm still around her to steady her. It felt sweet to be there, Miranda thought, and she stayed a bit longer than was absolutely necessary before she stepped away and shook out her riding habit.

"We'll turn right around and go back to the house," Uncle Rupert said, starting to mount.

"Not on my account," Miranda protested. "I'm fine, really. The worst that happened to me is that I was thrown, and that's happened before. There are no broken bones. I lost my breath for a moment, but that's back. There is no reason to cut short our expedition for a little accident."

"A little accident!" Uncle Rupert exclaimed, staring at her goggle-eyed.

"I told you, Uncle, she is not like other women," Devin said, laughter in his voice. "You know, Miranda, there is no need for you to go on. It isn't important."

"No reason to go back, either," Miranda pointed

out. "We have our lunch—unless the groom's horse stampeded, too."

"No, he's here," Rupert said faintly. "The food, as well."

"Well, I'd like to finish the tour. I think it is highly unlikely that another rock will drop on us, isn't it?"

"Well, yes, I suppose so."

"Good." Miranda dusted off her skirt. "Then let's go on."

So they continued to the bend in the river, a green, idyllic setting, and sat down to their lunch. Uncle Rupert and her father launched into a discussion of the properties of limestone, one of which apparently was its breakability. Miranda barely listened, content to sit and nibble at her food and let her nerves settle. It helped that Devin was beside her.

"And to think I found London dangerous..." she said lightly.

Devin turned and looked at her, his eyes narrowed. "What do you mean?"

"Well, two accidents since I moved here. I can't remember when I have ever been so accident prone."

"I see." He nodded, studying her face. "Why do you think that is?"

Miranda shrugged. "I'm not sure. The first time, I have to admit, I was careless. I leaned on a wooden railing even though I knew that much of the wood in the house had been eaten away by woodworm. That was a silly, impulsive mistake. But today—I truly cannot imagine how I could have avoided a falling rock. Should I have been paying more attention?"

"Thank God your father saw it in time. I don't

know how you could have avoided it, except to keep a careful watch. Limestone slides off the face of the cliffs and falls periodically. It is always good policy not to stand too close to the edge of them, I think.''

''I don't believe in signs or portents or living under a bad star or whatever you want to call it...but it does seem odd.''

''Well, safest to be extra careful,'' he said, with an easy smile. ''Just in case there is some sort of malevolent cloud hanging over us. Make sure you watch before you step. Darkwater is old and crumbling in many ways, and before it is restored, there are probably ample opportunities for accidents. You need to be careful. And if you go riding with Veronica or by yourself, make sure I am with you, or your father or Uncle Rupert. Or a groom, if there's no one else.''

She looked at him oddly. ''You sound very serious.''

''I am serious. You could have been killed today. Promise me that you will take extra care.''

Warmth stole through Miranda at the thought that he was concerned about her. ''All right,'' she agreed, smiling. ''I promise I will watch out.''

By the time Miranda went to bed that night, her nerves had been restored. She had been a little afraid that she would have trouble falling asleep or would suffer bad dreams as a result of the accident, but in fact she fell asleep rather quickly and slept quite peacefully until the middle of the night.

Then she came awake suddenly in the dark, her eyes flying open, her heart racing. She did not know what had awakened her, and she lay for a moment, listening, looking around. Then the shout came, and she knew that something like that that must have awakened her.

It came from beyond the connecting door into Dev's room, a man's hoarse shout. "No!"

Miranda hopped out of bed, impelled by the note of urgency and horror in the voice. She ran across the room, not even pausing to put on dressing gown or slippers, and opened the connecting door.

Dev's room was dark, but there was enough moonlight coming in around the curtains for her to make out his form in the large bed. Devin was moving restlessly, his sheets tangled about him. Miranda hurried to his side. He was asleep, but obviously in the grip of a nightmare. He groaned, his face contorted and sweating, and his hand shot out suddenly, making her jump.

She took his hand in both her own, saying, "Devin. Devin, wake up!"

His eyes flew open, and for an instant he stared at her sightlessly, his chest rising and falling in labored breaths.

"Devin, it's me, Miranda. Wake up. You're having a nightmare."

His eyes changed, became focused. He looked at her, and a long shudder ran through his body. "Miranda? What are you...?"

He sat up dazedly, leaning back against the massive headboard. Miranda sat down on the bed beside him, keeping his hand in hers. "You were having a nightmare. It woke me."

"Oh." He rubbed his hand over his face. "I see. I'm sorry."

"No need to apologize." She smiled. "All of us have nightmares from time to time. Are you all right?"

He nodded. "Yes. I—I'm just a little disoriented."

"What were you dreaming about?"

Devin shrugged. "I have it periodically. It's—" He ran his hand back through his hair and sighed. "I was dreaming about a girl I killed."

Miranda stared, stunned. "I beg your pardon?"

"Well, not literally. I did not take a knife and stab her through the heart, but I might as well have. She killed herself because of me."

"Oh my." She remembered the old man who had ranted at her in her house in London and the sad tale he had told. Obviously he was not the only one who was haunted by the incident. "What happened?"

"I seduced her," Devin said, his voice filled with self-loathing. "I was in Brighton—avoiding my creditors, I believe. And I met Constance. I thought she was an experienced woman. She was a friend of Leona's, older than most of the other girls. I assumed—well, I never realized she was a maiden. She was pretty, and I wanted her. Leona was keeping me dancing on a string at the time—teasing and baiting and not giving in."

He paused and looked at her a little guiltily. "I apologize. Hardly the sort of thing I should be saying to you."

"Why not? I am your wife."

"Not fit conversation for a lady."

"Ah, but you forget that I am not really a lady. Please, go on. I want to hear about it."

He nodded and started again, his gaze shifting away from her. "I was frustrated, and she was there and attractive. And I wanted her. I gave up on Leona. I thought that I would never have her. Oh, hell, my motives were even lower—I hoped, deep down, that if I chose another it would make Leona notice me, make her realize that she was missing her chance. So I paid court to Constance. I charmed her. I thought—I thought she understood the game, that she had done it before. Until she lay with me. Then, of course, I realized what a mistake I had made. I should have stopped then, but I did not." His mouth twisted grimly. "It was far easier to take my pleasure. Then Leona came to me. My scheme had worked, I suppose. She wanted me, and I stopped seeing Constance. Another evidence of my weakness. An honorable man would have asked her to marry him, having taken the virginity of a virtuous girl. But I did not. All I could think or see or feel was Leona."

Miranda's heart twisted at the recital of his passion for Leona, but she pushed the feeling aside. Devin's pain was more important right now.

"Then one morning Leona brought me a letter. She had been to call on Constance and found her gone. She had left me a letter." He paused, drawing a shaky breath, and his eyes came up to meet Miranda's, laced with agony. "She said that she was carrying my child, that she could not bear to live with the shame. She wrote that she was going to throw herself into the ocean and spare both herself and the baby the shame of its being born out of wedlock.''

"Oh, no!'' Miranda's hand tightened around his. "How awful.''

He nodded, his face drawn. "I went running over there like a fool, but of course she was gone, just as Leona had said. They searched for her, but they could never find the body, only the spot on the rocks where she had discarded her shawl and shoes. Her grandfather was devastated. He nearly went mad with grief. He blamed me, of course. Everyone did. Leona was the only one who stood by me. I don't know what I would have done without her. That was the scandal over which my father finally broke with me. He had forgiven many sins of mine before, he said, but he could not forgive that—that I had seduced an innocent girl and driven her to her death.''

"How could he have blamed you alone?'' Miranda asked, bringing his hand up to her chest and cradling it against her. "You were not the only person involved. Constance was responsible for what happened, as well.''

"Why did she not come to me?'' The words were torn out of him, soaked with the pain of years. "I would not have turned her away. I did not love her, but I would have done my duty if I had known she was pregnant. I would have married her. I swear I would have.''

"Of course you would have,'' Miranda agreed staunchly. "Your father could not have known you very well, or he would have known that.''

"He was only one of many who believed it,'' Devin

said flatly. "The things I had done, the manner of man I was...everyone found it easy to believe I would have played the cad. Obviously Constance never thought for a moment that I would have done the honorable thing." The corner of his mouth quirked up in an attempt at a smile. "Now you know what sort of man you married."

"I already knew what sort of man I married," Miranda replied. "This does not change my opinion. You have made mistakes—who among us has not? But you are not wicked."

"I don't know how you can even bear to look at me. Sometimes I cannot bear to look at myself."

Impulsively Miranda leaned forward and took Devin in her arms, resting her head against his and holding him close. "There is no need to keep grinding yourself into the ground about this. What you did was wrong, no doubt, but you were not alone in it. You did not force her. Constance was a grown woman, older than most of the girls, you said. She knew what she was doing and what could happen. She also could have told you. She did not even give you the chance to make it right. She should have come to you. She owed that to her child, if nothing else. There was her grandfather, too. She could have gone to him for help. Instead she chose to kill herself and her child. That is not the action of a fully sane woman. You cannot blame yourself because she was unbalanced. You do not deserve the entire burden of guilt."

Devin wrapped his arms around her tightly, burying his face in her hair. "You are an unusual woman, Miranda. Few would be so forgiving."

"What do I have to forgive you for?" Miranda pointed out reasonably. "It did not concern me. It is between you and God, and I think that you have punished yourself for it more than enough over the years."

They sat like that for a long time, holding each other, and Miranda could feel his taut body relax as the pain drained out of him. Gradually she realized the intimacy of their position, pressed tightly against each other, sitting in his bed. She wore only a nightgown, a flimsy barrier between his bare chest and her own skin. The warmth between them began to change and become more heated, and suddenly what had been only comfort and sympathy was now charged with sexuality.

Miranda released Devin and scooted back awkwardly. She looked at him and saw reflected in his face the same awareness of their position. Her cheeks flamed. She had scarcely noticed before how little Devin wore. Above the sheet his chest was bare. Miranda was unaccustomed to seeing a man's naked chest, and her eyes could not help running over his tanned skin, padded with muscle. She had to curl her fingers into her palm to resist the urge to reach out and touch the bony outcropping of his shoulders and collarbone, the rounded muscle of his upper arms.

She cleared her throat. "Well, ah...I should get back to bed now."

"Miranda..." He reached for her, laying his hand on her arm. He rubbed his thumb over her skin, searching for words. With a sigh, he released her and shook his head. "Never mind. Thank you. It was good of you to come help me."

"You're welcome. Good night."

Miranda slipped off the bed and walked across the room and through the connecting door to her room. But when she closed the door behind her, she did not lock it.

15

Miranda and Devin were in the library the next day, Miranda poring over old maps of the estate and Devin contemplating the way her dress fell over her hips as she stretched across the table, when one of the footmen entered.

"My lady, a package has arrived for you. A rather large one, from London. You had said to notify you—"

"Yes, of course." Miranda straightened up, her eyes bright and a wide smile curving her mouth. "Bring it in."

She turned to Devin excitedly. They were alone in the room for once, her father and the landscaper being outside walking through the overrun garden, the architect upstairs making notes to himself, and Hiram going over the books with Strong in Strong's office. Devin could not help but smile faintly at the happiness on Miranda's face; it was infectious. But he could not imagine what sort of package could have got her so excited.

"What is it? Dresses from London?"

"No. Better than that. At least, I hope it is. I hope you will like it. It is a wedding present."

"A wedding present? But you already gave me that." His hand went automatically to the ruby-and-gold pin in his ascot, part of a matching set with cuff links that she had given him on their wedding day.

"Yes, but that was different. That was a formal present. A— I don't know, something you expected. This is my own personal present."

Intrigued, he stood up as the footman came in, almost hidden by the large box he carried. With care, the servant set it down on the floor and bowed out of the room, closing the door behind him. Devin glanced at Miranda.

"Go ahead," she said, "Open it. If you don't like it, I promise I shan't cry. It is just a gift of...of possibility."

"Indeed." He cut the string that tied the package and opened the box. He went still, looking at the objects inside. He turned to Miranda, an odd, questioning look on his face, then reached into the box and pulled out an easel. Digging farther down, he brought up a wooden box containing tubes of pigment and glass bottles for the paints after they were mixed, then a palette, a box of brushes, pads of paper, a box of charcoal pencils, bottles of turpentine and linseed oil, until finally the library table was almost covered with the art supplies.

Devin stood looking down at the things on the table. He ran his fingers down a tube, touched the silken hairs of a brush. Miranda waited, watching him, wondering what he was thinking.

"You don't have to use them if you don't want," she said finally. "I just thought...you might miss it. While you were here, you might want to paint. To pass the time, at least."

He turned then and looked at her, shaking his head in puzzlement. "How did you know? I mean—I gave it up long ago."

"I saw your work at your sister's house," Miranda explained. "She told me that you were an artist."

He grimaced dismissively. "I dabbled."

"No. You are very talented. I saw the paintings. Your use of light, the colors..." Her voice picked up a little in excitement. "I couldn't believe it when I saw them. I realized then that you weren't just what one saw."

"A wastrel, you mean?"

"Well, frankly, yes."

Devin grinned faintly. "One can always count on you for honesty."

He looked back at the things on the table. "I can't believe...I don't know that I can do it anymore. It has been years. I lost interest."

"You might be rusty, but I don't believe your talent died. It is still there." She paused, then went on. "Rachel showed me the room in the west wing, the one where you used to paint. I've had it cleaned. You could use it again."

"It has good light in the afternoon," he agreed absently. Even when he had tried to sketch Miranda, he had not actually contemplated painting her portrait. He had assumed that he would never paint again. But now, suddenly, the idea tempted him. He remembered the smell of the oils, the feel of the brush in his fingers, the way light poured in through the windows of the room. He thought once more of the sketches he had done in private of Miranda.

"Why did you buy these?" he asked. "I mean, why do you care?"

"I hate to see talent wasted, and I think you have a tremendous talent. And I thought you might...find something you had lost."

They stood looking at one another for a long moment. Finally he said, "If I decided to paint, would you pose for me?"

Miranda's eyes widened a little in surprise. But she said only, "Yes. I would."

"Then perhaps I will."

Devin did not think he would begin to paint again. He had outgrown it years ago, as his father had always hoped he would. The supplies were a nice gesture and one that touched him, but he was not sure that he wanted to try them out.

However, later that afternoon, he found his steps turning toward the room Miranda had mentioned, the large, airy, sun-filled room that had been his studio when he lived at home. It had been cleaned, as Miranda had said, and all the supplies had been carried up and arranged on an old paint-bedaubed table there. The furniture in the room was minimal—besides the table, only a chair, a stool and a fainting couch.

He went to the box and opened it again, taking out the tubes of pigment one by one and laying them on the table, adding the small glass bottles. If he was going to paint, he would mix the pigments with linseed oil and put them in the bottles. He thought of mixing the oils together on his palette then, what colors he would combine, what mixture he would use to get the exact shade of Miranda's hair. What combination of white and black it would take to reach the gray of her eyes—and how to add the touch of silver to them.

Almost without thinking, he unscrewed the top from one of the tubes and squeezed out pigment into a bottle....

It was four hours later that one of the servants finally found him, standing in the studio, lamps lit around him, his coat off and his white shirt stained and smeared with paints.

"Uh, my lord...Lady Ravenscar sent me to find you," the footman said tentatively, never having seen the elegant Earl in such a state before. He had seen him tipsy, of course, buttons done up wrong or not at all, cravat rumpled and all askew. But as he had only been here five years now, he had never seen him with a smear of brown across the back of his hand and another of gray on his cheek—nor with that odd, distant look in his eyes, so that he stared at a man without really seeing him.

"What?" The earl frowned. "Miranda?"

"No, my lord. The dowager Lady Ravenscar."

"Oh. Why?"

"It is past time for supper, sir. The others are ready to sit down."

"Oh. Tell them to go ahead. Bring my supper up to me on a tray. I'm busy. And bring me more lamps. The light's damn poor in here."

The footman saw little sense in pointing out that it was nighttime and there was little likelihood of good light. He had long ago decided that the aristocracy were all mad, and this latest glimpse of the Earl of Ravenscar only confirmed that opinion.

When the footman relayed the news to the elder Lady Ravenscar, she frosted up. "We shan't wait on him. At least—" she turned to Miranda, acknowledging that she was now the lady of the house "—that is what I would advise, Miranda."

"Yes, I imagine you are right." But Miranda, unlike her mother-in-law, smiled when she said it, and the look she exchanged with Rachel was one of triumphant delight.

Devin painted through much of the night, finally going off to bed exhausted and disgusted by the rustiness of his skills. He would never recapture the ability he once had, he thought, though he knew he would try again.

The next morning, when he woke up, he was feeling less despairing and, given a fresh look at what he had done in the light of day, he thought that, while it was not worth keeping, it was not, at least, quite as horrible as it had seemed the night before.

He went down to the library, where he found Miranda in a discussion of numbers with Hiram Baldwin. He was growing more and more exasperated with his inability to get her face just right, and he reminded her that she had promised to pose. Miranda rose, smiling, and went with him without a murmur of dissent, leaving Hiram to sigh and return alone to the problem that had been vexing him.

Over the course of the next few weeks Devin was locked in his studio much of each day. Miranda sat for him two hours a day, one in the morning and one in the afternoon, all that she could stand of sitting still, she told him. The rest of the time he experimented with sketches and colors and still lifes or landscapes— whatever took his fancy. He was seized with a hunger, not quite the obsessive, unrelenting fevers that had often gripped him when he was younger, but still a need to create that made all other things recede.

How had Miranda known that this need still lived inside him? He had not even known it himself.

Had he thought about it, he would have been a trifle surprised to realize how little he missed the activity of London and the pursuits he had indulged in for years. Consumed in the excitement of painting, the need to do it, he rarely even thought of gambling or going out carousing for an evening. Even his drinking diminished as his boredom did, and he was surprised to discover the pleasantness of waking up of a morning without a heavy head and befogged mind. When he did want entertainment or fun, his thoughts turned naturally to Miranda. A few months ago he would have laughed at the thought that an evening playing cards with his wife and her sister, or even just sitting talking to her, would have more appeal than a night of frolic and liquor, but that was the truth of the matter now.

One thing he discovered, however, was that the sudden hunger in him to paint did not diminish the ever-burgeoning hunger in him for Miranda. He would not have thought he could be doubly obsessed in this way, but it seemed, strangely, as if the two desires fed on one another. He painted Miranda's face and form on canvas, trying to satisfy the need inside him, trying to wear out the fascination of her face, but in doing so, he wound up looking at her—the image and the reality—most of his waking day. At night, tired though he might be, he could not stop thinking about her. She was right next door, soft and warm, waiting for him.

Ever since that night in the library, he had known that she would allow him into her bed. She had made no pretence of disinterest, no calm statement that it was wiser to go their separate ways. All she had asked was his fidelity. If he gave her that, he knew she would be his.

It would be easy to say the words, he knew. It wasn't as if he had not lied a thousand times, as if he had not told countless women that he loved them, when in fact he barely cared about them. But somehow, with Miranda, he could not lie. He could not look into those clear, penetrating gray eyes and tell her something that he knew was not the truth. At the moment all he wanted was her. But he did not know if that would continue. Once he had slept with her, he might grow tired of her, as he had of every other woman he had ever known, except Leona.

And how could he tell her that he would be faithful to her, when Leona waited for him? Leona was, after all, the love of his life. He had known it at eighteen, and it had remained so for fourteen years. The strange disinterest he felt in Leona now was temporary, he was sure. It was something engendered by his irritation with her for wanting him to marry another and enlarged by his current dual obsessions with Miranda and his art. Guilt nibbled at him for the disinterest, no matter how much he told himself it was temporary. He could not honestly agree to giving her up in order to have Miranda. It would be an insult to Leona, even though she would never know it. And it would be an insult to Miranda, too, sleeping with her out of lust, knowing that he could not give her his heart.

Miranda deserved far better than that. Deserved far better than him, really. She had somehow returned to him his love for painting. She had comforted him, given him strength. With all her strange, irritating ways, she had wormed her way into his affections. He could not allow himself to be less than the man she thought he was.

Devin found it distinctly irritating that his noble intentions were not easier to carry out. It was, in fact, hellaciously hard to lie in bed each night, knowing Miranda was next door and that only his newly acquired sense of honor kept him from enjoying the pleasure of her body. It would seem only fair, he thought, that denying himself the pleasure would be somehow made more endurable by the knowledge that he was doing what was right.

Instead, each night he lay awake, remembering the taste of Miranda's lips, the soft give of her body in his arms, the shudder of response in her when he stroked her skin, and growing hotter and harder and more unable to sleep with each breath he took. He imagined undressing her, kissing her, caressing her—and he was cursed with a sensually vivid artist's imagination, so that each thought was almost unbearably real, except that there was no satisfaction.

During the day, as he looked at her, posing for her picture, the same thoughts intruded, winding through their innocuous conversation, tingeing his artwork with a undeniable atmosphere of sexuality. His breath came harder and faster; his skin warmed; his pulse quickened. He wanted her, but he knew he could not let himself have her, and the combination was slowly driving him mad.

The worst evening was at a party given by the local squire, a thin ascetic sort named Breakthorpe, whose wife was just the opposite of him, a jolly, plump, vocal woman. The party was small, containing once again the doctor and the vicar and his wife, as well as the Breakthorpe family and all those staying at Darkwater. However, after supper, when one of the Breakthorpe daughters began playing the piano, Mrs. Breakthorpe decided, after great wheedling by the Breakthorpe girls, to allow dancing while Catherine, the youngest and the quietest of the Breakthorpes, played the piano.

Devin had had no suspicion that the evening would be anything but dull. Instead he had spent the last hour of it dancing almost exclusively with his wife, and it had been the purest form of heaven and hell combined that he had ever experienced. He smelled the rose scent that she dabbed at her temples and between her breasts; he gazed down at the creamy, trembling tops of her breasts; he held her body in his arms, felt her skin against his. And desire pulsed dangerously in him.

Because of the size of their party, they had brought two carriages. Miranda's stepmother went home early, pleading a headache, with Joseph accompanying her, but this had left the rest of their party to crowd into the other carriage when they left the manor house. The result was that Miranda wound up sitting on her husband's lap, a satisfactory solution in everyone else's mind. Devin certainly would not deny that he enjoyed the ride, but by the end of it, after almost forty minutes of the rumbling vibration of the carriage, the constant fractional shifting of Miranda's buttocks against his body, the feel and smell of her so close to him, he was on fire and desperate for satisfaction.

He ached. His mind could fix on nothing except images of Miranda naked and writhing in his bed. His fingers itched to slide over her bare skin. He gazed out the window into the dark night, trapped in his own private pleasurable hell, the voices of the others swirling around him unintelligibly.

After they got home, he went straight to his study, where he downed two quick brandies. That seemed to help very little, so he made his way upstairs, passing Miranda's maid on her way down the stairs. That meant Miranda was undressed and in her nightgown, her hair taken down from its pins and falling free down her back.

Devin thought about the night she had come into his bedroom when he had had the nightmare; her hair had been unbound, tumbling down around her shoulders and onto her breasts and back, luxurious and thick. Just the memory made his loins tighten. He wondered if the maid had brushed out her hair, too, or if Miranda was even now sitting before her dressing table in her nightgown, brushing her hair out in long silken strands, burnished in the soft glow of the candlelight. He swallowed a low groan at the thought. *It was too much to bear.*

He went into his room, though his hand itched to knock at Miranda's door. He shrugged out of his coat, handing it over to his valet, then sent the man on his way, saying he would do the rest himself. He did not think he could stand another moment of anyone else's company. Ripping off his cravat in a way he knew would make his valet shudder, he tossed it over the back of a chair. He took off his cuff links and rolled up his sleeves, then unbuttoned his shirt, hoping to alleviate the stifling heat. It was not enough.

Devin walked to the window and opened the casement a little, letting the cooler night air waft in. It drifted over his face and chest, cooling his skin, although it could not ease the fire that burned within. He was not, he thought, up to being tried by fire. *He was a hedonist, for God's sake, not a man of the cloth!* He did not know how much more of this he could live with.

He stood for a long time, staring out into the night, then finally turned with a sigh and went to his empty bed.

Miranda awoke, heavy-eyed, and rang for her maid. Last night, she thought, had been the last straw. She wasn't sure how much more of this sort of marriage she could take. She had hoped to tease and goad and tempt Devin into wanting her so much that he would be eager to be a real husband to her. But somehow she had managed to get caught in her own trap.

Passion had been growing in her since their wedding day, throwing all her careful plans into a mess. Every day she wanted Devin more and more, yet he remained apart from her, not even trying to kiss her. She had even reached the sorry point where she had sometimes brushed up against him "accidentally" in the hope that it would stir him to action. But he had stayed maddeningly stoic.

Last night had been the worst...dancing with him all evening, riding home on his lap, feeling his hard muscle and bone against her side, his desire pulsing beneath her. She had been shaken to the core. As her maid had undressed her, all she had been able to think about was Devin's hand on her, his mouth pressing into hers. She had brushed out her hair, all the while listening for Devin's footsteps in the hall, hoping and praying that he would open the door between their rooms and come inside. She had not locked the connecting door in a long, long time.

But he had not entered her room. He never did, and it was driving her to distraction. She was beginning to think that she would have to be the one to give in. She thought about going to him and telling him that she no longer demanded his fidelity, that she was willing to share him with Leona and anyone else, as long as he would make love to her. Everything in her recoiled at the thought, of course. She was *not* willing to share him. However, if she was never to know the sweetness of making love with him otherwise, she was afraid that she might have to accept the arrangement, no matter how she felt about it.

This morning when she went into the breakfast room there was no one else there. She had slept later than usual after the difficult time she had had going to sleep last night. Most of the others had probably already breakfasted. She ate a quick, solitary breakfast, then poured herself a cup of coffee and strolled with it out to the terrace. She drank it, looking down at the gardens before her.

The landscaper had already made a good deal of progress in the backyard, trimming hedges and eradicating the weeds, hacking down and digging up bushes and plants that had grown wild. It was not a pretty sight yet, for it was too spare, and too often the bushes had been cut back to mere sticks. But the walks were being repaired and relaid according to the original plans, and soon they would start replanting wherever they could. Some of the plants and flowers would have to wait, of course, for fall or even the following spring to be planted.

With many of the larger hedges uprooted or trimmed, one could see much farther now, almost all the way down to the still-wild orchards of fruit trees. Eventually they would be pulled under control as well, of course, but restoring all the grounds to their original state was a task that would take years to accomplish.

As she stood there, a flash of movement at the bottom of the yard caught her eye. A woman had stepped out of the tangle of trees that was the orchard, and Miranda realized, surprised, that it was her stepmother. It was unlike Elizabeth to take strolls around the grounds, particularly one to the edge of the garden. Even stranger, a man came out of the trees behind her. Miranda stared, her first shocked thought that Elizabeth was having a clandestine rendezvous with a lover.

She quickly realized, however, that these were not lovers talking, but a person of higher rank talking to one of lower rank. The man nodded as Elizabeth told him something, looking down more often than directly at her. He was dressed in simple, serviceable clothes, the clothes of a working man. Miranda relaxed, scolding herself for even considering such a thought about her stepmother. Elizabeth was deeply in love with Joseph, as he was with her. Miranda was sure that the reason the idea had sprung into her head was simply because her brain was so occupied these days with thoughts of sex.

As Miranda watched, Elizabeth nodded to the man and began to walk back toward the terrace. The man stood for a moment longer, looking after Elizabeth, and Miranda saw his face clearly. It was an ordinary face, somehow familiar, but she could not place it. Then he turned and was gone, ducking back into the trees and disappearing from sight.

She sat down on the railing and finished her coffee. About the time she set the cup down, Elizabeth was close enough that she saw Miranda sitting there. She stopped and waved, then continued up the new gravel path to the terrace steps.

"Hello, my dear," she said, coming up and kissing Miranda on the cheek. "What are you doing out here?"

"Drinking a last cup of coffee and looking at all the changes in the garden."

"Yes, it is quite different," Elizabeth agreed, turning to look at it, too. "Rather barren now, I'm afraid."

"But it will look much better before too long. Mr. Kitchens assures me of that."

"I do hope so."

"Who was that man?"

"What?" Elizabeth turned to her. "What man?"

"The one you were talking to down by the orchards. He looked familiar."

"Oh. That is because he is one of the undergardeners. I am afraid I don't know his name. I was asking him about the fruit trees. I was not sure what kind they are. I was hoping there were cherries there, and I wondered when they would be ripe. I do so miss Hannah's cherry pie, don't you?"

"Yes, I do." Miranda smiled. "And what did he say?"

"Excuse me?"

"Are there cherries and when will they be ripe?" Miranda explained. She was beginning to worry about her stepmother.

Elizabeth had been acting odd ever since they had come to Darkwater. Elizabeth stayed in her room, pleading headaches and stomachaches and various other forms of ill health far more often than she had in the past. She had always been somewhat invalidish, but never this much. She was fond of eating and rarely missed a meal, but in the past few weeks she had eaten her supper on a tray in her room as often as at the dinner table. Miranda had more than once found her sitting in her room or somewhere else in a brown study, staring at the floor or off into space with a frown upon her face. This whole thing with the undergardener was odd, too. It was not like her to tramp through the garden and seek out one of the gardeners to ask about the cherries. True, she did love cherry pie, but she was not fond of exercise. It would have been simpler, and would have entailed far less walking, if she had sent one of the footmen to ask or had simply sent a note to Cook requesting a cherry pie.

"Oh," Elizabeth said. "Yes, there are cherries, and they are already ripe."

"Good. I shall tell Cook to make a cherry pie one night this week."

Elizabeth smiled. "You are a dear." Impulsively, she stepped forward and hugged Miranda tightly. "Have I ever told you how much I love you? You are like a daughter to me."

Miranda squeezed her tightly. "Yes, you have told me often, and I appreciate it. I love you dearly, too. However, you are far too young to have a daughter my age. I think you are more an older sister."

Elizabeth smiled. "All right. I shall be a very fond older sister."

They linked arms and strolled back inside. "I am going to the library. Would you like to join me?" Miranda asked.

The look of horror on Elizabeth's face was enough to make Miranda giggle. "Oh, no, I cannot. I, ah..."

"Never mind, you do not have to conjure up an excuse. I know you are not fond of reading. It is quite all right. I will see you at lunch."

"Miranda..." Elizabeth looked at her, her brow drawn into a frown. She seemed to be struggling to say something, but then she smiled and patted Miranda's arm. "Never mind. You go ahead."

She turned and walked away.

Miranda looked after her, puzzled, then shrugged and started toward the library.

Strong was waiting for her there, looking vaguely uncomfortable, as he usually did around her. In general she let Hiram handle most of the dealings with him, because he seemed unable to cope with a woman discussing business. He was not as tongue-tied around Hiram, which was fortunate, as many of his entries needed to be filled in verbally, being somewhat sketchy at best.

"Talking to him," Hiram said, "I think the man knows his job. It is just that he's not terribly good with the written word."

This fact seemed to Miranda to be something of a problem for the manager of a very large estate. She had asked Dev's uncle once what qualifications Mr. Strong had for the job, and he had looked at her blankly and said only, "His father was estate manager before him," as if this were answer enough. Since Devin had been with them at the time and had said nothing, only nodded in agreement, she supposed that to the British aristocracy this was apparently an adequate reason for someone to have a job. She suspected that once she started trying to turn the estate around, she would have to replace the man, although given Rupert and Dev's reaction, she would probably have to leave him as estate manager and invent a new title to give to someone to supervise Strong. In all fairness to Strong, she thought, perhaps the man sensed this opinion on her part and that accounted for his discomfort around her.

"Hello, Mr. Strong," she said, putting on as winning and reassuring a smile as she could. "I am afraid that Mr. Baldwin has a few affairs of my father's to attend to today, so I thought you might help me with a few questions."

"Yes, Lady Ravenscar."

"Good. Now, I was looking at a topographical map of the area the other day." She picked up a rolled map and spread it on the desk top, anchoring it at all four corners with books. "Now, this area of the estate."

"Yes. Apworth Mountain and the land around it." He nodded.

"What does the area look like?"

He looked nonplussed. "Well, rocks, miss—I mean, my lady. It is hilly and rocky. Not very good for anything that I know of."

"I understand it is part of the Roaches, which are in turn the tail end of the Pennines."

"That's right."

"What has this area been used for?"

"Used for? Nothing, my lady. I mean, people go to look at it. It's sort of grand, in a way, but it's not good for anything that I know of."

"You know, one often finds mineral deposits in this sort of terrain."

"I beg your pardon?"

"Coal, iron ore, even precious minerals. Has anyone ever tried to mine there?"

"No, my lady, not that I know of." He looked at her doubtfully.

"It's something I want to research. It would be nice

to be able to add to our revenues from the tenant farmers.''

''Yes, my lady.''

Miranda sighed inwardly at the man's passivity. ''All right, let's look at the books. I have been looking at the overview Hiram prepared for me, and I am definitely beginning to see a pattern. Take this Bigby land...''

The next two hours passed slowly. The maid came in toward the end of that time, bringing the cup of hot chocolate that was usually Miranda's treat after a few hours of working. She took a sip and decided that, delightful as it was, it could not possibly be reward enough for talking to Mr. Strong.

Devin came in at that moment, providing a welcome break. He looked tired, with shadows under his eyes, and she wondered if he had spent much of the night before as sleeplessly as she had. He was going to the abbey ruins today to paint, he told her, and would be gone much of the day, returning home after tea. Miranda nodded, thinking that she would love to go with him, but he did not ask her.

She wondered if the growing sexual frustration between the two of them was going to destroy the rapport they had been building the past few weeks. She remembered her thoughts of earlier that morning: that she should not demand fidelity of him before she would sleep with him. Even a half marriage like that would surely be better than his growing to hate being around her.

He left, and she returned to the books, taking a sip of the hot chocolate.

There was a tentative knock on the library door, and a moment later Elizabeth sidled in. She looked from Miranda to Mr. Strong as her hands clenched and unclenched. Miranda stood up, concern rising in her.

"Elizabeth? Are you not well?" She walked over to the older woman quickly and took her arm. "Here, sit down. Mr. Strong, would you be so good as to pour my stepmother a glass of water?"

Mr. Strong jumped up to go to the sideboard, where a pitcher and glasses stood. He poured out a glass of water and hurried over to Mrs. Upshaw with it, his forehead knitted in concern.

"Are you feeling all right, ma'am?" he asked.

"Yes, yes, I'm fine. Such a bother over nothing. Really. Oh, is this hot chocolate? Perhaps a little sip of that."

"Yes, of course." Miranda slid the cup over to her stepmother, and Elizabeth drank from it.

She set the cup back in its saucer and gave Miranda a forced smile. "I am sorry. I didn't mean to interrupt. I just thought we could talk a little. I can come back another time."

"No. Of course we can talk now." This was precisely the sort of odd behavior that Elizabeth had taken to exhibiting. She and Elizabeth had been together less than an hour or so earlier, and Elizabeth had indicated then that she was not interested in talking. Now here she was looking as if she was about to fall apart if she did not talk to Miranda.

Miranda turned to Strong. "Why don't you go back to work, Mr. Strong? I need to talk to my stepmother for a while."

"That is so sweet of you, dear," Elizabeth told her as Mr. Strong bowed and swept the books up under his arm, leaving the room. "But you did not need to. I could have come back another time."

"It's all right," Miranda assured her. "You have saved poor Mr. Strong another hour of pain, that's all. Think of yourself as his guardian angel."

"Poor man. He always looks so...distressed."

"I know. He thinks I am an ogre. I am finding that people in England have a grave mistrust of change."

"Yes, no doubt," Elizabeth agreed somewhat distractedly. She glanced around the room, looking up at the balcony, then quickly away.

"Now," Miranda said, "what brought you to see me? I know you don't enjoy the library."

"Well, I can't help thinking, every time I come in here, of you falling." Elizabeth waved her hand toward the balcony, where a sturdy new railing had been installed. "It is so dreadful."

"No harm done."

"Perhaps, but still...to think of what could have happened! It makes my blood run cold." She shivered as she took another sip from the cup.

"I know. But you mustn't worry about it. Nothing like that will happen again, I assure you. That sort of thing happens once in a lifetime."

"I supposed. It's just...I don't much like it here, Miranda. Joseph is so happy with his renovations, but, well, don't you find it a trifle boring? No parties or balls or opera or theater."

"Yes. It is a bit rural," Miranda agreed. "I am sorry if you are bored. Papa and I are busy working on the renovations. I didn't really think how little you would have to do.''

''It's all right. That's not what I wanted to talk to you about. I've been in my room, thinking. Miranda...'' She set down the cup and leaned closer to Miranda, putting her hand on Miranda's arm, looking intently into her eyes. ''Dearest, are you happy?''

''What? Yes, of course.'' Miranda smiled at her and patted the hand Elizabeth had laid on her arm. ''Why wouldn't I be?''

''I don't know. I worry. You looked so...tired and melancholy this morning when I was talking to you.''

''I did?'' Miranda said, surprised. ''I'm sorry. I didn't realize...''

Elizabeth nodded earnestly. ''It worried me. I went up to finish that crewel work I began the other day, but I found I could not concentrate on it. I kept thinking of your face. Is—is he making you unhappy?''

''Devin? Oh, no, Elizabeth, not at all. You must not think that. I am very glad I married Devin.''

''Really?'' Elizabeth looked doubtful. ''I worry that it was a mistake. I fear that Joseph pushed you into it.''

''Elizabeth, you know that no one pushes me into anything. I married Ravenscar because I wanted to. And I am quite happy. I am only a little tired this morning from the party last night.''

''Yes. I confess I am a little tired myself. I haven't danced that much for years. But I could hardly turn down that nice young doctor, and of course...'' she grinned like a schoolgirl confessing a secret, ''it is always magical dancing with your father.''

Miranda, who had danced with her father many times, found it an indication of Elizabeth's considerable love for him, that she could deem his dancing magical.

Elizabeth took another gulp of the chocolate. She had taken a handkerchief out of the pocket of her skirt, and she was worrying it between her fingers now, twisting and pulling and wadding it up. Miranda's gaze went down to the poor abused bit of linen.

"There is more, isn't there? That isn't all that brought you here."

"Well...oh, dear. I don't know how to say this."

"Just say it."

"I know you will say I am being foolish."

"I won't. I promise."

"Well, I—I—I'm just so worried!" she broke out finally, and Miranda realized with dismay that the older woman's eyes were swimming with tears.

"Elizabeth, please..." She leaned over and laid her hand over her stepmother's hands, to still them. "Are you in some kind of trouble?"

"No!" Elizabeth laughed a little shrilly. "It's not I who is in trouble. It is you!"

"Me? Whatever do you mean? I am doing quite well, I assure you."

"No. No, you aren't. Miranda, I think—" She turned her hands up and clutched her stepdaughter's, squeezing them as if they were a lifeline. She stared into Miranda's eyes, her own gaze filled with acute pain and fear. "Miranda, he is trying to kill you!"

16

Miranda stared back at her stepmother blankly. "What? Who? What are you talking about?"

"Your husband. Lord Ravenscar."

Miranda's jaw dropped. Had Elizabeth completely lost her wits? "Dev?" she finally gasped.

"Yes. Dev. Miranda, think!" The light in Elizabeth's eyes was a little unnerving. Involuntarily Miranda thought of the mad old man who had barged into their house in London, ranting about Devin murdering his granddaughter, and she shivered.

"There have been several attacks on your life since we came here," Elizabeth went on earnestly.

"What? Elizabeth, what are you talking about?"

"You fell from that balcony."

"Because I was foolish enough to lean on a railing that had been eaten by woodworms. That was all."

"What about when you went riding and the chunk of rock almost killed you and Joseph."

"That was an accident, too," Miranda said soothingly.

"How can you say that?" Elizabeth replied agitatedly. She finished off the cup of hot chocolate, her hand trembling so that the cup rattled in the saucer when she set it back down. "You could have been killed either time."

"Yes, but I was not. And there is nothing to say that they were not simply accidents."

"Two such 'accidents' in a row!" Elizabeth's voice rose to a squeak. "Don't you see? He is trying to hurt you. Get rid of you. The man is wicked!"

"Elizabeth!" Miranda straightened, her face growing cold and set. "I cannot allow you to speak that way about my husband."

"He has blinded you to his faults. I knew he would." Tears sprang into her stepmother's eyes.

"Elizabeth, please..." Miranda said more gently, putting her hand on Elizabeth's arm in a soothing gesture. She knew that she should not allow her stepmother to anger her with her comments about Devin. It was obvious that something was affecting Elizabeth's mind, and Miranda told herself that she must be gentle with the woman. "You are upsetting yourself over nothing. I know that Dev had a bad reputation, but that is not who he is. He is a good man. I am sure of it. He would not try to kill me."

"You don't know. You don't know *him!*"

"Neither do you," Miranda pointed out. "Besides, I think I know him much better than you realize."

"I knew you wouldn't listen." Elizabeth sank her face onto her hands.

"Of course I am listening to you," Miranda insisted. "I understand that you are very upset, and I am sorry for that. But there is nothing to fear. Really.

Both those events were accidents. I know it is a trifle odd for two accidents to happen in a row like that, but such things do occur. Haven't you ever noticed how you will seem accident prone for several days in a row? I am that way. The railing was old, and we all know that much of the wood at Darkwater was infested with woodworm. There is nothing odd about it breaking under pressure. And limestone rock breaks off and falls frequently. Everyone who lives here says so. Neither incident was unusual.''

"Yes, he is clever.'' Elizabeth sighed, looking weary.

"Besides, Devin could not have pushed the rock down on me. He was riding with us.''

"He could easily have had a cohort at the top of the cliff to dislodge the stone and push it down.''

"Endangering him, too?''

"Was he riding beside you?''

Miranda paused, thinking. "Well, no, he was a few yards ahead, talking to his uncle.''

"You see?'' Elizabeth exclaimed triumphantly. "It was you and Joseph who were almost killed, while Ravenscar was far from the danger.''

"Elizabeth, please, I don't know why you dislike Devin so. You hardly know him. You should come down to dinner more often, sit with us after the meal. Talk to him. I think you would find that he is a much nicer person than anything you have heard about him.''

"Oh, I know he is charming. That is not the issue.'' Elizabeth yawned, covering her mouth politely. "I'm sorry. I just…suddenly I feel very tired.''

"Yes, no doubt you need to rest," Miranda agreed.

"No. Not until you understand…" Her words were interrupted by another yawn. "Oh, dear me."

"Please, why don't you go up to your room and sleep?" Miranda suggested, eager to get her stepmother out of there. "You will feel much better when you wake up. You will see that you have gotten worried over the merest trifle."

"No, I won't." Elizabeth rubbed her hand across her face, looking confused.

Miranda frowned in concern. "Are you feeling all right, Elizabeth? Are you ill? Let me ring for a maid to help you up to your room."

"Oh, no, dear, don't be silly. I don't need help."

At that moment a footman entered the room, coughed politely to draw their attention, and announced, "Lady Vesey and Miss Vesey to see you, my lady."

"Lady Vesey?" Miranda looked up, surprised.

"Leona!" Elizabeth exclaimed. It was clear from her face, Miranda thought, that someone had informed her stepmother of what Lady Vesey was to Lord Ravenscar.

The servant came forward with the small silver tray, on which sat two calling cards, one for the spinster aunt and one for Leona. A faint smile touched Miranda's lips. She was never one to turn down a challenge.

"Why, yes," she told the servant. "Show Lady Vesey into the drawing room.

When the servant had bowed out of the room, Elizabeth turned toward Miranda, her eyes huge. "My dear, do you think you should? I understand from Lady Ravenscar that she is, well, not usually admitted into the best circles.''

''Yes, Elizabeth, I know. However, I have an interest in talking to Lady Vesey. I feel sure that it will not tarnish my reputation to receive her. Do you wish to come?''

''I believe that I will go upstairs and lie down, as you suggested,'' Elizabeth said quickly. ''I hate to think what Lady Ravenscar will say about this....''

''Don't worry,'' Miranda assured her. ''It won't be anything I cannot handle.''

Her stepmother rose and started out of the room, then paused, looking back at Miranda. ''Dear...please, you will be careful, won't you? Promise me?''

''Yes, of course I will.''

Elizabeth nodded, still looking unsatisfied, and left the library. Miranda straightened her dress and went out into the hall, stopping at the mirror a few feet away to check the state of her hair. Her cheeks were pink and her eyes sparkling in anticipation of the scene before her, so she had few qualms about her looks.

She continued down the hall and into the formal drawing room. She walked in to find Leona Vesey standing with Lord Vesey's aunt in the center of the room, facing a rigid Lady Ravenscar, whose nose and mouth were pinched into a pattern of disapproval. Rachel, seated beside her mother, looked less disapproving than furious.

It was clear that Devin's mother had questioned Leona's presence there, for as Miranda walked in,

Leona was saying, "...with Lady Ravenscar's approval—the new Lady Ravenscar, that is."

"Hello, Lady Vesey," Miranda said cheerfully, coming forward to take the other woman's hand and squeeze it.

Leona winced a little as she withdrew her hand from Miranda's. "Lady Ravenscar."

Miranda turned toward Rachel and her mother-in-law, greeting them pleasantly. "I am so glad you were able to entertain Lady Vesey until I got here. Please, sit down, Lady Vesey. Miss Vesey." She took the older woman's arm and guided her to a chair. "It is so pleasant when one's neighbors come to visit. I confess I had expected more people to call, but then I realized that no one wished to disturb us—our newlywed state, you know." She smiled in a secretive, self-satisfied way, doing her best to blush a little.

Leona's eyes narrowed. "Yes. Of course. I am so glad that you are settling in at Darkwater."

"Thank you. It has been most pleasant. Of course, so much of one's happiness depends upon one's husband. Don't you find that is true, Lady Vesey? Fortunately, Devin is the best of husbands."

"Indeed." Leona smiled faintly. "I confess," she said, amusement tingeing her voice, "that I had never really pictured Devin as a married man. He was always so...how shall I say it? Carefree."

"Yes, and such an attractive man," Miranda agreed, looking at Leona with wide, innocent eyes. "I am quite sure that many women were devastated when Devin entered the married state."

"No doubt." Leona glanced around. "Where is Devin, by the way? Surely the man hasn't gone out and left his bride alone so soon.''

Rachel's eyes flared with anger, but she managed to hold on to her temper and kept her mouth shut.

"He is out painting," Miranda said.

"Painting!" Leona's brows rose, and she let out a tinkling little laugh. "Oh, my, is he doing that again? I thought he had grown bored with dabbling in paints.''

"He had seemed to get off track for a few years, but he is painting furiously now.''

"You poor dear," Leona said in a condescending way. "It must be awful for you to have your new husband away all the time indulging himself.''

"I don't mind.''

"Really? How liberal-minded of you not to care. I really cannot imagine why Devin started again—of course, I suppose it does offer an escape, of sorts.'' Her tone was honeyed, but the look she sent Miranda was significant.

"Obviously you must not know Devin well, then,'' Miranda said with such a sweet voice and innocent look that Rachel had to cover her mouth to suppress a giggle. "He is a very good artist. I would not be surprised if one day he is famous the world over.''

Leona cast a suspicious look at her hostess, as if she could not decide whether she was being teased.

"Perhaps you would like to see some of his sketches," Rachel put in. "He has done any number of likenesses of Miranda.''

Leona's jaw clenched. "Oh, no, I wouldn't put you out to get them.''

"It's no bother," Miranda assured her, popping up. "I am sure Devin would not mind our going up to his studio to view them."

She went to Leona and put her hand under her arm, urging her up. Leona stood a little uncertainly, and Miranda linked her arm through Leona's. "Rachel? Lady Ravenscar?"

Lady Ravenscar's eyes glittered wickedly. "Why, yes, I do think I would like to see this."

Leona could scarcely get out of it now, and the three Aincourt women swept her up to the floor above and down the hall to Devin's studio. Leona stepped inside and came to a dead halt. Her eyes widened as they went about the room. A half-finished portrait of Miranda stood on an easel in the center of the room. Two more finished ones, one large and one small, were propped against the wall. A half-dozen sketches of her in charcoal were scattered across a table, and two watercolor sketches of her were lying on the floor to dry.

Leona's eyes grew bigger and bigger and her face paler until Miranda thought that she might faint. "Are you all right, Lady Vesey?" she asked solicitously.

Lady Ravenscar watched Leona intently, a faint smile touching her mouth, and Rachel unabashedly smiled.

"Yes. Fine." Leona spoke through clenched teeth, pulling her arm sharply away from Miranda's. "Dev has certainly been busy, hasn't he?"

"Yes. He has rediscovered his old love," Miranda said contentedly. "I am sure he regrets ever having given it up."

Leona offered her a brittle smile and left the room

abruptly, leaving the other women to follow her. Rachel glanced at Miranda and grinned.

By the time they rejoined Lady Vesey, she had recovered her pleasant demeanor, although Miranda, walking beside her down the stairs, could feel the tension radiating from her.

"So now Dev has gone on to other objects to paint?" she asked Miranda.

"Yes, the rest of the day. I can only pose for an hour or two a day. It gets rather tiring."

Leona's grin was a baring of teeth. "No doubt. And where is he sketching today?"

Lady Ravenscar, on the other side of Miranda, made a noise, but Miranda ignored her. Looking straight at Leona, a challenging light in her eyes, she said, "The ruins of the abbey. It is a very scenic spot."

"Yes. Of course."

Leona left as soon as they got back to the drawing room, practically pulling Vesey's elderly aunt from her chair and out the door. Miranda felt sure that she would divest herself of the aunt in record time and would soon be riding from Vesey Park to the abbey.

Almost as soon as Leona left, Miranda excused herself to go check on her stepmother. She walked out of the room, humming under her breath.

Lady Ravenscar looked at her daughter, a smile as broad as she ever allowed herself curving her lips. "I must say, Rachel, that was a splendid suggestion, going to look at Devin's pictures. I had no idea he had done such a number of Miranda."

"I did." Rachel smiled like the cat that had got into the cream.

"Very clever of you. I do wish, though, that Miranda had not told her where he was painting today. You know the witch is certain to go over there."

"Somehow," Rachel commented confidently, "I have a suspicion that our Miranda knew exactly what she was doing."

Miranda was not as confident as she had acted in front of Leona. The truth was, she had her doubts as to what Devin would do if Leona showed up at the abbey today. She knew she had taken a gamble by telling Leona where Dev was, but she needed to know what Dev would do. She had to let it play out, no matter what the consequences.

Lady Vesey's visit had raised her spirits, though. Miranda had not known for certain that Devin had not gone to visit Leona at Vesey Park since their marriage, although from the amount of time he had spent on his painting, she did not see how he could have managed it. But the fact that Leona had come here, transparently hoping to seek him out, indicated to Miranda that he had not seen his former mistress at all. Such a lack of interest was heartening, even if it did stem more from his new passion for his art than passion for herself.

She went up to her stepmother's room to check on her, as she had told the others. She met a maid slipping quietly out the door just as she approached.

"Oh!" The maid stopped abruptly when she saw Miranda and bobbed her a curtsey. "My lady."

"Is Mrs. Upshaw sleeping?" Miranda asked. Her stepmother had not looked well when she left her earlier, as well as having been acting very strangely. Miranda was a trifle worried about her.

"Not yet, ma'am. I think she is about to fall sleep now, though. She felt terrible sick when she came upstairs, ma'am. Her whole breakfast came back up, it did."

"Oh, dear." Miranda went past the girl into Elizabeth's room.

Elizabeth was in bed, her face rather gray against the pristine white of the pillow, her eyelids closed. They fluttered open when Miranda came to her bedside, and Elizabeth regarded her groggily.

"Miranda..."

"I heard you had a rather bad time of it," Miranda said, taking her hand and squeezing it. Her stepmother's skin was cool.

"Yes, it was an awful mess," Elizabeth murmured, stumbling over her words. "So silly—I didn't feel ill earlier this morning. But suddenly, just as I came into my room..." She shuddered.

"Perhaps now you will feel better," Miranda told her reassuringly. "I am sure if you take a nap, it will help."

"Yes. I can hardly keep my eyes open. I hope I will be able to sleep. I don't think there is anything left to come up."

Miranda patted her hand and sat down on the side of the bed. Elizabeth turned on her side, smiling faintly, and curled her fingers around Miranda's. She soon slipped into sleep.

Miranda looked down at her stepmother, a small frown on her forehead. She did not typically worry overmuch about Elizabeth's illnesses; she was always in the throes of some complaint or other, and they were usually brief and not very severe. Elizabeth certainly looked ill today, however.

"I think that I will sit with her for a while," Miranda told the maid. "Until she's feeling better."

Devin rode to the abbey ruins first and left his sketch pads and paints. He would come back afterward, he thought, and do some sketches. It was important, somehow, that what he had told Miranda not be a complete lie.

He had hated misleading her, omitting the important fact of where else he planned to go today. But he could scarcely tell her his true destination.

He rode in the opposite direction from the abbey, and in another forty-five minutes he was riding through the double row of lime trees that led to the entrance of Vesey Park. It sent an odd quiver snaking through him to look up at the front of the house. He had come here many times that summer he was eighteen, madly in love with Lord Vesey's new wife and unable to stay away.

He reined in at the front door, and a groom came to take his horse. A footman opened the door, bowing, but when Devin asked for Leona, the footman surprised him by informing him that her ladyship was not at home. Leona did not, Devin knew, have friends in the area; she was considered much too wild by the ladies around here, led by his own mother. The servant enlightened him by volunteering the fact that she had gone to see Lord Vesey's aunt.

That fact surprised Devin. Leona, he knew, found the old woman deadly dull, and he had assumed that Leona had been with her at the wedding feast solely because that was the only way she could get in. She must have been driven to visit Miss Vesey by sheer boredom; Leona could not abide living in the country. He was amazed that she had stayed as long as she had. He would have expected her to set out for London soon after the wedding.

He decided to wait for her, figuring that Leona would soon grow tired of the elderly aunt and return home. The footman, taking stock of his attire and demeanor, seated him in the formal drawing room to wait for her.

As he had hoped, he had been there only a few minutes when Leona came sweeping in, favoring him with a glittering smile and holding out her hands to him. She looked fetching in a green dress that set off her golden looks admirably. The material clung to her hips and legs, and the round neckline revealed the upper swell of her full breasts.

"Devin! At last. I never see you." She pulled her mouth into a provocative pout. "One might almost think that you don't like me anymore." She leaned toward him, her lips curving up in an inviting smile, her eyes glinting gold.

To her amazement, Devin took a step backward. Leona stopped, one eyebrow going up, and she said in irritation, "Whatever is the matter, Dev? Afraid of me?"

"No, of course not. Leona..." He paused. It was

desperately hard now to tell her what he had come here for.

Leona did not wait for him to continue. She turned away, saying in a contemptuous tone, "Your drab little wife told me you had taken up painting again. Really, Dev, I thought you had given up playing with paints."

"Miranda?" he asked in astonishment, distracted by her words. "You have talked to Miranda?"

"Yes. Aunt Vesey and I went calling on her. That is where I was just now. She told me you were out drawing at the abbey ruins." Leona cast him an amused glance and made tsk-tsking noises. "Lying to your bride already? Of course, I fully understand. You must be desperate to escape the provincial chit. My goodness, poor Dev... Are you terribly angry with me for persuading you to marry her?"

Devin's jaw set, and a light flared in his eyes. "No. I am not angry with you for that. If anything, Leona, you did me a favor. I am happier now than I can remember being for years."

Leona's eyes widened; then she relaxed and let out a little laugh. "Oh, you are teasing. I almost believed you." She came back to him, putting one hand on his arm and gazing up into his face in a way that had never failed to beguile him. "Why haven't you been to visit me? I would have alleviated your boredom."

"I wasn't bored," he replied and stepped back from her again. "I could scarcely call on you, Leona. Things are different now that I am married. It would be an insult to Miranda if I rode over to visit my mistress."

"Oh, her," Leona said dismissively. "What does it matter if she is insulted? She's a little nobody from America."

"She is not a nobody," Devin snapped. "She is my wife. I cannot allow you to speak about her like that."

Leona stared at him, shocked into silence.

Devin sighed. "I am sorry. But Miranda is my wife now." When Leona continued to stare at him, he went on irritably, "Didn't you realize how it would be? You were the one who urged me to marry."

"To get the money we both so desperately needed!" Leona lashed back. "Not to turn into some priggish country bumpkin. What has happened to you?"

He shrugged. "I don't know, Leona. I just—I changed." He paused then said, "I'm different now. My life is different. You and I—"

Leona put her hand over his mouth, silencing him. "Hush. You don't know what you are saying. All this bucolic living has softened your brain."

She moved closer to him, her body brushing up against his, her hand sliding away from his mouth to caress his cheek and neck. "I know you, Dev," she said in a low, intimate voice. "I know you better than anyone. You cannot fool me. You are still the same Devin, the man I love."

She took one of his hands and guided it to the open neck of her dress, holding his hand to the exposed swell of her breasts. "I know what you like..." Leona went on huskily. "Why don't we slip upstairs, so I can remind you of what you are missing?"

She raised his hand to her mouth, kissing the tips

of his fingers, taking the ball of his thumb between her teeth.

Devin looked down at her. Her eyes were golden, lit with a seductive glow, and her lips pouted in a way that was guaranteed to make a man want to kiss them. Her breasts were ripe and full. *And he was, amazingly, completely unmoved.* For the first time that he could remember in almost fifteen years, he felt no desire for Leona. Despite what he had come to tell her, he had not expected that.

"Leona, don't." He pulled his hand back and moved away. "I cannot do that. I am married now. It's different."

He turned around, his face and tone formal. "Let me tell you what I came here to say. I *have* changed, Leona. I don't know exactly how or why, but it is true. And I cannot undo it. I don't want to undo it. I cannot be the way I used to be, the way I was with you. I can't do the things I did or act the same way. I don't want to. I cannot be a husband to Miranda and keep you as a mistress. It wouldn't be fair to either one of you." He paused, then said the words he had never thought he would utter. "I cannot see you anymore."

Leona went pale with shock. Devin was filled with guilt as he watched her. He had loved her for years, and it was almost as much of a shock to him as it was to Leona that he had finally stopped. But he realized, looking at her, that he no longer loved her. He had made a decision last night to break things off with Leona, but he had thought that he still loved her. He had thought it would be harder for him to break with her, more of a struggle. He had expected to feel torn about choosing Miranda. But all he felt at the moment was relief. Leona seemed almost a stranger to him now, a little overblown in her provocative attire and manner, his memories of her and his love for her clouded by the haze of alcohol in which he had spent most of his time.

It occurred to him, startling him, how little time he had spent with Leona over the years and how little he really knew her. Their moments together had always been brief and stolen, tinged with the excitement of the forbidden and foggy with the amount of alcohol he had imbibed. There had not been hours spent together talking and laughing, as he had known with Miranda the past few weeks. He could have said a thousand things about Miranda's past, but for all the years he had loved Leona, he knew little more about her than that she disliked her two sisters and rarely saw them.

"I am sorry," he said inadequately. "But I cannot lie to you. You would not want that."

"I do not want *this!*" Anger contorted Leona's face, turning the soft, sensual lines into something harsh, and she made a sweeping gesture with her arm. "You are throwing me over for that—that—stupid, whey-faced American trollop?"

"She is not a trollop!" Devin's temper flared.

"How dare you." Leona shrieked. "I am Leona Vesey! Half the gentlemen of the *Ton* want me! You should be honored that I let you into my bed. I cannot believe—after all the years I spent on you! I could have had anyone, you know, and I chose you. There are scores of men who wanted to displace you over the years. All I have to do is snap my fingers, and they will come running.''

"I am sure you are right," Devin said, reining in his temper. "Any man would want you."

"Don't patronize me!" Leona's lip curled, and the words dripped from her mouth like acid. "You are such a fool, Dev. I don't know why it should surprise me. Men are always fools. You've found a new toy. She's shaken her hips at you and rolled those eyes, all the while acting as if she thinks your silly little paintings are great works of art. Now you think you will be a good husband and stay up here in Derbyshire, drawing and fornicating with that American ninny. Hah! In two months you will be dying with boredom. You will wake up one morning and realize what you've done. And you'll want me back again. You can't ever get me out of your blood. I *own* you, Dev. I have since you were eighteen and a flat straight from countryside.''

Devin looked at her, his eyes cold and flat. "You never owned me, Leona. I loved you. There is a difference.''

"Oh, please. You would have done anything I asked you to, and you know it. Because you wanted to be in my bed.''

"Is that all you think it was?''

Leona shot him a speaking look. "The only reason you married her, if you will remember, is because *I* wanted you to. I teased and enticed you until you would have done anything I said. Think about it, Devin. Your little milk-and-water miss won't be able to satisfy you as I can. You'll miss it. You know you will. And you'll regret it. You will come crawling back to me. But you know what? I won't be here. You will have missed your chance.''

Devin looked at her levelly. ''No, Leona. I won't be back.''

He turned and strode out of the house. Mounting his horse, he rode home to Miranda.

17

Miranda did not see Devin when he returned to the house that afternoon. She was still in Elizabeth's room, watching over her stepmother. To her surprise, Elizabeth had not yet awakened by late afternoon, so Miranda continued to stay beside the bed. Her anxiety grew as the afternoon turned into evening and Elizabeth was still deeply asleep.

Veronica relieved Miranda for a couple of hours, but she was only fourteen, and it was hard for her to sit still, so Miranda returned to take up her vigil. She didn't understand why Elizabeth still had not awakened, but it did not seem like a good sign. She told herself that it was only that the vomiting had simply worn her out. *It was good to sleep when one was sick; it gave the body a chance to heal itself.* But she could not suppress the feeling that there was something unnatural about Elizabeth's long nap.

She rang and told the maid to bring her supper to Elizabeth's room. To her surprise later, when there was a knock on the door and it swung open, it was her husband who carried in the tray containing her supper, not a maid.

"Devin!" Miranda exclaimed with delight, rising and going to him. "What are you doing here?"

"When they told me you would not be down to dinner, I decided to bring the tray to you myself. I haven't seen you since this morning."

He set the tray down on a low table and glanced over at the bed where Elizabeth lay motionless. "Is Mrs. Upshaw very ill?"

"I'm not sure. I don't think so. Still, it concerns me that she has not awakened yet. I thought I would stay until she does." She smiled up at Devin and reached out to take his hand. "I will miss seeing you at dinner, however."

He smiled and brought her hand up to his lips. "I, too."

Miranda wondered whether Leona had visited him at the abbey, but she could not bring herself to ask him straight out. "How did your work go today?" she asked instead, hoping that would lead naturally to his mentioning Leona's visit.

"It went well, once I got started." Devin started to say something more, then hesitated and glanced across the room at her sleeping stepmother. He raised her hand to his mouth again and kissed it, saying, "I will not disturb you. I only wanted to see you. I will talk to you later."

"Of course."

He left the room, and Miranda sighed in frustration. She wished she knew what he had been about to say. She wished she knew whether she had won the chal-

lenge she had thrown at Leona, or lost it—and Dev—
in the process.

Around ten o'clock, her stepmother woke up, mum-
bling incoherently, then opened her eyes and glanced
around in a confused way. Miranda got up and went
to her side.

"Elizabeth? How are you feeling?"

Elizabeth blinked at her groggily. "I—where—why
are you here? Oh, I remember. I was ill, wasn't I?"

"Yes, and you have been asleep all afternoon. Are
you feeling better?"

"I'm not sure." Elizabeth closed her eyes again as
if was too much effort to keep them open. "I'm so
tired."

"Would you like something to eat? Some broth,
perhaps?"

But Elizabeth was already asleep again.

The fact that her stepmother had awakened reassured Miranda. She had not gone into a permanent
unconsciousness, as Miranda had been beginning to
fear. No doubt her illness that afternoon had simply
worn her out. Sleep was, after all, the best curative.

Her father came in after that to check on his wife's
condition, and Elizabeth awoke at the sound of his
voice and said a few words. Feeling confident now
that her stepmother was better, Miranda decided that
she would not have to sleep on a cot in Elizabeth's
room that night, as she had been beginning to think
she would. It would be enough to have one of the
maids there.

So after ringing for the maid and instructing her to
awaken her if there was any alarming change in Eliz-

abeth's condition, she made her way to her own bed-room. Her maid was there and had already brought in a slipper tub and was filling it with warm water, an-ticipating Miranda's wishes. She helped Miranda un-dress and get into the tub. After a long soak, Miranda felt much better, though her mind still worried over the question of Leona's visit to the abbey that after-noon. *If Devin did not tell her about it, what did it mean?*

She pulled her nightgown on over her head and brushed out her hair, then climbed into bed. She was almost asleep when the door from Devin's room opened.

Her breath caught in her throat, and she tensed. De-vin paused at the door. He carried a candlestick in one hand, and it cast a flickering light over his planed face. His eyes were dark, his cheeks shadowed. His shirt was unbuttoned, hanging open down the front. Mi-randa watched, frozen, as he set the candle down, then crossed the room toward her.

He stopped beside the bed and stood gazing down at her for a long moment. The drapes at her window stood open, and enough moonlight came in that she could see his face.

He reached down and put his hand on her chest. His flesh was hot and faintly rough, and it trembled slightly with the thrum of his pulse. Miranda did not have to ask what he wanted. She knew.

She answered wordlessly, reaching up and putting her hand on his wrist, then sliding it upward.

"I want you." His voice was low and hoarse. "I

don't think I've ever wanted anyone the way I want you.''

His hand started a slow, enticing journey down her chest, sliding over her breasts and onto the plane of her stomach. Miranda did not speak, hardly breathed. She wanted him to go on. At this moment she no longer cared about her long-term plans for their marriage or whether he committed himself to her exclusively or what had happened today at the abbey. Right now, she knew, she would agree to almost anything as long as it meant that he would spend tonight in her bed. That was as much of their future as she could think of.

He spread his palm over her abdomen, spanning the width of it with his hand, then slid it over onto her hip and down her leg, coming back up and crossing to the other side.

"I want a real marriage," he said. "I don't want us to have a 'business' arrangement or go our separate ways. And I will not share your body with any man. I want you...and only you." He paused, then added, "I broke it off with Leona today."

Miranda drew in a sharp breath. "Devin..."

"Will you let me try to be a true husband?"

His hand slid back up her front, and Miranda could not contain a little shuddering moan. "Yes," was all she could manage to utter. "Yes..."

They came together with heat and urgency, tearing off their clothes and tossing them aside, the weeks of pent-up longing suddenly released into a flood of passion. His mouth was hot and seeking; hers no less so. They kissed and caressed, their eager bodies flush against each other, rolling across the large bed. Devin could not get enough of Miranda—the taste, the feel, the smell, of her. He had been hungering for her for weeks, and now she was in his arms, pliable and warm and as eager for him as he was for her. He kissed her over and over, his lips roaming her face and throat and down onto her chest, coming to rest on the sublimely soft mound of her breast. He cupped the orb with his hand as his mouth explored the bud of her nipple, teasing it with tongue and lips and teeth until Miranda was moaning and arching up off the bed, her fingers digging into his shoulders.

Heat exploded in Miranda's abdomen, desire pooling between her legs. She ached for him. Her hands swept over Dev, eager to learn all the textures of him—the hard bone of his skull and ribs, the thick curve of muscles across his back, the soft skin of his abdomen that trembled when her fingers roamed there, the coarse, curling hair on his chest that swept down in a thin line to his stomach, then lower…. Every part of him was enticing, intriguing, and she thought that she could have gone on for hours exploring him if it had not been for the ever tightening knot of urgency in her loins, the pleasurable ache between her legs that yearned for fulfillment.

She breathed his name, and he swallowed it with a consuming kiss. As he kissed her, his hand glided slowly down her body. His fingers moved over her abdomen and down her thigh, then back up, stroking and teasing, coming ever closer to the heated center of her passion, until finally, when Miranda thought she could bear it no longer, his hand slipped between her legs, finding the hot, moist center of her. A groan escaped Miranda, and she shuddered, stunned by the pleasure, greater than any she had ever experienced, yet, contradictorily, not enough. His fingers soothed her ache even as they increased it, both taming and emboldening her, giving and withholding, until she thought she would go mad with the wild hot delight he created in her.

His fingers separated the slick folds of her femininity, exploring and caressing, slipping inside her, then retreating. She moved her hips against him, urging him on to completion, but he continued his erotic caresses with maddening slowness. Something was building inside Miranda, wild and furious, a knot that tightened and grew with each caress, until she was almost sobbing, and then it exploded within her like wildfire. She gasped and arched her hips upward, her muscles tightening as pleasure swept through her in waves, until finally she collapsed, panting and filled with the most luxurious contentment she had ever felt.

"Devin..." His name was a sigh on her lips, and she looked up at him dreamily.

Desire speared him at her reaction, and he could wait no longer. He moved between her legs and slid into her. Miranda drew in her breath at the new sensation. She had thought she could feel no more pleasure after the storm that had just swept through her, but she found now that she was capable of even more. He filled her, bringing a completion and fulfillment that she had never known existed. They were joined, truly one, and for the first time she understood the unity of love. He belonged to her and she to him.

She wrapped her legs and arms around Devin, holding him tightly to her as he began to move inside her. Her breath shuddered out as he stroked in and out, building again that knot of desire within her. She could scarcely believe that it was happening again, only even more wonderfully this time, for he was part of her as she felt the waves of pleasure erupt in her again, and as she rode the crest of her passion, he joined her, shuddering and muffling his cry of passion in the crook of her neck.

They clung to each other, lost to the rest of the world, boneless and content.

Devin awakened slowly. He felt, for the first time that he could remember, utterly and completely at peace. He turned his head and looked at the woman who lay beside him. Miranda was still asleep, her dark lashes shadowing her cheeks, her face innocent and vulnerable in sleep, her vibrant hair a tangle upon the pillow. She was beautiful, he thought, and wondered how he could ever have thought she was anything less. Last night had been a first for him, as well as for Miranda. He had never felt such hunger and need, such pleasure, such satisfaction and joy. Even all of Leona's seductive wiles had never made him explode with not only release but also happiness.

He reached over and touched her cheek with his finger, slowly drawing it down to her jaw. Miranda's eyes fluttered open, and she gazed at him sleepily, a smile curving her lips.

''Good morning,'' she murmured.

''Good morning.'' He leaned over and kissed her softly on the lips. ''How are you?''

''Fine.'' Miranda's smile widened. ''More than fine, really. I am wonderful.''

''That you are,'' he agreed and kissed her again, more lingeringly this time.

Hunger stirred in him again, not with the razor-edge sharpness he had known the past few weeks, but deep and urgent. He enjoyed the feeling, knowing that it would be satisfied now. This morning, the fiercest urges satisfied, he could spend his time, could explore and learn her feminine secrets, teach her the wealth of delight that lay within her.

He could feel her smile beneath his lips as she curved her arms around his neck and gave herself up to the pleasure. They moved at a leisurely pace this morning, giving and receiving, enjoying every nuance of their passion. And when they reached their peak of desire, the explosion that rocked them was both familiar and new, as powerful as what they had experienced the night before.

It was, Miranda thought afterward, quite a lovely way to start off the day.

They lay together talking desultorily for some time after that. They talked about little of consequence, but it was sweet to lie in such a way, going over the intertwined bits and pieces of their lives. They talked about his painting of the abbey ruins and the shortcomings of Strong, the estate manager. Miranda pointed out that there were many things she still needed to see, such as the part of the estate that lay in the Roaches and some of the estate farms, not to mention parts of the ruined west wing and the house cellars.

"The cellars?" Devin repeated with a chuckle. "Why would you want to see those?"

"I want to see everything," Miranda replied simply. "Every part of the house."

"They are huge. They stretch under most of the central portion of Darkwater. And they're old. I'm not entirely sure they are safe."

"Are there dungeons?"

He laughed again. "There's your father's daughter speaking. As far as I know, they were used only for storing things—huge amounts of things. There are some small locked rooms, however...."

"Really?" Miranda turned on her side to look at him, intrigued.

"Yes, really. More storage rooms, where they locked munitions and valuables, I'm afraid."

Miranda grimaced. "You have no sense of romance."

"And here I thought I was terribly romantic." He smiled lazily, trailing his finger down her neck and onto her chest.

A little quiver darted through Miranda. "Well, in some respects you are...."

He kissed her, effectively ending the conversation.

It was some time later when they made their way down to breakfast. Everyone else in the family had already eaten and gone on their way, so the two of them were alone. It was not until they were almost through with the meal that Miranda guiltily remembered that her stepmother was ill and she had not even checked on her this morning.

As soon as Devin left for the abbey ruins, she trotted up the stairs to Elizabeth's room. The maid was dutifully sitting with her stepmother, just as Miranda had left her the night before. Elizabeth, on the other hand, was awake at last, sitting up in bed with a number of pillows propped behind her. She looked far better than she had the day before, though her skin was still pasty, her lips dried and cracked, and her eyes had large dark circles under them that were at odds with the long hours of sleep she had gotten the day before.

"How are you, Elizabeth?" Miranda asked, coming forward and nodding at the maid that she could leave.

"Miranda. My love. I am improved, I think." Elizabeth shook her head. "Still a little fuzzy, though. It is the oddest thing. I don't think I have ever felt quite this way before. I kept waking up last night and falling back asleep. I couldn't keep my eyes open for any length of time. My stomach hurts...and my head." She sighed.

"Well, thank heaven it seems to be over and you are on the mend," Miranda said encouragingly.

Elizabeth reached out and patted Miranda's hand. "Nan was just telling me how you sat with me all yesterday. Didn't even go down to eat. You are such a sweet girl."

"I was concerned about you," Miranda replied honestly. "You slept so much."

Elizabeth frowned. "Yes. I did. It's odd."

Miranda stayed for a few minutes longer, talking, but she could see that she was wearing Elizabeth out, so she left her to go back to sleep once again and Miranda went down to the library to work.

She found it hard going keeping her mind on the books and Mr. Strong's less than lucid explanations of the estate's workings. So that afternoon she went to the stables and had a horse saddled for her, and she rode out to the abbey ruins. She and Devin had ridden to the abbey before; it was one of her favorite places on the estate. But today it had an additional appeal.

Devin was there, painting, but he readily stopped when he saw Miranda. She had brought a small picnic lunch that Cook had made up for them, and they ate it, sitting in the shadow of one of the still-standing walls.

The abbey was an eerie place, stark and ruined, half-crumbled walls and flagstone floors overgrown with grasses and weeds. Many of the stones in the building's walls had been taken down and carted over to Darkwater to build the Aincourt mansion. Two walls of the central cathedral—one with a beautifully designed window, empty of glass—stood intact, large and imposing, with the customary medieval arches, but the other two walls had been reduced to rubble. Parts of the abbey were identifiable only by a line of stones half-buried in the ground, marking the shapes of rooms. In other places there were staircases leading upward to nowhere or empty gaping holes in the ground where the floors had fallen through into the cellars below.

Yet it had a unique beauty, too, Miranda thought, at once harsh and peaceful, defeated but at the same time unconquerable. After all this time and all that had been done to it, the abbey was still here, long after the men who had set out to destroy it were gone. When she looked at Devin's painting of the abbey, she saw that he had managed to convey the timelessness of the place, its haunting grandeur. She slipped her hand into his and squeezed it, smiling up at him.

At that moment, she did not think there was a happier woman on earth.

The days that followed did nothing to alter her opinion. Miranda spent much of her time with Devin. She was neglecting her work, she knew, but she didn't care. Her father was quite capable of dealing with all aspects of renovating the house, and between him and Hiram, they were also able to deal with any business concerns that came up. As for Devin's estate, well, that could wait for a few more days; it had been waiting for years. She told herself that she would get back to it soon, but dealing with the neglect of years was too melancholy a task when one felt as Miranda did, as if she was bubbling over with joy every minute of the day.

Everyone noticed the change in Devin and Miranda. Her father smiled smugly, as though to say he had been right all along. One evening at supper he remarked jovially, "I'm surprised you two haven't decided to take a honeymoon trip. Go to Vienna or some place like that."

"That's the thing," Uncle Rupert agreed, with a nod of his head. "Be alone for a while. Good thing, I should think. No nasty drafts, either."

Devin smiled. "I suggested it to Miranda. But she

would rather stay here and poke about a musty old house.''

"That's not true. I said I would love to go, but first I have to get the estate back on track. Papa can take care of seeing that the 'musty old house' is being renovated. But I still need to have a meeting with the tenant farmers and visit some of the larger farms.''

Devin cast a fond glance at her. "So I think our honeymoon will be a trip to the Roaches, in all likelihood. Miranda has a desire to see our land there.''

"You mean Apworth Mountain?" Lady Ravenscar asked in astonishment. "Whyever would you want to see that, Miranda?"

"It is beautiful in its own way, Mama," Rachel pointed out.

"But there is no place to stay," Rupert said, siding with his sister.

"That's not true, Uncle," Devin said. "I have gone there several times. Bert Jones is always happy to let me stay with him and his family. He would be doubly so if I brought a pretty wife with me. From there, it's an easy ride to Apworth.''

"Bert Jones?" Lady Ravenscar's eyebrows rose even higher. "You are going to put your wife up in a thatched-roof cottage?"

"I am sure I have stayed in worse, Lady Ravenscar," Miranda told her cheerfully. "Of course, we could always put up a tent. Devin says he has one.''

Lady Ravenscar looked as if she might faint. "My dear...camping...''

"It would be a wonderful place to paint," Devin went on, waxing enthusiastic about the idea.

"Really, Devin, you cannot go dragging your new bride all through the roughest country just so you can paint a landscape."

"But I want to see it," Miranda assured her. "I am interested in all areas of the estate."

Uncle Rupert shrugged. "Personally, I think I would choose Vienna for a honeymoon, but to each his own."

"We shall go to Vienna, too," Miranda assured them. "And Italy." The thought of a slow tour through Florence, Rome and Venice with Devin held a great deal of appeal for her. She looked over at him, and her heart swelled with emotion. "But we have a whole lifetime for that."

Devin left early the next morning for Darkwater Tarn. He had finished his series of sketches of the abbey ruins a day or two before, and he had decided to move on to the inky lake that gave the house its name. Miranda arose late and went downstairs to the library. She needed to finish up some correspondence with the manager of her real estate in New York, and then, she thought, she would get Mr. Strong to show her around some of the tenant farms. She had been doing a great deal of reading on improved methods of farming, and she wanted to see more of the land to get a better idea of what she would have to do.

But when she reached the library, she found a note sitting on the table, waiting for her, that drove all thoughts of Strong and the tenant farms out of her head. Her name was scrawled boldly across the back of the note. Miranda smiled. She had seen Devin's signature only a few times, but she immediately recognized the dark spiky letters as his distinctive hand. She broke the seal and read the brief note inside:

Beloved,
  Meet me at the cellar door in back of the house at 1:00. I have something to show you.

It was signed only with a large *R*. Below the message there was a crude map showing the location of the cellar door. Miranda read the note over twice, intrigued. She could not imagine what Devin wanted to show her or why he had chosen such a peculiar place. She had not even noticed that there was a cellar door located in that place. Besides, he was not supposed to be here today. He had said he was going to Darkwater Tarn. She wondered if he had changed his mind or if the tarn had been merely a cover for whatever surprise he had dreamed up. A smile curved her lips as she contemplated the afternoon. Whatever Dev had planned, she was sure that it would be far more fun than riding about the estate with Strong.

She sent the man a message that she would meet him the next day instead, then sat down to work on her correspondence, wanting to get it done before her appointment with Devin. It was difficult, for her mind kept wandering to the rendezvous with her husband.

She considered what she should wear. Should she change into an old dress more suitable to a visit to the no-doubt dirty cellars? Or should she assume that the cellars were merely a ruse and that he had some other ultimate destination in mind and that she should keep on what she wore, which was one of Devin's favorites of her dresses?

She finally came down on the side of vanity and did not go upstairs to change into an old dress. Instead, at one o'clock she slipped out the back door, walking as the map had illustrated in a westward direction. Almost halfway along the back wall of the house she saw the small inset door of the cellar, just where the map had shown it. It seemed odd that she had never seen it before. Then she noticed that the ivy around the door had been newly cut, and she realized that it must have overgrown the door before now, and Devin had had it cut aside especially for this afternoon.

With a smile on her lips, she reached for the door handle and pushed it open. She blinked, staring into the Stygian darkness inside, her eyes, accustomed to the summer light outside, unable to make out anything in the cellar.

"Dev?" she called tentatively, taking a step inside, still holding open the door with her outstretched arm. She peered into the gloom. "Are you here? I cannot see a thing."

At that moment a hand lashed out and gripped her arm, jerking her forward into the darkness. She stumbled, crying out a protest at his roughness, and in the next instant a hand pushed her hard in the center of her back and she tumbled forward into black, empty space.

18

Devin did not return from Darkwater Tarn until the light began to fail him. He had had a long and satisfying day, and as he rode home he thought with pleasant anticipation of showing Miranda the preliminary sketches he had made of the place. When he reached the house and handed over his horse to a groom, he headed straight for the library. It was empty save for Hiram, who was working at a sheaf of papers.

"Do you know where Miranda is?" he asked Hiram, who looked at him blankly. "Miranda," he repeated after a moment, wondering what was wrong with the man. "Do you know where she is?"

"But, I— Well, I thought she was with you."

"With me? No, I have been out at the tarn all day. Why did you think she was with me?"

"I— Well, I assumed it was you. She finished a letter to her banker in New York, then she handed it to me and said she had an appointment. Something about the way she smiled, I, uh, I thought she meant it was with you."

"No." Devin looked at him. "It must have been with her father or the architect."

The other man shrugged, but there was a doubtful expression on his face. "I suppose so, my lord. She didn't really say. It must have been my mistake."

Devin turned away and went upstairs. He checked her bedroom first, but she was not there. Something about the odd look on Hiram's face had set off an alarm inside him. The man had been certain that Miranda had been talking about him. *Why? Because she had looked the way she looked when she talked about him. That was what Hiram had meant. What other man would she look that way about? Obviously not her father...or anyone else that Devin could think of in this house.*

His mind leapt unbidden to the young doctor in the village, and for an instant jealousy surged through him. Then reason reasserted itself. He was as certain of Miranda as he was of himself—probably more so. If she had decided to take a lover, she would have told him so outright. He told himself that Hiram must have been mistaken, but he could not quell the fear that was burgeoning in his chest. He had grown complacent over the last few weeks because nothing untoward had happened. And in any case, he had never thought that the danger threatened anyone but himself....

He whirled around and charged out of his room. He went first to the Upshaws' room, where he found both Joseph and his wife.

"Miranda?" her father said in surprise. "Why, no, I haven't seen her since luncheon. Have you checked the library?"

"She left there long ago."

"Where is she?" Elizabeth's voice rose hysterically. "Has something happened to her?"

He glanced over at the woman. He was rarely around Miranda's stepmother, who usually kept to her rooms, but as he looked at her now, an odd feeling swept through him. Then it was gone, as quickly as it had come, and he saw only a frightened woman.

"Did you do something to her?" Elizabeth went on, her voice almost a shriek.

"Elizabeth! Dear, what are you saying?" Joseph turned to his wife with a horrified look. He put his hands on her arms and turned her aside, leading her over to a chair. "Please, I am sure there is nothing to worry about. Miranda can take care of herself. She often goes off on her own. She will turn up before supper."

He returned to Devin, saying in a low voice, "I apologize. My wife is not feeling well, and she worries so over the girls. She has been, well, very anxious for weeks now. I'm not sure why. Let's go out and see if we can track down that girl."

But Elizabeth would not be left behind. She insisted on going with them as they looked for Miranda. They went first to Veronica's room, where they were informed that she had not seen her stepsister all day. Devin went from door to door throughout the house, his fear swelling with each passing moment as he opened and closed the doors on empty rooms. *Something had happened to her. He had been careless, unthinking, and Miranda had paid the price for it.*

*   *   *

Miranda's scream pierced the air as she pitched forward into utter darkness. For one blind, panicked moment, she was certain that she was dead. Then she slammed into a hard wall and slid along it, her feet stumbling on the stone stairs. Her legs buckled under her, and she came down hard on her knees and banged her side into the wall once more. She stopped, crumpled against the wall, and for a long moment she just lay there, stunned.

Gradually the pain in various parts of her body pierced through the shock that had overtaken her. Her head hurt, her legs were twisted in an untenable position under her, and the palms of her hands stung, as did her left arm. Gingerly she moved, reaching up to brace a hand against the unseen wall as she swung first one leg, then the other, out from under her. She breathed a sigh of relief when her feet met stone steps and not mere air beneath them. A little more comfortable, she leaned against the wall, wrapping her arms around herself in an attempt to stop the shivering that had seized her entire body.

Someone had attacked her! It took some time to get her mind around that thought. But clearly someone had lured her to this cellar door with a note, then jerked her inside and pushed her down the stairs. The assumption must have been, of course, that she would die. And so she would have, if the push she had been given had not propelled her to the side as well as forward, so that she met the wall beside the stairs instead of hurtling straight forward down them.

Miranda wished she could stop shivering. It was cold and damp in the cellar, and combined with the cold clutch of fear, she was chilled through and through. She huddled against the wall in the darkness, trying to think. *How had this happened? More than that, who would want her dead?*

Her mind went unbidden to her stepmother's warnings the other day. She had dismissed them out of hand, assuming they were simply the sort of unfounded anxieties Elizabeth often suffered from. But now she could not help but think of them, take them out of the back of her mind and look at them. The note had come from Dev, directing her to this place of likely death. And who would benefit the most by her death? Well, her father and Veronica, if the truth were known, but she would have believed them as capable of trying to kill her as she was of flying. Dev, while he might not inherit the total of her fortunes, had been given a large lump sum under the terms of her will, enough, as Elizabeth had pointed out, to make it worth his while to get rid of her—especially if it would also get rid of the unwanted burden of a wife.

Tears sprang into Miranda's eyes, and she let out a choked sob. Was it possible that Dev had been merely acting a role the past few weeks, pretending to be happy with her, pretending to have broken it off with Leona, all so that he would look blameless when she was found dead at the bottom of the cellar stairs?

Miranda pressed a trembling hand to her mouth, on the verge of giving way to hysteria. She held herself quite still for a moment, tensing every fiber of her being. *It was not Dev! It simply could not have been Devin!*

She gritted her teeth and took a firm hold of her

emotions. *She was not going to break down. She re-fused to give way to this fleeting moment of doubt and fear. She was too strong for that.*

Sternly she shoved aside her raging fear. It was not Dev who had done this to her. That was ridiculous. Her heart knew it, even if her head had panicked for a moment. She knew Devin. He had not lied to her. He had never lied to her. He had been honest from the first when he told her that he did not want to marry her. He had not been playing false with her the past few weeks. She was certain of that. Whoever had done this to her, it was not Devin.

And she was acting like a fool, sitting here, trembling and doubting Devin. She had not even climbed the stairs to see if she could open the door and leave.

She stood up carefully, mindful of the fact that on the other side of the stairs there might very well be empty air all the way down to the bottom of the cellar. Keeping both hands on the wall, she began to inch her way back up, feeling with her foot for each step and sliding it upward. It was utterly dark except for the tiny line of light that showed between the top of the door and the door frame, barely enough to pinpoint where the door was. With every step she took, she was reminded of her aches and pains. The sleeve of her dress was in tatters on the left side where she had scraped along the rough stone wall, and there was a large rent in the left side of her skirt, as well. Her upper arm was scraped and stung like mad, for she had lost a good bit of skin from it to the life-saving wall, as well. Seemingly every muscle and bone in her ached from the jarring fall, and she was sure that the next day she would be a study in black-and-blue bruises.

Finally she reached the door and felt for its handle. All she encountered was an old-fashioned iron ring. She hooked her hand through it and pulled, but as she had expected, the door did not budge. Whoever had shoved her down the stairs had locked the door behind him, too. It would have been foolish of him to do anything else, of course.

She leaned against the thick wooden door, fighting off another swell of panic. *How long would it take someone to find her?* She had not told anyone where she was going, only saying to Hiram that she had an appointment. It could be hours before anyone even realized that she was missing, given the size of the vast house. They might not begin to worry until she did not show up for supper. Then they would have no idea where to look. She had slipped the note into her pocket; there would be no hope of anyone finding it and following her to the cellar. *And who would ever suspect that that was where she had gone?*

Panic rising inside her again, she began to pound on the door and kick it, screaming at the top of her lungs. After a few minutes she sagged to the floor, exhausted. Her effort had been useless, she was sure. The door was very old, but sturdy, built of thick planks of wood, and the cellars were made of even thicker stone. She was certain that all the noise she had made had been immediately swallowed up. She drew a few deep calming breaths and tried not to give way to despair.

Devin would come looking for her when he did not

find her at home. He would not give up until the house and surrounding area had been thoroughly combed. And there was a whole houseful of family and servants to look for her. She would be found eventually. It might take a while, and it was not pleasant sitting alone in the dark, dank cellar, but she could endure it. It was only a matter of time.

In the meantime, she decided, she would occupy herself with considering who had done this to her.

The note had been a trick, obviously. It had looked like Devin's handwriting, but there had been very few words, and she was not that familiar with his handwriting, having seen it only a couple of times. It was a distinctive hand, probably easy to copy, with its bold, spiky letters. Someone had sent her a phony note, then waited for her to come running, counting on her love for Devin. *But who? And why?*

No one would gain by her death except her father, Veronica and Devin, and she refused to believe that it was any of them. There must be some other explanation. Yet she could think of none.

She leaned back against the door, bracing her elbows on her knees and dropping her face into her hands. Dev would come for her, she told herself. *He would come.*

Miranda did not know how long she sat in the chilled, damp dark. It seemed like a lifetime. She passed from determination to despair and back again half a dozen times. She thought about her life, her family, about Dev. She remembered the first time she met him and all the times they had been together since then. In retrospect, it did not seem like much time. Yet she loved him as she had never loved anyone else. She had known instinctively, she thought, that very first time she saw him. She remembered the sudden clutching in her gut when she had looked into his eyes and the strange feeling that she knew him. She *had* known him. She had known him on some basic, primal level that had told her this was the man for her, the man she loved.

Others would doubtless have told her that she was mad to marry him as she had, based only on that instinct. They would have said that she had been swayed by his wicked good looks and that it was infatuation, not love, she felt. But Miranda had known differently. She had loved him, if not quite from the first, at least from the night of Rachel's party, when he had dizzied her with his kisses and then she had looked at his paintings and seen into his soul. She had known then that there was no one else for her. Everything that had happened since had only made her love him more.

She was not as sure of his love for her. He wanted her, she knew that. He had committed himself to her. But he had never told her that he loved her. That emotion, she feared, was still given to Leona.

But someday, she told herself, he would realize that it was she he loved. She would erase Leona's image in his mind and replace it with her own. Provided that she ever got out of this cellar, of course, she reminded herself wryly.

She was slumped back against the door when she heard a noise. It took a moment for it to register; then she stiffened, sitting up straight. It was muffled, but surely that was the sound of a voice.

Miranda jumped to her feet, wincing at the pain in her ankle, and began to beat at the door again, shouting. She paused to take a breath, and as she did so, she heard a muffled call outside the door. It was Devin, and it was her name that he yelled.

Miranda screamed back. A moment later something heavy thudded into the door. It thudded again and again, but the door barely rattled in its frame. It had been built to last an age. She heard Devin's voice again, cursing colorfully, and she smiled. A few minutes later there was a creaking sound, a grating of metal on metal, and she realized that he must have turned a key in the lock.

Miranda stepped aside just in time as the door swung open with a bang. For an instant Devin was silhouetted in the door frame, ducking his head to come inside, and then he was on the step with her, his arms going around her like iron and holding her to him.

"Miranda," he breathed into her hair. "Miranda, thank God. Thank God. I thought I had lost you forever."

"It's my fault," Devin said, pacing up and down his bedroom floor.

It was three hours later, and Miranda was ensconced in Devin's huge, sheltering bed, having taken a bath, been fed, and had her various scrapes and scratches patched up. Devin had insisted on her drinking a restorative brandy, so now she felt pleasantly warm and slightly tipsy as she watched him stride restlessly across the floor. They had spent some time explaining to each other exactly how they had gotten into their relative situations, with Miranda telling him of the note and the push down the stairs, and Devin sharing how one of the housemaids had happened to see Miranda walking behind the house close to the door, thus saving them a good many hours in their search for her—and saving Miranda a long, cold wait in the dark. Devin had looked at the note in Miranda's pocket and immediately declared it a forgery, but Miranda had already figured that out. Unfortunately, it yielded no clues. It was merely a piece of notepaper, which might be found anywhere about the house—or any other house, for that matter. There was nothing to say who had penned it, or even whether the person lived inside the house with them—a harrowing thought—or was a complete stranger who had somehow managed to sneak in.

"But why would anyone want to do away with me?" Miranda had asked reasonably.

Devin's response had been his terse statement that it was his fault.

"I beg your pardon," Miranda responded. "How is it your fault?"

"I knew there was something going on," he said flatly. "I should have been more careful. I should have watched out for you better. The thing was, I thought it was me they were after."

"Who?"

"I don't know who. Whoever did this...and the railing in the library...and the rock on the cliff."

Miranda shivered. "So you think all those things were planned, too?" During her long, cold hours of waiting, she had been forced to agree with her stepmother's analysis of the "accidents."

"Of course. Rocks do fall from limestone cliffs. I have seen them lying about before. But how likely is it that one would happen to fall right when you were riding beneath it—especially just after the railing in the library had been sawed through so that you fell?"

"It was sawed? It wasn't just rotting wood that broke?"

"No. That wood happened to be solid. I was pretty certain of that, for I had been up on that balcony only a couple of days before, looking at the wood, and I knew there had been none of the telltale wormholes in it. That is why I went up there to check after you left. And I found that it had been sawed almost completely through at both ends."

"Why didn't you say something?" Miranda asked. "Why didn't you tell me?"

"I didn't want to alarm you. And I didn't realize that you were in danger. I thought it was an accident that you had been the one leaning on the rail. I assumed it was intended for me."

"Why?"

"Because of the other attacks. The ones in London. The night we met, and the other time at Vauxhall Gardens. Both times, they came after *me*. So when the railing was tampered with, I thought they intended to harm me. The same thing when the rock came crashing down. I was in the same party, and I assumed that they were inept and had pushed it too late to hit me.

I tried to watch over you because I was afraid that you might get hurt simply by being around me, as you were those two times, but I did not realize that you were the target. I still have absolutely no idea who has been doing it or why. Was I wrong? Were they really after you the other times? Or was it me they wanted to harm, and they later decided that they could harm me by hurting you?''

"But who would want to harm you?" Miranda asked.

He smiled ruefully. "Any number of people, I'm afraid. That first night, I thought they were overzealous bill collectors, frankly. Some ruffians that someone to whom I owed money had sent to frighten me into paying. The second man seemed much more intent on killing me, however, and I don't know how that would benefit a bill collector." He paused, looking at Miranda. "What is it? What's the matter?"

"Nothing," Miranda responded. "Why do you ask?"

"I don't know. You looked quite odd for a moment."

"Oh. Well, I suppose it was thinking of that man who came at us with a knife."

Miranda hoped that her voice had come out normally. The truth was that when Devin had mentioned the man who had come out of the dark at them with a knife, it had struck her like a bolt of lightning: their attacker that night was the same man whom she had seen her stepmother talking to not long ago down by the old orchards!

She felt cold, as if all the blood in her had drained

away somewhere. She had to struggle to pay attention to what Devin was saying. "But there are many people I have offended over the years," he was continuing. "It could be any one of them. I have scarcely led an exemplary life. What I can't figure out, though, is why any of them should wait until now to try to do me in. On the other hand, if it is you they are really after, then why did those men attack me the first night? You were not with me. I had never even met you. Even more to the point, why would anyone wish to do you in?"

Miranda did not answer. The answer, she thought, was sitting right in front of her. If Miranda died, her estate went to her father and her stepsister. Elizabeth would not inherit directly, but she would be giving her daughter a rather large present. And with Miranda gone, when Joseph died, Elizabeth and her daughter would inherit all of his money, not just part of it.

But she could not bring herself to believe that her stepmother had actually hired someone to kill her. Elizabeth had been the closest thing to a mother Miranda had ever known. *Had Elizabeth been merely pretending to love her all these years? Had she secretly wished her out of the way?* She remembered how Elizabeth had come to her the other day, warning her against Devin. *What better way to throw any possible suspicion away from herself?*

She could not believe it. There had to be some other explanation. Elizabeth could not be evil. Perhaps the man had been hired by someone else and he was here pretending to be a gardener so that he could be near Miranda and find an opportunity to kill her. In that case Elizabeth would have known only that he was a gardener. Or else... Well, she could not think of another possibility at the moment, but surely, if she worked on it, she could come up with something. Veronica's mother could not be a would-be murderess. Her father could not be married to a killer. It was clearly absurd.

She sneaked a glance at Devin. She wanted to tell him her thoughts, but she knew that she could not. He would immediately assume that her stepmother was trying to kill her, and he would do whatever he had to to stop her. Miranda could not bear the idea of Elizabeth's being exposed as a criminal and sent to gaol. It would kill her father, and the shame of it would dog Veronica the rest of her life. She knew that she would simply have to settle the question of Elizabeth's guilt by herself.

"Until we can figure this out, we have to do something to make you safe," Devin was saying, and Miranda agreed absently.

"You have to promise me that you will not leave this house alone," he went on. "I intend to stay by your side every possible moment, but if I am not here, then you must not ride out alone—or even go for a walk in the garden. Agreed?"

Miranda nodded. "Agreed. I shall wait for you inside like the frailest of females."

"I need to get you away from here. There are so many possibilities of attack in and around Darkwater. Obviously the fellow has no problem gaining entrance to the house. I think we should leave for Apworth

Mountain as soon as possible. There is no way anyone can come at you without my knowing it out there.''

"But how can we find the person responsible for the attacks if we are stuck out there?'' Miranda argued reasonably.

"You have a point.'' He studied her, his face falling into thoughtful lines. "Perhaps...perhaps we can lay a trap for our culprit.''

"A trap?'' Miranda brightened. The thought of doing something active to find the killer appealed to her much more than passively hiding out. *Unless, of course, the killer they trapped turned out to be Elizabeth....*

"Yes.'' Devin smiled faintly, warming to his idea. "If we tell everyone that we are going on a trip to Apworth, to get away by ourselves after your ordeal in the cellar, then the killer will think that we are out there alone, vulnerable, unsuspecting, and he might come after us. Try to kill us with no witnesses around and make it look like another of his accidents. Except we won't be alone or unsuspecting or vulnerable. We will be waiting for him. I can arrange for the game-keeper and his son to meet us there. I trust both of them with my life. They can stand guard secretly, and when the killer comes, they will spring the trap.''

"All right,'' Miranda agreed.

She only hoped that things would turn out so that they needed to use Devin's plan. But first, tomorrow, she intended to have a little chat with Elizabeth.

19

To Miranda's surprise, she found her stepmother waiting for her when she walked into the library the next morning. She paused on the threshold, hastily rearranging her plans.

"Miranda!" Elizabeth popped to her feet. Her face was white and set, determined. "I—I wanted to talk to you."

"Good," Miranda replied. "I wanted the same thing."

Looking at her stepmother, it was difficult to believe any of the thoughts that she had entertained last night. Still, there was no getting around the fact that Elizabeth had been talking to the man who had attacked her and Devin.

"I know you will not want to hear this, but I have to say it," Elizabeth began resolutely.

"All right." Miranda walked over to the library table and sat down, her eyes fixed on Elizabeth's face.

Elizabeth swallowed. "I—I hope that yesterday made you think again about what I said to you the other day. About your safety."

"Yes. It made me think a great deal about my safety."

"Someone lured you into the cellar, where you could have broken your neck. Or lain broken and bleedy for days—for who knows how long!" Elizabeth's voice caught, and she paused for a moment, struggling visibly to gain control of her emotions.

"Yes, I know." Miranda forced back the instinctive pity she felt for Elizabeth and faced her coolly.

"Do you believe me now? Do you see how Ravenscar is—"

"Yesterday did not make me suspicious of Devin," Miranda said pointedly. "After all, it was he who led the search party for me."

"No doubt he assumed you were already dead from the fall, or near death, and he would cast suspicion off himself by seeming to be looking for you frantically, worried about where you were." Elizabeth paused, then added, "And that wasn't the only attempt recently. The other day, when I drank your cup of chocolate, do you remember? I was terribly ill and sleepy afterward. I was so sleepy that I could barely keep my eyes open. I almost fell asleep walking up the stairs to my room. It was not natural. I didn't know what to think. But yesterday I began to put two and two together. I realized that that had been another attempt on your life. Someone had put something in your chocolate, but their plan was foiled because you gave that cup to me."

A chill ran through Miranda as she considered her stepmother's words. She remembered how they had tried to awaken Elizabeth but had been unable to, and how she had worried that Elizabeth was ill. However, she also felt a stirring of hope. If her stepmother had been drugged, then she could not be the person responsible for trying to kill Miranda. *Or perhaps Elizabeth had really been ill, and she had seized on it as a means of throwing suspicion off herself.*

"But you just slept," she pointed out. "I mean, you felt bad, I realize, but it obviously did not kill you. It was a soporific...if anything."

"Perhaps he intended to do something with you when you were in a drugged state. Also, you know I have a weak stomach. If you remember, I regurgitated most of what I had drunk, to be indelicate about it. So perhaps there was not enough left in my stomach to kill me. You, on the other hand, might have been able to keep down the whole dose. It might have been enough to kill you."

"Elizabeth, Devin did not try to kill me. I know it."

"Why?" Elizabeth cried in an impassioned voice. "Because he told you so? Don't be deceived by him. He is a liar. A deceiver!"

Miranda stared in astonishment as Elizabeth began to pace the room in an agitated way. Her hands were clasped tightly together at her waist, her face twisted, and she seemed to be struggling with some sort of inner demon as she walked.

"Elizabeth, stop this." Miranda said harshly, going to her and taking her by the arm, turning her stepmother to face her. "You have been against Devin from the very beginning. You tell me that he is bad, a deceiver. But I think that it is you who has something to answer for.''

''What?'' Elizabeth backed up as far as she could, looking at Miranda uncertainly. ''What are you saying?''

''I saw you, Elizabeth,'' Miranda said flatly. ''I saw you with that man in the orchard the other day. At first I could not place him. I only knew that he looked familiar. But last night I remembered where I had seen him before. He was the man who attacked Devin and me in London.'' She gave Elizabeth's arm a shake. ''What were you doing conversing with the man who attacked us?''

''No!'' Elizabeth cried out in horror. ''Not you! He wasn't supposed to attack you!''

She realized as soon as she said it how she had given herself away, and she stopped abruptly, the blood draining from her face.

Miranda dropped her arm, staring at her stepmother as if she had never seen her before. ''Then you did hire him? You sent him?''

''I didn't mean for him to frighten you,'' Elizabeth said agitatedly. ''Certainly not to attack you. I would never harm you—you must believe that. It was only Devin.''

''Only Devin?'' Miranda repeated. ''Elizabeth! Why?''

''I was trying to keep him from marrying you! The first time he was just supposed to keep Ravenscar from appearing that night. I knew how charming he was. I was afraid if you met him you would agree to marry him. So I found Hastings. He said he could keep Ravenscar from showing up at his mother's house for supper. Then, the second time, I knew I had to do something more. Hastings was supposed to frighten Devin, tell him that he had to stay away from you or he would die. I wasn't trying to hurt him. I just wanted to keep him from marrying you!'' Elizabeth cried.

"Oh, God!'' She clapped her hands to her temples, tears spilling from her eyes. "I have been so stupid. I've made such a horrible mess of it. I was wrong, so wrong. I should have told you earlier, but I was too scared! I couldn't bear for you and Joseph to know the truth. And now it's almost gotten you killed. And now you think that I—that *I* am the one who has been trying to kill you.''

"So you are saying that you hired this man to...frighten Dev away, but he is not the one who lured me into the cellars yesterday?''

"No! No, of course not!'' Elizabeth raised her head, her hands dropping away, and she stared intently into her stepdaughter's face. Her eyes were red-rimmed and wild, and for just an instant Miranda felt a flicker of fear. "I told you, I would never hurt you. You are as dear to me as Veronica. I was only trying to protect you from Ravenscar. The reason Hastings is here at Darkwater is because I hired him to protect you after those two 'accidents.' He has been watching you— obviously not well enough, given what happened yesterday.''

"But why?'' Miranda asked gently, reaching out a calming hand to her stepmother. "I don't understand.''

"No. You wouldn't. You couldn't. You have no idea what I'm really like. What I've done.'' Her stepmother drew a long, shuddering breath and stiffened her back.

Looking straight into Miranda's eyes, she said, "Everything I have told you is a lie. My entire life is a lie. I am not really Roddy Blakington's widow. Indeed, Roddy Blakington never existed. I was not married before I met your father. Veronica is—she is illegitimate. And her father is Devin Aincourt."

Miranda felt as if the wind had been knocked out of her. Her mind whirled, and she could think of nothing coherent to say. After a long moment, she managed to say faintly, "What?"

Elizabeth sagged and sat down abruptly in a chair. "I never wanted anyone to know," she said softly. "I am so ashamed. I was not loose...I swear I was not. But one day I met Dev, and...I wasn't the same person after that. I had lived a sheltered life. I had never met anyone so urbane and charming, so witty and—and handsome. I lost all good sense. I felt madly in love with him, and then I was so foolish and wanton as to sleep with him. I thought...I thought he loved me as I loved him. I did not realize that I was just a plaything to him, a brief fling while he was summering in Brighton. When he learned that I was pregnant, he tossed me aside like a used shoe. He refused to marry me."

Miranda pressed a hand to her temple. "I—I cannot believe..."

"Are you saying that I am lying?" Elizabeth asked fiercely. "Do you think that I would reveal something like that about myself just for fun? The man is wicked!"

"No, of course I don't think you are lying," Miranda protested. "It is just—there must be some other explanation. "This is all—"

"Constance!" Dev's stunned voice came from the doorway to the library, and the two women swung around to face him.

"Dev!" Miranda had not heard him come in. She wondered how long he had been standing there. It was obvious that he had heard at least the last part of their conversation, for he looked stunned.

"Yes," Elizabeth replied, lifting her chin a little and looking him in the face. "I am Constance. I had been afraid that you would recognize me. I tried to stay out of sight."

Miranda remembered how often her stepmother had pleaded sick instead of coming down to dinner, and how when Dev was around she usually seemed to fade into the woodwork. She rarely even looked straight at him. It had never occurred to Miranda that her stepmother had been acting the way she had because she knew Dev and was afraid he would recognize her.

Elizabeth went on in a bitter voice. "But clearly I need not have troubled myself. I was not important enough for you to remember."

"But—how can—you are dead!" he finally blurted out.

Elizabeth's brows lifted. "Perhaps that is what you hoped."

"No! Good God." He turned to Miranda. "This is the woman I told you about—the girl whom I got pregnant, who killed herself and left me a suicide note."

"What?" Elizabeth exploded scornfully. "Is that the story you told this innocent girl?"

"It is what happened! Why did you write me that note? Why did you run away and pretend to be dead? Why didn't you come to me and—"

"Just a minute." Miranda turned to her stepmother, whose eyes were lit with an unholy fire. "Did you know that old man, Elizabeth? The one who came to visit me a few days before we left London?"

"Yes, of course. It was..." Elizabeth's voice roughened. "It was my grandfather. He raised me after my parents died, and then I shamed him before the world. I shouldn't have been surprised when he didn't come after me. I had destroyed all his trust in me. I was a fool to think—"

"Wait. That man came to tell me not to trust the Earl of Ravenscar. And the reason he gave was because Ravenscar had seduced his granddaughter and she had killed herself."

"What?" Elizabeth blinked, confused.

"That is what he told me. He believes that you are dead, too."

"You left notes, Elizabeth!" Devin came closer to her. "I— You wrote me a note telling me that I had ruined your life and you despised me. You said that you would rather die than live with the shame of bearing an illegitimate child. You disappeared. They searched for your body for days. And I was so...so furious that you had not even come to me and told me about the child. Do you honestly think that I would not have married you?"

"What are you talking about?" Elizabeth stood, and

her voice rose hysterically. "You refused me! You denied that the child was yours. You said you would bring witnesses against me to prove that I had been promiscuous if I tried to force you to marry me. You—"

"I did not! How can you say that? You never even told me about it!"

"Of course I did!"

"When? Where? I was often drunk, but I know I could not have completely forgotten that."

"I did not tell you face-to-face. I hadn't the courage. I was afraid, ashamed. And you had—you had stopped coming to see me. So I wrote it in a letter and gave it to Leona to deliver to you."

"Leona?" Devin's face went white. "You gave it to Leona?"

Elizabeth nodded. "Yes. She was my friend, as well as yours."

"The only letter she gave me was the note you left saying that you were going to throw yourself into the sea to avoid the shame of what you had done."

There was a long silence. Elizabeth's mouth began to tremble, and she crumpled more than sat back down in her chair. "Dear God."

"How did you learn that Dev rejected you and your child?" Miranda asked pointedly.

"Leona..." Elizabeth's voice was barely above a whisper. "She was my friend. She had been so kind to me from the moment she came to Brighton. She was dazzling and sophisticated, and I was thrilled that she even took any notice of me. I was just a country nobody. I couldn't tell my grandfather about my pregnancy. I couldn't face Dev. So I went to her and told her all about it. She said that she would deliver a note to Dev if I wrote it, so I did. The next afternoon she came back and sat down in the music room with me. I remember I was practicing the piano. And she told me very gently that Dev had read my note, then had torn it up and thrown it into the fire. He said he was going to leave for London, and I was not to follow. He said that—the things I told you, that he would deny and shame me if I pursued the matter. I was devastated.''

"Of course you were." Miranda went to her stepmother and knelt down beside her, taking her hands in hers. "Anyone would have been."

"I didn't know what to do, and she said that the only course left to me was to leave. She suggested that I go to America or India or some other colony, where no one would know who I was. She gave me money because she was my friend and felt sorry for me. And she said that in a new country no one would know who I was. I could change my name, I could pretend to be a newly bereaved widow, and no one would ever know the difference. She was so kind. She helped me to pack and to leave. She even hired the post chaise for me, and sent her maid with me to help me.''

"More likely to make sure you didn't change your mind and decide to come back," Miranda corrected. "And to steal a shawl to leave beside the sea."

"I—I suppose so. My God…" Tears formed in her eyes and spilled over. "Even after all this time, it hurts. I thought she was my dearest friend, and she betrayed me.''

"She betrayed everyone." Miranda's voice was hard with anger. "Your grandfather has been nearly driven mad with grief. He has mourned you all these years. Everyone thought you had died. People blamed Devin for your death. It was a terrible scandal, and Dev's father disowned him. Leona recklessly destroyed three lives." Miranda stood up, her gray eyes like steel. "And I know why. She wanted Devin for herself. He had been pursuing her, and she had been teasing and putting him off, but she always meant to have him, I'm sure. However, when you told her you were pregnant, she knew that he would do the honorable thing and marry you. She would lose him, and she did not want that. It would ruin her plans. So she lied to you. And she lied to him. She lied to everyone."

Miranda stood up and turned in Devin's direction.

He was pale with emotion, and there was a stunned hurt in his eyes that tore at her heart. Miranda thought that if Leona were there right at that moment, she would have gone straight for the heartless woman's throat.

"Veronica is my daughter?" Devin asked, his eyes going from Miranda to Elizabeth.

Elizabeth nodded, brushing at the tears that still trickled down her cheeks. "Yes. She—she has no idea. I have always told her that her father was Roddy Blakington. A wonderful man I made up. She—I—" Panic filled her eyes. "You won't tell her, will you?" She looked from Devin to Miranda and back, her hands clenching nervously in her skirt. "I don't know what it would do to her. I—she would be bound to hate me.''

"I am sure she wouldn't hate you,'' Miranda began soothingly.

"I won't tell her,'' Devin added, his voice rough with emotion. "Keeping silent is the least I can do after all the pain I caused you. Caused everyone. But I will also look after her as a father would, I promise you that.'' He hesitated, then went on. "Constance...Elizabeth, I am sorry. I know no amount of words can make up for the suffering you went through. Please, believe me, I did not know. I would not have— I know I have never been the model of a gentleman, but I would not have behaved so dishonorably.''

Elizabeth nodded, pressing a hand against her lips, tears running down her face.

Miranda looked at her with concern. "Let me take you to your room, Elizabeth. A nice, soothing lie-down would be good, don't you think? I'll ring for your maid, and she can put a lavender compress on your forehead.''

"Yes,'' Elizabeth choked out. "Please. I—I need to be alone.''

Miranda did as she had suggested, taking Elizabeth's arm and helping her up and out of the room. She led her up the stairs to her bedroom and over to the bed, then rang for Elizabeth's maid.

"I was a fool,'' Elizabeth whispered. "I was a fool back then, and I am still one now.''

"You are not a fool. You simply trusted the wrong person. That is all. I am sure many women would have acted just as you did.''

"Not you."

"I wouldn't be so sure. Most people are not very wise when it comes to love."

"You didn't marry for love. You were very practical about it."

Miranda smiled. "You think not?"

"Are you saying that you love him? That you loved him before you married him?"

Miranda nodded and took her stepmother's hand. "He really is a good man, Elizabeth. Those things you thought about him all these years were false."

"I know. But I—I hated him so long that it will take a bit of adjusting to feel differently. Oh, Miranda! Will you ever forgive me? I have been half-mad with fear the last few weeks. I was so afraid he would hurt you, but I could not bear to tell you the truth. And I sent Hastings to hurt him! I have been such a fool, such a coward and— Can you ever forgive me?"

"Of course I can. I know you have been—well, you haven't been yourself."

At that point Elizabeth's maid came in, and Miranda left Elizabeth to the girl's ministrations. She was sure that Elizabeth was not the only one in a state of shock and needing to talk right now. Devin had looked as if his world had been turned inside out.

She started toward the stairs to go back down to the library, but she found Devin sitting on the top step, waiting for her. "Miranda." He stood up and turned to face her. There was a bleak look on his face that tore at her heart. She went to him and wrapped her arms about his waist, leaning against this chest. His arms went around her, and he hugged her to him tightly.

"God, Miranda! What a fool I've been!" he burst out, echoing Elizabeth's words. "All these years... Leona's been lying to me. Toying with me."

Miranda's arms tightened involuntarily around him. Devin's pain hurt her, and it hurt even more that his pain sprang in large part from the fact that he had loved Leona. But she put her own emotions aside for the moment.

"Let's go to my room." She took his hand and led him down the hall to her bedroom. Devin sat down on a chair with a sigh, leaning forward and bracing his elbows on his knees, his chin on his hands.

"That was when she let me have her," he said, staring sightlessly at the wall as his thoughts turned back to that time fifteen years before. "I had been chasing Leona for over a year. She would tease me, offer more and never fulfill it. When I went to Brighton, she introduced me to Constance. Leona knew that I was mistaken about Constance's being experienced, and she did not correct it. I think she wanted to see what would happen. Leona would come to my apartments late at night and want to know what had happened with Constance. It was a kind of triumph for her to know that my telling her about it made me crazier with desire than anything Constance and I had done."

He shook his head, then plunged his fingers back through his hair. "I am sorry. I should not be telling you things like this."

"You can talk to me about anything," Miranda said

calmly, despite the hot anger against Leona that burned in her.

"But I guess when Cons—when Elizabeth told her that she was pregnant, Leona realized that the fun and games were over. I had taken her to task over not telling me that Constance was a virgin, and she must have suspected that I would marry Constance even though I loved *her*. She didn't want that. So she made up those lies—convinced Elizabeth to flee to America, made all the rest of us believe that Elizabeth was dead so that we would not try to find her."

He paused, and when he spoke again, his voice was rougher. "I think that she wanted me to feel to blame for Constance's death. She knew that my sinking deeper and deeper into wickedness would bind me to her even more. It would make me more like her and less like my family and the other people I knew. The more I separated myself from the rest of the world, the more I was tied to her. Does that make sense?"

Miranda nodded. "Yes. She didn't understand the good parts of you, I am sure, and they frightened her. She knew that it was the goodness inside you that would make you likely to leave her."

"She ruined Elizabeth's life without a second thought." He shook his head. "She watched me suffer with guilt. She stood by while my father and I broke over Elizabeth's death. I never spoke with him again. He died despising me. And she never said a word to me about what really happened." He looked up at Miranda, tears shimmering in his eyes. "How could she have been so heartless?"

Miranda's throat closed with sympathetic tears, and she could only whisper, "I don't know."

"She never really loved me," he went on.

"I don't think she is capable of love," Miranda agreed.

"It is no wonder she never felt jealousy. Her heart wasn't in danger. All she cared about was having power over me. She even urged me to marry you. She did not realize—" He stopped abruptly and looked at Miranda. "Dear God…"

"What? What's the matter?"

"Of course. It is she who—"

"Who what? Devin, what are you talking about?"

"It is Leona who has been trying to kill you."

"What? Why? What would she get out of it?"

"Everything. Don't you see? You have interfered with her power over me far more than Constance ever did. I told her the other day that I was not going to see her again. Even before that, she was bound to realize that her control over me was slipping away. I haven't been with her since I became engaged to you. She's lost me." He grimaced. "More importantly for her, no doubt, is the fact that she has lost her chance at your money."

"What?"

"I told you, she wanted me to marry you. She thought, as I did, that your money would be under my control. She no doubt still thinks that. I never told her any differently. Her idea was that I would spend your money on her and the things we liked to do. She told me that Vesey was curtailing her spending. So to her way of thinking she has lost a great deal of money. If you were dead, however, she would assume that I would inherit your money. And with you out of the way, I am sure she thinks that she could get me back under her spell again. No doubt it was she who arranged for all your 'accidents' to happen.''

''You really think so?''

''Who else? It makes sense now.'' Devin rose to his feet. His eyes glittered with an unholy light. ''I'm going over there. I'm going to make sure that nothing else happens to you.''

''Dev!''

But he had already turned and was striding from the room.

Devin rode to Vesey Park, impelled by a white-hot fury. He reined up in front, turning his horse over to a groom, and went to pound on the front door. A startled footman opened the door, then hastily stepped back as Devin pushed his way through it.

"Where is she?" he growled, and when the footman began to stutter out a response, he yelled, "Leona! Leona! Where the hell are you?"

"Sir!" The footman gaped at him. "I shall announce you if you—"

Devin did not spare the man a glance as he strode through the entry hall to the staircase and began to take it two steps at a time, bellowing Leona's name. The footman hurried after him, wringing his hands and calling out, "Sir!" ineffectually.

Leona appeared in a doorway halfway down the hall. A smile curved her mouth, and she sauntered toward Devin, waving back the footman. "It's all right, Portman. I will see Lord Ravenscar."

She waited for Devin, arms crossed beneath her breasts, a smug smile firmly in place. "Well, well,

Devin, even sooner than I thought... I told you that you would come running back to me, didn't I? Now, the question is, how much should I make you crawl before I take you back?''

"Don't flatter yourself." Devin hooked one hand around her arm and dragged her into the sitting room.

"What do you—" Leona yelped in protest. "If you think *that* is going to win me back, I can tell you that you are fair and far off!''

"I don't give a damn about winning you back. I came here to tell you that I am on to your scheme. And I swear to you that if you harm one hair on Miranda's head, I will not rest until I have hunted you down and put you in the ground."

Leona gaped at him, her preconceptions tumbling down around her with a thud. "What? Miranda? How dare you!''

"Oh, I dare!" he shot back. "Don't think that you can twine me around your finger again. I know you. I know all the things you did—the lies you told me, the games you played."

"What? Don't be absurd. I have no idea what you're talking about."

Devin opened his mouth to explain about Elizabeth, but stopped. He was not about to give Leona any ammunition to use against Miranda or anyone connected to Miranda. He would have liked to spew out what he thought about her and what she had done to both him and Elizabeth, but he knew that Leona must never know who Elizabeth was or that Veronica was his illegitimate daughter. So he shoved back his grievance and said only, "Oh, yes, I think you do. You have played me for a fool for years, Leona, and you may think that I will never hurt you because I've been your lapdog for so long. But I am not anymore. You have seen how I am with others who cross me. You know what I'm capable of.''

''I know that you have gone quite mad,'' Leona snapped back, trying to wrest her arm away from him.

''No, not yet. But I can promise you I will if any harm comes to my wife.''

''You keep prating on about her! I have no idea what you're talking about.''

''The 'accidents' that have been befalling her, that is what I am talking about. I realized that it was you who must be behind them. So I came here to tell you that it will do you no good. I will never come back to you, no matter what might happen to Miranda. The thought of touching you again makes my skin crawl. And should she be hurt, I will know that you are the one who caused it, and I will make sure you pay for it. Physically, socially, every way possible. Do I make myself clear?''

''Perfectly!'' Leona seethed. ''Now let go of me. I hate you!''

He released her abruptly, and she staggered back a little. ''Then the feeling is mutual,'' he told her bitterly. ''Just remember what I said. Leave Miranda alone.''

''I wouldn't touch your precious little wife!'' Leona cried, her voice cracking with fury. ''Now get out of my house.''

''Gladly.'' Devin knew that he had made an implacable enemy of her, but he also knew that Leona was far too interested in self-preservation to discount his words.

He took a last long look at her, wondering how he had thought himself in love with her for so long. Then he turned on his heel and strode out.

After Devin left, Miranda went down to the library. It had been a taxing day, and she was glad to seek the solace of her work. Hiram was not there, being upstairs closeted with Joseph and the architect, going over the expenditures for the renovation of the house. Mr. Strong, however, was there, and she remembered that yesterday she had told him to meet with her almost an hour earlier. He jumped to his feet when she came in.

"My lady."

"Oh. I'm sorry, Mr. Strong. I forgot our appointment."

"That is perfectly all right, my lady," Strong said with alacrity, getting to his feet. "I will come back another time."

"No, we should go ahead," Miranda said. "I need to get it done before Lord Ravenscar and I leave for Apworth Mountain."

"Apworth Mountain, my lady? Are you sure? I mean, are you still planning to go after, well, your ordeal yesterday?"

"Of course. Why not? Now, where were we? The final set of books?"

"Yes, my lady. But, ah, I was thinking. Perhaps we might ride over to one or two of the tenant farms today. You had been wanting to go to them, you said."

"That's true." Miranda considered the idea. It was tempting to think of riding out instead of staying cooped up in the house today. And now that Devin had figured out that it was Leona who was to blame for the "accidents," she supposed there would be no problem with leaving the house. She sighed. "No, I had better not. I need to get through with this or I will find it hard to enjoy our excursion."

"Of course." He started to sit down, then stopped. "Oh, wait, I left part of the papers in my office. If you will excuse me for a minute."

"All right." Miranda sat down at the table and pulled the ledger book to her as he left the room.

She was deeply engrossed in an examination of the accounts some ten minutes later when the door opened again.

"Ah, there you are," she began, swinging around to look at Strong. To her surprise, it was Devin's uncle who had come into the room. "Oh! Uncle Rupert. I thought you were the estate manager."

"No. Sorry." He smiled. "How are you doing, my dear? All recovered from your fright yesterday?"

"Oh, yes." She smiled. "I am rather resilient."

"Yes, I can see that you are. I was going out for a ride, and I thought I would stop in and see if you would like to go with me. Over to the abbey ruins, perhaps?"

"No, I had better not. I'm waiting for Mr. Strong to return. We have to finish the books today."

"Oh, surely that can wait," the older man said jovially. "It is a beautiful day for a ride."

"No. I'm sorry. I cannot."

"Oh. Pity." Uncle Rupert reached into his jacket and, much to Miranda's amazement, pulled out a pistol. He leveled it at her. "I am afraid that I must insist, my dear."

Miranda stared at him, her brain suddenly numb. *Uncle Rupert?* "It is you?" she asked. "You are the one who—"

She broke off, turning as the door opened, and Strong stepped into the room. "Mr. Strong!" she cried with relief. "Help me."

But Strong only glanced at her nervously, then looked toward Rupert. "People will see the gun," he said agitatedly. "You cannot walk out of here carrying that, sir."

"I am afraid you're right, Strong." Uncle Rupert started toward Miranda.

Miranda stared at them, stunned. *The two of them were in on this together!* Suddenly it came to her like a blow to her skull.

"The estate!" she cried. It was the only thing that connected the two men. "You have been cheating Devin on the estate!"

Uncle Rupert sighed. "That is your problem. You see? You are simply much too clever for your own good."

He stopped beside her, and before Miranda knew what he was about to do, he raised the pistol and brought the butt end down sharply on her skull. Everything went black, and she crumpled to the floor.

It was completely dark when Miranda came to, and for an instant she was terrified that she was back in the dreadful cellar again. But then it impinged on her consciousness that there was light coming in through some large cracks in the ceiling. She knew that the cellar had not looked like that.

Her head was splitting. She sat up gingerly and looked around her. There was a little more light than there had been yesterday in the cellar, and she was able to see that she was sitting on an earthen floor, earthen walls all around her. The light from above came through in four lines the shape of a rectangle. A vague shape of stairs went up to the rectangle. She was again underground, she thought, this time with a trap door instead of a regular door and earthen walls instead of stone ones. She supposed it could be another part of the cellars, or perhaps even some other outbuilding of Darkwater.

Or it could be the abbey ruins.

That thought took hold of her mind, and the more she contemplated it, the more she thought that the abbey was the likely answer. They would not want to risk her being quickly discovered again, as she had been yesterday. No doubt they would think it better to get her away from the house. *But how had they managed to carry her unconscious body out of the house without anyone noticing?*

She sat for a while longer, gathering her strength. She knew that she would have to make the attempt to open the trap door, but right now she felt too sick and weak from the blow Rupert had given her to do much of anything.

Sighing, she leaned back against the wall. Rupert had accused her of being too clever. The truth was, she thought, she hadn't been clever enough. After weeks of going over the books and looking through the estate business matters, she had not caught on to the fact that Rupert and the estate manager were cheating Devin. No doubt they had a false set of books which they had shown her. They must have been collecting more money in rents than they showed in the books and pocketing the difference. The estate must not be in the terrible shape the two of them had pretended.

She remembered now her questions about one of the tenant farms and how much more prosperous it looked than the records indicated. Why hadn't she realized what that meant? It had been foolish in the extreme to simply take Strong's explanation on faith.

The fact was, she had been too distracted to give the estate the full attention she should have paid to it. There had been the renovation of the house and grounds, of course; those things had taken away a good deal of her time. But the biggest distraction had been Devin himself. She had been too busy trying to get him to fall in love with her to really notice much of anything else.

Unfortunately, it looked as if she might have to pay for that inattention with her life.

She thought about the first "accident." It had happened immediately after she met the estate manager. She recalled his amazement when she had told him that she would be running the estate herself. No doubt until then he and Uncle Rupert had expected to be able to continue the same game that they had been playing with Devin's estate all along. Perhaps they had even thought that they would now have her money at their disposal, as well. Upon hearing the truth, Strong must have rushed to arrange the first "accident," knowing that she would be exploring the library that afternoon.

When that failed, Uncle Rupert had invited her out for a ride along a trail where a limestone rock could conveniently split her skull open. Then there had been a lull of a few weeks without accident. Perhaps when their books had held up to her inspection they had decided that murder would not be necessary. But in the past week or so, they had now tried to kill her three times: the drug in the hot chocolate, which Elizabeth had drunk; the cellar; and now this. Something had frightened them into renewed action. She wondered what it was.

Of more immediate importance, of course, was when Devin would return home and when he would set up another search for her. Given the fact that he had become convinced that Leona was the culprit, she had to wonder if he would even worry about the fact that she was not in the house. All she could do was hope that he would. But even if he was worried about where she was, how could he realize that she was at the abbey?

No, she thought, she could not afford to trust in Devin's rescuing her. She had to make plans for herself. The first thing, of course, was to find a weapon that she could use against them when they came back—*provided they were planning to return, of course, and had not simply thrown her into this room to die a slow death of thirst and starvation.* She shoved aside that discouraging thought and began a slow perambulation of her prison. One hand trailing along the earthen wall, she walked, sweeping the floor beside her with one foot, searching in the almost non-existent light for something she could fashion into a weapon. A few times she came upon small rocks, which she pocketed, but after circling and crisscrossing the room, that was still all she had.

Miranda sat down on the bottom step and examined her discoveries: three rocks, two a little larger than pebbles and one that would fit into the palm of her hand. She thought for a moment, then removed her handkerchief from the pocket of her dress. Spreading it out on her lap, she centered the three stones on it and neatly tied them up in it so that she had a small sack with the rocks firmly lumped together, and therefore larger and heavier than they were singly, and with the advantage of having a knot of material beneath the rocks by which she could grasp and wield the makeshift weapon. It was not, perhaps, the most dangerous weapon she could have—she wished sincerely that she had decided to carry a pistol or a knife strapped to her leg—but it was better than being unarmed. Besides, she would have the element of surprise on her side. Uncle Rupert and Strong would not expect her to have a weapon; she was obviously not the sort of female they were accustomed to.

She heard a sound above her head and went still, listening. There was the neigh of a horse, then the faint sound of a voice. She thought about shouting—it could, after all, be a stranger, or even Devin looking for her. But common sense told her that it was Rupert or Strong, or both, come to finish the job, and the best thing for her to do was to appear as weak and helpless as possible.

Therefore she hurried back to the wall where she had been when she came to, and she slumped down upon the floor, closing her hand around her weapon and thrusting it into her pocket.

At the top of the stairs, the trap door opened and fell back with a crash. A moment later, a man's legs appeared, then the rest of his body. It was Rupert, carrying a lantern that cast light around the small dank room. Down the stairs behind him came Strong, looking distinctly unhappy.

"I don't know why we can't just leave her," Strong was saying, his voice close to a whine. "She will die without our help."

"Yes, but what if my nephew takes it into his head to search the abbey?" Rupert snapped. "It seems just the sort of thing he would do. We can't risk anyone finding her before she's had time to die. She could tell everyone all about us. We just discussed this, Strong."

"Yes, but..."

"Buck up, man," Rupert went on impatiently. He had reached the bottom of the stairs now and turned his lantern's light on Miranda. "Well. I see you're awake."

He did not look happy about that fact. Miranda supposed it would have been much easier to finish her off if she were not awake and watching. She sat up, trying to appear groggier than she felt. "Uncle Rupert..."

"Oh, don't try to get around me by being all female and helpless now," he said, his voice cantankerous. "If you were like other women, this never would have happened. I don't understand why you had to be the way you are. Always poking and prying into everything... If you had just left it alone, there would have been no problem.''

"True," Miranda replied dryly. "You could have continued robbing Devin blind. No doubt you were hoping you could do the same to my fortune, as well.''

"Well, it isn't as if he noticed...or cared," Rupert argued petulantly. "Devin never had any idea what went on up here.''

"Made it easier to embezzle money from him, I'm sure," Miranda said sarcastically. "But, you know, I think you have gone too far this time, Rupert. Devin is bound to notice that something is amiss when his wife dies in yet another mysterious accident. He will begin searching for what reason someone had to kill me. Don't you think eventually he will find out?''

"Nonsense. He will be the main suspect. Who else would want to kill a rich wife except the husband? I am sure it is he who Mr. Upshaw will concentrate on.''

Miranda's hand tightened on the rock. "So you are not content with stealing from your nephew? You intend to get him sent to the gallows for murder, as well?''

Behind Rupert, Strong made a noise, turning pale.

Rupert frowned at her. "No. Of course not. With luck, no one will suspect anything. This wouldn't even be necessary if you were not such a damnably prying, bullheaded female! Pushing me out of the way. Taking over. Having to go see the tenant farms yourself. And going to Apworth Mountain! Who would have dreamed you would take it into your head to see that godforsaken place!''

"Apworth Mountain." Miranda stared at him. "You mean...you have to kill me to keep me from seeing Apworth Mountain? Is that it?''

"Of course," Rupert replied pettishly. "Devin knows nothing about the contract. Even he would be bound to notice the mines.''

"The mines? My God, of course! I was right. There are minerals there, aren't there? You have been mining it, and Devin doesn't have any idea.''

"Oh, stop yammering," Rupert said irritably, bending over to grasp her wrist and pull her to her feet. "As if Devin deserved any of it anyway. He is a wastrel and—''

Miranda did not resist the older man's tug at her arm. Instead, she came up with it, propelling herself forward with all her strength as she whipped her hand out of her pocket and flung it upward. The sack of rocks connected smartly with Rupert's head. He made an odd noise and collapsed, going over backward under the force of her forward movement.

She tore past him and up the stairs, blasting into a surprised Strong on the railingless steps. He staggered backward, flailing his arms, and fell off the side of the stairs, landing with a thud a few feet below on the earth. Miranda did not stay to see what happened to either him or Rupert. She was already up the stairs and out onto the ground.

The bright sunlight outside blinded her, and she staggered forward, shading her eyes. *Where were the horses she had heard?* She heard a noise behind her and whirled around. Two horses stood just beyond the low stone wall, loosely tied to a bush. At her sudden appearance, however, they skittered nervously, and when she whipped around and rushed toward them, they broke and ran, tearing free of their loosely tied reins. Miranda ran after them uselessly, cursing herself for her impetuous plunge toward the animals. Behind her she heard a roar, and she knew that Uncle Rupert must be up and after her.

She took her to her heels, jumping over the low stone wall and darting around another higher wall. It was not long before she was completely lost in the ruins. She stopped, panting, and leaned against a wall, listening for the sounds of pursuit. She heard nothing, and cautiously she edged around the corner of the wall. If she could just get away from the abbey and into the woods, she felt sure that she could elude Rupert and Strong.

As she slipped around the corner, however, she heard a cry. She whirled around and saw Strong in the distance, running toward her. Rupert was not far behind him. Miranda whirled and took off at a run. She was in the large open square that had once been the abbey courtyard. A half-fallen wall loomed before her, and beyond that, she knew, there was a large empty field between her and the hiding places that the woods offered. She thought she might be able to outrun Uncle Rupert, who was, after all, getting up in years and had also been hit in the head. Strong, however, was a different matter.

She scrambled over the wall and ran full tilt. Behind her she could hear Strong yelling. And then, in the distance, she saw the figure of a horseman approaching them. Joy swept over her.

"Devin!" she cried and ran toward him now instead of the woods.

The horse leapt forward, bearing down on her in a run. Miranda dropped to her knees, sobbing for breath. She felt the rush of air as the horse tore past her, and she turned to see Devin launch himself off the steed straight at Strong.

After that, it was all over in a matter of moments. The force of their collision knocked the air from Strong, and Devin followed it up with a right upper cut to the chin that sent him into unconsciousness. He leapt to his feet and ran toward his uncle, who decided to turn and run in the opposite direction. It was of no use. Devin was on him in a moment, and he, too, hit the ground, unconscious.

Miranda staggered to her feet as Devin turned and ran back to her, sweeping her up in his arms.

"Are you all right?" he asked, holding her so tightly to him that she could hardly breathe and kissing her all over her face. "Oh, my God, Miranda! To think I almost lost you! Tell me you're all right."

Laughing, gasping, she managed to answer in the affirmative. "Yes. I'm fine. Thank heavens you got here in time. But how did you know? How did you get here?"

He hugged her, held her at arm's length to inspect her and make sure she was all right, then pulled her to him again. "When I got home and you were gone, I knew something was wrong. I had already realized as I was riding home that I had been wrong about

Leona—I mean about her trying to kill you. She looked utterly blank when I accused her of it. She is skilled at deception, but I knew that look was real. She didn't know what I was talking about. So I questioned the servants, and one of them remembered seeing Strong and Rupert heading out the back with a rolled-up rug, which they put in a wagon. That seemed decidedly odd, and it looked even odder when a groom told me they had brought back the wagon and rug, then gone out again on horseback. I followed them. And when I got close enough, I saw you running. What happened?''

He held her out at arm's length again and looked at her. ''What is going on? Why in hell were Uncle Rupert and Strong trying to kill you?''

''Well, it's a long story.''

Devin glanced toward the two prone figures on the ground. ''That's all right. I think we have a while before these two wake up. Tell me.''

Quickly and concisely, Miranda related what had happened that morning after he left for Vesey Park to confront Leona. Devin listened in amazement.

''But why?'' he asked, when she had finished telling him how Rupert had threatened her with a gun, then knocked her unconscious and taken her to the abbey. ''Why would Uncle Rupert want to hurt you?''

''They thought I was about to discover their secret—although I'd been so stupid about the whole matter, I rather wonder if I would have. In short, they were cheating you, Dev. I think they must have been taking money from the estate for years and pretending that it was actually losing money. In reality, only *you* were losing money.''

He stared at her. ''I can't believe it. The estate was actually prospering?''

''I think so. I knew that the entries were incomplete. I thought Mr. Strong was stupid…a bad manager. In reality he was quite clever. Perhaps I would have caught on if I hadn't been so, well, caught up in you, but I'm not sure. Anyway, they were afraid that I would find out. And they didn't want us to visit Apworth Mountain.''

''What?''

''It was something that Rupert said when he was talking about why he had to kill me. He's set up mines on your estate that you know absolutely nothing about.''

''I can scarcely take all this in.''

''I know. It is so bizarre.'' Miranda shivered. ''It's amazing, the lengths that people will go to for money. Rupert intended to kill me.'' She leaned against Devin's broad chest. ''But then, fortunately, you came along and saved me.''

''It seems only fair, my love,'' he said lightly, holding her out from him and looking into her eyes. ''After all, you saved me.''

He bent to kiss her, and, with a happy sigh, Miranda surrendered her lips to his.

Epilogue

Miranda rose and stretched. Pushing back her chair, she left the estate manager's office, locking the door behind her, and strolled across the yard into the main house. It was quiet inside Darkwater now that the day was ending and the workmen's hammers and saws had stopped. The renovation of the house was proceeding nicely, but Miranda had to admit that she would be grateful when she and Devin left for their belated honeymoon trip to Italy and she would no longer have to hear the sounds of the workers rebuilding the house. They would have left long ago had she had not felt the need to spend the last month making sure that the estate's affairs were all in order.

But that was all settled now, she thought, and she could turn her attention to packing. Also, Joseph and Elizabeth had gotten back yesterday from their extended trip to Scotland, and Joseph could tend to the renovations now, while Miranda and Devin spent the next four months traveling.

Time, Miranda knew, would heal all wounds. She could and would forgive Elizabeth for the attacks on

Devin. But it had been much less awkward with Elizabeth gone for the last month, and it would be easier, too, for them all to deal with each other after a few more months. Devin had spent the last month getting better acquainted with his daughter, though, of course he had not—and would never—let Veronica know even by a hint that she was anything other to him than a younger sister-in-law.

Rupert and Strong were both now in prison. Miranda had suggested letting them emigrate to a colony, instead, to avoid scandal for the family, but Devin had insisted on turning them in to the authorities. "They tried to kill you," he told her, his eyes bright and hard as stones. "If they were not to go to prison, I couldn't let them live." Miranda had quickly agreed that prison was called for.

Miranda went up the stairs and along the corridor to Devin's studio. It was where he could usually be found. He turned at the sound of her footsteps and smiled.

"Miranda. Come look. I finished your portrait."

Miranda smiled and went forward obediently to look. It was the fifth of her portraits he had finished and, according to Devin, his favorite. It would hang, he had decided, in the entryway downstairs. In the painting she was wearing a bloodred gown, vivid against her white skin. Like all of Devin's paintings, it was filled with light and color, and it made Miranda look, she thought, more beautiful than she really was. However, she never complained to Devin about his paintings in that regard.

"It's lovely," she told him, slipping her arm around his waist.

"I still haven't quite captured that quality," he mused, studying the portrait.

"What quality?"

"The quality that is uniquely you." He grinned down at her. "That is why I'll keep on trying."

"People may get tired of your painting my face over and over again," she teased.

"Ah, but you see, that's the beauty of it—I don't care. I don't have to sell my paintings. I am, after all, a wealthy man. You told me so yourself."

"You are indeed," Miranda agreed. "I think I have all the estate's affairs in order now."

"That's good. Then we can leave for Europe soon."

"Do you want to hear the sum total of your assets?" Miranda asked.

He smiled at her. "It won't mean much to me. I think I shall leave all that in your capable hands."

"It was that sort of attitude that got you into trouble in the first place," Miranda scolded him playfully.

"Ah, but the difference, you see, is that I can trust you."

"Yes."

"I love you," he said simply and bent to kiss her.

Miranda took his hand, and they strolled out of the studio and along the corridor to dress for dinner.

"You know, the ironic thing is that Strong was actually quite a good estate manager. Your estate prospered under him as it had not for years. The farms were producing enough rents for you to live well. And he made a deal with a coal company to mine your land in the Roaches that makes you a very wealthy man indeed. You could have renovated Darkwater yourself.''

They reached Miranda's bedroom and went inside. Miranda turned her back to Devin, and he began to unhook her dress.

''Have you ever thought about that?'' she asked. ''You had plenty of money. It was never really necessary for you to marry me.''

''Oh, yes, it was,'' he contradicted her, bending down to place a kiss at the base of her neck. ''It was very necessary—for my happiness. I could have had all the money in the world, but if I had not married you, I would never have known love.''

Miranda turned and smiled up at him, letting her dress slide down her arms and pool at her feet on the floor. ''And you know it now?''

''Oh, yes.'' His smile was slow and rich with promise. ''I have a very intimate acquaintance with love now.''

''Then why don't you show me?'' she asked, sliding her arms up the front of his shirt and around his neck.

Devin pulled her close to him, his mouth coming down on hers. ''I would be happy to.''